So Long As It's Wonderful

A ROOSEVELT COUNTY NOVEL

SHEILA QUINN

Printed in the United States of America

ISBN 979-8-9899176-0-0

Cover design and illustration by Bruce Deroos, Left Coast Design

With gratitude to Zane Grey and the legacy of his work.

"For some reason the desert scene before Lucy Bostil awoke varying emotions—a sweet gratitude for the fullness of her life there at the Ford, yet a haunting remorse that she could not be wholly content—a vague loneliness of soul—a thrill and a fear for the strangely calling future, glorious, unknown.

She longed for something to happen. It might be terrible, so long as it was wonderful."

from *Wildfire*

Dedication

For Henry and Josephine, always my motivation.

These are our stories.

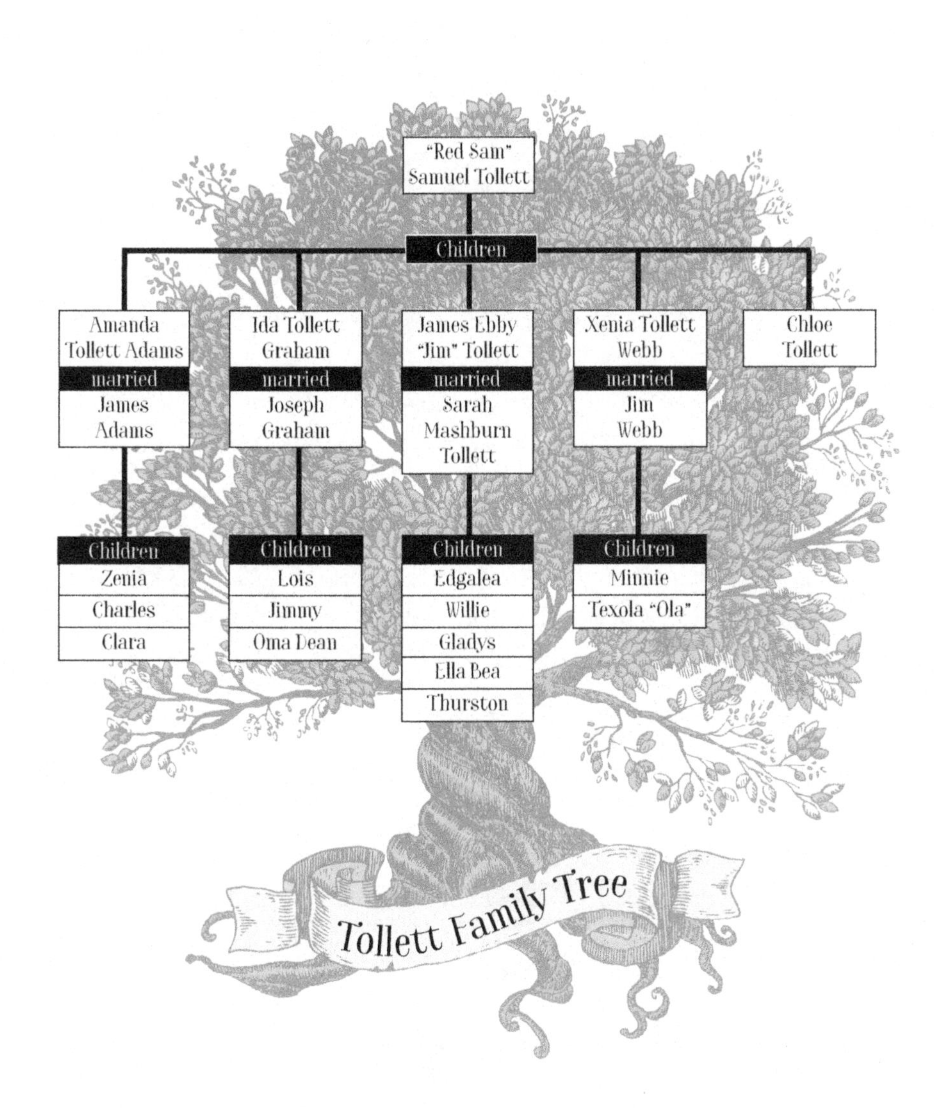
"Red Sam"
Samuel Tollett
Children
Amanda
Tollett Adams
married
James
Adams
Ida Tollett
Graham
married
Joseph
Graham
James Ebby
"Jim" Tollett
married
Sarah
Mashburn
Tollett
Xenia Tollett
Webb
married
Jim
Webb
Chloe
Tollett
Children
Zenia
Charles
Clara
Children
Lois
Jimmy
Oma Dean
Children
Edgalea
Willie
Gladys
Ella Bea
Thurston
Children
Minnie
Texola "Ola"
Tollett Family Tree

Chapter 1

They say redheads are the wild ones, but Willie's hair was as black as her mother's. Her sisters inherited the soft, red curls of the Tollett clan, while hers leaned more to the wiry side. She wore it tied back and covered with a scarf, but nothing could be done about the unruly strands coming out around her face. The wind blowing over the dry plains whipped the strands across her cheeks, and she tried once more to tuck them behind her ears.

Fashionable hair was the furthest thought from the sixteen-year-old's mind. She stood with her father, watching their small herd of Polled Herefords. When Willie came out to feed last night, she'd noticed the pregnant heifer, Rose, standing alone in a corner of the cow lot, an early sign of labor. She and Father both kept an eye on her as they completed the morning's work and returned to the lot as soon as they finished dinner.

Willie's father bought six heifers of the new Hereford breed at a sale in Amarillo the previous summer. Her grandfather, called Red Sam for his bright hair, bought a bull.

They'd immediately bred them, and now five of the six heifers would give birth to their first calves within days of each other. Two healthy calves already stood nudging their mothers for milk. The sixth heifer, who hadn't managed to get pregnant, would be butchered by the end of spring. Willie understood that death was part of the business, but she felt a throb of sadness in the back of her throat any time she thought of it.

The Herefords were bred to be hornless, as well as docile. More than any of that, Father had bought them for their resilience to harsh weather and limited grazing, both realities on the eastern edge of New Mexico. After they arrived, Willie spent countless hours studying the herd, talking to the heifers and learning their individual patterns. She'd named each one after a flower and went into the pen almost every day, stroking their necks, sharing bits of sweet sorghum, and raising them up as pets. She knew it was foolishness. It wasn't something other farmers or ranchers, and certainly not her father, would do, but she could not tend to a creature without coming to love it.

Despite the cattle's promise, Jim Tollett's friends thought he was crazy. Of course, most households in Roosevelt County kept cows, but only enough to provide milk and meat for their families. Willie's father was known for telling everyone the wheat prices wouldn't hold. They shrugged off his warnings as the prophetic gloom typical of Brother Tollett and plowed more land for wheat production.

Jim and his brothers had arrived in the New Mexico Territory in 1907, only five miles from the Texas state line. They had done well during the Great War when demand for American wheat was high. In the five years since the war ended, Jim had bought land from other nesters who couldn't keep up the game. In sixteen years, he'd gone from living in a dugout to an accumulation of land and relative wealth. Willie's dream was to manage a farm and a small herd, just like her father.

"I'd better get the coop mended before we lose our flock to a fox," Father said. No one knew how the wire around the bottom of the chicken coop had come loose, but Willie suspected her six-year-old brother, Thurston, of having something to do with it. She wished he were out here now to help with the repair.

On the other hand, she enjoyed working alone with their father. He carried out every movement of his lean body with purpose. He grew his hair long enough to cover his neck, and a short beard covered his face. His intense blue eyes never relaxed under the shadow of his hat. A strict man, James Ebby Tollett expected things to be done right with little instruction, and Willie admired him as much as she differed from him. Jim was a serious man who prized order above all else. Willie laughed easily and challenged expectations. Still, nothing gave her more satisfaction than pleasing her father with a job well done.

Willie went about her chores, checking in on Rose every time she passed the cow lot. Each time, she expected to see a new calf on the ground or at Rose's teat, but labor continued without delivery.

Rose tilted her white head one way and then the other. She bawled, kicked the ground, and shifted the weight of her bulging red body forward and backward, all signs of straining, but without the regularity of final contractions. Tulip and Daisy had gone from restlessness to labor within a few hours.

Rose turned toward the fence and Willie noticed the calf's hooves sticking out under her tail. Delivery had started but stalled. If it didn't continue soon, Rose and her calf would die.

Willie ran to the chicken coop. She'd seen plenty of births on the farm. She'd even assisted her mother, who often served as a midwife to cousins and neighbors when their times came. Experience taught her that some mothers and babies needed assistance. And sometimes, it didn't make a difference. Around here, the line between birth and death was razor thin.

Willie was surprised to find that her father was not at the chicken coop. The mesh of wire around the bottom was once again intact. He must have moved on to his next task, but she wasn't sure what that was. Her heart pounded in her chest. She turned a desperate circle, scanning the flat horizon marked with nothing but grass and fences. Seeing no sign of him, she hurried to the barn. As she passed the horse pen, she saw Buck standing alone and realized that her father must have ridden Buster to inspect one of their distant fields.

Grabbing ropes from the barn, Willie hurried back to the heifers' pen, where Rose was now lying on her side. Perhaps the heifer only needed more time. The first labor often took longer, and intervening too soon could complicate matters. But so could waiting too long. She stood and scanned the barren horizon again. No sign of her father. Willie could feel her heartbeat in her left temple as sweat formed on her brow. Delay would result in tragedy.

She opened the gate gingerly. The last thing she wanted was to spook the heifer and cause her to get up and run. She kept her distance at first, standing with her back to the gate. Hands shaking, she built a loop with one rope and held it by her side.

Willie took a small step toward the struggling mother-to-be. After a pause, she took another. Rose's small brown eyes followed her movements. They widened with fear. Willie took a slow step backward. She reached her left hand into her pocket, pulled out a piece of sweet sorghum and held it out to Rose.

"Whoa, Rosie," Willie crooned. "It's all right. I'm here to help you." Hoping her voice was steadier than her stomach, she took another step. The heifer knew her voice. It also knew her habit of sharing sorghum. She continued taking slow steps as she spoke. "Easy, girl. Easy."

When she was close enough to feel the moisture expelled from each labored breath, Willie reached out and stroked the rippled skin of Rose's neck. She held out a sorghum piece with her left hand as her right hand slipped the rope over the heifer's neck. Rose wasn't interested in the sorghum, but it served as distraction enough. She secured the other end of the rope to the nearest fence post. As she did, she thought of her classmates' eagerness to get married and have babies. Would they be so eager if they understood what it meant for their young bodies?

Willie approached again, praying the heifer wouldn't try to bolt. She gathered her skirt and knelt at the heifer's tail end.

Rose bawled and strained against the rope but didn't get up. A long red strand of afterbirth clung to the calf's hooves. It would be dead soon if it wasn't already. Willie had to act fast.

She squatted behind the heifer and tied the second rope around the calf's exposed hooves. She gripped the rope tight and pulled with all her weight, leaning back until she fell back clumsily. She let the rope go slack and waited, praying that natural contractions would begin. A moment later, she saw the sign she'd hoped for. Rose's abdomen swelled as her back end tensed. Willie began to pull the calf when Rose pushed, and then they rested together between contractions. After three rounds of pulling, the hooves had scarcely moved, and the head still wasn't visible.

"I know you can't appreciate this now, but you've got to trust me," Willie told Rose as she rolled her sleeves up to her shoulders. She repositioned herself behind the heifer and cupped her hands as she'd seen her father and grandfather do in rare cases when a calf was lodged in its mother's narrow pelvis. She slid her hands in over the wet hooves, past the calf's head, and down the neck, reaching inside until she had a hand on each of its shoulders. She tightened her grip and pulled down with a twist.

The calf came with a whoosh and a slurp and landed in her lap. A rush of amber liquid spilled out and splashed onto them both.

The calf didn't move.

Willie noted its stillness with horror. It should be twitching and gasping. Here was evidence she'd done her job correctly, but not quickly enough. Her throat tightened and her eyes burned. Anger and frustration clouded her thoughts, even as she wiped the calf's face and stroked its shiny coat.

Rose got to her feet and started licking the calf's face and body. Her movements weren't gentle, but it struck Willie as tender all the same. Willie scooted back and watched, irritated by the new mother's rough persistence. They both needed to accept the reality of their failure. A tear ran down Willie's cheek, and she brushed it away. If she was going to be taken seriously as a landowner and business woman, she had to learn to control her emotions.

In her lifetime on the farm, she had seen many stillbirths and animals that needed to be put down. It was never easy, but she had never felt the weight of responsibility before today. She considered the financial loss. At least she'd saved the heifer.

Rose abandoned all tenderness now and nudged the calf forcefully, lifting its slick hind end and tossing it inches above the ground. She was determined to bring her calf to life, not for financial gain or a man's approval, but because it was in her nature to give birth. She knew it wasn't supposed to end this way.

Willie wiped tears away, but more filled her eyes. She grieved for the mother in front of her, and it seemed right to do. A new life was gone from the world before it ever drew a breath. If there was anything worth crying for, surely this was it.

Through the blur of tears, Willie saw movement on the ground, a trick of the eyes. Then she saw it again and was certain it was no illusion. The calf shook its head suddenly and gasped, filling its chest with new air. The heifer gave another rough nudge, and the calf bawled.

Abandoning any regard for composure, Willie continued to let the tears roll down her cheeks as she stood up. Then she held her arms out wide as she yelled, "They made it! They both made it!"

Rose looked at Willie. Willie recognized it as a warning and backed out of the pen, leaving the mother and baby to get acquainted.

When her father arrived, Willie was still at the fence watching, unable to take her eyes off the living, breathing calf she'd thought dead.

"How 'bout that?" he said. "No matter how often it happens, it's always a miracle."

They stood together then, enjoying a rare moment of stillness rather than moving on to the next task. The heifer continued licking and nudging while they watched. Finally, the calf lifted its back hooves and after two lurches forward, stood on all four feet. Its body swayed from side to side while its feet struggled to stay underneath. It stumbled to its mother's side and began nursing.

Jim Tollett gestured at his daughter's clothes and said, "Looks like you had a hand in this one."

"More than my hand," Willie said. She spoke loudly and gestured as she spoke, wanting to make sure her father heard and understood despite his hearing loss. "Nearly to my shoulders." She explained what had happened while he was gone, and smiled in anticipation of her father's commendation.

"Whoa! Is that a brand-new calf?" Willie turned around and saw Thurston standing barefoot outside the pen wearing his Sunday clothes.

"It is," Father said. "Could be yours someday."

Willie winced at the reminder. For nine years, she had been their father's only interested beneficiary. Her sisters wanted nothing more than to be married off and have babies clinging to their skirts, but Willie wanted the farm. She'd been given a man's name, and she wanted a man's life.

Willie had been working beside her father and learning the business for as long as she could remember. He was agreeable to giving her a quarter section of his land when she finished school.

Even as a child, however, Willie had sensed the shift after Thurston was born. Jim Tollett had continued treating Willie like a son regarding the work she was expected to do, but when it came to talk of inheritance, Thurston became the new heir apparent. Willie knew their father was inclined to hand over the farm she'd worked so hard for to a boy who'd been in long pants a shorter time than she'd been in high school. Still, she clung to her father's promise of the first one hundred sixty acres.

Now, her brother had shown up at the moment of her greatest accomplishment and stolen her father's attention. Thurston stepped forward for a closer look at the calf, belly full and sleeping on the ground with its mother standing nearby.

"Thurston!" Willie yelled. "If you get your church duds mucked up, Mother will have your hide!"

"Oh yeah!" he said. "That's why I came out here. Edgalea sent me to tell you both it's time to get to the social."

"Great day in the morning!" Willie said. "Run and tell Edge we'll be right in!"

Chapter 2

As soon as Willie stepped into the house, she wished she could return to the cows. The urgency of the delivery and poignancy of mother and calf were replaced by a different sort of commotion. The pungency of lye soap stung her eyes, and the voices of her three sisters deliberating over hair styles carried from their bedroom to the kitchen. She eyed the murky water in the washtub and regretted not only that she needed a thorough scrubbing but also that she'd be the fifth person to use the bath water.

She was certain Edgalea had taken advantage of the first bath. At eighteen years old and in her last year of high school, her oldest sister was desperate to catch a husband. Though their parents rarely mentioned the matter, it seemed to be the only thought on Edgalea's mind. The list of eligible bachelors dwindled as her friends put the finishing touches on their bridal trousseaus. Meanwhile, Edgalea would graduate high school without a marriage prospect. Willie secretly hoped she could be so unlucky in love.

"Ooh, Willie! What is that smell? Is it coming from you?" Gladys asked. Her fourteen-year-old sister came out of the bedroom wearing a hand-me-down dress to which she'd added a fashionable new collar. Everyone agreed that Gladys was the prettiest of the Tollett girls. She had a kind smile and green eyes to complement her wavy auburn hair.

Willie looked down at her soiled clothes. She hadn't noticed outside, but now she was aware that even though she'd rinsed her arms in the stock tank, she was filthy, covered in the mixture of fluids and blood that come with new life. A bath, even in dirty water, became more appealing.

"Willie helped a calf get borned!" Thurston said when he walked in the door.

"Well, she smells terrible," Edgalea said. "Where's Father?"

"Washing outside," Thurston answered.

"Just as well. Go wait with Mother while Willie gets her bath."

Thurston burst into their parents' room telling their mother about the calf, and Edgalea returned to the girls' room, leaving Gladys and Willie alone in the kitchen.

"Did you really help?" asked Gladys as Willie undressed and stepped into the washtub. "I'm glad Father didn't make me go out there."

"Yes, I did. I was afraid we'd lose the heifer and calf if I didn't. But Father didn't make me go out. I wanted to. It's the only way to learn everything I'll need to know when I have my own place."

"Do you really want to do that? Wouldn't you rather have a family? What if you wind up like mean ol' Aunt Chloe?"

"Aunt Chloe is mean because she wanted to be married but isn't. I won't be mean because I don't want to be married."

"Good thing! No man will come around with you smelling the way you do!"

Willie splashed water at her sister, who squealed and ran to the safety of their bedroom. She scrubbed until she was sure the only thing anyone could smell was lye. She pulled on a clean shift and went into the bedroom the four sisters shared.

Ella Bea laid face down on the bed, clearly in a pout. The ten-year-old was spoiled and rotten. She had the tightest and brightest of red curls, making her the darling among the Tollett kin, but she had a habit of tattling on her siblings, which made her the target of their pranks and derision. As the youngest girl, but no longer the baby, she was doted on and neglected in turn.

"It's not fair!" Ella Bea muttered into the pillow. No one bothered to ask what she was referring to. They'd endured enough of Ella Bea's tantrums to be skilled at ignoring them. Edgalea only pushed her glasses further up the bridge of her nose.

Willie took a plain black dress from the wardrobe. Edgalea, whose red curls were pinned back in precise rows, secured Gladys's waves in a pile at her neck. They both wore their best dresses, newly embellished for the occasion. Ella Bea groaned once again.

"Willie, why won't you wear the blue floral one? It's so much more flattering," Gladys said. "You wear that black dress to school every day. Don't you want to dress up a little?" she asked.

"What for?" asked Willie. "They're all the same people I see at school and church. They've been looking at me my entire life."

"Exactly! Wouldn't you like everyone to see a different side of you?"

"Sure I would. I'd like them to see me as a future landowner, not a bride-to-be."

"You've done a fine job of making sure no one will see you as a bride," Edgalea said.

"They probably think you'd make a good hired hand," Gladys teased.

"Father's made us all into hired hands," Edgalea said. "Though I don't suppose there's much difference," she added.

"The pay is different," Willie said. "If I'm gonna work as hard as a man, I'd like to be paid like one."

Ella Bea moaned again, louder this time.

"Ella Bea! What is wrong with you?" Willie demanded.

"I don't want to talk about it!" she cried, and she buried her head in the pillow once more.

Despite her sisters' protests, Willie stepped out of the bedroom with her coarse hair standing on end and wearing same black dress she wore every day.

Father was dressed in his Sunday britches and a clean muslin shirt. His long, thin hair was combed straight back. He must have made several trips to the windmill to get water for Mother before he changed clothes. She'd emptied the washtub and started to heat fresh water on the stove.

"You look mighty fine, girls," Father said as he put his arm around his wife. "Are you sure you don't want to come, Sarah?" he asked her. "We don't mind waiting, do we?"

The girls, other than Willie, minded very much but knew better than to say so.

"Ah, Father. I've been waiting so long already!" Thurston said. Father silenced him with a look.

"I'll come if you want me to," Mother said. They all knew she would rather soak in a bath than cause a stir at the church social.

"No, you stay here and enjoy the quiet," Father said.

Willie watched her parents embrace. Jim Tollett kissed the top of his wife's head as she leaned against his chest. They each seemed so old and weathered individually, but in moments of closeness Willie could imagine them as the lovestruck young couple they once were.

Chapter 3

It took half an hour to get to the church in their horse-drawn buggy. The days were getting longer as April got underway, and the mild weather made for a pleasant ride. Jim Tollett owned a Ford truck, but preferred his horses and buggy. They were quieter, and Father was more confident in his ability to identify and solve any malfunction that might arise. Willie wished she were spending the evening watching over the new calves and their mothers. She felt less comfortable in her fitted school dress than in the gathered skirt and denim blouse she wore to work at home.

The sun lingered in the west before making its final descent, but women had already lit the lanterns in the churchyard by the time they arrived. Church was the central gathering place for Sunday worship, as well as weddings, funerals, and community meetings.

Jim Tollett was one of the founding members of the Inez Methodist Church, which sat at the intersection of the original Clark, Greathouse, and Tollett homesteads. They'd all donated land to the Methodist church in 1909 and, after meeting in Miss Edith Sanders's home for several years, built a small A-frame worship hall. They gave it a plaster finish and purchased a piano from Lindy Mason's family on the afternoon of her funeral. On the south side of the building was the church yard, the site of picnics, musicals, and dances, and on the north side, a graveyard. Life and death held together by the church.

The church held the spring social every year while the wheat still lay dormant and before spring planting began. Everyone in the community was invited, even those who didn't worship with the Methodist congregation. Men brought guitars and fiddles, women prepared their best dishes, and everyone forgot their work and worries for a time. It was the highlight of the year.

The older Willie got, though, the less appeal the spring social held for her. As much as she enjoyed exchanging news and stories with her friends, she felt more and more as though the events were organized as opportunities for young women to showcase their charms and young men to claim their prizes. Willie preferred sizing up cattle to being sized up by her classmates.

Makeshift serving tables, wide wooden planks laid across barrels, were set up along the south side of the building to keep the wind from blowing so much dust into the food. Along with the moon and stars, kerosene lamps cast light and shadows across the ground. Colorful quilts were spread over one end of the yard, leaving the other open for dancing. Women sat in clusters, as did the teenagers, while the children played games of tag and the men lined up along the hitching posts.

While Willie spent the afternoon in the cow lot, her sisters had been in the kitchen frying chicken and baking biscuits. She helped carry their dishes to the table and exchanged greetings with the elderly members of the community as she reached between them to make room on the table for her family's contributions. Apparently, they'd arrived so late the blessing had already been said. She wondered whether her father would be disappointed that he hadn't been able to offer it. He and Mr. Greathouse had an unspoken rivalry regarding who could lead the longest, most pious prayers.

An ad hoc band warmed up as people continued filling their plates. Traditions of respect dictated the oldest members of the congregation enjoy the first choices of the abundant spread. Other adults and children young enough to eat from their mothers' plates were next. The remaining children and unmarried adults, equal in social status, were left to scrape the bottom of dishes and get whatever meat they could manage, usually chicken breast and pork bones.

When it was her turn, Willie helped herself to generous portions of bratwurst and kraut provided by the Shotzinger family. Their sausages were flavorful, and they could work wonders with cabbage, salt, and time in a crock. Willie considered herself lucky that others passed over their dishes, as she had a large appetite.

Across the table, Carl Martin was searching in vain for a platter of chicken with dark meat remaining. Willie avoided looking straight at him, but even at a glance she recognized his dark hair. It was combed back so slick, she imagined him running a lard-covered comb through it. He fancied himself as slick as his hair.

As Willie returned the serving spoon to the plate of sausages, his hand brushed against hers and she looked up instinctively, meeting his dark eyes. Unlike many of the girls in town, Willie did not avert her gaze. Carl didn't seem surprised. He locked eyes with her and grinned. She did not smile back, but Carl was not deterred. His grin widened, revealing a set of teeth that were straighter and whiter than seemed natural.

"I'd love to have a bit of whatever you brought, if there's any left," he said, still smiling and maintaining eye contact. She didn't like the brazen way he was looking at her now, but she refused to be the first to look away.

"I carried in those biscuits, but my sisters deserve the credit."

"Don't be modest. I'm sure your touch made all the difference."

"Truly, I wouldn't know. I was up to my elbows in the business end of a heifer while they cooked."

Carl looked away, and she knew she'd won the exchange. Willie carried her plate to an empty quilt closest to the band. She loved all music, but at socials she most enjoyed the jigs when everyone could join in the dance together. She tried to clear out during the slow songs with romantic themes, lest any boys get the wrong idea. When she was younger, she'd danced with her father, but last year he'd started leaving her without a partner. She suspected it was intentional.

"Mind if I sit next to you?"

Willie knew the voice without looking up. Floyd Beaman had been the tallest boy in the fourth and fifth grades, but he hadn't grown an inch since. Unlike his family, he was small statured and rotten to the core. He'd begun getting in trouble when they were in grade school and had continued a life of idleness and dishonesty. Now that everyone was partnering up to get married, he approached the young women as though they'd never met and tried to present himself as a reasonable prospect. Even the most desperate of girls wouldn't accept an advance from Floyd Beaman. Willie was both surprised and encouraged that none of her classmates had been foolish enough to accept his pretense.

"Actually, I'm waiting for someone."

"I'll join you until she gets here," he said. "Then I bet we can make room for three."

"No, that won't do." Willie looked past Floyd's shoulder. The answer to her dilemma was standing within earshot. "I'm waiting for Harold," she said, a little louder than necessary. "I promised I'd save him a seat and a dance."

"Oh, well, now I see." Floyd turned away, clearly scanning the room for another quarry.

"A dance, is it?" Harold said as he took a seat next to Willie. "You know I'm gonna hold you to it." His blonde hair stood on end; she'd never seen it otherwise, though usually he wore a hat. He grinned at her, making the scar on his cheekbone dance. He'd gotten that scar when she dared him to pick sandhill plums from her Grandpa Sam's homeplace when they were ten years old. Red Sam's hound had come out, as Willie had known it would, and scared the pudding out of him. He ran straight into the barbed wire fence in his hurry to get away.

Willie couldn't help smiling at him. "I was afraid I'd be dealing with Floyd all night."

"I wouldn't wish that on anyone."

"Remember last fall when he set his sights on May Bell? I thought he was going to follow her to the privy."

"As I recall, though, that was the night Glenn decided to make his intentions for her known. He didn't know he had them until he watched Floyd's attempts."

"I believe you're right."

"It might work to your advantage to have him stalking you tonight. Could draw out your secret admirers."

"I don't want other boys' attention any more than I want Floyd's. You'd better be careful though. If your mother sees us together, she'll be hauling you out back to get a switch!"

"I'm twice her size now, and I bet she'd still try! I still don't understand why I'm the one that got in trouble. You were the one who took your dress off!"

"I wanted to swim in the stock tank with you. At seven years old, I didn't see any difference between your body and mine. How was I to know you'd get in trouble?"

"Or that my mother would consider you a dangerous woman from that day forward?"

The two friends laughed and continued eating without talking, caught up in the music and the ease of each other's company.

Willie believed Harold Parrish might understand her better than anyone else, not only because she'd known him all her life, but also because he also had plans that didn't fit the county's expectations. His father was a land-wealthy man, and Harold would inherit every acre and dollar, making him a coveted young bachelor, but he wasn't interested. He wanted to leave Roosevelt County. He'd planned to attend university since he'd learned such a thing existed.

"Can I take your plate for you?" Willie asked as she stood up.

"I know that trick, Miss Tollett. You'll disappear, and I'll never get the dance you lied about promising me."

Willie laughed. That was exactly what she had in mind. "In that case, can we go ahead and get the dance over with?" she asked.

"It's no wonder you have to beat the fellas back with a stick. You're the picture of charm!"

Harold took her plate and put it on the quilt with his own. When he bowed slightly and held out his hand, Willie took it with a smile and they joined the other couples. The band began playing a slow song. Willie's cheek was level with Harold's chest, and she caught a whiff of lye soap and peppermint. She guessed there was candy in his pocket.

"What will you do after you graduate next year?" he asked her.

"Get married and start having babies, I suppose."

Harold laughed. "The church ladies will be relieved to hear it," he said. "But really, what do you have in mind?"

"A quarter section of land."

"You know, I'm graduating this spring."

"Of course, I know."

"I'm planning to go to university. In Tennessee."

"Yes, I know." Willie couldn't understand why Harold was acting as though they'd never spoken of these things.

"You've never struck me as the type to be satisfied as a farmer's wife." Again, he was stating things that were well-known between them.

"No."

"So, how about coming with me? Next year, after you graduate, of course. Think of it. You could explore the city, have new adventures. Once I finish school and start working, I could buy you a small farm so you could keep your calluses thick."

Willie smiled but didn't say anything. She had thought dancing would save her from unwanted talk of marriage. Now she was slow dancing with a marriage proposal.

"It would be nice to have your company," Harold said. "It will take me three years to finish my courses. I'll start out living with my uncle and working at the bank in town. By the end of the first year, I'll have saved enough to rent a small place. Once I graduate, I'll be able to take a good position at any bank."

Willie considered what he was offering. She had never imagined a life away from Roosevelt County. She'd only wondered whether or not she would be in charge of her own life. As much as she liked Harold and was tempted by the idea of an adventure, she was afraid marriage in the city would be the same as marriage on a farm. And it wasn't for her.

"That's sweet of you to ask, Harold, but it won't do. By the time you finish school, I could have my own herd growing on my own land. I figure I'll stay around here."

"I had a feeling you'd say that," he said. "But you can't blame me for trying." He placed a strand of hair behind her ear as she inhaled his peppermint-lye familiarity. They continued dancing, even as the next song began. Neither was anxious to separate, since they were both aware of the finality it would represent.

Halfway through the second song, Willie felt a tap on her shoulder.

"Mind if I have a turn?" It was Roger Harris, and his question was not directed to her but to Harold.

"You'd better ask Willie" Harold said, "unless you're wantin' to dance with me."

Roger posed his question again, this time to Willie. She sighed. At least the song was close to ending. If she was going to have to dance with someone other than her friend or her father, at least it would only be for a little while. And Roger was harmless. There was nothing notable about his character or his looks. He was nice enough, smart enough, and handsome enough. Average in just about every way. She was sure he could have his pick of girls by the time fall came around.

After a beat, she answered. "Sure."

Roger took her right hand in his, and she placed her left hand on his shoulder, keeping her arm straight enough to maintain distance between them. She couldn't think of anything to say, and she wondered if she might get through the dance without having to speak at all. She watched Bill Carter and Joyce Moss float by as though the stars and music had been arranged specially for them. Willie wondered how it might feel to be so at ease with the script other people wrote for you.

"Your hands are sure rough," Roger said. It was the kind of comment that would have made Edgalea cry, but Willie accepted it as a compliment.

"Yeah, they rarely blister anymore," she said.

"My mother has cream she puts on her hands every night." It was becoming clear why Roger, a perfectly average boy, hadn't procured a betrothal. His conversational skills left something to be desired. Neither of them lingered when the song came to an end.

As Willie walked toward the food tables, she saw Gladys dancing with Carl. It looked as though a queue of their classmates were waiting for their chance to impress her. Roger approached Edgalea and extended his hand. Willie hoped he'd thought of something more interesting to talk about than hand cream.

Willie left her sisters to the dancing and walked to the front of the building. She needed a break from the courting rituals. A crowd of grade school girls ran by, and for a moment she envied their ability to run and play so freely. Then Thurston and his friends ran by, chasing the girls, and it occurred to her that they were rehearsing for the games of pursuit her own peers played.

Willie rounded the corner to the north side of the church building, where the glow of the lamps could no longer reach her. With the sun down, the breeze over the Staked Plains gave her a chill. It felt refreshing when she'd first stopped dancing, but now she wished she'd grabbed her sweater. She leaned against the building with her arms folded over her chest. She could make out the outlines of crude tombstones marking two generations of settlers' graves.

A tiny flame flickered only a few yards away. For an instant, she saw the outline of a man with sunken eyes and weathered skin drawn over high cheeks. She half-gasped, half-screamed at the sudden appearance of an unfamiliar man.

"Sorry, miss," he stammered. She couldn't tell from his voice whether he was also rattled or suppressing a laugh. She watched red embers being drawn up the end of a cigarette. "Really, sorry," he said again. "I didn't mean to startle you. I was surprised anyone else would be looking for a hiding place at such a fine party."

"It's okay," Willie said. She was irritated at the man's presumptuousness. "I'm not hiding."

"My mistake." The man took another drag of his cigarette. Willie studied the outline of his face from the cover of darkness. She didn't recognize him. "I'll move down," he said. "There's plenty of dark on this wall."

Willie felt her irritation being replaced by curiosity. He hadn't asked why she was hiding in the dark or questioned her denial of the obvious fact. His only response was to offer her space. And though she'd come over here to be alone, she discovered she wanted the company of this peculiar man. "It's okay if you want to stay here," she said. "I don't mind."

"All right, then." He lifted the cigarette once more.

"Mind if I try that?" She surprised herself with the question. She'd never had a desire to smoke before. The dance, Harold's proposal, and now this strange man made her feel reckless.

"You sure?"

"It's not my first," she lied. The man handed her his cigarette. She took it in her thumb and forefinger, lifted it to her lips, and drew a breath. She could feel the man watching her just as she had watched him. The burn went from her throat to her lungs, but she resisted the impulse to cough. She returned his cigarette and choked out her thanks.

"Not your brand?" he asked. Willie couldn't tell whether he was being genuine or condescending. She decided he was a hard man to read. In the darkness, it was difficult to tell anything about him except that he was old. She shook her head, afraid that if she tried to speak, the cough she'd been trying to swallow would make its way out.

"I don't think I've seen you around here," Willie said.

"No, I'm not from these parts."

"Visiting or planning to stay?"

"I'll stay a while. Came from East Texas. Came West hoping to get on with an uncle in Causey, but he didn't have anything for me, so I joined up at the Greathouse Ranch. It's why I'm here. Boss thought I might feel at home with church folks."

"And do you?"

"Church folks make the best food," he said. "And the people aren't bad, so long as it's not Sunday." Willie laughed. She didn't know anyone who wasn't church folk.

"Did you bring your family with you?" she asked.

"Pop died a year ago. My brothers and sisters stayed near Mother back east."

"I meant your own family. Wife and kids."

"That life wasn't meant for me. My friends married off a decade ago while I was playing baseball and trying to make my way on the farm. Then I went away for a while. Reckon I came home too old and broke to go lookin' for a wife."

"I didn't know men could get too old for marriage," Willie said. "I thought that only happened to girls."

"When you get to be my age, the only girls interested are the ones whose first husbands have died and left them with a passel of kids to raise."

"Sounds like a bargain," Willie said. "How old are you, anyway?" She knew her parents would not approve of such direct conversation, particularly with a man, but he didn't seem bothered by it.

"Thirty." He held his cigarette out toward her. She hesitated, then took it, determined to get it right. Again, she inhaled. This time, she didn't breathe in quite so quickly or deeply and so avoided becoming choked.

"That's not too old," she said. "You should meet my sister. If you want to get married, she'd probably go for it." Then she added, "There's no dead husband or kids either." Her eyes had adjusted to the darkness, and she noticed the man looked younger when he laughed.

Willie saw a book tucked under his arm.

"What's that?" she asked.

"A Zane Grey."

"What's a Zane Grey?"

"A book. By the Western writer." Willie shook her head. The only things she'd seen men read were the Bible and the weekly newspaper.

"Do you read a lot of books?" she asked.

"I do. Mostly Westerns."

"Why?"

"Why do I read books, or why do I read Westerns?"

"Well," she considered, "both, I guess."

"I like to read because it occupies my mind. I like Westerns because the good guy always wins."

Willie thought that was a fine answer. After several minutes of silence, he dropped the butt of his cigarette to the ground and stamped it out with the toe of his brogan. Willie couldn't think of anything else to say to the stranger.

"I better get back to the social," she said. "Good luck with everything."

Willie found the dance going on just as she'd left it. She returned to the spread of food, served herself a slice of buttermilk pie, and found a seat where she hoped to go unnoticed. A shadow came over the blanket.

"A girl as pretty as you sitting alone?" Willie looked up as her father sat on the blanket next to her.

Willie smiled. "My own doing."

Jim Tollett turned his head to the right, offering Willie his better ear. Unfortunately, as her mother often teased, her father was *deaf in one ear and can't hear out of the other.* "Surely you'll accept a few dances tonight."

Willie leaned closer and answered. "I will," she said. "Already have, in fact."

"That's right?" he said. "How about one with me?"

Willie set her plate down and stood took her father's hand.

"Any dances with Harold Parrish?" he asked.

"Yes," she said.

"He's from good stock, you know."

"Mm-hm," she said. She was beginning to understand his meaning, but she refused to satisfy his curiosity right away.

"Did he have anything interesting to say?"

"Not that I recall."

Jim Tollett furrowed his brow, and his blue eyes lost a bit of their twinkle. He twisted his mouth as though deciding whether to speak or keep silent. He muttered something under his breath, and Willie understood enough to know she'd better come to Harold's defense.

"I guess you knew Harold was going to ask me to go to Tennessee with him?"

"Yes. Though the part that most interested me was that he wanted you to go as his wife."

"That was part of the deal, yes."

"Either you turned him down or you're holding back excitement on my account."

Willie paused before she answered. She didn't want to disappoint her father and it seemed in this instance there was no avoiding it.

"I told him I couldn't go. What would I do in the city? We've been working to build our herd here. And our grain crops get better every year. If we rotate the fields like we've planned, we'll be looking at our best year yet. I couldn't stand to sit in some city apartment and miss it all." Willie tried to read her father's expression. She watched it change.

"As the one who's taught you everything you know, I'd love to keep you on the farm forever. As a father, I'd love to see you settled with a good man. I s'pose you're right though. Your mother said you'd refuse. All that book learnin' of Harold's won't satisfy."

Willie didn't know what to say, so she nodded. Dances came with a cost, no matter who the partner was. As the song came to an end, her faither said, "I wouldn't dance with Carl Martin again."

"Oh?" Willie asked. "Why not?"

"You smell like an old cigarette."

Chapter 5

Willie didn't tell her sisters about Harold's proposal. She needed time to understand it herself, and she didn't want to hear their opinions. Once they were in bed, she did tell Edgalea and Gladys about the man she'd met in the dark. Of course, she didn't mention she'd shared his cigarette. Or that he appeared to like books more than dancing. Edgalea had been scandalized by her impropriety as it was. Still, once she was convinced that Willie had no intention of pursuing him romantically, she wanted more details than her sister could provide. It had been so dark after all, and Willie hadn't been gauging his marriageability.

All the talk at church the next morning was of the social. The high school girls were certain they'd sealed their fates, either as brides-to-be or as spinsters. Boys and girls who'd become so familiar the night before now stole shy glances at each other as they walked into the worship hall with their parents. The ladies repeated the compliments on cooking and dresses they'd offered the night before while the men continued their speculations about the wheat crop soon to come out of dormancy.

The worship hall was arranged into two rows of wooden pews, leaving a center aisle down the middle. Willie's family filed into their customary seats on the left side of the lectern, third pew from the front. Her grandfather, best known as Red Sam, but referred to in church as Brother Samuel, sat in the pew in front of them with Uncle Owen, Aunt Dell, and their three children.

Father sat on the end of the row, both so he could stretch his legs during the preaching and so he could get out easily when the time came to lead a prayer or make an announcement. Thurston, still prone to foolishness during the service, sat between Father and Aunt Chloe, who listened to the young people's chatter with her head tilted, the way their dog did when she caught an unfamiliar scent. Ella Bea, the next youngest, sat on their aunt's left side. It was another source of El's perpetual indignation. According to her, Aunt Chloe was not only mean, she also smelled bad. The older girls made it a point not to get close enough to confirm the claim. Gladys, Willie, and Edgalea completed the row. Willie noticed her sister scanning the room as they walked in and knew she was hoping to see a tall stranger with a drawn face and sunken eyes.

Mother did not attend church with the family. There were a few members of the congregation who did not welcome the presence of a Cherokee woman, and Sarah Tollett was never one to kick up dust. It was a wonder to Willie that her mother could recite so much of the Bible. The book of Isaiah was her favorite, and she could recall a passage to suit any circumstance.

Mr. Greathouse broke through the noise with a welcome, and the hall filled with the familiar echoes of the pews settling against the wooden floor as the last congregants took their seats. Willie guessed that since he'd helped start the church, it was his privilege to start the service every Sunday. Knowing the routine, everyone bowed their heads for the opening prayer, and at first it seemed like silence had come over the room. After a moment, however, Willie noticed her brother's deep breathing, Mr. Harris's foot tapping the floor, and Mrs. Lancaster patting her sleeping baby's backside. A church house is never quiet.

Mr. Greathouse filled the remaining space with his voice. Willie tried to focus on his words, but she was overcome by his sonorous baritone. As the prayer went on, Willie's head bobbed. Someone should have cautioned him to keep it short on the morning after the social. Willie felt the jab of Edgalea's elbow in her ribs and sat up with a start. She had clearly missed the amen.

Willie thought Mr. Greathouse would have made a great preacher. Instead, they had to listen to the nasal droning of Pastor Westbrook week after week. Her family still pined for the days of Pastor Thurston, her brother's namesake, but he'd traded the pulpit for a position at the Portales Bank.

Pastor Westbrook took his place at the lectern and invited the few members who had Bibles to open them to the book of Hebrews. Father turned to the appropriate page then held out the large volume as though inviting his row of kinfolk to look on. The only one close enough to see was Thurston, and he hadn't yet learned to read. Still, they all turned their heads toward the book in a pantomime of following along.

Willie did her best to remain attentive throughout the service, but her eyes grew heavy, and her mind wandered. She imagined a future for herself in Aunt Chloe's position, sitting next to Thurston and his children in church. This image did not seem natural, so she tried for a moment to imagine her family coming to visit her and Harold in Tennessee. That wasn't a fit either. Whenever she imagined herself as an adult, she couldn't figure out who else belonged in the picture.

Her mind drifted to thoughts of the calves in the pasture. She'd gone out before sunup this morning to check on the newest one. There was no evidence of the difficulty of the day before. He stood at his mother's side drinking eagerly from her swollen udders. Iris and Holly showed no signs of laboring yet.

Willie realized she hadn't absorbed a word of Pastor Westbrook's message when she saw him gesture for the congregation to stand as he began singing. They remained standing as Father led the closing prayer. Willie shifted her weight from one foot to the other. She opened her eyes and noticed movement on her right. Turning, she saw Thurston crouched on the floor. She watched as his nimble fingers untied Aunt Chloe's boot laces then retied them to each other. It was a bold move as there would be no way for Thurston to deny what he'd done, and his punishment would be severe.

Aunt Chloe had no sense of humor, and Father never carried his into the church building. Willie made a note to herself to try teaching her brother the art of subtlety.

When Father finally said his amen, Thurston was standing upright, head bowed, and eyes closed. Aunt Chloe, anxious to get to her Sunday School pupils, attempted a quick step into the aisle. Her body, anticipating significant forward motion, lurched forward while her hobbled feet stayed put. She half-grabbed, half-fell into the pew in front of them. When she'd righted herself, her eyes bored into Thurston, but his eyes were full of incredulity and his gaze rested on their cousin Marvin in the pew in front of them. In this moment, Willie recognized her brother's cunning. Of course, Aunt Chloe would never imagine that the child sitting right next to her could have done such a thing without drawing her attention. Her eyes landed on Marvin, and Willie knew his day would be the worst for it. Edgalea was already shuffling out the other end of the pew, and Willie followed her, putting distance between herself and their ill-fated cousin.

As the senior high pupils entered their classroom, the boys and girls gathered in opposite corners of the small space. The girls sat in a cluster of chairs and occasionally looked over their shoulders at the boys, hoping to make eye contact with any of them who might have turned to steal a look at the girls. The boys leaned against back the wall or stood with one foot propped on a chair and body curved forward, an arm on a knee and chin in hand. Before Willie had a chance to sit down, May Bell said, "Ask Willie. They're chums, and I bet she'll know."

"Know what?"

"Is Harold sweet on anyone?" Willie thought of their conversation during the dance.

"If he's sweet on anyone, I bet it's Eula Baker," May Bell said. "He's planning to go to university in Tennessee, and she's so refined. Her mother pays a woman in Fort Worth to make all of her dresses. He'd never settle for a country bumpkin, isn't that right, Willie?"

"Oh, I don't know about that," Willie said. "I'm sure he'd like a farmer's daughter just fine." She was glad her friend wasn't here to suffer such foolishness. His family was two miles away at the Baptist congregation.

Seeing that Willie was not going to confirm her theory, May Bell moved on. The girls continued their roll call of eligible young men, speculating who was sweet on whom. By watching their faces, Willie could tell who hoped to be named in relation to each boy. Good news for one meant heartache for another. Gladys's name came up more than once. Edgalea feigned disinterest, but Willie could see she was absorbing every word. As her interest in the girls' conversation waned, Willie began to catch bits and pieces of the boys' talk.

"My dad says it will be good for all the businesses in town," said Glenn.

"It would keep my uncle from having to go so far to place a bet," Leon added with a laugh.

"My pop says it'll be nothing but a den of thieves," Ralph said.

As usual, Willie found the boys' conversation much more intriguing than the girls'. She leaned back in her chair, hoping to hear more and wondering what they might be talking about.

Mr. Greathouse walked through the door, and a hush fell over both sides of the room. The young people immediately turned their chairs back into straight rows. They followed their teacher's voice with both their eyes and ears as he extoled them with the blessings and curses outlined for them in the second letter to the Corinthians. Willie did her best to pay attention. She knew it was important to her parents that their children be well-versed in the Bible, but as in the service, the combination of a late night, quiet room, and somnolent voice made it hard to stay awake, much less alert. The minutes dragged on until they were dismissed at last.

Aunt Chloe walked to church from her house in town, but she rode home with Willie's family for Sunday dinner every week. As usual, the two adults spoke in serious tones in the cab while the children sat in the truck bed.

When they arrived home, the girls each took an apron from a nail on the wall, and Aunt Chloe did the same. It bothered Willie that their aunt behaved as though it was her own kitchen. She went to the counter that ran half the length of one wall where she sifted flour from the bin and added soda from the tin. Edgalea handed her a block of butter and took tin plates and cups down from the open wooden shelf above the counter. Mother stood at the wood burning cookstove stirring a skillet of onions and potatoes.

As expected, Aunt Chloe began recounting poor Marvin's transgressions as soon as she had an audience. Willie was afraid her aunt's indignation would lead to tough biscuits.

"He's a lively child," said Mother. She'd always had a sense of humor about children and their hijinks.

"I hardly think that's an excuse," said Aunt Chloe.

"Yes, of course you're right," said Mother. "But it is a fact."

"Well, I don't know what Owen and Dell are going to do with that boy, but they better do it in a hurry." Mother agreed to appease Aunt Chloe, Willie guessed.

The two women were close, and Willie believed it was because they were both outcasts of sorts. It was the only thing she could see that they had in common. Her aunt was excluded from most social functions in town, even when she was invited to attend. Outside the family, there was no place for an unmarried woman of her age.

Mother was married to a prominent citizen, but even his family referred to her as "Jim's squaw." Because of Jim's relative wealth, most people in the community kept their opinions to themselves, but their behavior was such that Mother never felt comfortable in social gatherings or even in church. The women avoided sitting next to her, and their children dared each other to yank on her skirt before running away.

The Tollett girls had endured their share of ridicule when they'd started school. Because she favored her mother's looks, Willie was a particular target when they were young. Once, when she first started to school, she got in a fight in the school yard because a boy asked what she was doing off of the reservation. At the time, Willie wasn't even sure what his words meant, but she knew they were meant to insult. She never told anyone what prompted her to punch the boy, not wanting the rest of the family to know what was said about them.

The girls all learned to ignore the looks and comments, and as they grew older and their father grew more successful, their classmates seemed to have forgotten their earlier derision. Thurston had avoided the teasing all together. Still, though she would never say it out loud, Willie wondered whether Edgalea's lack of a suitor was related to their mother's Cherokee heritage.

Aunt Chloe gave Mother a synopsis of the sermon every Sunday as they made final dinner preparations. The two women dredged pieces of chicken through eggs and flour then dropped them into a skillet of hot lard. Edgalea removed the fried onions and potatoes from another skillet and added a scoop of flour to its black bottom. She tossed in a bit of salt and dragged the spoon through as the residual fat coated the grain and formed a thick paste. She added milk and stirred the gravy until it thickened. Gladys cut biscuits and put them in the oven. Willie poured milk into glasses and helped Ella Bea set the table. The aroma of Sunday dinner filled the house.

They took their seats around the kitchen table, Father and Mother at each end with Willie and Thurston on each side of Father, Aunt Chloe and Edgalea on each side of Mother, and Ella Bee and Gladys in the middle. Father had constructed the oak table when they first moved into the house. For most of the day, it was only large enough for six people, but at dinnertime they raised a leaf at each end so that all of them could sit together.

"By the time the cooking is finished, I don't even feel like eating anymore," Aunt Chloe said after the amen.

"I do!" said Ella Bea. "All those smells and goodness have been tempting us for so long."

"Exactly. It's a temptation to excess," said Aunt Chloe. "And on the Lord's Day no less. I have a mind to begin fasting every Sunday."

"And miss out on fried chicken?" Thurston asked incredulously.

"I think it's a fine idea, Sister. We would all do well to consider the temptations of the flesh and how we might thwart the plans of the Great Deceiver," said Father.

"It's worth noting that sin first entered the world in the form of food," Aunt Chloe added. "The Devil's always known it was our greatest weakness."

Gladys rolled her eyes without the notice of the adults. All three of her sisters saw her, however, and snickered quietly. They were accustomed to the odd behavior of their aunt and her tendency to consider everything enjoyable as a threat to their souls. Father had the same inclination.

"I think that's just fine," Mother said, even as she served Aunt Chloe an extra helping of potatoes.

Mother was a peacemaker by nature, but she was from a long line of strong women, healers among their people back east. She bent over backward to make others feel comfortable, so her own opinions were expressed in ways so slight they were easy to miss.

"Father, I heard talk from the boys this morning that a pool hall could be opening in Inez," Ella Bea said.

"Come again?" Father said, either because he didn't hear or didn't believe her.

Willie didn't mention she'd heard the same in her class. She hadn't realized exactly what they were talking about at the time, but now she was able to make sense of it. She braced herself for Father's reaction. He refused even to walk by the pool hall in Portales, choosing instead to cross to the other side of the street in order to avoid associating with the likes of its patrons.

"No one has mentioned such a plan to me," Father said. He did not raise his volume, but everyone at the table heard the change in his tone. It was the sound of righteous fury rising.

"It's no wonder. They know you won't abide such corruption," said Aunt Chloe.

Jim Tollett had been part of the 1916 vote to make Roosevelt County dry. As early as ten years prior there had been seven saloons in Portales alone. He'd alerted everyone to the evils of drinking or supporting establishments that sold liquor. Willie could imagine him doing the same regarding gambling.

"They'd turn our town into a bunch of good-for-nothings, handing hard-earned money to the Devil," Father said. "I won't have it." He turned to Mother. "I'll call on a few folks after I take Chloe home. We'll get this shut down right away."

The rest of the meal was spent in disciplined silence. No one dared speak of frivolity when a battle for the soul of the town was at hand.

Chapter 6

The three oldest Tollett girls attended high school in Portales. Two years prior, several county schools had consolidated so the children in the Inez community were expected to attend school in Rogers, a community six miles away. It was an unpopular decision that frustrated many families' efforts to have their children educated. The walk was too far, and the bus was so bumpy it could have churned butter. When she was in the tenth grade, Willie and Edgalea left home before the sun rose and returned well after it set. This year, Edgalea, Willie, and Gladys stayed in Portales with their Aunt Xenia during the week and attended the high school in town.

True to his word, Father made two stops between Aunt Chloe's house in Inez and Aunt Xenia's house in Portales. The Hollinses and Bishops were original homesteaders in Inez. As such, they had control over much of what happened in the community. The Armstrongs were also among the town's first citizens, but Mr. Armstrong got his start as a bartender in one of Portales's seven saloons. Although he wouldn't patronize such establishments now, but he wouldn't speak out against them either. The girls were instructed to remain in the Ford while Father called on the influential, like-minded men of the town.

"I don't understand what the issue is," Gladys said.

"Gambling establishments attract the sort of riffraff that ruins a town's prosperity," Edgalea explained as though she were many years older.

"Portales seems prosperous enough, and they have saloons and a pool hall," Gladys said.

"Father is looking out for our best interest," Edgalea insisted.

"Yes, he's worried we'll all start gambling," Willie said, rolling her eyes.

"Don't be silly," Edgalea said. "They'd never let girls in a billiard hall."

"Sure they would," said Willie. "Certain girls."

"Oh, Willie!" Edgalea said. "If Father heard the way you talk—"

"She'd still be his favorite," Gladys said.

"Father is protecting the moral well-being of our town," Edgalea continued. "This is a Christian community, and he doesn't want to give the devil a foothold."

When Father returned to the truck, the girls leaned forward, hoping to hear his report over the rumble of the motor, but he offered no comment. Instead, he drove to the Bishops' place in silence.

While he was inside, Edgalea got out of the truck bed.

"What are you doing?" Gladys asked.

"I'm going to sit by Father so I can find out what's happening."

"You'll tell us everything tonight, won't you?" Gladys asked.

"If it's appropriate for children," she said. Gladys and Willie exchanged a look.

When Father returned, he looked at Edgalea without any comment, started the motor, and drove on. Willie and Gladys leaned forward enough to hear Edgalea yell, "Father, how did the visits go?"

"Fine," he answered. They couldn't hear what Edgalea said next, but it didn't matter since Father did not reply. He probably hadn't heard her either. They rode the rest of the way without speaking. Portales was a much larger town than Inez, and Main Street was bustling. The streets that surrounded the courthouse square were home to a drug store, boot shop, and billiard hall, as well as a theater that featured both live performances and picture shows. Further down Main Street, there was a cafe, George McCormick's filling station, and the general store the McCormicks opened the year before.

Aunt Xenia's house was located on Railroad Street, just off of the newly paved Main Street, one block east and two blocks south of the high school. The road was wide enough for four wagons or motor cars to pass each other comfortably. Each home was set far enough from the next that two more could have fit between them. Aunt Xenia lived in a white craftsman with two bedrooms, a sitting room, and a kitchen. Unlike others on the street that had been hauled in from their original farm sites, her house was built where it stood now. She refused to cut down anything that dared to grow, so the yard had a wild look about it when compared to the surrounding houses. The front yard was closed in by a rough picket fence, and every inch of the backyard was planted for food.

Despite their nearly identical physical appearances, Aunt Xenia was the opposite of Aunt Chloe, though the girls didn't dare let on to their father, who assumed they were in a household of high decorum. She expected each of the girls to behave properly, but both her definition of proper and her enforcement of it were more lenient than Jim Tollett's. Xenia and her husband, Jim Webb, had come to New Mexico with the same wagon train as her father and brothers when their daughter Minnie was only two years old. Ola was born three weeks before they made it to their claim in the New Mexico Territory.

Jim Webb died within months. He'd gone to Portales to pick up lumber to add a second story to their original homestead house. A sheep farmer found him in a gully, crushed by the weight of his load. Xenia lived on their claim for the three years required to be awarded the title and deed, then left her quarter section to her father's management and moved to town with her two young girls.

When her sister Mandy died in 1915 and her husband sent their three youngest children away, it was Xenia who volunteered to take them in. They had arrived at the train station with nothing but the clothes they wore. Then four years later, when Xenia's sister Ida married a widower, she opened her doors to his teenage daughters, Lois and Jimmie.

Jimmie and Lois graduated high school soon after moving in, but without husbands, they had nowhere else to go. Mandy's children had joined their oldest brother in Idaho two months prior, leaving Xenia with a household of five women, eight when Willie and her sisters joined them. They lived together as cousins and sisters, drawn together by their losses and the hospitality of a widow.

Father stopped the truck in front of the house, and the girls climbed out of the bed. Willie retrieved their small bag as Aunt Xenia came out of the house.

"I'd begun to wonder whether the girls were coming this week," she said. Indeed, it was hours past the time when they normally arrived.

"I had to make a couple of stops on the way. The devil is on the prowl, and I aim to fend him off."

"Yes, I'm sure. Well, we already had supper and cleaned up. All the chores are done, and the other girls are getting ready for bed." Willie saw the criticism land on Edgalea. It came so infrequently from their aunt that it stung her sister, who thought of herself as above reproach. In exchange for room and board, they completed their chores faithfully, without complaint. Breaking their commitment would be a difficult pill for Edgalea to swallow.

Normally, Father would come in for a few minutes and get news from Portales before continuing home. Tonight, he didn't even come inside the house. He thanked Aunt Xenia for staying up, reminded the girls to be virtuous, and restarted the engine. They watched his truck putter around the corner.

When it was out of sight, Aunt Xenia smiled as they turned and walked inside.

"I'm sorry we weren't here sooner," Edgalea said.

"It's no bother," Xenia said. "We left a few biscuits on the table in case you came along, and the girls took care of all your chores in case you didn't." Willie marveled at this. At home, there would be plenty of chores waiting, but no biscuits. As her father was fond of saying, "He that tilleth his land shall have plenty of bread, but he that followeth after vain persons shall have poverty enough."

"We'll be right along to bed," Edgalea said, still apologetic in her tone.

"That's not necessary," said Xenia. "I only made a point of saying everything was put away so your father wouldn't come in. I have no interest in fetching his coffee while he explains the devil's latest scheme. I'd rather put my feet up with a magazine."

Willie was surprised to see everyone still sitting up. Lois poured over *Ladies' Home Journal*. Aunt Xenia had issues going back years, and Lois perused them nightly, "for recipes," she said. Jimmie mended a skirt while Ola crocheted and Minnie brushed her straight, black hair. No one, it appeared, was ready for bed. Only Aunt Xenia would be bold enough to brush off Jim Tollett. Indeed, she seemed beholden to no man.

"I thought you all would never get here!" Ola said, dropping her afghan and standing to greet Willie with a hug. "I want to hear all about the social!" Ola was the closest to Willie in age, and Willie thought of her as another sister. She was the most petite of the cousin group. Even her facial features were small. The exception was her ears, and Ola always kept her curly auburn hair brushed forward to hide them.

"Yes, tell us all about it, since we weren't able to go," Jimmie said.

"It wouldn't have been appropriate without escorts," said Edgalea.

"So, the fatherless are cursed to be without husbands as well?" Jimmie asked. From her cheeks to her hips to her tone of voice, Jimmie was all edges.

"You're not fatherless," Minnie said. "You have a living, breathing father only two miles from here. I don't even have a memory of mine before he died."

"But isn't it easier to have never known your father than to be put out by him when a new wife and baby come along?" Jimmie asked.

"She's right," Lois said. "Little Oma Dean is the one with a father now, and we are left without."

The question of whether it is worse to have no memory of your father who died or to have been put out by a father who was still living came up often in this house.

"How are we supposed to find husbands if we never get out of the house?" asked Jimmie.

"Who cares about finding a husband? I only want to dance and eat pie!" Lois said.

"Jimmie, you get out of the house every day," Ola said.

"Cooking and cleaning for Red Sam doesn't count."

"Speaking of cooking," Willie said, "How about one of those biscuits?"

"Yes," said Edgalea. "And talk of the social will have to wait. It's already late."

"I doubt Willie has anything interesting to report anyway," Minnie said. "She probably stood around with the old men speculating on wheat prices."

Willie thought of her time standing with the older man on the side of the church building. She laughed to herself but would not share this memory with the ladies of Railroad Street. They would judge it unwise at best and scandalous at worst.

Instead, she went into the kitchen, followed by her sisters, while their cousins continued arguing. Edgalea took down three plates. "Don't bother with dishes, and you won't have to wash them," Aunt Xenia said as she refilled her coffee. In a display of crudeness their parents would never allow, they ate their biscuits standing and leaning over the pan. "What calamity has got your father worked up this time?" Aunt Xenia asked.

"There's talk of a pool hall opening in Inez."

"Oh, is that all? I don't know why he gets so worked up about folks having a good time," Aunt Xenia said. "Maybe if they didn't have to come all the way into Portales, they'd have an easier time staying awake during the Sunday service."

"Oh my!" Edgalea said.

Willie choked on her biscuit. From the way her father talked, pool hall patrons were the sort of miscreants who engaged in mischief all night and stayed hidden away during daylight hours. She had never imagined them being the same people who sat in church pews.

Their aunt only shrugged.

"Maybe she's onto something," Gladys said. "If we watch for the men who nod off during the prayers, we'll know who's been out gambling all night."

"The way your father goes on in his prayers, I don't know anyone who could stay awake," said Aunt Xenia.

"Aunt Chloe does," said Gladys.

"That settles it then," said Aunt Xenia. "My little sister is definitely not at the pool hall on Saturday nights." The girls laughed out loud, but stopped abruptly and looked over their shoulders, as though their spinster aunt might have heard them. "Now that's decided," Xenia continued, "I believe I'll go to bed."

Gladys ate the last biscuit and Edgalea wiped the pan while Willie returned to the sitting room and rolled out the mattress she shared with her sisters. Ola was the only other one still up, and she kneeled beside Willie as though to help, though it wasn't necessary.

"So, tell me all about it! Who did you dance with?" she said quietly.

"Not many, really."

"I bet Harold asked you to dance."

"Actually, I asked him to dance with me. Or told him he would. Or told someone else."

"You beat all, Willie! Did he talk to you about going to Tennessee?"

"How did you know?"

"He told me he was going to. Wanted to know what I thought you'd say."

"What did you tell him?"

"I told him there was no way you'd marry him! Guess it didn't keep him from trying."

"No, it didn't," Willie said. At that moment, Edgalea and Gladys came into the room, and Willie ended the conversation with an almost imperceptible shake of her head.

"More later," Ola whispered. "Good night, all!" she said with a bright smile. She went into the bedroom she shared with Minnie and closed the door. Jimmie, Lois, and Zenia shared the other bedroom. Aunt Xenia slept on the sofa in the sitting room when she slept at all.

Gladys spread two quilts over their mattress and flopped onto the bed. "Take off your dress before you wallow around," Edgalea told her. Gladys complied with her sister's request. Raising herself to her knees, she lifted the shapeless dress over her head and tossed it into a heap on the pillows. Edgalea picked it up, shook it out, and draped it over the back of a chair with her own.

"How could our two aunts be so different?" Gladys asked as she burrowed under the quilts.

Willie looked from Edgalea who was tidying up their corner of the room, to Gladys, who didn't give tidiness a moment's thought. "Do you mean sisters should all be alike?" she asked.

"Not that they should be, just that they *would* be."

"Hmm," Willie said, getting into the bed. "And which sister in our family might we all become more like?"

"I don't know," she said. She added in a whisper, "I only hope none of us becomes the unbearable one."

"Shush, now, you two!" Edgalea said as she laid down on Gladys's other side. "None of our aunts are unbearable. They're all making do with what they've got."

"You're only afraid Aunt Chloe might be listening all the way from her house," Willie said. Gladys put a hand over her mouth to stifle a giggle. It was cut off by a knock at the front door.

The girls froze.

"Great day in the morning," Willie whispered. "Who would be calling this late at night?"

"You don't think—" Gladys said.

"Don't be ridiculous," Edgalea whispered.

They heard their aunt's soft footsteps move toward the door.

"Sorry to bother you, Mrs. Webb." It was a man's voice. "We wanted to let you know there's been some disturbance in town tonight. We advise you all to stay inside and not open your door to anyone."

"If you didn't want me to open my door, Deputy, you shouldn't have knocked on it," she said. "What sort of disturbance?"

"We're not ready to say yet. Only that you and your girls should stay in."

"At this time of night, we've no reason to go out, I'm sure. What about in the morning?"

"By daylight, everything will be fine." They exchanged parting words, then the sisters heard Aunt Xenia close the door and go into the kitchen.

"What do you think that was all about?" Willie asked in a whisper.

Edgalea sat up.

"What are you doing?" Gladys asked.

"I'm going to ask Aunt Xenia what she thinks is going on."

"When will you ever learn, Edge?" said Willie. "If you really want to know something, don't ask."

"What do you mean?"

"If you ask an adult a question, they'll know you're interested and begin whispering things behind closed doors. Let them assume you don't know anything and don't care, and they'll speak openly."

Edgalea laid back down as she considered her sister's words. "I'm an adult, you know."

"Not without a husband, you're not," Willie said, cringing in the dark at the taunt that fettered them equally if in different ways.

"Stay here, both of you," Gladys said. "I won't be able to sleep if one of you is missing." Edgalea pulled the quilts over her shoulders. They all got quiet, but it was a long time before they slept.

Chapter 7

As usual, Willie and her sisters were the first ones up on Monday morning. Perhaps it was because they'd been raised on a farm with work that needed to be completed before breakfast. Or maybe it was because they could hear Aunt Xenia get up and could smell the coffee she brewed before sunrise. The sisters would be up and dressed with their bed rolled away before anyone else appeared.

Willie loved this part of the day because they had their aunt to themselves. Xenia told stories of Tennessee that were as fantastic as fairy tales. Willie could hardly imagine the green Sequatchie Valley or the feud with the Swaffords, things the rest of the family never spoke of. Today, however, Willie wanted to know if her aunt had any suspicions about the disturbance last night.

"How did you sleep?" Willie asked as she and Gladys carried their cups of coffee to the round wooden table.

"Just fine, thank you. I hope you girls weren't bothered by the knock on the door."

"Oh, did you have a visitor?" Gladys asked. Willie thought she might be laying it on too thick.

"Only the deputy," said Aunt Chloe. "He didn't say enough to be helpful, so I wish he hadn't said anything at all."

"Good morning!" Aunt Xenia called as Jimmie shuffled past. She winked at her nieces. The girls gave Jimmie wide berth in the mornings, but their aunt was unfazed by her sour disposition. Jimmie wore a tattered housecoat that might have once been blue. Her dark, wispy hair was still under a cap. She answered inaudibly and carried her coffee back to the bedroom.

Willie wondered how they could get their aunt back to the topic of the deputy's visit, but then Lois came in, wearing the tidy cream-colored blouse and brown skirt that she wore every day. Her thick, brown hair was twisted into a bun at the nape of her neck. "How would you like your eggs this morning?" she asked as she tied on her apron. They ate eggs every morning.

For two years Lois had been keeping books for the Portales schools, but she didn't leave the house until after breakfast. Willie was glad, because she was the best cook among them. She was a full-figured woman, generous in all the places her sister was spare.

"I tried to get Minnie up, but she's still laying like a lump!" Ola said as she entered the kitchen.

Jimmie returned looking more alive, if not softened. She pulled on a sweater and refilled her coffee cup. Then she cut a chunk of bread, smeared it with butter, and folded it in two. Lois handed her two boiled eggs which she tucked into a muslin sack.

"Wonder what Red Sam has in store today," Aunt Xenia said.

"It's a Monday. Laundry day," she said. "Goodbye, girls. Thank you, Lois," she added on her way out the door.

Minnie came in as the other girls finished their breakfast. Willie and Ola washed the dishes while Gladys packed them each a lunch of buttered bread and baked sweet potatoes. Despite being the last one to the table, Minnie was the first one out of the kitchen. She didn't eat enough to support a field mouse. Willie suspected a strong gust would knock her over some day.

Minnie and Edgalea stood in front of the only mirror in the house while Willie, Gladys, and Ola crowded in around them. The older girls patted and preened to no effect that Willie could see. Minnie's hair was always straight and black as a raven, regardless of her efforts to add curl with heat and oil. Edgalea, in contrast, had ringlets to spare.

"Ola, your ears are still sticking out," Minnie said. "And Edgalea dear, your hair is so curly, I don't think there's anything that can be done for it." Willie pressed her lips closed tight. Ola's ears looked fine. And her sister was self-conscious about her curls. Though they were a point of pride among the older generation of family, they'd brought on a fair amount of teasing when the girls were young. Edgalea rarely stood up for herself, but Willie was ready to fight anyone who came after her sisters—even if it was another family member. She silently dared Minnie to say another word.

Ola tried to catch her own reflection in a corner of the glass.

"Ola, back up," Minnie hissed. "Wait your turn."

"You are the only one who ever gets a turn. You spend almost as much time in front of the mirror as you do in bed," Ola said.

"It's important that I look good. I don't plan to be living here with you all next year. I need to make sure Joe is ready to get married before the summer's end." Minnie had set her sights on Joe Beck last spring. He worked at the Greathouse Ranch and was four years older than Minnie, but she'd finally caught his attention, and they'd been seeing each other regularly since Christmas.

"Surely he knows what you look like by now," Willie said.

"The poor man who marries you will likely starve," said Ola.

"The point is, I'll be married," Minnie answered, "which is more than you all will be able to say." She looked at Edgalea's reflection.

"Joe may be less willing to marry you if he hears how often you pluck the hair out of that mole," Willie said.

"You wouldn't dare."

"I love a dare."

Minnie walked toward the bedroom in a huff while the three sisters finished pinning their hair.

At the sound of the first school bell, the girls grabbed their satchels and dashed out the back door. In grade school Willie had walked three and a half miles to the dugout that served as the Inez School. When her father bought the quarter section of land adjacent to their homestead and dragged their one-room house onto it, her walk had been reduced by three-quarter miles. Willie still marveled at their proximity to the high school It took less than five minutes to walk from Aunt Xenia's front door to the dusty school yard.

Despite the nearness, the girls struggled to get to school on time. They ran behind the house, waving at Mr. Mullins where he stood in his garden, cut through the Tarvers' backyard, turned left, and quickstepped across the school yard, hoping they wouldn't hear the final bell until they were inside the building.

Portales High School had opened its new building the year before and was a source of great pride in the community. The symmetrical two-story building with red brick and white stone accents was the largest, newest school in the region. Unlike the dugouts where Willie had attended classes before, the building had wooden floors and glass windowpanes in every classroom.

Willie sat in her second-story home economics class staring out one of those glass panes. She was supposed to be adding buttons to the dress she'd made as her final project, but all she could do was dream about the farm. Willie was conscientious about her handwork only to the degree that her garments were functional. She added pockets to skirts where the patterns didn't call for them and reinforced the elbows of all her blouses. It was a shame there were no prizes for the best patches on trousers. Scalloped hems, lacy collars, and fashionable sleeves held no interest for her.

Willie enjoyed the convenience and socializing that came with town life, but she missed the homeplace during her days away. She envied the boys who were allowed to drop out of school to work for their dads.

She'd named the new calf Carl when she checked on it after dinner yesterday. He had pranced around his mother, showing off, Willie thought. She had a greater fondness for the calf than for her eager classmate, but there was something about its shiny coat and eagerness that brought him to mind. Her father believed naming animals was silly, but he'd indulged the habit since Willie was a small child. She noticed that although he never gave them names, he would call them by the monikers she assigned.

Willie counted on her father keeping his word to give her a quarter section to begin farming. She didn't know of any other way a young woman could get started. In one more year she would be free of the textbooks and classrooms, and if not farming, then what?

"Willie, I believe you've picked up the wrong button."

Willie looked up at Joyce Moss, whose comment had interrupted her thoughts, then down at the work in her hands. It was true the button she was adding was black, not pearl like the last two she'd attached. However, she had not picked up the wrong button. She'd simply run out of pearl buttons in her notions bag. Rather than wait until she could find more or replace the first two so they'd all match, she'd decided she would have two pearl buttons and six black ones on this dress. A black button worked as well as a pearl one after all.

Rather than explain all this to Joyce, Willie said, "Oh, thank you."

Joyce's dress was flawless. Ever since grade school, she had bested the other girls in handwork. As a result, she wore the finest-looking clothes. Even when Eula Baker, the wealthiest girl in town, ordered a dress from Amarillo, it didn't compare. Joyce had been accused of wearing store-bought clothes, but she insisted they were her own creations and even turned up her sleeves and shirttails on occasion to prove the stitching was her own. Willie could already tell the rose-colored dress she was embellishing now would be a lovely complement to her fair skin and blue eyes.

"I could help you, if you'd like," Joyce offered. Willie resisted the urge to make a smart remark, since Joyce had never been anything but kind to her. Even when the other children shunned her in grade school, Joyce never joined in. Willie had to remind herself of this fact whenever Joyce's sweetness tempted her to be mean.

"Thank you," Willie said, "but it's all right." Joyce gave her a half smile, and Willie knew the deliberate mismatch of buttons would gnaw at her. "Really, it's how I want it," she added. Joyce exhaled the breath of a friend who knows better than to argue.

"You and Bill made a handsome sight Saturday night," Willie said, knowing the new subject would take Joyce's mind off her buttons.

"Thank you," Joyce said. It was a sigh more than a statement. Willie worried that she was about to start crying. Her eyes were red and puffy.

"Is something wrong?"

"Only that Bill thinks we should be married this summer. After graduation next week his father is giving him a quarter section that's already growing up with wheat. He could use my help, especially with the harvest coming. After the social Bill told my parents there's no reason to wait."

"I guess your parents didn't agree?"

"No. They think I should graduate. I've always been top of the class, so they think I should finish."

"And what do you think?"

"I used to agree with them. I love school. It's something I've always been good at, but really, what use does a farmer's wife have for so much learning? Bill already waited a year for his own graduation just to keep his mother happy. It seems unfair to make him wait another."

"You'll be married your whole life. Seems unfair if he can't wait one more year."

Joyce sighed again. Willie regretted she couldn't give her friend an easy answer. For the first time she could remember, she was relieved to see May Bell coming toward them.

"Did you hear what happened to Gussie McCormick?" Joyce and Willie looked at each other, then shook their heads.

"Oh, I forget you don't really live in town." Willie was certain she hadn't forgotten. Irritation replaced the relief she'd felt when May Bell first interrupted. "I've just been praying so much for them." She paused. Willie refused to respond.

"Oh, really? Why is that?" Joyce asked. Willie wanted to kick her under the table.

"Well, surely you know George owns the service station." The girls nodded. George was only a few years their senior but already had a wife and thriving businesses. In addition to the service station he owned, he drove and serviced the only school bus in the county.

"Apparently, two nights ago Gussie walked next door to the service station to grab a particular wrench for George. While she was inside, she heard a wild animal howling and carrying on. She had no way to defend herself other than the wrench in her hand."

"What did she do?" asked Joyce.

"What kind of animal?" asked Willie.

"She had to wait it out. She stayed crouched behind the counter until the sound stopped for a while. Then she ran across the yard as fast as she could to get back home."

"So, she didn't see it?"

"No, George heard it too and went out to look, but by that time the animal, or whatever it was, had gone. Of course, I don't know why he sent Gussie over there in the first place. A young lady has no reason to be out past dark, and he should have never put her in that position."

"What do you mean, 'whatever it was'?" Willie asked.

"That's the crazy part. No one who heard the sound that night could say for sure what sort of animal it was. Some said it sounded unnatural. A howl of sorts, but not like any coyote or wolf anyone's ever heard before.

"I think I'll make a pie to take over to Gussie today. I'm sure she's still a fright."

Willie rolled her eyes. A pie and a prayer were May Bell's way of getting the gossip and placing herself at the heart of the action.

"And that's not all," she went on. "Yesterday morning, the Perkinses, on the other side of the filling station, said their garden was all torn up, like a hog had gone and wallowed in it."

"That doesn't sound like something a coyote would do," Joyce said.

"No," May Bell said, only pausing for a breath, "and when I was helping Mrs. Thompson carry in linens this morning, the teachers were saying that some folks heard the sounds again last night."

Willie thought about the deputy's visit to Aunt Xenia's house. She wondered whether May Bell knew he had been out last night, knocking on doors and warning people to beware. She wasn't about to give up this bit of information.

When the school bell rang at last, the girls packed up their notions and put away their garments, each with her mind returning to what she wanted: approval, independence, significance.

As Willie walked to her aunt's house, she thought again about the calf. Surely, it would be the start of her own herd. She'd helped calve it, after all. She resolved to get a commitment from her father this weekend. Her mind worked over the ways she could bring it up, the arguments she might use, and Father's likely responses. By the time she reached Aunt Xenia's door, she'd prepared herself for a half dozen ways he might refuse.

She walked in to find everyone gathered in the sitting room.

"We've had a letter from Zenia," Lois said. "Edgar's wife had the baby, and they're happy to be together. Everyone is doing fine.

"That's good news," Willie said.

"Yes," Jimmie said. "I reckon it's better to be called for than sent away."

Willie felt an impulse to roll her eyes at Jimmie's self-pity, but she took in the sight of the four fatherless women in the room. They shared a bond Willie hoped she would never know. Her father fetched her home every Friday. And while they didn't always see eye to eye, she'd never doubted his love for her. Willie slipped unnoticed into the kitchen and out the back door.

Chapter 8

The rest of the week passed without a visit from the deputy or further word of nighttime disturbances. At school, Willie continued the finishing touches on her dress. She worked slowly in order to finish at the same time as her classmates who were being meticulous and adding embellishments to their work. She hoped Mrs. Thompson wouldn't notice her choice to stick with the basics until the term was over.

In her English class, she dutifully recited *O Captain, My Captain*. They would perform their recitations at the graduation ceremony at the end of the month. Though she didn't see what it had to do with the close of a school year, it was a tradition that the sophomore and junior classes had carried out since the school opened.

The repeated refrain, "fallen cold and dead," still echoed in her mind as she sat in Mr. Thompson's class. Willie was not a natural when it came to her math courses, but she worked at them, trusting her father's word that they would be important for every aspect of farming from inventory and profits to building and repairs. She completed the problem Mr. Thompson had written for them on the blackboard and waited while her classmates finished.

"Psst! Willie!"

When she heard her name being whispered from behind, she knew she shouldn't turn around. She knew who sat in that seat. Yet when she heard it a second time, she looked over her shoulder despite herself.

"I can help you," Carl whispered.

"With what?" she asked, with no attempt to hide the irritation in her tone. In answer, he tilted his slate up for her to see.

"The thing to remember is to take the square root at the end."

Willie turned back around. She couldn't tolerate Carl or his arrogance.

Mr. Thompson rapped his knuckles on his desk as he stood up. It was his way of signaling the time for working the problem was over.

"Miss Tollett," he said, "please share your answer with the class."

"Thirteen feet," she said.

"Well done. I hope the rest of you also came to that conclusion. If not, I'd advise you to revisit your assignments from this week. For now, it looks as though our time is up." Willie had noticed that Mr. Thompson only spoke in formal tones like this at school. When he gossiped with the men outside the general store or talked over wheat prices at community picnics, he sounded like everyone else. The change appeared so effortless that Willie wondered if he was even aware of it.

As they filed out of the room, Willie heard Carl calling her name. She tried to ignore him and keep walking, but he was not deterred.

"Good thing I helped before Mr. Thompson called on you." He grinned, both chin and chest puffed out. She could tell he was waiting for her admiration and gratitude.

"I already had the answer," Willie said.

"You don't have to thank me," he said. Willie was stunned by his commitment to ignorance. Before she could respond, he added, "I'm just glad I could help."

"I have to go," Willie said, and she hurried away.

There was no real hurry since the students usually lingered in the school yard on Friday afternoons. She found Ola among a group of girls admiring Eula Baker's new shoes. Ola also looked disinterested, so they met up with Edgalea and Gladys before crossing the road toward Aunt Xenia's.

Willie was glad she and her sisters would go home this afternoon. Sometimes she felt out of place among the other young women at her aunt's house. She and her sisters could not imagine the losses they had all suffered, and their presence felt cruel at times, as though the very fact of their two living, loving parents mocked the other women's circumstances.

Their father was already waiting at the house when they arrived. The girls gathered their few belongings and took them to the truck. "Jim, don't forget about those jars," Aunt Xenia called out. "And careful how you load them. Broken glass won't do Sarah any good."

As they arranged the rattling crates in the truck bed, Father asked, "How did you all do in your lessons this week?"

Each of the girls gave their father a report of what they were learning. None of them mentioned the deputy's visit.

"You were in town earlier than usual," Edgalea remarked.

"I had a meeting this morning with William Terry's wife."

"I didn't think you liked Mrs. Terry," Willie ventured. Edgalea shot her sister a disapproving glance over her shoulder.

Gladys, however, gave Willie the side-eye of a co-conspirator and said, "Right. I believe you said she needed to 'tend her affairs at home and leave the important work to the men.'"

"I reckon I did say that. And I meant it, too. But Mrs. Armstrong and her so-called League managed to keep Roosevelt County dry when there weren't enough men to get the job done. If they could get it done in Portales, I suppose they have friends who could help us in Inez." Then, in the voice he reserved for public prayers, he added, "The Lord works in mysterious ways."

"Did you all make a plan?" Edgalea asked. The girls were climbing into the truck bed now, finding places to sit that would allow each of them to stabilize a crate.

"We have the beginnings of one," Father said, standing with his hands on his hips. "I have to admit, those ladies are cunning. It's no wonder they got the vote, despite the absurdity of it." As he stepped toward the cab of the truck, he added, "Their husbands have their work cut out for them, sure enough."

In moments like this, Willie wondered what she was missing. Her father was the smartest man she knew, but in some regards, she found him dumb as a post. She could not reconcile the wisdom of the man she admired with a stance like this one. Why was it surprising that a group of women would be resourceful enough to solve a problem? And why would this be considered "work" for their husbands? Willie assumed she must not have all the relevant information. Surely, her father didn't mean that women were inherently less capable or that capable women were somehow problematic.

As they turned off the main road toward their farm, Willie's thoughts turned to the calves and their new mothers. She thought of her pet, Carl, in particular, wondering whether he'd been eating well, if his mother was patient with his nursing, and how much he might have grown in the days she was gone.

She didn't wait long to find out. She knew she needed to help unload the truck, but empty glass jars weren't going to spoil. She tossed her bag toward the stoop on her way to the pens.

She was standing at the fence admiring the even newer calf when Father joined her.

"How did it go for that one?" she asked.

"Easy. Came yesterday while I was eating dinner."

Willie smiled. The heifers had finished calving successfully.

"It's been a good spring," Willie said.

"It has indeed. And no surprise to that. As I've said before, you reap what you sow."

Willie watched the new mothers nursing their calves. "It's amazing that the heifers know what to do."

"It's in their nature. And it helps that I selected these carefully from the herd in Amarillo. In fact, I've spent years getting everything in place for this spring, and I've kept watch to ensure that each calf would be born healthy."

"It was sure something to help with Carl's arrival," Willie said, wanting to remind her father that she, too, had played a role in the success of this spring.

"Nothing remarkable about it. I've been teaching you these skills all your life." Willie thought her father might give her a compliment, but when he continued, he said, "Truly, the Lord's hand was over us that day."

Her father's refusal to give her credit stung, and she was simultaneously embarrassed that she was so hungry for it. The closer she moved toward independence, the more desperately she needed his approval. That the former should depend so much on the latter stirred feelings in her she hadn't made sense of yet.

Thurston walked toward the gate and started to slide the latch.

"Whoa, boy!" Father called out. "What do you think you're doing? Get in that pen between a bunch of mommas and babies and you're liable to regret it."

"But I want to pet them."

"Once we separate them. Not until then."

Thurston shrugged and ran in the other direction.

"Sometimes I wonder about that boy," Father said. "He can't hold a thought long enough to let it settle."

Willie didn't respond. She continued watching the drama playing out in the pasture. Her favorite, Carl, pranced near the newest calf, inviting it to play. He paid for the invitation when the newest mother's head bumped roughly into his side. Carl ran to hide behind his own mother and peaked out from under her belly. After a time, he latched on to her and soothed his pride with her milk.

When they were young, Mother had a habit of narrating conversations between animals. Father had dismissed her attribution of emotion and drama to livestock, but Willie had picked up the habit, and like calling the animals by her pet names, her father had eventually joined her.

"Momma, help me! That cow is mean!" Willie said, imitating the voice she believed best matched Carl's.

"Just wait, son," Father answered in his imitation of the mother. "One of these days she'll see you're not all bad and wish she'd been nicer to you."

Willie ignored any double meaning her father might intend. She couldn't bear to think he was urging her toward marriage. During her days at school, she felt disconnected and out of place. Every week she worried that her brother would gain a greater share of their father's favor. But on Friday evenings as they surveyed their work and progress, she was reassured of her status. This was her place.

She only had one more year to endure school and hold her father to his promise. Her resolve to suggest Rose's calf as the start of her own herd waned. She would leave well enough alone for now.

"I 'spect we better get to work while there's plenty of daylight."

"Yes, sir."

"Carry those jars in for your mother. Then those pens need cleaning and the stove needs fuel. Get your clothes changed and come back out with a shovel."

"Yes, sir."

Willie grabbed her satchel on her way into the house. On her way back through the kitchen, she grabbed a cold biscuit off the table and took a bite.

"I declare, you eat like a grown man," Edgalea said, trying to catch the crumbs as they fell from Willie's hand.

"Leave her alone. She does the work of a grown man, too," Gladys said.

"I wish I could be outside instead of stuck in here with these math lessons," said Ella Bea.

Mother came in with a bushel basket of potatoes and onions in time to hear Ella Bea's whining.

"Best learn to be happy where you are," she said.

Mother used this phrase often, and it fit her. Willie had rarely seen her mother look unhappy. When Sarah Tollett joined her husband's family on the wagon train from Indian Territory to Roosevelt County, she believed she was leaving Egypt and heading for the Promised Land. In many ways she was. The land was fertile, and her husband prospered, while the place she'd left behind had meant death for so many she loved.

She'd made it out of Egypt, but Willie couldn't say whether her mother had made it to Canaan or was still wandering through the desert. In the last eight years, she'd received letters reporting the death of her oldest two sisters and two younger brothers. Her oldest brother had simply disappeared. The community's mixed response to her Cherokee lineage and the distance between homesteads made it hard for her to make friends. Despite all her trials, Sarah never complained. She took it all in stride with a straight back, broad shoulders, and enigmatic smile.

Willie knew the kitchen was about to be a frenzy of chopping and cooking, so she hurried out the door. She preferred the endless possibility of farm work, even in something so mundane as collecting cow patties. At least it held the potential for life and death extremes, unlike the apparent sameness of household chores. She didn't understand how Joyce or any of the girls could be in a rush to get married. The only advantage she could see was that she'd only be cooking for two. By the time the crates were stacked in the cellar and the pens were clean, all thoughts of weddings and town life had disappeared. She came in for supper feeling simultaneously hungry and satisfied.

When the girls climbed into their bed, there was a flurry of talk now that they were alone. Ella Bea was anxious to hear all of the news from town. She complained every Friday that she was left alone with Thurston during the week, but Willie suspected she enjoyed being the oldest child at home. She'd had to cover more of the household chores while her sisters were gone and seemed to believe that made her grown enough to be included in the older girls' conversations and intrigues.

"A letter came from Zenia," Willie reported to Ella Bea.

"She sounded happy," Gladys added.

"She'd never seemed happy here," Willie said.

"I never heard her complain," Edgalea said.

"But that's not the same as being happy, is it?" asked Willie.

"Her prospects for marriage are probably better there," Edgalea said.

They continued talking while Ella Bea listened intently. Once again, no one mentioned the deputy's warning. They all seemed to know, without having discussed it, that bringing it up would jeopardize the freedom they had in town.

When there was a lull in the conversation, Ella Bea sat up straighter and raised her eyebrows, indicating she had something to say. Willie could see she was delighted to have her own significant news to share, and she must have been waiting all day for this moment. "You won't believe the way Father is talking about this pool hall affair!"

"If he's seeking the help of the Ladies' League, it must be sending him over the edge!" said Willie.

Ella Bea's countenance dropped. Their father's partnership with the League must have been the news she'd been anxious to share, and now she'd been robbed of the opportunity to be the center of attention.

"The Lord works in mysterious ways," Gladys said in a perfect pantomime of their father.

"It isn't mysterious at all. Women get the work done, and the Lord gets the credit," Willie said.

"Willie Josephine! It will be no mystery when the Lord strikes you down!" Edgalea said, pushing on her glasses. Gladys snickered behind her hand, but their eldest sister's face was all seriousness.

"Fine. The Lord can have the credit. I'm only tired of seeing men take it all."

Chapter 9

Spring passed in a flurry of births and blooms. The greens and squash in the garden were already plentiful while the tomato vines searched for new holdings. Nearly two hundred fluffy yellow chicks pecked and scratched as they made their way from roost to range. The calves put on weight and challenged each other to contests of speed and strength. Orderly rows of ducklings glided across the playa lakes. The wheat in the fields looked like golden rippling water, and grain sorghum filled the air with sweetness.

The presence of spring was also evident among the students of Portales High School. The teachers struggled to maintain order in their classrooms as their pupils' attention turned to farming, fishing, and each other. Now, finally, the school year was coming to an end.

Willie and her sisters asked to have one more night at Aunt Xenia's before moving back home for the summer. Willie hadn't been keen on the idea, but she knew it mattered to her sisters, and they believed Father would be more agreeable to the idea if she were the one to ask. At first, he said no. He thought it senseless to have to fetch the girls out to Inez for the baccalaureate in the morning. Aunt Xenia reminded him that she would be attending anyway, and the girls were welcome to ride with her. And, in fact, this would keep him from making trips to Portales on consecutive days. He couldn't argue with her reasoning.

A graduation would be held at Portales High School as well as at the other consolidated school districts in the county, but each congregation, Baptist, Presbyterian, and Methodist, would host morning baccalaureate ceremonies for the seniors of their number. The Inez Methodist church boasted nine graduates from four different high schools. Carl Martin's family didn't attend church, but he was invited to all three baccalaureate ceremonies. In the end, he was likely the most prayed-over graduate in Roosevelt County.

When they returned to Aunt Xenia's house on the afternoon of the last day of school, they found Lois sweating in the kitchen. In the warmer months, they avoided using the oven except early in the morning, but the fire was stoked.

"Why is it so hot in here?" Minnie demanded. "Where is my mother?"

"She's gone to see if any blackberries are ripe enough to pick," Lois said. "We noticed some on the Bledsoe Road that were starting to turn."

"Why not wait a week when she could get a bushel in minutes?" Willie asked. "She's gonna tear her arms up searching."

"Special occasions are meant to be marked," Lois said with a grin.

Minnie dropped her book bag on the table then walked to the front porch fanning herself.

Gladys pushed up her sleeves and started washing the dishes. Edgalea began cutting biscuits from the dough Lois was patting out. Ola skimmed the cream off a jar of milk and whipped it with sugar. Even Willie, who wasn't as proficient in the kitchen, knew enough to start a pot of coffee. They worked together in the way women familiar with each other can do. Everyone saw what needed doing and moved with an ease that denied probability for five people in a small kitchen.

When Jimmie and Aunt Xenia returned, the ladies of Railroad Street treated themselves to a supper of sweet biscuits topped with berries and cream. The house was too hot to be comfortable, so they carried their dishes out the front door. Aunt Xenia had a concrete porch raised two steps above the yard and spanning the length of the house. Two wooden rocking chairs sat on one side of the door, and a straight-backed, cane-bottomed chair sat on the other. Aunt Xenia and Lois took the rockers, Minnie took the straight-back, and the other young women sat on the concrete. It felt cool compared to the late spring air.

Mr. Mullins, the widower in the next house over, was also taking supper outside. "Hello to you!" he called out, standing and waving.

"Hello!" Aunt Xenia called back.

"How many girls have you got now?"

"Oh Lordy," Aunt Xenia said quietly. "He's on the porch watching for us all day. He knows exactly how many of you there are." They all giggled, and she called out, "About to lose a few!" To the girls she added, "Maybe that will encourage him to take his morning coffee inside."

"Maybe it's you he's most interested in," Lois said.

"No!" Minnie and Ola said in their mother's defense. Aunt Xenia's expression echoed their sentiment.

They settled into a quiet evening. A few neighbors walked by and waved or called out. The women of Railroad Street would wave or holler back, but each was occupied by her own thoughts, and they were content to be alone together.

As the sun brushed the horizon, a roll of dust came down the road, and Joe Beck's truck screeched to a stop in front of the house. As they'd anticipated, he had agreed to marry Minnie, and they'd chosen the first Saturday in July before the wheat harvest would begin. Minnie put her bowl down; Willie guessed she was trying to hide it.

"Evening," he said, coming into the yard.

"Evening," Aunt Xenia answered.

"Mind if I walk with Minnie for a bit? We won't be long."

"I s'pose that'd be all right. But she needs to be in before dark."

"Yes, ma'am," he said.

Minnie hopped up and smoothed her skirt then ran her fingers through her hair. She wasn't aware of the berry stains at the corners of her mouth. Willie thought of getting her attention but decided against it. Gladys, always the better soul, cleared her throat and pantomimed wiping her face, but Minnie paid her no mind. She stepped off the porch and took hold of Joe's elbow, claiming her prize.

The remaining women lingered as the sun went down and they watched the sky turn dark. Gladys yawned, setting off a succession of yawns through the group. They couldn't deny their weariness any longer.

"I'll do the dishes tonight," Lois said. "You all get to bed."

"I'll help," said Aunt Xenia. "I'll be watching for Minnie anyhow."

After they'd carried in their dishes, the older cousins retired to the bedroom while the Tollett sisters rolled out their mattress and prepared for bed.

"What's the matter, Edge?" Gladys said once they were settled under a thin quilt. Her voice was so soft it didn't quite penetrate Willie's sleepy mind.

"Nothing," Edgalea said.

"It's not nothing," Gladys said. "I can tell you're crying."

This reply broke through Willie's fog, and she came fully awake. Why was her sister crying on the night of her graduation?

"It's nothing you'd understand," Edgalea said. "You're still young, and you've always been beautiful." She sniffed. Willie couldn't decide whether to feign slumber or speak up.

"You're also young and beautiful," Gladys told her. "Did Minnie say something terrible?" At the mention of her cousin, Willie couldn't keep silent. She threw the quilt aside and put her feet on the floor.

"I'll go settle this with her right now," Willie said, forgetting her cousin was still out with Joe Beck. "I'll teach her to keep her thoughts to herself."

"No, Willie!" Edgalea said, forcing herself to whisper. "It's nothing to do with Minnie! And even if it was, I have no interest in your defending me. Get back in bed." Willie sat on the bed but did not get back into it.

"Well, what is it then? What are you being such a ninny about?" Sisters could turn from fierce defenders to harsh critics on a dime.

"It feels like the end of opportunity. As long as I was in high school, I still felt as though I had a chance at finding a husband."

"Oh, Edgalea, you can still find a husband!" Gladys patted her sister's back. They were all sitting up now.

"Or you could appreciate the fact that you escaped," Willie said. "Better to be a maid and wish to be a matron than be a matron and wish to be a maid."

"That's easy for you to say. You don't want to get married. I want to have babies and have someone to make a home with."

"Ha! Make a home for is more like it."

"I'm destined to become Aunt Chloe!" Edgalea said. Her voice cracked again, and she resumed her crying.

"That's up to you! Look at Aunt Xenia. She's not married, and she's happy enough."

"But she was married. She knew love. And she got to have babies."

Willie sighed. She didn't know what to say, so she relented. "I'm sorry," she said, her sympathy returning. The three sisters sat in silence, feeling tired, but not wanting to be the first to lie down. Gladys and Willie waited for Edgalea to break the tension.

Instead, their silent vigil was interrupted by the creak of the front gate.

Edgalea slid down and pulled the quilt up to her chin. Her sisters followed suit. A moment later, they heard the front door opening, soft footsteps, and the click of bedroom doors closing.

Despite her exhaustion, Willie doubted she'd be able to relax into sleep. She was mad at Minnie for picking at her sister's vulnerability, if not tonight in particular then for her lifetime of vanity and careless comments, but she was also mad at Edgalea for making her vulnerability so obvious. And she was mad at a world that made arbitrary rules and deadlines for girls that didn't exist for boys.

She squeezed her eyes shut, willing her mind to rest, but the night sounds grew into a din she couldn't ignore. Her sisters' breaths were slow and heavy. A cricket had taken its place under the window and played its song. Wind pushed the hollyhocks against the wall outside. From far away she heard a howl.

Then the howling got louder, but maybe it wasn't howling after all. Perhaps it was singing. Or crying? Willie sat up again.

"Did you hear that?" she whispered. The only answer was continued steady breathing. She strained her ears to identify the sound. She shivered and considered sinking back into the bed.

Instead, she got up and crept toward the front window.

"You heard it too?"

Willie yelped. She hadn't expected anyone else to be up, but there stood Aunt Xenia at the window, shotgun in hand.

"What is that?" Willie asked. "What animal makes a sound like that?"

"I don't know," Aunt Xenia answered. "No one does. Deputy's been trying to figure it out for weeks."

"Is it dangerous?"

"No one knows."

"Has it caused damage?"

"Nothing serious."

"What about livestock?" Willie asked, thinking of the calves back home.

"No livestock lost. And no clear tracks. Nothing more than some roughed up yards and gardens. And that sound. Makes a soul feel like dying. Or like it's already dead." Willie nodded in agreement.

"Go on to bed, Willie. I'll stay up to keep an eye out."

"Won't be able to sleep. It's like you said; that sounds gets into the soul."

"Put the kettle on the stove and we'll have some tea."

Willie did as she was told and returned with two cups of tea, each with a splash of milk. Aunt Xenia motioned for her to set her cup on the fireplace mantle. Willie was comforted by the heat of the warm cup as much as by the tea. It stilled the shiver the sound had first induced. By the time her cup was empty, the noise had stopped. It didn't gradually get quiet as it moved away; it simply stopped.

Without saying a word, Aunt Xenia returned the gun to its perch above the back door, and Willie returned to the bed, where her sisters had never stirred. In the morning, she wondered whether it had all been a strange dream.

Chapter 10

Aunt Xenia didn't mention the howling at breakfast the next morning, so Willie didn't either. The kitchen would have been still and quiet if not for Aunt Xenia drumming her fingers on the table and Willie bouncing her leg underneath. They sat together as though their coffee were the only thing to be interested in.

Jimmie came in and joined them at the table to eat her boiled egg. She went to Red Sam's an hour later on Saturdays. Willie wondered why boiled eggs never smelled as good as fried eggs. One by one the other young women came in to get their coffee.

"I'm off to work," Jimmie said. "Congratulations, girls," she said, looking at Minnie and Edgalea. "Although I'm not sure life gets any better once you graduate. In fact, it's probably downhill from where you stand."

"Don't listen to her, Edgalea," Lois said. "There's still plenty of joy to be had if you choose it."

Jimmie grunted and opened the door. "I'll see you at Minnie's wedding if not before," she said as she walked out.

Minnie stood without a word and went to the bedroom, leaving her plate behind for someone else to take care of. The other young women began clearing the table.

"I'll take care of cleaning up," Lois said. "You girls better get dressed!"

Edgalea had been working on a new dress for the occasion for months. Father had given her a generous length of light blue silk for Christmas, and Edgalea was determined to create a fashionable garment. She had embraced a traditional dress style with a fitted bodice. Mrs. Thompson said girls should accentuate their waists while they still had them. As a special touch, she'd splurged on a one-inch lace trim around the cuffs and collar.

"Does it look okay? It's nothing fancy, but I think it turned out nice."

"Of course it did," Aunt Xenia said.

Willie didn't care one way or another about fashion trends, but when Edgalea came out on the morning of her graduation, she had to admit that the effect was lovely. Her sister was as attractive as any of the silly girls who were adding lace to wedding dresses.

"It's beautiful, Edge," Willie said. Despite their differences, she believed her sister should be engaged by now if that's what she wanted. Her oldest sister was smart, strong, and capable.

Lois stepped out of the kitchen and smiled. "Oh, it's beautiful!" she said with a smile. Willie loved that when Lois said something, it was easy to believe she meant it.

"It's perfect!" Gladys squealed, and she gave her sister a hug.

Minnie came out from the bedroom where she'd been in front of the looking glass for most of an hour. Willie was sure she'd only been drawn out by the sound of compliments being bestowed on someone other than herself.

She entered the sitting room and twirled around so they could all see her dress. It was black with a dropped waist. There were no buttons, save the clasp at the back of the neck. The only embellishment was the flare of the asymmetrical sleeves. She wore a black belt low on her hips and a long, beaded necklace with a knot tied two thirds of the way down.

The look was something out of a catalog, but Willie only saw the same smug cousin she'd known all her life. She exchanged a look with Ola and saw that she was also unimpressed. Then she saw their mother's face.

In fact, Aunt Xenia's entire body transformed as she filled with admiration and pride. She tilted her chin up, drew her shoulders back, and inhaled deeply as she took in the sight of her daughter. Her face glowed and tears filled her eyes. She rarely showed any particular preference for her own daughters over the other young women living in her house. In fact, she was often more frustrated with Minnie's antics and attitude than with any other's. But in this moment, Willie saw the incomparable connection of a mother to her daughter. It had nothing to do with the dress, and Minnie was no better behaved than usual.

Willie understood in her aunt's expression that the intensity of a mother's love for her daughter was not in proportion to her performance or behavior. It was a force of nature that ran through her bones, perhaps through the bones of generations of women before her, calling out to the very blood they shared. For all the ways a daughter may be rejected by her father or the ways she may falter in her quest to please him, the power of her mother's love called her to rise again. Willie was certain she had glimpsed an invisible mystery in that moment. She was equally certain Minnie had missed it.

"You look beautiful," Edgalea said.

"Thank you, Edgalea. You look nice, too, though I don't know why you've chosen to dress more like a matron than a maid."

Willie watched her sister shrink before their eyes. Edgalea pushed her glasses up her nose but did not speak up for herself. Willie felt anger rising inside her throat.

"But then, I guess it doesn't matter," Minnie continued.

"Minnie!" Aunt Xenia hissed, the magic of earlier gone.

"What? All I'm saying is she can wear whatever she wants, since no one will be looking at her anyway."

"Hold your tongue," Xenia said.

"Or maybe they will look, only to wonder how in the world she could be kin to me."

Willie stepped toward her cousin with the intent of ripping the dress and its smug wearer apart, but Ola anticipated the move, grabbed Willie's arm, and stepped between her sister and her cousin. Minnie was unfazed, but now included Willie in her verbal attack.

"Neither of you will ever find a husband," she said coolly. "You'll be as old and alone as my mother!"

The sound of the slap reached all of their ears full seconds before understanding came to their minds.

"I need to check my hair," Minnie said, though she raised her hand only as high as her cheek, and she walked slowly, deliberately back into the bedroom.

"I declare," Aunt Xenia said when the door had closed. The five young women stood staring at her.

"Momma!" Ola gasped. She'd never known her mother to strike anyone.

Whether it was shock or the pure satisfaction of the moment, Willie couldn't conceal the smile that started in one corner of her mouth and spread across her face. It was Gladys, however, who let out the first quiet giggle. She clapped her hand over her mouth in the way she always did when she was tickled, but that was all it took for the room to erupt into laughter. Lois's loud guffaws were complemented by Ola's cackle. Gladys and Willie leaned shoulder to shoulder as they laughed all the way to the floor. Aunt Xenia bent over with her hands on her knees, wheezing to draw a breath. Even Edgalea, who would carry the wound of those words for years, doubled over with laughter, surrendering to the absurdity of the moment.

They carried on until their sides were sore and their cheeks were wet with tears. "Oh, that felt good!" Aunt Xenia said when she was able to breathe, and Willie couldn't tell whether she was referring to the slap or the laughter. Xenia stood upright and beat the hat she'd crumpled against her thigh. The young women followed suit, standing and straightening their hair dresses.

Minnie did not come out of the bedroom until they'd recovered their composure. "I hope you're all satisfied," she said with her chin jutting forward. "I'll have a rosy cheek all day." Willie noticed her eyes were also red but decided not to comment.

"Don't be silly," Aunt Xenia said. She was still smiling. "You look fine. Now, get your things and let's load up. You know my brother doesn't like to be kept waiting." With that, she took up her handbag, adjusted her hat, and led a march to the car.

This was the first baccalaureate ceremony Willie recalled attending. She didn't know whether the occasion would be somber or celebratory. She heard a cheerful melody from the piano when they arrived at the church building, and it gave her hope the mood would be light.

The group from Portales gathered with the rest of her family in the churchyard. Thurston stood with his arms folded over his chest and his chin pushed forward in a defiant pout. Ella Bea scowled at him behind their mother's back.

Pastor Westbrook was the first to greet them as they entered. "Good morning, folks. It's good to see you this fine day. I'm sure you're proud of Miss Edgalea."

"It's her fault we're at church on Saturday," Thurston said. Father thumped him behind the ear and ushered him inside.

"And Mrs. Tollett, what a pleasure to have you here with us," the pastor said without missing a beat.

"Thank you," Mother said. Her posture didn't change, but her eyes titled downward ever so slightly. Even though it wasn't Sunday, the family filed into their customary pew. The only difference was that Edgalea took a seat in the front row with the other graduates, and Mother took the place of Aunt Chloe, which pleased Thurston very much. Their aunt's store was open on Saturdays, and the boys she hired to help were participating in graduation events, so she'd conceded to closing the shop for an hour, but no more. Willie suspected the spinster wanted to be gone before any fun might be had.

Each young man from the graduating class was highlighted in the ceremony's program. Ralph Greathouse said the opening prayer and Roger Harris led the congregants in a hymn. Leon Moss delivered a speech on behalf of the graduating class. He had announced earlier in the year his plans to become a preacher. His daddy said that was fine, as long as he still made time to work the farm on the other six days of the week. His message was brief, with a different tone than Willie was accustomed to hearing on Sunday mornings; he sounded glad.

The elder Mr. Greathouse then called the name of each graduate as they stood and turned to face their families and guests. While they stood, he stated their plans for the future. Most of the boys planned to build homes on their families' land and continue farming. Leon also wanted to preach, and Ralph fancied himself a mechanic-in-training.

Mr. Greathouse might have said, "The girls are all getting married, except Edgalea," but he didn't. He announced the wedding date of each one and to whom she was betrothed, as though the community didn't already know. Willie expected Minnie to gloat at the first public announcement of her engagement, but she managed a demure expression. When Mr. Greathouse came to Edgalea, he said, "The Tollett family is lucky not to be losing Edgalea just yet. She'll continue to help at home for now." It was about the kindest way he could have said it, but Willie watched her sister's cheeks flush. She cast her eyes downward, and Willie knew if she looked up, they would be glistening with tears.

Leon said what Willie assumed to be the final prayer, but then Mr. Greathouse stood again to pray over the graduates, their marriages, and their children who would bless the community in the future. Willie imagined him tallying a point for managing a public prayer when her father hadn't. When the amen was finally said, the graduates formed three short rows. J.B. Mason returned to the piano, and his mother led the class in a hymn they'd prepared.

Again Willie thought the service was over, but then her father stood. "Ah," she thought, "evening up the score." He gave another final benediction, and at last they were dismissed to enjoy a light lunch before they would continue on to their respective schools for the graduation ceremonies.

The ladies set up a spread of ham sandwiches and pickled vegetables across tables in the front lawn. Willie made her way to Harold, who was struggling to retrieve a cucumber tightly packed in a jar.

"What are you doing here?" she asked.

"I came to see you," he answered, not looking up from his task. She wondered if he avoided her eyes because she hadn't accepted his offer of marriage.

"Would you like help with that?"

"No, I can get it," he said, his tone conveying more than his words.

"Harold?"

"I said I can get it."

Willie felt her chest tighten, and heat come to her cheeks. He had never spoken to her like this, and she couldn't tell whether she might deserve it or if he was being unfair. She turned to get away.

"Willie," Harold said, and he reached for her hand. "I'm sorry," She let him take her hand, but now she'd decided she was angry with him. He was the one who had made things uncomfortable. They had always been friends and still would be if he hadn't had the idea of marrying her. She planted her feet and made him take the step to fill the gap between them.

"Willie, I don't want to leave like this. I really am sorry. I only wanted you to be a little sorry, too."

"Then you don't know me very well, Harold Parrish. What on earth would I have to be sorry for? Having dreams and plans of my own? Wanting more than to follow a boy around? Is that what I should apologize for?" Willie knew her voice was getting louder, but she didn't care. Mrs. Mason was at the sandwich table now and turned to look over her shoulder. Willie forced herself to smile.

Harold shook his head and laughed, which only fueled Willie's anger.

"This is exactly how I will think of you. Full of fire and never a thought of backing down."

"Well, why should I back down?" Willie said. Her voice had returned to normal, and she felt the heat receding, but she didn't want to let him off the hook.

For the first time since she approached Harold, she looked into his eyes. She thought she saw a flash of sadness, but it passed before she could be sure.

"I'm leaving tomorrow," he said.

"Tomorrow?" she repeated, and she was surprised at the way her throat constricted as she said it. "What's the hurry?"

"I need time to get a job before my classes begin. My parents are going out with me; it's been years since they've seen Momma's family. They need to be back in time for the harvest. It's why I wanted to stop here before my ceremony.

"And I wanted to give you something," Harold said.

"A gift for me?" Willie asked. "But you're the one graduating."

"I'm the one leaving," Harold said. "And it's less of a gift than settling a debt." He reached into his breast pocket and pulled out the pocket watch he'd received for his thirteenth birthday.

"Are you late?" Willie asked.

"No." Harold laughed a little. "I want you to have this." He took the chain off the fob and handed her the watch. Any time the friends bet or swore on something, Harold used the timepiece as his highest stakes. No matter how many footraces Willie won, how many times she bested him in cattle knowledge, or how many times he'd backed down from a challenge, he'd never handed over the timepiece. Willie knew he wouldn't, but it hadn't stopped her from harassing him about it.

"I couldn't," she said.

"I should have given it to you a long time ago."

"That's true." Willie said. "Many times over. But I can't take it."

Harold took her hand, placed the watch in her palm, and closed her fingers around it. "You can't let me leave with unpaid debts."

"Fine," Willie said.

She wasn't sure what to say next. They stood in silence, neither showing much interest in their sandwiches.

"You'll write to me, won't you?" Harold asked.

"Of course," Willie said. "And you'll write back?"

"Cross my guts," he said. Willie smiled. When they were grade school children, she'd told him she never felt things in her heart the way people talked about. When she was sure of something, it came from her guts. They'd sealed many promises by saying "cross my guts," but it had been years since either of them had used their childhood oath. They didn't say anything more but sat together until they noticed everyone else was finished eating.

"I'll take your plate for you," Willie offered.

"Thanks," Harold said. "Guess you'll be heading to Portales soon."

"Yes."

"Guess this is goodbye then."

"Yes. Goodbye, Harold."

Willie could see Harold wanted to hug her. She held their plates like a shield in front of her body. Unable to bear the sight of Harold's eyes ringed with red, she turned toward the row of makeshift tables set up for rinsing and scrubbing dishes. A few ladies from the congregation, organized by the pastor's wife, had volunteered to clean up after the event. Willie refused to cry here. She wouldn't allow anyone to assume she wanted to marry Harold Parrish or that she was brokenhearted over him. Her heart was her own business.

Willie caught up with Mother and Edgalea as they walked toward the wash station. Sarah Tollett was not accustomed to being served, so rather than hand her plates to Mrs. Lancaster, she stepped behind the table with the other women and plunged her hands into the washtub.

"Oh no, you don't need to do that!" said Mrs. Burton. "You're the mother of a graduate. Go and enjoy your family." It was not lost on Willie that she hadn't refused help from Mrs. Harris or Aunt Xenia, also mothers of graduates. She was certain her mother noticed too, despite her smile and expression of thanks to Mrs. Burton.

They'd seen rejection veiled as kindness before. Publicly, some women were sugary sweet, but Willie could tell which ones considered her mother to be below them. As a young child she'd wanted to call out their duplicity, but her mother wouldn't allow it. "People's hearts don't change when they're embarrassed," she'd always told them. Willie was less interested in changing hearts than repaying hurt, but she knew this was not the time or place to say so.

Aunt Xenia came to their sides, having left her dish-drying post.

"I'll get Father and tell him we're ready to go," Willie said. "We need to hurry to Portales."

Edgalea's relief was visible, but Mother hesitated.

"I should stay to help," she said. "I could clear the serving tables."

"I'll stay to help and ride over with Aunt Xenia," Willie said, with a pleading look to her aunt.

"Yes," Aunt Xenia said. "You all go on and save us a few seats."

Mother recognized Edgalea's urgent desire to leave and realized that agreeing with Xenia was the most gracious way out.

When every dish was washed, dried, and returned to the basket of the woman who'd provided it, Willie made her way to Aunt Xenia's car. As she rounded the corner to the side where cars were parked, Minnie stepped in front of her. Between the unspoken goodbye with Harold and Mrs. Burton's insult to her mother, she'd forgotten her anger toward her cousin. At the sight of her now, she felt it rising again. Willie tried to step around her, but Minnie took her arm. Willie tried to shake her off, but Minnie pulled her back. Her nerves were raw, and she was ready to fight by the time her cousin spoke.

"Where's Edgalea? I need to talk to both of you."

"She rode with our parents," Willie said. "I think she's had enough of your nastiness for one day."

"About that," Minnie said. "I'm sorry." It was almost a whisper.

Willie looked at her cousin. The mark from the slap was gone, but her eyes were still red. Willie wasn't sure whether she'd been crying or was about to start. "Fine," she said. "Truth be told, it was worth it to see you get your due."

Minnie looked at her feet. "I guess I deserved that."

"Yes, you did." Willie started to the car again.

"Joe called it off," Minnie said quickly.

Willie turned around to face her. "What do you mean, 'called it off'?"

"I mean, he's moving to Amarillo without me."

"Why would he move by himself?"

"Not by himself. But not with me."

"You don't mean?"

"I do. He wasn't even going to tell me, but his brother told their aunt, who's married to Uncle Nathan's hired hand. Uncle Nathan put it to him that he better tell me himself. That's why he came by last night. He's marrying a girl from Amarillo, and her daddy gave him a quarter section with a soddy to get started. I wonder if he's not marrying her just to get the land."

"Minnie, I'm sorry," said Willie. And she was. She knew most of her cousin's spitefulness was the result of her own worry over being alone.

"I haven't told my mother yet," Minnie continued. "I know she was relieved to have me married off. I wanted to give her one more day to be proud of me before she finds out I'm a disappointment." She paused and sniffed. "At least—that's what I'd planned to do."

"You? What about Joe? It sounds like he's the disappointment."

“That’s not how people will see it.”

“It’s how I see it.”

“You don’t see things the way regular folks do.”

“Well, I won’t tell anyone.”

“But could you tell Edgalea? Please? I don’t think I can bear to say it all again, and I want her to know I’m sorry.”

“Sure.”

“I envy you, Willie.”

“Why is that?”

“You don’t care about anything.”

“I care about plenty. Just not marriage.”

“What else is there?”

The rest of the day was a blur of speeches, prayers, and awards. For such an exciting occasion, Willie found it tiresome. She dreaded the conversation she needed to have with Edgalea and wondered why it even mattered. She was relieved when they finally made it back to the comfort and predictability of the farm. The place made more sense to her. And she’d get to be there all summer.

Chapter 11

In the first weeks after school ended, the Tollett family shifted from school routines to the centrality of farm work. Edgalea took over the household, with Gladys and Ella Bea as her charges. Thurston was expected to work beside their father, his days of being mothered having come to an end. He would begin school in the fall, but the initiation into his responsibility to the farm started now. He was a sharp boy and would have learned a great deal more if he'd had any interest in it.

Willie joined her parents in the fields from sunup to sundown every day but Sunday. Her sisters missed the ease of the classroom, but her body craved the sweat and effort of farm work. She had to admit, though, that she also longed for the company of her classmates and the companionship of the house on Railroad Street.

Willie suspected her mother was as glad to be back outside as she was. With Edgalea home, she returned to being her husband's right hand on the farm. As much as Willie learned the mechanics of farming and livestock from her father, she sensed there was much to learn from her mother as well. Her approach to cultivation was gentler somehow. She seemed to be working with the earth rather than at odds with it, always whistling or humming a tune in contrast to Father's grunting and muttering.

Willie hoed around the perimeter of the garden. Chickens ran over to peck at the exposed roots and overturned soil. The sky was clear, and the day was getting hot. Her bonnet and long sleeves protected her from the intensity of the sun, and her skirt, though it clung to her legs with dirt and sweat, allowed the occasional breeze to provide moments of cooling relief.

Willie thought of the townsfolk as she worked and wondered what news her father might have tonight. Every Saturday Father met with the community leaders who opposed the opening of the pool hall in Inez, which made Saturday evenings the most exciting time of the week. Jim Tollett would give the family detailed updates on the effort and its moral imperative. Then, if they were patient, he would eventually give reports on the general goings-on of the county.

Willie appreciated a good story even though her father was not a good storyteller. Last week, he'd had word of Harold from Mr. Parrish. He'd been getting along well after his move to Tennessee and had found work in the law office of one of their Tollett kinfolk, thanks to a letter her father had written on his behalf. Willie imagined Harold walking from his rented bedroom to the stone front of the law office wearing a dapper suit. She wondered now and then what it would have been like to have said yes to his proposal, and every time she knew it would have been a mistake. She considered the callouses on her palms and the sun on her back. It wasn't for everyone, but this was where she wanted to be.

"Willie!"

Willie looked up to see Thurston running toward her. She pushed her bonnet back to remove the shadow from her eyes. He was running as though chased by the devil himself. She dropped her hoe and ran to meet him.

"Willie!" he gasped as they met.

"What? What's wrong?"

"Nothing's wrong! Why would anything be wrong?"

Willie replaced her bonnet and turned back to the garden.

"Wait! Willie! There's a baseball game this afternoon, and John Musick is playing second base for Elida in the game against Inez. Mother said I could go if you'll take me! Will you take me, please?" The words spilled out of his mouth like water from a pump.

"Why do you care who's playing for Elida?"

"Because he's the best pitcher and second baseman in the country!"

"If he's so good, why doesn't he play for the Dodgers or something?"

"No one knows. They've tried to get him up to the big time, but he won't do it. He only moved out here last fall, so this is his first season in Roosevelt County. Come on, Willie! I'll do your chores for you tonight!"

"How do you even know about this man?"

"Everyone knows about him!"

"And why would Mother give you permission to go? You know I'm going to check with her, and if I find out you're lying, I'll have your hide for wasting my time!"

"I promise. But she said only if you take me." Willie wondered why their mother specified her as Thurston's chaperone.

"Fine, I'll take you. But I'm not leaving until the garden is weeded, so you might as well get another hoe and help me."

Thurston took off toward the barn and came back shortly. He whacked at the ground with such fervor that Willie had to remind him that much of the green coming up was edible. When she was satisfied that he'd kept his end of the bargain, she followed him into the house. Most days, they would be sitting down to a dinner of meat, potatoes, biscuits, and greens. Instead, Ella Bea handed her a cloth sack.

"A couple of biscuits with ham steak," she said.

"Thanks," Willie said.

"It's not much of a dinner," Thurston said. Willie was aware of her own hunger and shared Thurston's disappointment but would never say so. She was careful not to criticize anything that came out of the kitchen.

"It's what Mother said to do," Gladys explained. "She said since Father is gone and you two are leaving, there was no need to fuss over a big meal." Willie assumed this was sufficient confirmation of their mother's permission. Thurston took his biscuit and headed for the door.

"Where is Mother now?"

"She and Edge went to visit Mrs. Belcher. Me and Ella Bea were supposed to tell you that and then head over there."

"Why am I the one who has to go with Thurston?"

"Edgalea doesn't want to be around all the newlyweds, and I told Mother you needed to go more than me."

"What does that mean?" Willie bristled at her sister's presumption and especially at the idea of her talking about it when she wasn't around.

"You get grouchy when you don't get a good dose of people now and then."

"I do not!" Willie said.

Gladys raised her eyebrows and tilted her head forward, inviting Willie to examine the evidence between them.

"Fine. I'll take him," Willie conceded. She gave her sister a half smile. "But I can't promise I'll be in any better mood when I return."

Gladys and Ella Bea tied on their bonnets, and Willie followed them out. Ella Bea's eyes took in Willie's appearance from head to toe.

"Surely you're going to change clothes," she said. It was a statement more than a question.

"Why?" Willie asked.

As her sisters made their way across the pasture, Willie and Thurston rode toward town on the old gelding, Buster. He prattled on about the player from Inez, but Willie mostly ignored him. As they got closer, Willie found herself wondering who else might be at the game and what word she might get of her friends, teachers, and neighbors. She felt energized and admitted to herself that perhaps Gladys knew her better than she knew herself.

The Inez township consisted of one main road that boasted Aunt Chloe's general store, Dr. Burton's hospital, and a post office. At the end of the main road, cars and wagons had pulled off onto the prairie grass. Inez was not as large or prosperous as Portales, but the people were unrivaled in the pride they had for their community.

Willie hitched the horse and walked toward the baseball field. Her grandfather, Red Sam, had taken the girls to the ballpark often when they were younger. The infield was greener than she remembered seeing it in past years, but the outfield was still mostly dirt. A man from Inez was at bat in front of the chicken-wire backstop. The players who weren't on the field sprawled out along each baseline under the shade of discarded army tarpaulins.

Willie was surprised to see the size of the crowd gathered at the park. Men and women of every age sat in the backs of their wagons or trucks along the outfield or on large quilts where they could be closer to the action. Willie scanned the crowd to see whether any of her friends were there. She delivered Thurston to the park and felt no further duty except to see he got home when the game was over.

The girls her age were more interested in their male companions than the men on the field. Willie was glad to see her friend Joyce waving at her. As Willie got closer, she noticed everyone dressed as for a Sunday picnic. Joyce had on the dress she'd made for their final assignment in home economics, and the rose color was as flattering as Willie had imagined it would be. Willie was relieved that it hadn't become her wedding dress.

Even the young men looked like they'd taken care to clean themselves up. Willie thought it was strange they'd taken so much time from their work, not only to attend the game, but also to get gussied up. And wouldn't they have to change again to return to their work when they got home?

"Oh, hi, Willie! Who are you here to see?" May Bell asked. May Bell and Glenn were sharing a quilt with Bill and Joyce. Willie knew May Bell's motive was to point out for everyone that a single had interrupted a party of couples. Joyce smiled and made room for her on the quilt.

"I guess I came to see the second baseman," Willie answered. Even though she wasn't bothered at being without a date, she wasn't going to give May Bell the satisfaction of confirming it for everyone.

"See, May Bell. I told you everyone's heard of him," Glenn said. May Bell narrowed her eyes at Willie. Her flippant comment had had the unintended effect of deflecting May Bell's slight and garnering the approval of her sweetheart. May Bell would stew over it for weeks. Willie decided this baseball game might amount to more fun than she'd expected.

The sound of the crowd shifted from indistinct chatter to concerted cheering as the visiting team took their places. Willie followed their gazes to the field. The famed second baseman was thin as a rail. Mother would say he needed to get some meat on his bones. He wore his cap low on his forehead so that his face was nothing more than a shadow.

Somehow, through that shadow, he could catch the ball whether it came bouncing on the ground, falling from the sky, or driving straight at him. His long arm stretched out and his foot remained on the bag. He swept his glove down to the runner's back before you even realized he had the ball. The only time Inez scored was when their heavy hitter managed to send the ball out of the park.

Willie found herself engrossed in the action of the game. She'd never seen someone with as much athleticism as the man from Elida. Standing still, he looked lanky and awkward, but when the action started, he transformed. He was powerful, quick, and agile.

When May Bell's chatter failed to keep Glenn's attention, she turned to Willie. Willie knew she was trying to engage her, but she was surprised to find herself even less interested in her gossip than usual. She couldn't take her eyes off the second baseman, so she tried to satisfy her with a series of nods and "mm-hms." When it was Elida's turn to bat, Willie finally registered May Bell's words.

"Of course, they were a mismatch from the beginning. Him coming from a wealthy family and all."

"Sorry, what are you talking about?" Willie asked. She felt bad for being rude, but only a little.

"I said, it was a shame about Minnie's engagement," May Bell said.

Willie recognized May Bell's attempt to bait her, and

she did not want to give her that satisfaction, so she didn't respond.

"Of course, I've wondered if they were ever engaged at all."

Still, Willie did not respond.

"Maybe it was all a big misunderstanding."

"A misunderstanding?" Willie couldn't help it. She wanted to know what May Bell was getting at if only to know what the townsfolk might be saying.

"Sure. Joe is such a sweetheart. Minnie must have misinterpreted his general kindness. Wishful thinking, you know?

"Apparently, he'd been planning to marry the girl from Amarillo for over a year. They only eloped because her father was anxious to have help for the harvest."

Willie had seen enough of Joe's "kindness" toward Minnie to know there was only one way to interpret it, but sharing what she'd seen would only damage her cousin's reputation. There was nothing she could say without betraying her confidence. Joe's version of the story would be the only one remembered.

"Maybe so," she said, hoping May Bell would move on to another subject.

"Anyhow, we've sure been praying on her behalf."

As much as Willie had looked forward to seeing her classmates, she already needed a break. She excused herself and walked to George McCormick's makeshift stand, where he and Gussie sold soda pop and roasted peanuts. Seeing the McCormicks brought to mind the nighttime disturbances that had been happening just as school ended. Wasn't it Gussie who'd had such a fright? Willie had forgotten all about it in the weeks she'd been back home.

She hadn't brought any money, so she walked on until she spotted Thurston and his friends loitering behind the visiting team, hoping to catch a foul ball. She watched long enough to confirm her brother wasn't getting into any trouble. With nowhere else to go, she returned to her classmates.

May Bell was still trying to shift the attention from the baseball field toward herself. Willie took a deep breath and braced herself for another round of nosy questions disguised as Christian concern. May Bell wasn't directing her comments to anyone in particular. She was open to anyone who would pay more attention to her than to the game.

"May Bell, did anyone catch the creature that was making all the noise and tearing up yards?" Willie's question had the effect May Bell had been wishing for all day. It helped that Elida was up by seven runs in the ninth inning. Everyone turned to respond.

"You mean the Howler," May Bell said.

"My dad says the deputy has taken too long to get to the bottom of it," Joyce said.

"I agree," said Bill. "I'm not even allowed to sit on the porch after dusk. Mother is terrified I'll be attacked." Standing over six feet tall and built like an ox, the thought of Bill being attacked was ludicrous, and they all laughed.

"Is the Howler dangerous? Has it attacked anything?" Willie asked.

"Of course!" May Bell answered.

"What?" Glenn asked. "When? I haven't heard about any attacks."

"Oh, I'm sure I have. I don't remember the exact details, but I'm certain someone has been attacked."

"It's strange that the howling's only heard in town. Seems like it would be out on the farms where there'd be more easy targets," Glenn said.

"Plenty of dogs, cats, and chickens in town," Willie said.

"Maybe the Howler's not an animal," Bill added.

"Haven't you heard it? There's no way it's human!" Joyce answered.

"Maybe it's something in between!" Bill said. "Like one of those werewolves!" As if on cue, the boys tilted their heads back and began howling.

"Werewolves only come out during a full moon," Joyce said. "The Howler comes out all kinds of times."

"Not just any time," corrected May Bell. "Only at night."

"Well, if the deputy isn't going to get the job done," Bill said, "I say we get a group together to go after it. I bet we could find it."

"As long as your mother lets you out of the house," Glenn said.

The last pitch of the game hit the catcher's mitt, and the conversation ended with the game. Willie regretted not bringing up the Howler sooner. She would have liked to have heard more about it.

Now that the game was over, Willie felt the need to return to her duty as her brother's keeper. She scanned the crowd for the boys his age and saw them moving as a single form toward the visiting team's dugout. She pushed her way against the movement of the people who were trying to leave the park until she was close enough to call out.

"Thurston! Come on! We need to get home!"

"Ah, Will! I just want to shake John Musick's hand. It'll only take a minute, promise!" Unable to reach him, Willie had no choice but to follow.

"Fine, but only a minute!" she called. "We have work to do!"

Willie watched as other not-so-lucky boys were dragged away by their parents and older siblings. By the time Willie reached Thurston, only a short line of men stood between them and the famous player. Thurston hopped forward when it was his turn to say hello. Up close, the man was taller than he'd appeared on the field but every bit as thin. Thurston put out his hand, and the second baseman shook it firmly and said hello as though greeting a grown man.

"I'm John Musick," he said.

Thurston was struck dumb in the presence of his new hero.

"Introduce yourself," Willie whispered, and she nudged her brother forward with a knee from behind.

"Thurston, sir."

"Do you play baseball, Thurston?" John Musick asked. He took a pack of Camel cigarettes and a match out of his hip pocket. He tapped the pack on the heel of his hand and slid a slender cigarette out. He struck the match against the dugout fence and lit it as Thurston explained that he wanted to play but didn't have a glove. When the man looked up, he noticed Willie for the first time and smiled.

"Care for one?" he asked her.

"No, thank you," Willie said. She couldn't believe this baseball player was offering her a cigarette. She hoped her brother wouldn't mention it to their father. It would mean the end of future outings to the baseball field.

John Musick must have noticed her shock because he winked and said, "Not your brand?"

Willie's face burned with sudden recognition. Between the darkness of the church building and the shadow of the baseball cap, she had not known the man in front of her as the same one met she at the church social two months ago.

"You played real well," Willie said, hoping her cheeks were only red from the sun.

"Kind of you to say so," he said. "Thurston, I hope you can make it to another game. Maybe you could help me warm up."

Thurston's eyes went wide, and he gave Willie his sweetest, pleading look.

"Only if your chores are done," Willie said. Then she added, looking again at John Musick, "Next time, we'll bring my sister. The one I told you about."

Thurston looked up at her and wrinkled his nose.

When they got home from the baseball game, Willie had to remind Thurston of his promise to help her complete the evening's chores. Luckily, daylight and warmth now stretched well into the night. They didn't come in until supper was almost finished.

"We're having trouble with a few of the business owners in town. Seems like Armstrong got to them," Father said. Willie guessed her mother had asked about the meeting in town.

"What has Mr. Armstrong told them?" Mother asked.

"He has them convinced that any business that doesn't compete with their own is good for everyone. And the town will vote the way the owners do, so it could mean trouble. Hollins had a few ideas for changing their tune, but I'm not sold on 'em yet."

"Why would any of them want a pool hall next door?" Ella Bea asked.

"It's beyond me," Father answered.

"Couldn't the billiards players bring them more business?" Willie asked. "If people have another reason to come into town or if folks come from surrounding towns to play, won't they also eat and maybe shop?"

"Nonsense," said Father. "It's nothin' for you girls to concern yourselves with."

Willie recognized this line. Her father used it when his daughters asked a question he'd rather not, or perhaps could not, answer. Willie regretted she'd asked her question so soon in the conversation as it meant they would hear little else about the meeting tonight.

"Was Matthew Cash at the meeting?" Mother asked.

"He was."

"How are Andrew and Violet?"

"Fine, I guess."

"The baby will be here in a few weeks. Right around harvest, I imagine. How's Violet feeling?"

"Don't rightly know."

"Matthew didn't mention it?"

"Not the sort of thing men talk about."

"No, I guess not," Mother said. "I just pray a little joy to their family after all they've been through."

"They got Andrew home," Father said. "I'm sure that's all they'd thought to hope for."

"But Violet's lost her parents."

"Not everyone can handle the West," Father said. "They're better off in Georgia.

"Why did it take Andrew so long to get home?" Gladys asked.

"He had to stay in a hospital in France before he could make the trip back over," Mother explained. "Then he was laid up in a hospital in New York before he was released on a train back home.

"And all that time, Violet raising Ruth on her own while she waited for word of his whereabouts," Mother said. "Such a sad way to start a family. But those who hope in the Lord will renew their strength."

"She wasn't completely alone though, was she?" Edgalea asked. "She's been living with Mr. and Mrs. Cash since Andrew went to the war."

"She was alone in her own way," Mother said.

"Was Mr. Parrish at the meeting?" Willie asked, hoping to reengage her father and get news of Harold.

"He was," Father said. Willie waited, but he didn't say any more, and Willie knew better than to ask another question once her father's mood turned sour.

"Father, you should have seen the ball game today!" Thurston said.

"I'm sure I had more pressing work to do."

Thurston's face sank. Once again, Willie regretted she'd asked her question so soon. She also regretted her father didn't like for her to ask questions.

"Willie, did you notice any plums on the road?" Mother asked.

"Yes, the sandhill thickets were loaded."

Mother aways knew the right question to ask. Everyone at the table was soothed by the promise of jelly and pies.

Chapter 12

All year the farmers prayed for rain, but for one week in June they begged God for clear skies. Cut wheat would rot if left on wet ground. As the wheat neared ripening, every farmer watched for signs and patterns and planned their harvest days accordingly. Important decisions might be made only because cows decided to lie down or the sky took on a green hue at dusk.

While they waited for the perfect convergence of ripeness and weather, families tried to get ahead on every other job possible. Once the harvest was underway, it would become their singular focus until the last shocks of grain were taken to the mill, and the straw was stored for the winter.

Jim Tollett gave assignments to his wife, daughters, and young son every morning at breakfast, expecting by dinnertime his small crew would have them completed and be ready for a second round to be given over the noon meal.

As they finished dinner on Monday, Father laid out the afternoon's priorities. "The barn roof needs to be patched," he said.

"Oh! I'll do that!" Thurston said. He was already jumping up from his unfinished dinner and heading for the door.

"Sit down, son," Father said. "It's a job that requires care and self-control."

"I got loads of that!" Thurston said.

Jim turned his attention back to his wife. "I need Willie to get the Hereford and their calves moved to the south pasture, so you'll have to see to the roof."

"I better hurry then," she said. "Storm's a comin'."

Willie trusted her mother's judgment. For all that the men speculated about the weather, her mother knew it as a matter of course. The weather was an extension of the body of living things Mother seemed to inhabit. Willie knew her father counted on his wife's intuition to plan his harvest, though he'd never admit as much.

"Willie, when you finish, go help your mother."

"What should I do?" Thurston asked.

"You'll be plantin' corn seed with me," Father said.

"Will we have time to go fishing?"

"Not today, but when the harvest is done. It'd be nice to have a mess of catfish for Sunday dinner."

Willie left her sisters to clean the kitchen and beat the rugs while she stepped out into blue sky. She was grateful for the assignment she'd been given. It was work that would typically fall to a son. Moving a handful of cows and their calves would be simple enough. It was only matter of pushing them along the fence and closing the gate. As long as she got the mothers moving, the calves would follow their swinging bags of milk.

Even Buck seemed to understand that the job would not require much effort. He loafed along in the heat, stopping to sniff and snort at clumps of grass. The herd moved without concern. As long as they made steady progress, Willie didn't feel any need to rush them.

They'd made it halfway to the south pasture when Willie welcomed a breeze on her sweating brow. As the wind picked up, however, it began carrying the dry earth across ground, and Willie noticed a shift in the Herefords' energy. They became less somnolent, now and then bawling a call and response with their calves as they walked. Willie felt a sudden urgency to finish her job, and pressed the herd to pick up the pace.

"Hope we don't get a duster," she said into the wind.

As if in answer, Willie heard the rumble of distant thunder. She adjusted her position to the back of the herd where she could keep them moving along.

"Git on now!" she hollered. They made good progress in this way, despite the increasing jumpiness of the cows.

Willie saw in the sky what her mother had known was coming. A wall of dust was rolling toward them. Behind the dust was a solid black thunderhead. As the dust rose up, the cloud bore down, so it was hard to tell where one ended and the other began. It was evident both would be on them in short order. Willie knew she wouldn't outrun the dust, but the gate was just ahead, and she was sure she could get the cows safely behind it before the full force of the storm hit.

Willie felt the dust clinging to her sweaty brow and stinging her cheeks with greater force. She blinked her eyes against the assault, to little effect. The dust was so thick she could hardly see anyway. The first Hereford, Tulip, balked at the gate with her calf, but Holly didn't stop and gave them no choice but to go through. Then it seemed they would all follow suit.

Willie felt another change in the air as she watched them. The temperature dropped several degrees. The darkness on her now was not from dust. The storm cloud had completely blocked the sun. The cows had nearly all cleared the gate when a simultaneous flash of light and crash of thunder split the air. Willie watched through the haze as the split-second erupted with chaos. The last cow turned and attempted to run back the way they'd come, only to collide with the last calves who were following behind her. After the flash, they were shrouded in darkness again, and Willie could only hear the continued rumble of hooves. She took a gamble and dismounted, hoping she could close the gate without being trampled. Not sure whether the last calves had made it in, she pulled on the wooden slats and swung the gate around. Then she got behind it and pushed, leaning her weight against it to nudge the calves out of the way. She secured the latch and leaned against the gate, squinting her eyes to identify any calf-shaped silhouettes on the wrong side of the fence. She strained her ears to determine which side of the gate all the bawling came from.

Satisfied her job was done, Willie stumbled toward Buck. Rather than get on his back, she walked beside him, allowing his broad body to shield her from the wind as they walked toward the barn. Their barn was not the red, round-roofed style popular in railroad advertisements. It was more like Mother's quilts, a patchwork of building materials salvaged from other projects. It was only large enough for two stalls in one half, a storage area for tools and farming implements in the other half, and space to store straw in the loft. The two ends were made of wood brought on the train from Albuquerque to build Red Sam's first house. The broad side had boards from the upper portion of a half-dozen soddies whose occupants had abandoned the promise and perils of homestead life. The rest came in bits and pieces her father acquired by helping raise and fell homes, barns, and fences in the sixteen years since they'd arrived. She could only guess where he might have collected the wooden shingles necessary for a roof repair.

Rain collided with dust to create heavy, muddy droplets. Willie knew her mother wouldn't be on the roof, but she might need help getting the ladder and tools inside. She couldn't see far in any direction, but she trusted Buck to lead the way, since he'd surely be anxious to move toward shelter.

Willie called out to her mother but heard no reply. When she was close enough to make out the solid shape of the barn, she tripped and landed on her hands and knees. As she scrambled to get out of the mud, her hand landed on something hard, and she closed it around the wooden handle of a hammer. Reaching behind, she realized she'd tripped over the ladder. She got to her feet, and in the next flash of lightning, Willie saw her mother's body only inches from where she stood. The thunder that followed could have been her pounding heart.

She had to look away and catch her breath before she could bear to bend down for closer inspection. Sarah Tollett was lying face up on the ground, her hair swaying in the puddle that had formed around her head and her left leg bent at an unnatural angle. Willie lowered her cheek to her mother's face and was relieved to feel warm breath coming from her open mouth. She tried to check for blood, but between the mud and darkened sky, it was impossible to know what had happened.

She pushed the hair from her mother's forehead and was relieved to hear her moan. She looked over her shoulder and yelled for her father. Sarah muttered something, but Willie couldn't make out the words. Deciding to move her out of the rain, she sat back on her heels and slid her arms under her mother's shoulders, prepared to drag her into the barn.

"No," Sarah said. Her voice was so soft Willie wasn't even sure she'd heard it. She paused, then started to pull again. "No," Sarah repeated. Willie was certain she'd heard it this time. She removed her arms and rocked onto her heels again, cradling Sarah's head in her hands to keep it out of the mud.

Getting her mother out of the storm was the only thing she could think to do. Out here she couldn't assess her injuries or give her any help. The wind continued its assault, though the rain was being replaced by streaks of sunlight as the storm was blown east. Willie looked around for something that could provide shelter, but nothing materialized.

She stepped to her mother's feet and worked to untie the laces of her worn boots, taking care not to move her injured leg more than necessary. The job proved nearly impossible.

The laces were swollen with water and Willie's fingers could not get a good hold on the slippery leather. Finally, she bent her head over and used her teeth to loosen the knots. At last, she was able to slip the boots off her mother's feet. She spat out mud and grit as she returned to her mother's head and placed the boots side by side underneath to keep her face lifted out of the water.

Willie stood again and took a few steps toward the barn. She covered the same number of steps in the opposite direction and put her hand on Buck's back. She looked toward the house, to the corn field, then back to the barn. Finally, she returned to her squatting position next to her mother.

"What do I need to do?" She was alarmed by the quaver in her own voice. She looked again toward the corn field and wondered what her father would do. That thought was followed by another, more worrisome one. What would he expect her to do?

Willie looked at her mother. Sarah's lips moved, but Willie couldn't make out the words. She leaned closer, putting her ear to her mother's mouth.

"Jim," she said. He was the primary concern for both of them. Willie watched her mother take another raspy breath. Her brow tightened and her lips parted, preparing to speak again. Willie leaned close once more.

"And Doc," Mother added. It was more breath than voice, but Willie understood. Willie kissed her mother's forehead and stood up. As she did, Sarah closed her eyes, and her face went slack. Willie yelled for her father again, but she knew it was no use. Even without the wind, her father would not have been able to hear her.

Willie lifted her skirt to her knees and ran across the pasture, calling out as she went. She tripped over tufts of buffalo grass and slipped in the mud until her clothes became heavy with it. The short distance felt impossible to cross. She could see her father on the tractor and Thurston walking beside it, making their way back to the barn. Either they had finished planting before the storm or it was too wet now to continue. Thurston looked up the next time she yelled, and he drew the attention of their father. When Jim saw his daughter running, he jumped down from the tractor. When Willie saw him running toward her, she turned and headed back to her mother.

Willie's legs and lungs burned, but she didn't slow down until she'd led her father to where she'd left Buck standing beside her mother.

Jim Tollett tried to rouse his wife, but with no luck. He placed his ear over her mouth and his hand over her heart. Even as he stroked her hair and whispered, "You're gonna be fine," Willie saw his eyes were wide with fear.

Thurston appeared at her side. "Willie?" he asked.

"Go to the house," she said. "Tell the girls that Mother's hurt and she'll need her bed. Maybe bandages." Thurston didn't move.

"Go," she said again, and he took off running.

Willie watched as her father ran his hands over her mother's limbs, pausing here and there to feel more carefully.

Willie was grateful now that her mother was unconscious, as this would be a painful process if she were awake.

"Fetch Doc Burton!" Father finally said. Willie's heart sank. Her mother had already told her she needed the doctor, and now she'd wasted precious time. She gathered her skirts once more, put her foot in the stirrup, and swung her leg over Buck's back.

"Willie!" her father called out. She paused. "Don't mention it's for your mother. Just say there's been an accident."

"What if he asks questions?"

"Tell him I need him. That's true as anything."

Chapter 13

Willie urged Buck along though his hooves sank in the sandy mud. When they reached the road, she went as fast as she dared and did not let up until she'd covered the six miles to town. By the time she arrived at the hospital in Inez, the rain had stopped, and the sun shone through the clouds.

Doctor Burton's hospital was connected to his home. The two wings formed an L-shape where they met at a common a sitting room and front door. Willie left Buck standing in the road while she yanked on the door. She found it locked. She tried knocking, but no one came. She pounded the door with more force, then realized the hospital might already be closed.

Willie ran around the building to the back door of the Burtons' private residence and knocked again. She was relieved to see the solid wood door standing ajar. Through the screen door, Willie could see the petite Mrs. Burton wiping flour from her hands onto her apron. She looked startled when she took in Willie's appearance.

"Oh my! What's happened to you?" she asked through the screen. Willie hadn't considered how frightful she must look.

"Not me," Willie said. "My m—" Then, remembering her father's caution, she said, "There's been an accident at our place. My father needs the doctor!"

"Oh my!" Mrs. Burton said again. "I'll get Dr. Burton." Mrs. Burton turned and shuffled so slowly Willie was tempted to push through the door and fetch the man herself.

The doctor's wife had not invited Willie in, so she remained on the stoop as the rain continued to fall. She watched as rivulets of muddy water ran over her soiled skirt, pooling at her feet. Finally, she saw Doc taking quick strides across the kitchen with his black bag in hand. He didn't stop as he passed her on the steps, so Willie matched his pace and followed him across the yard.

Like his wife, Doctor Burton was short in stature and more round than lean. He wore a vest that stretched across his barreled chest and a mustache that curled up at the ends.

"Leave your horse and get in the car with me. You can tell me what happened on the way out."

"He's still saddled," Willie said, "and I'm—" She looked down at her clothes and back up at him.

Doc yelled at a boy who was tossing sticks into the bar ditch to watch them be carried away. Willie thought he looked like one of the youngest Clark boys. "I'll give you a nickel to take care of that horse," Doc yelled. The Clark boy's face lit up, and he hurried toward them.

"I'll pay you back," Willie said.

"No need," Doc answered. "Now tell me what's happened."

Willie hesitated. She understood the importance of her

father's warning. Doctor Burton had always been kind, despite his wife's poor manners. She'd learned from a young age that no matter how kind and generous a person might seem, they might only extend their kindness and generosity so far. Willie chose her words carefully.

"There was an accident. The roof needed to be repaired, but then the storm hit. It was so dark; it was hard to make out exactly what happened."

"Your father's hurt?" Dr. Burton asked.

Willie didn't answer his question but continued to explain, "There's no blood that I could tell but maybe a broken bone—or bones."

"Your mother is about as capable as I am. She'll probably have him set straight by the time I get there. Surprises me a little that she sent for help. That's how I knew it must be urgent."

"Yes, sir," was all Willie could think to say. If Doc Burton could acknowledge her mother's skill, surely he wouldn't hesitate to help her. Willie almost told him the rest of the truth, but she trusted her father's judgment.

"My father sure needs you," she repeated.

"I'll do what I can," he said.

They rode the last two miles in silence. Willie couldn't get the image of her mother's limp body and slack face out of her mind. Almost as bad was the memory of her father's expression. She'd never seen fear in his eyes before, and she hoped she never would again.

When they turned down the Tolletts' road, Willie was surprised to see her father still kneeling by the barn. He must have heard Doc's Packard approaching, because he stood up and waved his arms over his head.

"Is that your daddy out there?" Doc asked. Willie didn't answer.

"Miss Willie, is it your mother that's hurt?" Again, Willie didn't answer. She got out of the car and ran, praying he would follow her. She was relieved when he overtook her and continued running across the yard to her mother. He knelt to the ground with no regard for his nice suit or the mud soaking into it.

By the time Willie reached the spot where her mother laid on the ground, the doctor was giving his prognosis.

"I don't see evidence of injury to the head. Probably passed out for the pain. There's probably a break in the leg. Hard to tell. Let's get her into the house, and I'll use the salts to bring her to. Might as well let her sleep for the transport. It's not going to be comfortable." Doc secured Sarah's arms to her side. Jim slid a board under her left leg, and they secured it with strips of cloth from Doc's bag.

Willie watched the men load her mother onto the wagon. She winced as speed took priority over gentleness. She was grateful her mother slept through the ordeal, even as she longed to see her open her eyes. Doctor Burton led the team to the house while Father sat beside Mother in the wagon with his long legs stretched out, serving as a secondary splint to stabilize her body.

Willie didn't have instructions for what to do next. The job she'd been assigned was finished. The adrenaline that had carried her across the furrows, into town, and back home was gone. Her legs wobbled. She put her hands on her knees and heaved, emptying the contents of her stomach. The storm had cleared and taken the dust with it, leaving a clear sky above them. She straightened up and looked at the barn.

Thurston came out of the back door and nearly ran her over.

"Where are you going?" Willie asked. She was afraid something else had gone wrong.

"Everyone told me to get out, so I came out."

"How is Mother?"

"Doc woke her up and she started moaning something awful. That's when everyone started yelling for me to get out."

Willie looked toward the house. She didn't want to go in.

"Come on, Thurston," she said. "We need to finish repairing the barn roof."

"Ah, Will. I need to dig up worms in case we go fishing tomorrow."

"I don't care what you think. You're not going fishing and the roof has to get fixed."

Willie didn't know whether it really mattered, and she doubted seriously that Thurston was going to be any help doing it, but she'd decided to finish the job, and he was going to help.

The certainty in her voice was convincing enough. He kicked at the dirt, then followed her as she lifted one end of the ladder and dragged it to the side of the barn. She retrieved the hammer, then started up the ladder with strict instructions to her brother to hold it steady.

As soon as Willie was on the roof she felt better. She didn't know whether repairing the roof was the most important thing to do, but she knew it was a good thing to do. If something more urgent came up, her sisters would come to tell her. Thurston delivered shingles and nails as Willie needed them, and she made steady progress.

She didn't know how much time had passed when she saw Doc Burton walking to his car. Shades of dark blue and purple streaked the sky as afternoon turned to twilight. The doctor waved to her, and she nodded her head toward him, not wanting to risk her balance. Soon after, she saw Ella Bea collect eggs from the henhouse and Gladys carry pails of milk from the barn. She never saw her father or Edgalea.

Willie watched her shadow grow longer every time she raised the hammer. Eventually, the shadow and light began to play tricks on her eyes. The nails weren't where they appeared to be, and she brought the hammer down on her forefinger and thumb more than she ought. She realized with some surprise that she was working by moonlight. Still, with only three more shingles remaining, she was determined to finish the job before she went in.

Chapter 14

Willie entered the house ready to collapse, work and worry finally given their due. She washed at the basin and dropped into her seat at the kitchen table. The house was quiet, and only one lamp remained lit.

"I wondered when you'd come in."

Willie hadn't noticed Gladys sitting in the rocking chair in the corner of the sitting room. She sounded as though she'd been sleeping, but she got up and joined Willie in the kitchen.

"I wanted to finish up." Willie couldn't say any more than that. She didn't know how to explain her need to be useful or her belief that if the roof were finished, it would be as though her mother hadn't fallen.

"I know," Gladys said. She removed the towel from a bowl of black-eyed peas and put it in front of Willie.

"How's Mother?"

"Sleeping. Doc left laudanum for the pain, and I put a bit of it in her tea."

"And Father?"

"Hasn't left her side." This news surprised Willie and increased her worry. Her father was never one for idleness or coddling.

"How bad is it?" Willie asked. "What did Doc say?"

"He said the swelling was too bad to tell for sure, but she probably broke the leg bone up by her hip." Gladys allowed Willie to take her supper and the information in silence. They sat together until Willie got up to wash her dishes. Then they both went to bed.

Willie struggled to sleep. Her mind replayed the flash of lightning and the sight of her mother's body on the ground. Her muscles were stiff, and she couldn't get comfortable. She didn't want to disturb her sisters, so she laid as still as she could and waited for morning. At the mockingbird's first song, she got up, dressed in the dark, and put the coffee on.

Willie moved quickly. They'd be shorthanded now, and she needed to cover the work of two people. As she stood at the barn door, though, she realized she didn't know what she should do. Father hadn't given her the day's assignment. Left on her own, she was confident she would have made the right choice, but this was her father's operation, and he would have in mind what needed doing first. She only hesitated for a moment before changing course and calling in their dairy cows. She would finish the milking, then check in with Father.

The jerseys were agreeable to being milked a bit earlier than usual. As Willie sat on her stool and milked Polly, her mind returned to the sight of her mother in the mud. She blinked away the memory. By the time Willie stood up, it was nearing daylight. The chickens were off their roost and snatching the worms that materialized with the rain. The calves in the south pasture were awake and nudging their mothers' swollen udders.

Father's vigil was over. Willie saw him on the ladder inspecting the roof, and she was glad she'd finished the job. Yesterday, her body needed a task to occupy her mind, but today she took pride in the fact that she hadn't let them fall a day behind. The roof would be ready for the harvest. She resisted the urge to go to him, choosing instead to carry the heavy buckets of milk to the separator.

When she got into the house, Gladys and Ella Bea were finishing breakfast. Father came in just after her, and they sat at the table. Willie winced at the sight of one chair missing and another empty. Edgalea must be sitting with Mother.

"Willie, I saw your work on the roof," Father said. She hadn't done the job for a compliment, nor had she expected one, but she was grateful he was at least acknowledging what she'd done.

"The last row looks like a child was swinging the hammer. When you've got a job to do, set your mind to doing it well. There's no use in a job poorly done."

Willie thought about the long shadows, the weakness in her arms, and the weariness in her mind, but she didn't mention these things. They would only be excuses. Father was right. She'd known at the time that her work wasn't precise, but she'd kept going.

"I'm sorry, Father," she said.

"Your sisters will need your help in the house today, tending to your mother."

"But there's more to do before harvest."

"Thurston will help me."

"Yes, sir," she said. She might have been able to hear his criticism and her new assignment to the house as unrelated, but she saw the truth on her sisters' faces. She had been judged and found wanting. Her punishment would be exile.

"Willie," said Gladys, "Edgalea has been with Mother for a good while. Why don't you go in so Edge can eat breakfast?" Willie recognized her sister's kindness and carried her plate to the basin. She refilled her coffee cup, needing something warm to hold.

Edgalea was sitting by their mother's bedside reading from the Bible. Willie didn't need to look to know it was the book of Isaiah. Mother's eyes were closed.

"I'll sit a while so you can eat," Willie said. Edgalea, who had surely heard the conversation coming from the kitchen, nodded and stood. Willie took her place in the chair, but she did not take up the Bible. Instead, she held her coffee with both hands and willed herself to settle down. In her place, her sisters might have been disappointed or had their feelings hurt, but Willie was filled with anger. She felt the heat from the coffee rising to meet the heat of her mood. Both threatened to spill over.

How her father could take Thurston out and leave her in the house was unthinkable. Where was Thurston yesterday when the repair needed to be done in the first place? Where was Thurston when Doc Burton needed to be fetched or when it was time to put on the coffee and milk the cows this morning? Willie was better than a son; she was nearly a grown woman!

Willie stayed in the house as her father had directed, though she felt out of place and in the way at every turn. Her sisters had routines they followed every day. Willie knew the things that needed to be done, but it seemed that someone else was always a step ahead of her. The only task that wasn't already assigned was to care for their mother, so Willie committed herself to it, though it didn't require much. It was mostly a matter of sitting next to the bed, ready to answer whenever their mother woke up.

Edgalea came in with a cup of tea and instructions to encourage their mother to drink it. It smelled awful, but Willie didn't question her eldest sister. Mother was still sleeping, so Willie set the cup next to the kerosene lamp on the bedside table, the only light in the room. The flour sack curtain over the single window had been left closed this morning. Willie guessed it was so her mother could sleep, but it made the room feel lifeless. Sarah slept under a wagon wheel quilt of her own making. Her father had built both the table and the bed. The only thing in the room not made by their hands was the desk in the corner. It had been left behind by nesters who'd abandoned their claim.

Willie wasn't good at sitting. Her sisters all had pieces of handwork they could set their hands and minds to, but Willie shunned such projects with pride in the fact that she was never sitting down long enough to finish anything. She wished she'd brought in Harold's watch to keep track of the time. If only her skirt had pockets, she'd always have it with her. She took up the needle and quilt pieces from the basket Edgalea left under the chair and worked at stitching them together. It did help pass the time. She even felt a bit of satisfaction at having been productive. Then she held the pieces under the lamp to inspect her progress. The stitches she'd made were uneven, and she took them out, not wanting to ruin her sister's fine work.

Willie returned to sitting in uncomfortable stillness, listening to her sisters in the other room, Edgalea giving instructions, Ella Bea complaining, and Gladys mediating between the two. She heard them moving about purposefully, putting away dishes, opening and closing drawers, and sweeping the floor. She heard the door open now and then as one or more of the girls took her work outside. Laundry or tending the garden, Willie guessed.

"Drink this, Jamesy," her mother said. Her voice was barely more than a whisper, but it startled Willie. She'd forgotten she wasn't alone in the room.

"What's that, Mother? Do you need a drink?" Willie picked up the cup of tea, ready to hold it to her mother's lips, relieved to have something to do. Sarah's eyes were still closed. She appeared to be dreaming.

"I know it's awful, but you need to drink it," Sarah said, her eyes still closed. Willie had heard her mother say these words many times to those in her care. Now she must be encouraging herself.

"Come on, Jamesy." Sarah's voice was pleading. She wasn't talking to herself, Willie realized, but who was Jamesy? Willie knew everyone in their community, and this name didn't sound familiar. Her mother drifted back into quiet sleep.

Willie thought surely it must be close to dinnertime. She went to the window and pulled the curtain back just enough to look outside. The sun was in the eastern sky and morning birds were still singing. She did what she could to pass the time. She rerolled the quilts that had been placed under her mother's legs to keep the swelling down. She took up the needle and thread again, this time concentrating on the precision of her stitches, doing her best to make them match her sister's. Mostly though she paced the length of the small room, feeling very much like a caged animal.

As the day went on Mother stirred more often, running her hands over her face, pulling the quilt up then down, or attempting to move and grimacing with pain.

Throughout the morning, Mother asked what was wrong. Willie reminded her she'd fallen, then she would drift back to sleep.

"Willie, what's wrong?" her mother said again with her eyes still closed.

"Remember, Mother? You fell yesterday and hurt your leg."

"Not me." With effort, she cleared her throat. "You."

"No, I didn't fall. Nothing's wrong with me."

"Something's wrong. Your leg's shakin' the whole room." Willie was suddenly aware of her bouncing leg, a trait that showed up whenever she was upset. Is this what her mother had been asking about all morning? She felt bad that her anger had disturbed her mother's rest.

"I'm sorry. It's nothing," Willie said. "Do you need anything? Would you like more tea? Maybe a bite to eat?" Willie realized she was nervous now that her mother was more awake. She wasn't sure what she should do. Mother or Edgalea had always been the one to sit with someone who was sick. The sitting was uncomfortable, but Willie was even more unsure of how to sit with her mother now that she was awake. "Should I get Edgalea?"

"I'd drink some coffee."

Willie went to the kitchen and started to pour her mother coffee, but Edgalea handed her a cup of tea instead. Willie wrinkled her nose at the foul-smelling liquid and started to protest.

"Tea for now," Edgalea said. Willie grabbed a biscuit too, in case her mother felt like eating.

"Oh, a letter came for you," Edgalea added. "From Harold."

Willie balanced the tea and biscuit in one hand and took the envelope with the other. She recognized her uncle's Chattanooga address and Harold's neat handwriting.

Sarah was asleep again, so Willie opened Harold's letter, noticing the weight of the paper. It was nearly opaque. Willie caught a hint of peppermint scent.

Dearest Willie,

Hope this finds you well. I've settled in, much as I can. It's a busy city. Trees and mountains enough to make you dizzy. I sweat all day, not from work, but from the air itself. I shouldn't say so much. You might think I'm complaining. It's beautiful country. Green like I'd never imagined. Lots of folks raising hogs and chickens. And cows grazing on mountains. It's a wonder they don't fall off.

How are you? Bet you're glad to be home for the summer. How are the calves? Nearly grown, I suspect. Feel like I've been gone a lifetime. Let me hear a word from you.

Your truest pal, Harold

Willie reread the letter until she heard her mother stirring.

"Coffee?" she asked.

"Edgalea said you can only have tea for now," Willie said.

Sarah raised up on her elbow, and Willie held the cup to her mother's lips, but she only took a sip before she laid back. Willie thought she was asleep, but she spoke again.

"Is your father all right? I know I gave him a fright."

"I suppose." Willie had no sympathy for her father just now.

"Poor Jamesy."

"Did you say Jamesy?" Willie asked. Willie had never heard her mother call anyone by anything other than their given name. She was the only one who called her father James, rather than J.E. or Jim. She couldn't imagine her mother using a pet name or her father answering to one. There was no reply. Her mother was asleep again.

The next time Sarah woke, Willie said, "You called Father Jamesy."

Mother gave the hint of a smile. "That's been years."

"What has?" Willie asked.

"Needed a bit of tenderness, close as he was to crossing over."

"Father?"

"Laid up for weeks. I could make a tea or poultice for near 'bout anything but wasn't much left but to show kindness on his way out.

"Tolletts were a rough bunch. Chloe was the only one who showed me any welcome. They loved Jamesy, though."

Willie couldn't make sense of the story her mother was telling; perhaps there was no sense to be made.

"What was wrong with Father? How did he get better?" Willie had so many questions, it was hard to choose where to begin. In response to her questions, Willie heard her mother snoring.

Willie was surprised to realize she'd eaten the biscuit. She dusted the crumbs off her lap and paced another circle around the room. She knew her parents had met in Oklahoma when their families had been neighbors. Proximity was the circumstance that brought most marriages to bear. As Aunt Xenia said, "A mule can only go so far." She had never guessed there was more to her parents' story. Now, she wondered what other stories she didn't know. She also wondered why she'd never bothered to ask.

Willie thumbed through her mother's Sears Roebuck catalog for a page with the most open space, tore it out, and began filling the margins with a letter to Harold. She recounted the story of her mother's injury and her confinement in the house. As she began, she felt her anger rise again, but as she wrote about her mother, it subsided. "I don't recall having ever been alone with my mother. I suspect I might have missed something."

Willie sighed as she closed the letter. She folded the page and slid it into one of the thin, wax-covered envelopes from her father's desk. She wrote the address from memory and planned to send it with the mail truck that afternoon.

Willie put her elbows on her knees and rested her head in her hands. She imagined Harold sitting at a desk copying down the names of dates and legal cases. According to his last letter, this was how he spent most of his days. In the evenings, he took his supper in the house of a widow woman who took pity on him and was grateful for the small pay he gave her each week. An uninvited image came to Willie of her being the one who had supper waiting for him. What a cruel trick it would be if she'd turned him down, then lived out her days in domestic captivity anyway. Perhaps she should tell him she'd changed her mind. She wouldn't even have to finish high school. Plenty of girls didn't.

"Another letter for Harold?" her mother asked.

"Yes," Willie said, and she realized she'd been tapping the envelope against her leg as she thought about her friend.

"Nice boy. Not right for you, but nice."

"Why wasn't he right?" Willie asked.

"Don't you know?"

"Sometimes I think I do. Other times I think I'm a fool."

"You're no fool, Willie Josephine. Impulsive as a pup, but not a fool."

Willie expected her mother to say more, but she closed her eyes and drifted back to sleep. Willie felt the urge to shake her mother awake. If she'd known Harold wasn't right, why hadn't she said anything? Willie had always believed her family all thought she was a fool for refusing his proposal. It was another loneliness she carried, but her mother had known. Only a moment before, Willie had been ready to board a train to Tennessee. She smiled to herself. Perhaps her mother was right to call her impulsive.

If Harold wasn't right for her, did that mean someone else was? Willie had always assumed *she* wasn't right for marriage, not that she simply hadn't found the right match. Unable to tolerate this new line of thinking, Willie stood up and carried her mother's cold tea back to the kitchen.

"Pour it back in the pot," Edgalea said as she dropped handfuls of chopped potatoes and onions into a skillet. "We'll try to get her to drink more later."

"Can I help?" Willie asked. She hadn't done anything useful all day. She craved a job, even if it was in the kitchen.

"I doubt that very much. When's the last time you quartered a chicken?" Edgalea asked.

"When's the last time you wrung a hen's neck?" Willie asked.

"Ohh," said Ella Bea. "Why do you have to say that?"

"I'm only saying, I do my part in getting dinner on the table," Willie said.

"And all I'm saying is you might not know what to do with a chicken once its head and feathers are gone," Edgalea retorted.

"Ugh!" Ella Bea said, this time putting her hands over her ears.

Willie turned toward the back door. Edgalea was right in pointing out that she didn't know as much about cooking as her sisters. She usually stayed out of the kitchen unless it was time to eat. She belonged outside. She would have to confront her father and convince him to let her get back out.

She opened the door to find him, but was startled by Gladys, who stood red-faced and white-knuckled, a bucket of water in each hand. Willie usually hauled the water when she came in for dinner.

"Give me a hand, would ya?" Gladys asked.

Willie took one of the buckets from her and raised it up to pour into the washbasin while Gladys set the other on the floor.

"How's mother?"

"Mostly sleeping," Willie said. She was tempted to share what her mother had said, but she felt protective of her. She didn't know what it meant anyway. It could be the result of her fall or the laudanum. Or both.

"I think I'll see if Father needs my help."

"They're already washing up," Gladys said. Willie noticed the urgent tone in her voice. A warning that Willie needed to comply with their father's directive to stay inside.

Willie assumed she would take her meal with Mother, but Father carried his plate of fried chicken and a fresh cup of tea for Mother into their bedroom and closed the door. Half an hour later, while the girls were clearing the table, he reemerged, told Thurston to get his hat, and went back to work.

"I can sit with Mother a while," Gladys offered.

"I'll do it!" Ella Bea said.

"You only want to get out of finishing the laundry," Edgalea said.

"It's okay," Willie said. She hoped Mother might say more about Harold or her own life as a young woman. "I don't mind."

Edgalea and Gladys both looked at her with disbelief, but they didn't argue.

"I've made more tea for Mother," Gladys said, "without the laudanum this time."

Willie poured a half cup and carried it in to her mother. Sarah was sleeping again, so Willie placed the cup on the table and looked around for something to do. She regretted she hadn't accepted Gladys's offer. She stepped out and grabbed the broom from its nail on the kitchen wall.

"You must be kin to your father," her mother said as Willie started sweeping. Her eyes were still closed, but her voice was stronger than it had been in the morning. "You've convinced yourself that moving will keep you from getting caught."

"Caught by what?" Willie asked as she continued swishing the broom across the floor.

"Whatever's on your mind."

"The floor needed sweeping, that's all. No good being idle."

"There's a difference in being idle and being still," her mother said. "You don't always have to be busy to be useful."

Willie held the broom still and repeated her mother's words in her mind. They made no sense to her, but she understood that her mother wanted her to stop sweeping, so she leaned the broom against the wall and returned to the chair.

"Don't get settled yet. I need your help with the chamber pot. All that tea you've been bringing me."

When Willie had her settled and comfortable again, she tried to pick up the threads of the morning's conversation.

"Tell me more about how you and Father met. Did he marry you because you took care of him?"

"Our families were neighbors. You know that. As I recall, I married him because he took care of me."

"But you went over to tend to him when he was sick. You were the one taking care of him."

"That was the beginning, but marriage is more than beginnings. We've taken care of each other."

"I can't imagine Father taking care of anyone but himself." Sarah winced, and Willie knew her anger had slipped out with her words.

"Your father can be harsh, but it comes from care. He has an idea of how the world ought to be, and he'll go to any length to bring it about. Reminds me of someone else I know."

Willie didn't respond. She didn't like to think about how similar she and her father were while she was angry with him. And she wasn't ready to let go of her anger.

"I need to close my eyes for a spell," Mother said.

Willie readjusted her mother's pillows and the splints around her legs. She finished sweeping, then passed the time reading from Isaiah.

After so little work, Willie didn't have an appetite when Edgalea called her to the table for supper. She picked at her cornbread and moved the beans around in her bowl.

"Better eat up, Willie," Father said. "We have a lot of work to do in the morning."

"We do?" Willie asked. It sounded like a foolish response. Of course, there was a lot to do. She only wanted to make sure she was being invited to do it.

"That storm washed out some fence posts in the south pasture, and we need to get them reset before we let the Herefords out to graze. I'll start on the far west end, and you start on the east. We'll need to meet each other by dark."

"Yes, sir." Willie knew she'd been reinstated as her father's right-hand man.

"You did right to finish the roof," Father said. Then he got up and went to bed.

Willie never expected him to apologize. Her father was a hard man in matters of pride and righteousness, and he was right about the quality of her work. She was satisfied to be back where she belonged.

Chapter 15

Mother tried every day to get out of bed but couldn't manage it. Doctor Burton came back on the third day and confirmed that she'd fractured a bone near the hip joint. He said there were some city doctors who could put in a glass joint, but that he'd bet on a regimen of exercises to be as effective. It was less risky and more affordable. He said if she did them faithfully, she'd be good as new over time.

"How long will it take?" Mother asked.

"As long as it takes," he answered. When she frowned, he added, "The sooner you get started, the sooner you'll get better." With that pronouncement, Doc turned to leave, and Father followed him out, speaking in hushed tones. Willie guessed it was going to be a long time before her mother was good as new.

As soon as the men were gone, Sarah called Willie and Edgalea to her bed and instructed them to help her to a standing position. The girls stood on each side of their mother, holding one hand and keeping another at her back, prepared to catch her. Sarah's first task was to trace a small arc with her right toe, beginning a few inches in front and ending a few inches to the side of her leg.

Willie watched her mother's face. She didn't wince or grimace, but after two repetitions, there was sweat forming on her brow and creases around her eyes. Willie and Edgalea's eyes met.

"Why don't you take a break, Mother?" Edaglea asked. "It doesn't have to be done in one day."

Willie was annoyed with her sister. She didn't want to give their mother an excuse to stop.

"I think you can do one more," Willie said. "I know you can." Edgalea frowned at her, but Sarah nodded.

She put her foot out but it only trembled. Despite her fierce brow and tight jaw, the leg refused to make the circle. She groaned, and her eyes filled with tears. Edgalea's tears spilled over, and she looked with pleading at Willie.

Willie relented. She wasn't trying to be cruel. She only wanted their mother to push herself. "You'll get that one next time," she said, looking at Edgalea. The girls took their mother's elbows and prepared to lower her back onto the bed, but Sarah squeezed their hands and planted her left foot.

"One. More." she said, breathing as though she'd finished a foot race. The girls looked at each other but did not speak. They stayed beside their mother as sweat dripped from her hair. She forced her trembling foot to travel the three-inch path along the floor with nothing but the force of her will.

"Now," Sarah said, "I believe I'll lie down for a spell."

Willie always assumed she'd only taken after her father. Now she wondered how much of her spirit was an inheritance from her mother. She'd never had any ill feelings toward Mother, but as she became more interested in farm work and spent more time with her father, her mother drifted to the background of her life. She was constant and essential but not central to the action of Willie's everyday life. Willie now understood she'd underestimated Sarah Tollett.

Willie didn't have any more days in the house, but for the rest of the week she brought her mother coffee and sat with her before going out.

"Mother, you said marriage is about more than beginnings. But how do you know whether to begin?"

"Are you asking about Harold?"

"I guess. Not only Harold, but the whole of marriage. It seems like you have to give up everything."

"You give up a lot, but you get a lot in return. There's freedom in letting go of a little control."

"That's not how it looks to me. It looks like women hand over their whole lives, and men just go about doing whatever they had in mind to do. I want to choose my own life."

"Do you think I didn't? I chose this life. Choosing doesn't mean you get everything you want. You have to decide what you want most and what you're willing to give up to get it. I chose to leave my family, knowing I might never see them again. Your father didn't make me come. He knew I'd been without a home for most of my life and that I wanted my children to have a place where they could stay for a lifetime if that's what they wanted."

Answers like these only brought up more questions. Willie wanted to ask more, to get a complete story, but there was never enough time. Her coffee cup was empty, and the sun was over the horizon. Although Edgalea and Gladys kept the household running smoothly, Willie knew their mother's role in the farm work would be harder to cover. She was determined to try.

She got up even earlier than usual and completed as many of her chores as she could so she'd be available after breakfast to do whatever Father asked of her. Once the harvest began, they would only have a few days to get all the wheat cut, and then they would have two days with the threshing machine. Planting would resume two months later.

Willie was making herself indispensable, and she knew it. She decided she should not return to school for her senior year. Now she had to figure out how to get her father to agree. Being back in her father's favor softened her toward him and raised her curiosity about the relationship between her parents. One morning, she asked, "Mother, can you tell me about a time Father cared for you?"

"He cared for us both on our way here. You were born only a few days after your brother Lavern passed on. Our wagons had only made it as far as Hereford on our way here. Brokenhearted as I was over losing my baby boy, I couldn't stop to grieve. Edgalea still needed tending, and you were spirited from the start.

"Your father insisted we stay awhile in Hereford. He took on odd jobs, building houses and working on farms. The folks at the church gave Lavern a proper burial. The women welcomed Edgalea into their homes and cared for her as though she were one of their own. They gave me space to grieve, even before I knew that's what I needed. If it hadn't been for the kindness of the people in Hereford, my body would have kept moving, but my spirit would have stayed behind. Your father made sure I had both before we moved on."

Willie thought about this story all morning as she and Thurston cleared Russian thistle from the corn fields. What might have happened if they hadn't spent their time in Hereford? Had her parents considered staying there forever?

When they finished the job, Thurston made himself scarce, but she met her father at the pen of Herefords. The calves were running together, and the calf she called Carl was interrupting the game with his own attempt to get their attention.

"Hey, girls! Look at me!" Willie said, using the voice she'd designated for her favorite calf.

"Go away! You have slick hair, but you're too eager!" she went on, using a higher-pitched tone for one of the young heifers.

"Someday, you'll appreciate me!" she whined in a mock-hurt voice.

Jim Tollett laughed. Willie decided to take advantage of her father's good humor and the beautiful day.

"I was thinking I wouldn't go back to school."

"What do you mean, not go back?"

"Mother's leg will take a long time to heal. She'll need to take it slow, but she won't if she knows you need her help. She'll push herself more than she should. I know almost everything there is to know about the farm and the herd. This will give me the chance to learn the rest. I'm a good worker." Willie paused. "And I'll be working my own land next summer."

"That's still some time away," Father said. Then he fell silent. At least he hadn't argued.

Chapter 16

On a Friday morning two weeks after Mother's accident, Father announced that the harvest would begin the next day. Willie finished her breakfast quickly so she could get out of the house. The kitchen was about to become the hub of preparation as the women prepared bread and pies to feed the harvest hands.

Father took his hat from the nail by the door, and Willie stood to follow him outside, but he said over his shoulder, "Willie, your mother has a job in mind for you today."

"Today?" she asked, but he was already out the door. Willie imagined herself rolling out pie crusts and cutting biscuits. She felt the anger rising. Was she being punished again? Her work since Mother's accident had been flawless, everything done with precision and exacting standards. She looked to her mother for explanation or defense.

"You and Ella Bea are going to do some cleaning for me."

"Cleaning, Mother?" Willie tried to keep her voice steady, but she felt the tremor of rage in her throat.

"Your father's had a recommendation for a hired hand, a man that's been working at the Greathouse place. Frank says he's a good worker who knows farming and doesn't need watching. Anyhow, Father's promised him lodging so he can get early starts and put in long days. He'll need a place to lay his head tonight."

"But where?" Thurston asked. It was reasonable that he would be most concerned, since he was the one who could end up sharing a room.

"Willie and Ella Bea are going to clean out the dugout, and he'll board there," Mother said.

"Eww!" Ella Bea said, "The dugout gives me the shivers."

"He's an old bachelor, accustomed to sharing a bunkhouse," Mother said. "The dugout will do just fine."

"I wouldn't want to sleep in there!" Ella Bea said.

"Willie, you go on and get started," Mother said. "I'll send Ella Bea out as soon as she's finished in here." There was no mistaking the finality in her tone.

Willie opened the door to the dugout with caution. She understood now why she'd been taken off the farm duty. Her sisters lacked the physical strength to remove the heavy tools and equipment stored in there.

It was hard to believe she'd lived in the small shelter when they first came to Roosevelt County. Her father had proven up their claim by digging a well and building this dirt-walled home, signs to the government that they planned to stay on the land. Willie was only an infant then and Edgalea a toddler, but by the time they'd moved out, Willie was four and Gladys was the toddler.

Before Ella Bea's arrival, their father, with help from his brothers, had built their house with wood shipped by train from Amarillo to Portales. Since that time, the dugout had served as storage. For such a small space, it held an unbelievable amount of detritus. Now Willie was tasked with tunneling through the piles, finding new homes for everything, and making the space livable once again.

"What is all this stuff?"

"Things Father's saving."

"What for?"

"Later, I guess." She wasn't trying to be obtuse. Her father saved everything, included broken tools and implements. He might need the parts or metal to be remade into something later.

Seeing no better strategy, Willie settled on dragging everything out and taking stock of what was before her. Of course, the things closest to the door were the most recent deposits: rakes and hoes with broken handles that would be repaired and used again. A step inside revealed a plow disc that a neighbor had discarded and an assortment of out-of-commission cream cans, machine parts, and miscellany. Willie carried, rolled, and dragged it all outside.

The ceiling and walls were covered in newsprint intended to keep the dirt from breaking off or sliding down to the floor. The bachelor's stove, an old single belly where Mother had cooked for a family of five, stood in the corner. Their round wooden table was in the center of the room, its rough top now stacked with crates of canning jars.

Willie lifted the first crate and carried it outside. Mice had left a trail of debris in and around the crates. She winced. She hated mice, but it was inevitable she'd encounter them in here. After many loads, Willie had the first room completely emptied out, and she still hadn't seen any mice.

The room was starting to resemble a living space again. With it cleaned out, Willie got the sense she was looking at an old memory. She imagined her father sitting with his Bible opened on the faded blue tablecloth while Mother held Gladys on her hip, swaying as she stirred an iron pot of beans. She could smell cornbread and hear her father's voice reciting the scriptures. She imagined the ridges of the rag rug under her hands and knees as she and Edgalea played train with wooden spools. Looking down, she could make out the rug's swirling pattern buried under layers of dust.

Willie used her foot to find the edge of the rug. She bent over and took the edge in both hands. As she lifted one side, dirt cascaded to the ground, freeing it from the weight of years. The rug had always been heavy, but now it was all she could do to drag it backward toward the open door. When she got there, panting and sweating, she extended her arms to each side of the rug and tried to fold the edges enough to get it through the door. When that didn't work, she walked to the side of the room, raised one edge, and began rolling it. When the rug was in a long roll, she took hold of one end and dragged it backward out the door.

As she stepped through the doorway, she bumped into Ella Bea. Startled, she yelped and dropped the rug. Alarmed by her sister's reaction, Ella Bea screamed.

"What?" Willie said. "Did you see a mouse?"

"There's a mouse? Get it away!"

"I didn't see a mouse! You're the one who screamed, so I thought you saw a mouse!"

"I screamed because you screamed!"

"I didn't scream!"

"You did!" Willie looked at her youngest sister standing with her hands on her hips, chin tilted back, and eyes boring into her.

Laughter spilled out of Willie. Her fear of mice, her sister's deep need to prove this point, and her own need to defend her pride were all so ridiculous that in this moment, Willie found it hilarious. She doubled over and crumpled to the ground, overcome by the laughter that wouldn't stop now that it had started. How long had it been since she'd felt such release?

Ella Bea maintained her challenging gaze at first. Then she dropped her hands and tilted her head while she watched. Finally, because she couldn't help it any longer, she laughed, too. When Willie was finished, she stood back up, shivered like a dog after a swim, and smoothed out her skirt.

"So, there's no mouse?" Ella Bea asked.

"No," Willie said. "Well, yes," she added. "Probably a lot, but I haven't found them yet."

"Do you think we will?"

"I'm certain of it. Come on. We need to finish."

The second room of the dugout wasn't as cluttered. Over the years, they'd rarely taken more than a few steps inside the dugout to make a deposit. Until today, access to the second room had been blocked by clutter. The mattress had been removed from the bed when they moved into the new house, but the frame stood against the wall with neat rows of crates stacked on top. Next to the bed was a small table with an old kerosene lamp. Willie and Ella Bea stood in the doorway for a full minute as Willie took in another rush of memories.

"I think the hired man ought to do his own cleaning," Ella Bea said.

Willie didn't respond to Ella Bea's suggestion, but it did bring her out of her reverie. "You clear everything off the bed, and I'll get everything else. Then you can help me move the bed," she said.

Ella Bea kept the pout on her face, but when Willie picked up the table in one hand and lamp in the other, she walked to the bed and lifted a crate. After a while, Ella Bea began singing as she worked. Willie recognized the songs from her days on the grade school playground and joined in. They reminded her of jumping rope. She thought of those days as recent, but she had the feeling that childhood was in the distant past. Boys and girls she'd played with were getting married now.

Her thoughts were interrupted by a crash.

"That one!" Ella Bea screamed, pointing to a crate.

"Mice?" Willie didn't need to ask, but she did anyway.

"The jars started moving when I picked up the crate!"

"You better hope all those jars aren't broken. Can you carry the crate out of here? Otherwise, they're going to scatter and hide and we'll have to find them again."

"Them?"

"Yes, them. There's never just one mouse."

"Why don't you carry out the crate?"

"Fine," Willie said. She hated mice and dreaded the thought of scaring one out of the crate and up her arm. Unable to bring herself to pick up the crate, she grabbed one of the rakes she'd already removed from the dugout and hooked it over the top of the crate. She pulled on the crate and dragged it across the dirt floor and out the door. She heard the glass jars rattle but couldn't tell whether it was from the movement of the crate or the movement of the mice.

"Uh, Willie," Ella Bea said. "Willie!" Willie jumped at the unexpected sound. She turned around, expecting to see mice scurrying across the ground. Instead, a gray snake slid across the ground. She could see two feet of the body, and it wasn't out of the crate yet.

"That explains why we never saw mice," Willie said. If the size of the snake was any indication, they wouldn't find any rodents. Willie didn't care for snakes, but she'd prefer one to a mouse any day. She hoped the new hired hand didn't mind snakes too much, as this one would probably try to return to his home sooner or later.

The sisters worked quickly removing the rest of the debris from the dugout. Willie used an old broom to dust the outside of the stove, sweep off the bed, and clear cobwebs from the newsprint covering the walls. With the interior as clean as necessary for a hired hand, Willie stepped back outside. The brightness and heat of the sun bore down on their faces. She told Ella Bea to clean the furniture that would be moved back while she carried the farm and gardening equipment to the barn.

It took both girls to carry the rug. They laid it across a fence and Willie picked up two brooms and handed one to Ella Bea. They stood on opposite sides of the rug and alternated turns beating it. With every strike, clouds of dust filled the air and settled around them. Willie's standards for a hired hand's quarters lowered another notch. She declared the job "good enough," and they rolled up the rug, carried it back into the dugout, and rolled it out on the floor. They carried the table and two straight-backed wooden chairs back inside and examined the room.

"What about a bed?" Ella Bea asked.

"Thurston sleeps on the mattress now. Let's hope this fella carries his own bed roll," Willie said.

"Looks like we're finished, then," said Ella Bea.

"Not so fast. All the things we dragged out have to be carried to the barn."

Ella Bea moaned.

"We'll do it after dinner. It's probably time to clean up anyway. Edgalea's not letting you inside looking like that," Willie said.

"What do you mean?"

"We've collected more dirt and cobwebs than the root cellar."

"Gross! I thought it was only you that looked so bad. Do you think Mother will let me have a bath tonight?"

"If you haul your own water. Meantime, we better head to the windmill."

The girls walked toward the windmill and stock tank. Willie noticed a man standing next to her father. As she got closer, a now-familiar silhouette triggered recognition.

"Here's two of my daughters now," Father said. "Willie, Ella Bea, say hello to Mr. Musick."

"Hello," Willie said. She put out her hand to shake it. Mr. Musick didn't skip a beat like many men did when she greeted them in this way. He put his hand out and shook. Mr. Musick wore a loose-fitting cotton work shirt, denim overalls, and brogans. It gave him a different look than his baseball uniform.

"I expect you have Mr. Musick's quarters ready?" Father asked.

"Yes, sir," Willie answered.

"John, you can take your belongings in and get settled. I need to check on my wife. As I mentioned, she's been laid up." Willie noticed the wooden trunk at the man's feet.

She didn't wait for the men to walk away before dunking her head into the stock tank. The coolness of the water took her breath away. She rubbed her hands over her face, wiping away the dust and grime. She opened her eyes to see Mr. Musick making his way to the dugout. Judging by the sway in his back, the trunk must have been heavy. She walked toward the familiar stranger.

Chapter 17

Willie caught up with Mr. Musick as he reached the dugout door. She took a quick step and opened it for him. She caught the lingering scent of his last cigarette as it mixed with the dust that hadn't quite settled.

"It's kind of you to have got the place ready. I told your father I didn't mind cleaning it out myself."

"Mother wouldn't have stood for that. And I had my sister's help."

"You must all be very kind, then. Is this the sister you mentioned? The one without a dead husband?" Willie's face flushed. How bold she'd been in the dark!

"No. My youngest sister, Ella Bea."

"Another sister? How many of you are there?"

"Four girls. And my brother, the one you met at the baseball game."

"Yes, Thurston, I recall?" Willie was impressed he'd remembered her brother's name. He seemed to recall everything of their conversations.

Willie felt bad now. She'd imagined preparing the space for a stranger, but Mr. Musick was familiar and she liked him. She was embarrassed that she hadn't done a more thorough job of cleaning his new home.

"I'm afraid we didn't do much but get the farm equipment out. Well, that and a snake, but there's not even a mattress. Thurston sleeps on it now." Willie could feel herself beginning to ramble.

"It's better than the last dugout I lived in," he said. Willie noticed his voice and his eyes look to the horizon. She followed his gaze, unsure of what he might see. "I imagine the work will be better, too." His voice trailed off.

When Willie looked at him quizzically, he came back into the moment and said, "France" as though that explained everything. Willie nodded knowingly but hadn't really understood. "I'll be comfortable here, I'm sure. Thank you again."

"I hope so," she said. She was curious about the formality of his speech. He didn't put words together like folks around here.

As she walked from the dugout to the house, Willie wondered how much her father knew about John Musick. She doubted he would hire a man who read Western stories, played baseball, or went to the pool hall on Saturday nights. She considered telling him, but there was a depth to John Musick's gray eyes that made her want to protect him.

Willie felt the heat of the kitchen coming from the open back door even before she smelled the biscuits. The girls kept the front and back doors propped open to allow a breeze to pass through the house, but it didn't do much good. Ella

Bea took one pan of biscuits out of the oven as Edgalea cut another batch. Gladys removed ham steaks from the frying pan and added coffee to make a red-eye gravy. Mother sat at the table, where judging by the clean circle inside a dusting of flour, she'd been making pie crust. Willie took tin plates down from the cupboard.

"Get an extra plate," Mother said. "The new hand will join us for our noon meals."

"Every day?" asked Ella Bea.

"Every day that he cares to. And we'll wrap a couple of biscuits for him to take for his supper."

"But why? Isn't Father going to pay him enough for grub?" Ella Bea asked.

"Of course he is, but he's a bachelor and might not know how to cook. He'll do hard work and need good food to get it all done."

"And have you seen him?" Edgalea asked. "He looks like he hasn't had a proper meal in months."

"I bet you could help fatten him up," Willie teased. Edgalea cut her eyes, but Willie noticed the hint of a smile that followed.

Edgalea started to clear the mess from the table.

"It's too hot in here," Mother said. "We'll take our dinner outside."

"Are you sure?" Edgalea asked. She looked at Willie and pushed her glasses up the bridge of her nose. They were all hot, but they also shared an unspoken concern. Mother had only started taking steps two days before. With the help of a cane, she could get from one room of their small house to another, but she hadn't attempted the steps from the back stoop to the yard.

"I'll have to do it soon enough," Mother said, in response to their hesitation.

The girls finished putting food on all the plates then carried them outside. The sun neared the horizon, making its glare less direct. The breeze across the Staked Plains cooled their skin. No matter how hot the day got, she could count on the evening to give them relief. Willie thought of it as God's blessing on their work.

Edgalea and Gladys carried the men's plates, and Ella Bea carried Thurston's though no one had seen him all morning. Willie carried a chair for her mother to sit in, even though she was skeptical of her mother's ability to get to it. Father and Mr. Musick met them at the back door.

"Your mother?" Father asked, nodding at the chair. They all knew what he meant. He would not allow his wife to eat alone or be separated from everyone else. If she couldn't come out, they would all go back in.

"It was her idea," Willie said. "I'll help her," she added, but it was too late. Father was already inside the house. Thurston showed up then, like the cows at feeding time, but Edgalea sent him to the stock tank since he was muddy up to his elbows. The girls sat on the ground and Mr. Musick squatted, sitting back on his boots the way Willie had seen the cow punchers and ranchers do. With his long limbs, he reminded her of a frog.

The back door opened, and they all held their breath as they watched Jim holding his arm out to support Sarah's shuffling steps. She made it to the edge of the cracked concrete stoop and paused for a moment before putting her right foot out. It hovered in the air for an agonizing beat. Willie looked from the foot to her mother's face. It showed no obvious emotion, but Willie had learned this summer that the tiny wrinkles around her eyes told the truth of her mother's feelings. She was scared but determined.

Jim stared at his wife's face, and Willie realized he was also reading her eyes. He leaned in and said something none of the rest could hear. It was uncommon for them to demonstrate such closeness. Sarah smiled and her foot touched the step. She let out a gasp as her weight shifted from the back leg to the front. Willie instinctively leaned forward, as though she could catch her mother, but it wasn't necessary. Her father had his arm around her waist and delivered her safely down one more step and to the ground. He kissed her temple then moved his arm back to her side, offering as much support as she might need but letting her choose whether to take it. Only Sarah evoked such tenderness and restraint from Jim Tollett. She took a sidestep to her chair and lowered herself into it.

Thurston returned just then, having missed the excitement. "I'm so hungry I could eat a whole hog!" he said as he grabbed his plate from Ella Bea.

Mother looked relieved to have the attention taken from herself. "Go ahead and say the blessing, James."

When Father finished his prayer, Edgalea turned back to

Thurston. "What have you been doing all morning? Where did you get into mud?"

"I want to go fishing, so I've been looking for worms. Father said they'd be where the ground is wet, so I've been hauling water and building a place for them to come."

"You were supposed to be hauling water for the house!" Edgalea said.

"Where do you fish around here?" John Musick asked.

Thurston was so taken with his hunger and explanation of the worms he hadn't noticed the extra man squatting in the yard. When he saw John Musick, he dropped his fork and his jaw.

"What're you doing here?" he asked. His eyes were wide as he stared at the baseball player from Elida.

"James Thurston," Mother said. "Where are your manners? Your father hired Mr. Musick to help with the harvest." Willie waited for Thurston to tell them about Mr. Musick's baseball fame, but he didn't. He cleaned his plate in silence, boldly staring at the man the whole time. Mr. Musick didn't say a word but met Thurston's stare with kindness.

"Willie, you have a letter from Harold today," Father said.

"Looks like he's not giving up," Gladys said.

"There's nothing to give up on. We've always been friends. We're still friends."

"Until he finds someone with enough good sense to marry him," Edgalea said.

"Girls, not in front of Mr. Musick, please," Mother said.

Their guest kept his eyes on his empty plate, but even in the shadow of dusk, Willie could see the corners of his mouth lifted. She stood to carry her plate inside, trying to appear casual as she collected plates from the others.

When she reached her father, she asked, "May I have the letter, please?"

Father took the small envelope out of his breast pocket and handed it to Willie. She carried it into her parents' room, where she thought she might have a moment of privacy.

My Dear Willie,
Forgive my saying so, but your mother is right. You should finish school. You have your whole life to farm and the day will be here sooner than you know. I'm sure you're feeling cross with me already. It gives me a laugh to think of it. But you'll see. In a matter of months, you'll be on with your life and that with the satisfaction of having completed your courses. If you don't, you'll fuss at yourself for all time. I know you.

You all must be getting ready to harvest. I miss the excitement of it, but not the worry. I'd like work that doesn't depend on something so fickle as the weather.

Willie, I'd still like for you to join me. We'd only be a couple of years here. Then I'd start saving to buy you a farm. Don't you like the sound of that? Tell me you'll at least think about it?

Your truest pal, Harold

Willie folded the letter and returned it to the envelope. She tucked it in the pocket of her skirt and sat on the edge of her parents' bed. She took the letter out and read it again. Then she read it a third time. She wondered if Edgalea was right. Maybe she did lack good sense. Did the longing she felt for her friend mean that she should marry him? She stuffed the letter into the envelope and walked out of the bedroom determined not to follow that train of thought.

When she entered the kitchen, her sisters turned from their dishwashing to study her face. Willie refused to give answers to their silent questions. She walked out the door and toward the barn. The sliver of moon didn't provide much light, and Willie hadn't thought to grab the lantern in her hurry to escape her sisters' watch. Still, every step was so familiar, she could have done it blindfolded. The only surprise was the light coming from the dugout window. That would take some getting used to.

As she made her rounds, she became more and more confident she'd made the right choice. This was where she belonged, and this was the work she wanted to be doing. What kind of work would the wife of a lawyer even do? Willie realized the answer was in the question. She would have the job of wife. And then mother. And by the time Harold had an established practice and money saved, she would have no chance of working her land.

Chapter 18

Aunt Chloe arrived before sunrise on Saturday morning, signaling the beginning of the wheat harvest. It would be hot, dusty work outside and steaming labor in the kitchen. Despite that, the air was filled with excitement. The girls hadn't even finished greeting their aunt before she had her apron on and was refilling Mother's coffee. Aunt Chloe's way of making herself at home in their kitchen used to bother Willie. Now she recognized it as a sign of her full acceptance of her mother, a signal of equality that most of Father's family did not convey. It was her most redeeming quality, perhaps her only one.

As a young girl, Willie looked for escape from the kitchen by carrying ham-filled biscuits, coffee, and water to the men in the field. When she was thirteen, she joined her parents among the golden rows of wheat, working to prove her worth outside of the kitchen. That was the year Edgalea turned fifteen and hoped to take the lead in their kitchen, but Aunt Chloe had come instead, and there was no question who was in charge.

Aunt Chloe's posture was different this year. Maybe it was because Edgalea already had her apron on and was positioned at the stove. Or perhaps Aunt Chloe was giving respect to the fact that since she'd graduated high school, Edgalea was an adult. Whatever the reason, Aunt Chloe looked to Edgalea when she said, "Don't let my hands be idle, now." Edgalea straightened to her full height, gave her glasses a quick nudge, and started assigning tasks of peeling, chopping, and fetching.

Willie took this as her cue to head outside. Thurston made it as far as the kitchen before he sat down. She pulled him up by the elbow and told him he better get the cows milked and eggs gathered. They had a long day ahead. Willie fed the livestock and made quick work of carrying water to the garden for Gladys, who'd be in the kitchen all day.

Every hand was necessary during the days of harvest. It was essential to get the wheat cut, stacked, and threshed before the next rain. Even though rain chances were remote, the threat loomed in everyone's mind. Men and boys of all ages poured into the fields. Some women worked alongside them, those without sons and widows trying to hold on to their land. The other women and girls worked long days to keep everyone fed and full of coffee.

Even those who lived in town came out to help. Willie knew that her cousins would be at Grandpa Sam's, cooking for the widower and his hired hands, and Aunt Xenia would be out in the field, helping bring in the harvest from her land. Her father had hired Andrew Cash, the son of his friend Matthew, to help John Musick. His family lived in Portales, next to the McCormick filling station, but Andrew had dreams of farming.

The prosperity of the entire community depended on the success of the wheat harvest, so it was in everyone's interest to get it done. It was long, grueling work, but it was a social time, too. Special bonds formed when everyone was working toward one goal, and Willie suspected the townsfolk didn't want to be left out. Much of the local lore, from Mr. Mason's missing thumb to the elder Carters' courtship, had its origins in the harvest days, and everyone wanted to take part in history-making.

The sun came over the flat horizon, and it wouldn't be long before there would be no place to escape its intensity. Willie circled back to the house for breakfast. Already, it was so hot in the house that it would be more comfortable to eat outside. Willie noticed that Father was already gone. She was anxious to join him in the work of the day, so she pulled a biscuit apart, slid two fried eggs between the halves, and turned to go outside. That was when she noticed her mother.

An hour ago, it looked natural for her to be sitting at the table drinking coffee. The sight of her still seated now that it was time to go outside pained Willie. She turned back and stepped toward the table.

"It's gonna get hot out there," she said.

"Yes, you'll be glad for your hat this afternoon," Mother said, without looking up from the paring knife and potato in her hands.

"I'm sorry you won't be out there with us."

"Nothing to be sorry for. Mr. Musick will do what's needed. I'll be helpful in here."

Willie hesitated, hoping her mother would say more or that she herself might think of something to say, but when the silence lingered, she took her breakfast outside. Her father already had two horses hitched to the binder. He stepped into the metal seat and gave her a wave. It was time to get to work.

Willie was as strong as many of the young boys helping their fathers, and her strength was put to good use. As her father bounced behind the horses, the blades on the machine's long rotating arms cut the stalks on his left. A wide belt collected them as they fell and deposited them in piles on the right. Willie walked behind the binder, tying the bundles and tossing them into the windrows. She envied the men their long pants as the fullness of her skirt wrapped around her legs and restricted her movement. She wore one scarf over her hair and another over her mouth and nose to minimize the amount of dust and chaff she inhaled.

They measured time by Thurston's hourly appearances with water, coffee, potatoes, and biscuits. Father slowed the horses enough for Thurston to make the handoff but never completely stopped. He wouldn't stop until he saw that dinner was ready, and they ate later than usual on harvest days. Willie continued walking behind him, tying and tossing.

By the time they finally stopped, the comparative silence following the hours-long rumble of the binder was startling. Willie could feel the sound lifting from her ears. It would take a minute to recognize that the initial silence was filled with the sounds of birds, wind, and other binders in the distance.

During these days of harvest, they didn't eat a noon meal together. The workers in the fields ate the sandwiches and potatoes their wives or children brought out to them throughout the day. Dinner was brought out in the evening, marking the end of the day's cutting. Willie saw that Edgalea was driving the buggy, and only her brother and sisters were coming out. Aunt Xenia must have stayed back with Mother. By the time Willie and Jim reached the wagon, the girls had laid out a spread of fried chicken, beans, squash, and biscuits on the back end of the wagon. John Musick and Andrew Cash arrived at the dinner site just as Willie was filling her tin plate.

Tired as they all were, there wasn't much conversation over dinner. Father had questions for Andrew and Mr. Musick about their progress, but after a brief back and forth, they all fell into silence, savoring the food and the moment of rest.

"Well, thank you, girls," Father said. He wiped his hands on the sides of his pants as he stood. It was the cue they'd been waiting for. The ladies made quick work of loading the dishes and driving the wagon away. Mr. Musick and her father drove the binders toward the barn, where they'd unhitch the horses for the night. Willie and Andrew returned to their respective fields. Walking in the reverse order that she'd started this morning, they stacked the wheat into shucks of ten to twelve bundles to continue drying out. They would have to retrace every step they'd walked before their work for the day was done. Willie guessed she had two hours of daylight left. At least the sun's heat wouldn't be so intense.

When she was more than halfway finished, she saw Mr. Musick stacking wheat in the place where they'd started cutting this morning. Despite her sore feet and weary arms, Willie was annoyed that he was doing some of her work. If anything, he should be helping Andrew. This was her field.

When they reached opposite ends of the last row, Mr. Musick gave her a nod and she returned it. Then she forced herself to work faster, determined to get further in the row than he could. Neither spoke, even as they worked together to stack the last bundles.

"I didn't need your help, you know," Willie said.

"I know," said Mr. Musick. "Your father sent me over here. I suspect he wanted to check the other section and ask the young Mr. Cash about my work without me around."

Willie nodded. She knew that was exactly what her father would be doing.

"Do you work in the field often?" Mr. Musick asked.

"Yes, sir. Father didn't get his son until six years ago. We all do our share of farm work, but I guess I took to it more than the other girls."

"I'd say. You rival many of the boys."

"They're not much to compare to."

John Musick laughed. Willie noticed the way he tilted his head back and opened his mouth when he laughed, like there was no reason to hold it in or save it up because there would be plenty of laughter for later. She'd never seen a man laugh like that. It contrasted with his usual quiet and the shadows under his deepset eyes.

"I'll see you tomorrow," Willie said when they reached the point where he would veer off toward the dugout and she would go into the house.

Willie felt as though she'd only lain down long enough for her muscles to stiffen when it was time to begin again in the dark of the morning. This was the only time of year when it was acceptable for them to miss church. No one else would be there either.

Father had secured first place in line for the threshing crew, but that meant their cutting had to be finished in three days. The second day was hotter than the first, and the third was suffocating. When Willie wiped the sweat from her brow with the back of her sleeve, it scraped dust and chaff across her skin, creating tiny cuts across her cheeks and brow. She could see the heat coming off the ground, and her canteen seemed to be empty well before Thurston came out to refill it. She refused the biscuit and the egg he brought out, but when he brought her a raw potato, with instructions from Mother that she had to eat it, Willie was shocked to discover how delicious it was. It was cool from the cellar and as juicy as a cucumber. It awakened her hunger, and by dinnertime, Willie was ravenous. When she smelled the fried chicken, her stomach lurched with hunger, and she filled her plate with every good thing.

After the meal, she reversed her path to start piling the bundles. Willie finished stacking the wheat on dead-tired feet. She was accustomed to hard work, but usually her chores provided more variety in the demands she made of her body. The repetition of walking and tossing all day was harder than a normal day of pushing, pulling, and lifting. She wondered how many miles she might have walked these last three days.

She gazed down the rows ahead of her and realized she was hoping to see John Musick. She scolded herself for wanting to be spared the full job. Of course, he had no reason to come tonight. Father was satisfied that he'd done good work the past two days. She walked the rows alone, thinking of the threshing that would begin in the morning.

Willie stopped at the stock tank to wash. The skin of her knuckles cracked and bled. Her sisters' hands were in no better shape after their long hours of cooking and scrubbing. Mother passed around a jar of petroleum jelly to work into their irritated skin before they went to bed. The women would begin cooking even before the men were awake in the morning.

Chapter 19

The days of threshing were hard, but they also doubled as a weeklong social event. The homesteaders of the plains knew that their survival depended on welcoming one with the other. The threshing crew set up their steam-powered machine in one location for as long as it took for the grain in that area to be sorted from the chaff. Then the crew moved on to the next location. This year, they began at Red Sam's place. Willie's family would go over, and so would the men and women working Aunt Xenia's land, as well as the Belchers, Parrishes, and Clarks.

The farmers sharing the thresher loaded bundles of wheat onto their racks and brought them to the thresher, where all available hands used pitchforks to toss them into the noisy machine. The straw would come out, ready to use for stuffing mattresses, lining the henhouse, and keeping livestock warm in winter. Grains of wheat dropped out of the other end into a large barrel to be taken to the mill to make flour. Chaff that wasn't blown away by the wind landed in a separate barrel.

Jim Tollett and John Musick each drove a horse-drawn bundle rack to the Tollett farms and back. Once again, Willie and Andrew Cash walked beside the older men, this time throwing the shocks of wheat onto the rig. While one team was in the field loading, the other would be unloading at the thresher.

By the time Willie and her father arrived with their first wagonload, her sisters had already laid boards across barrels to make two rows of tables for the food that arrived throughout the day. The back of Aunt Xenia's wagon carried a small stove and food stores, much like the chuck wagons of the cattle drive days. They set up two tubs of water for workers to wash up and two other tubs for cleaning the tin dishes between each shift of workers coming to eat. Willie could imagine what a grueling task hauling all of that water must have been.

The farmers and their crews all helped each other. They split the cost of the thresher and its crew on a per day basis, so it was to their advantage to get their neighbors' wheat through as quickly as their own. "Many hands make light work," as Mr. Clark was fond of saying. With plenty of hands working, there were also plenty of breaks when they could get a cup of coffee or a plate of food and exchange news and stories.

After getting her father's first load through the thresher, Willie went to the wagon to see about a cup of coffee. She thanked her Aunt Xenia then turned to see Luke Parrish, Harold's father, standing behind her. He was so much like her best friend that it warmed her heart to be near him even as she felt an ache that Harold was not here. He smiled.

"Good morning," she said, returning his smile.

"It's good to see you, Willie," Mr. Parrish said. "Looks like you're still your daddy's best hand." Mr. Parrish winked. He'd always been kind to Willie, even when she'd led his son into shenanigans.

"Yes, sir. What do you hear from Harold?"

"Got a letter last week. He's busy with his work and studies."

"Too busy to lend us a hand, I guess," said Kate Parrish. Harold's mother had come to stand beside her husband just after he'd spoken to Willie. Mrs. Parrish was a severe woman with a head full of gray hair that made her appear older than her thirty-seven years. Willie was always surprised by her small stature since her presence loomed large. She had been less generous than her husband toward Willie. She had also been against Harold's move to Tennessee. Willie didn't know how to respond, since anything she said was bound to be wrong. Over her shoulder, she could see Grandpa Sam's wagon coming up the road.

"I better go help with that load," Willie said. "I'm sorry Harold's not here," she added. It seemed the safest remark she could offer, but she turned to walk away before she could see Mrs. Parrish's reaction.

In midmorning, the ladies began bringing over platters piled high with fried chicken, ham steaks, beans, squash, biscuits, and potatoes. As space became available, they laid out apricot and plum hand pies. Everyone ate sitting on the ground or squatting on their heels. No one minded manners except to say thank you to the women who brought out the food. The men who owned the threshing machine left it in the hands of the local men several times throughout the day so they could help themselves to the local fare. The way the women competed to impress them with their fried chicken and hand pies, Willie figured they must be the best-fed folks in the county.

In years past, she and Harold had helped each other's families at the thresher and taken their breaks together. This year, Willie watched for her cousins taking their turn for dinner and joined them.

"Gladys says your mother's doing well," Ola said. Like everyone else, her clothes were soaked with sweat and her hair stuck to her temples.

"She's getting along," Willie answered, "though not as quickly as she'd like."

"Edgalea says your father took on a good hired hand," Jimmie said. Willie noticed Edgalea push her glasses up the bridge of her nose. Of course, they slid down again, riding the beads of sweat.

"Mm-hmm," Willie said through a mouthful of fried potatoes. "Mr. Musick has been a lifesaver." She didn't understand why they were repeating everything her sisters already told them.

"Sounds like a good man," Jimmie said. "Why isn't he married?"

"Says he's too old," Willie said.

"He hasn't always been old," Minnie quipped.

"Spent his younger days in the war," Willie said.

"How exciting!" said Ola.

"He doesn't speak of it," said Willie.

"Sounds like he could use a woman's touch," Lois said as she scanned the crowd. Willie followed her gaze and saw John Musick filling his plate. She noticed he loaded his plate with yellow squash.

"Yes, we should all have the chance to meet him," Jimmie said, looking over her shoulder to follow Lois's gaze.

Willie didn't like the sudden interest this henhouse was taking in Mr. Musick. The poor man wouldn't know what hit him if they all came at him. Anxious to change the subject, she said, "What's the latest on the Howler?"

"You know, a couple of a weeks went by when there wasn't any talk of it," Ola said. "Folks were beginning to think it had moved on or been killed or something. But then, early last month, folks started hearing it again."

"Why hasn't the deputy got it yet?" Willie asked. "Seems like it wouldn't be that hard. It doesn't sound as if it's sneaking around. Can't they just follow the noise?"

"They've tried. But once they get close, it goes quiet," said Lois.

"No one's heard it this week," Ola said.

"Mark says they're going about it all wrong. Says they should be calling in experts from Santa Fe who've dealt with supernatural creatures." Mark was Minnie's new beau. After Joe's betrayal in the spring, she hadn't wasted any time investing in her future and had attached herself to a railroad man.

"What do you mean, supernatural?" Ella Bea asked.

"Don't listen to her," Ola said. "Mark's been filling her ears with stories."

"Mark says it's the only explanation for why no one has caught it."

"Or even found it," Ola added.

"Hasn't anyone seen it?" Edgalea asked

"There are some that say they have," Jimmie said. "I don't believe them."

Willie listened to their continued speculation as she ate her apricot pie, relishing the way sweet and tart mingled on her tongue. She was tempted to get a second helping but decided against it. She had many hours of hot work ahead of her, and it wouldn't do to be overly stuffed. Besides, she would have the opportunity to fill her plate again later in the evening.

Her father and Mr. Musick arrived with the next bundle rack of wheat. She got up to help them unload but saw that they were walking toward the food wagon. As she watched John Musick, she was suddenly concerned that he might come toward their quilt to say hello. She didn't want him to be subjected to the scrutiny of this gaggle of maids, old and young, who would be appraising him like a cut of meat. She got up quickly, carried her plate to the wash tub, and walked past Mr. Musick to say hello to her father before going to help the crew at the thresher.

At the end of the day, as she rode with her father and Mr. Musick in the wagon, Willie could feel the numbness in her arms and shoulders that she knew would turn to soreness by morning. She relished the feeling, knowing it was a sign of increasing strength. Willie knew her sisters, aunts, and cousins would remain in the field until the other families finished their last loads of the day. And then they would face the enormous task of cleaning the kitchen and getting prepared to do it all again tomorrow. Theirs would be the last heads to fall on pillows tonight.

Over the next two days, Willie enjoyed more time working and catching up with her cousins. She'd eaten her fill of every good thing the ladies put on the table. By the last day, she was exhausted and satisfied in the equal measures known to anyone who has worked to weariness and watched the fruits of her labor piled up in stores.

They had one more run to Jim Tollett's farm and to Red Sam's to complete the year's harvest. Willie sat down for the last feast with her family before fetching the final loads. She listened to the men talk of the quality of their grains, speculate on wheat prices, and make their predictions about the next year's crop.

Aunt Xenia approached them then.

"Andrew! Better get to town," she said as she wiped her hands on her apron. She lowered her voice so only their small group could hear. "Your momma just rode over to fetch Sarah. Says Violet's time came on last night. It's been rough going and no baby yet. Violet's asking for you. I'm taking Sarah over, and you can ride with us."

Andrew looked to Jim Tollett, who nodded his assent. "Better hightail it, son," he said.

There was a moment of silence after Andrew left.

"That puts us a hand short," Jim said. "I'll let you take John for the first run, then he can come with me."

"Hope Andrew gets a boy this time," Red Sam said. "Bunch o' daughters won't help when it's time to get a harvest in."

Willie thought of her mother, sisters, aunts, and cousins, who had been up before the men this morning and even now were standing in the heat of the stove, trying to replenish platters as quickly as the crews cleared them.

"How's your ham, Grandpa?" Willie asked. "And your potatoes, biscuits, beans, and squash? Did you get any pie?" She knew it was sass, but she also knew he wouldn't recognize it. She wasn't certain, but she thought she saw John Musick smile before he concealed his face with his hand.

"It's all fine, Willie. Just fine."

While Grandpa Sam chewed his meat, Willie formed a plan. "I could bring the last load with you, Father." He looked up at her. "Mr. Musick could go with Grandpa, and you could drive our rig while I load. Then you could go on in, and I'll bring the rig over here to unload while you finish."

"Well, now I don't know about that," her grandfather said. He chewed and swallowed another forkful of meat.

"Say, Red," her father said, "If Mr. Musick drove your rig, I could drive my own. Willie can handle getting the load back here."

Willie saw no difference in what she had suggested and what her father was now proposing, other than the mouth the words came from, but her grandfather nodded his agreement.

As Willie drove her family's last load down the furrows, onto the dirt road, and across Red Sam's field to the thresher, she imagined her father expressing his pride, if not with words, then at least with a nod and a smile. She was imagining how she would accept his approval with equal nonchalance when a snake, disturbed from its nest, rose up and rattled its tail. Dolly jumped and turned. Willie pulled hard on the reins to keep her from taking off across the furrows, but she continued pulling, toppling the rig and tossing Willie against the rack. She righted herself, then took hold of the bit, cursing and consoling the horse in equal measures. The snake slithered away, and Willie was both relieved and disgusted to see that it was only a bull snake impersonating its deadly doppelganger.

With great effort, Willie righted the rig. Most of the load had been thrown, so she began the work of reloading what was lost. She wanted to get to the thresher without anyone noticing a delay, so she urged Dolly to make quick time of the return trip even though it meant a rougher ride with the full load.

As she pulled the rig next to the thresher, John Musick came toward her. She hopped down from her seat, ready to begin the work of throwing the bundles into the cylinder.

"You okay?" he asked over the sound of the machine.

"Of course I'm okay," she yelled, continuing to swing the pitchfork up and over. The last thing she wanted was for him to have the impression that she didn't know what she was doing or couldn't handle the work. Surely he'd seen her working all week. She waved her arm to indicate she was ready to continue working.

To her frustration, he stepped closer to her, so close that she had to stop the swing of her pitchfork. "Great day in the morning," she muttered to herself.

"You sure you don't need to sit down? Looks like you've got a goose egg coming up."

Willie's free hand went up. In her hurry to get the load to the thresher, she'd ignored the throbbing on the side of her head. Worse, she'd disregarded the fact that it would surely leave a visible mark as evidence of her imperfect errand. Even through her gloved hand, she could feel the knot forming. She pulled her hand away and saw blood on the glove. No wonder Mr. Musick was narrowing his gray eyes at her.

Willie decided to ignore both the blood and the hired hand. She wiped her shirtsleeve across her temple, refusing to flinch, and resumed her motion with the pitchfork, wagering John Musick would be smart enough to get out of the way.

He did step back, avoiding her swinging tines. Then he grabbed his own pitchfork and began helping. He didn't speak again, not when the load was through the thresher and not as he followed her to the wagon. His quiet made her own silent treatment less effective than she'd intended.

Finally, she broke the silence. "You don't have to help me. I'm fine."

"I know you're fine," he said. "I also know you took quite a wallop."

Willie did not want his sympathy, so she resumed her silence.

"I don't know many girls who could finish a job after that," he said, jerking his head toward her temple.

Willie couldn't tell whether he was condescending or complimenting her. John Musick walked away silently as though nothing had happened. She couldn't figure him out. And a small part of her regretted that she hadn't thanked him for his help.

Willie drove the rig home, grateful that twilight would hide her injury even though the shadows made driving difficult. She found herself fighting ruts and furrows all the way in. She unhitched Dolly and brushed her off then led her to the pen and gave her a bucket of oats. When Willie returned to the barn to clean the binding rack, Father and John Musick were already there.

"Willie, come look at this," her father said. Willie walked to the side of the wagon. Jim pointed to an axle. "This wasn't bent when you drove away with the last load."

Willie looked at the place where he pointed. She thought about the rough ride and the pull of the wagon. She'd been foolish not to recognize the problem. "I'm sorry, Father. A snake spooked the team, and they tipped the wagon. I got the wheat reloaded and back to the thresher quick as I could and didn't realize there'd been damage."

"Horses will only spook if they don't think anyone is in control. How many times have I told you, you've got to lead horses; you can't let them lead you. We can't afford such carelessness."

"Yes, sir."

Father left the barn without another word. If he saw the dried blood or swelling on her temple, he didn't mention it.

"Is he always so hard on you?" John Musick asked.

"Do you always listen in on other people's conversations?" Willie knew he couldn't have avoided hearing her father's reprimand, but she was embarrassed, and it made her mean.

"I'm sorry," he said.

Willie could see by the crease between his eyes that he

meant it, but she wasn't certain what he was sorry for. "It's his way," she said. "I'm the only one he's got, at least I was, so he's had to make sure I know what I'm doing. I don't mind. I need to learn all I can."

"You talk like you're running out of time."

"I'll finish high school in a year."

"You don't expect your husband will know what's needed?"

"You expect me to have a husband? I don't plan to work anyone's land but my own," Willie said. "Not that there's anything wrong with working someone else's land," she added quickly. Why did everything she said to him sound so impertinent?

"A woman working her own land?" Mr. Musick said. "That's something I've only heard in fiction." Once again, Willie couldn't tell if the hired hand was admiring or mocking her ambition. She finished her tasks and returned to the house without speaking to or looking at John Musick again.

The next morning, Willie woke to the throbbing of her head, and she felt the knot as soon as she brought her hand to her hair. She was grateful for Sunday. Since many folks would be taking their turn with the threshing machine, the church would not gather. Tomorrow, they would spend part of their day helping those families, but today they would rest.

After their chores were done, Father would read from his Bible, and the rest of the day would be hers to spend as she chose. After the flurry of cooking and eating over the past days, even the girls would be given a break from their heavy kitchen duties. Meals today would be simpler fare.

Willie slipped out of bed and dressed in the dark. Her mother was already sitting at the table, Bible open to the book of Isaiah, so Willie poured herself coffee and joined her. She took a seat on her mother's right side, hoping to avoid questions about the goose egg she was sure would be visible, even in the dim lantern light.

"Turn around so I can see your head."

"My head?" Willie asked. It was impossible her mother had seen already.

"Your father told me you'd hit your head. Said I should take a look."

"He did?" Sarah took Willie by the chin and turned her head. She slid the lamp closer to her daughter's face, studied her eyes, turned her head, and studied them again. She traced the bulge on her daughter's temple with the slightest pressure of her index finger. Willie tensed but didn't flinch.

"Bulging out. Eyes change in the light. That's good."

"Did Father tell you about the axle?"

"He did."

"Was he mad?"

"He takes things seriously. That sometimes looks like mad, but it's not."

Willie drank her coffee, unsure of what to say next. Sarah didn't speak either. After the week of her mother's accident, silence didn't make her nervous the way it used to. She finished her cup and went outside.

Willie took her time going through her chores. The chickens followed her, hoping she'd throw out more scraps, but she couldn't even offer acknowledgment. Despite the successes of the week, she still felt the sting of last night's failure. When she got to the barn, Father was standing by the axle again. It was unlike him to reprimand her for the same offense more than once, but harvest was a high-stakes time.

"Do you have an explanation for this?" he asked.

"It's like I said last night, Father. A bull snake spooked the team. I must not have had a good handle of them and—"

"I know how the axle got bent. I'm asking if you know how it got repaired."

Willie walked around to where he stood and bent over to see for herself. Sure enough, the axle was straight and sturdy. She wondered if perhaps it had never been bent. She hadn't looked for herself last night, and it was possible that in Father's tired state, in the shadow of dusk, he had made a mistake. She wondered but did not speak her thoughts out loud. There was only one other possible explanation for what they were looking at.

"I don't know," she said. Her father grunted and went about his work while she finished preparing for hers.

Willie didn't see John Musick until she was bringing in water after supper that night. He was at the windmill, splashing water on his face. She spoke softly, but firmly.

"Did you fix that axle?"

"I did."

"Why?"

"Because it was broken."

"I mean, why did you do it overnight. And without telling my father."

"Because I didn't do it for your father."

"I don't need any favors," Willie said. She walked away.

Before she made it to the house, John Musick was by her side. "I know you don't need favors. You've proven that. All you want is to please your dad, but he doesn't give you much credit. My dad was a lot like that, too. I meant to do you a kindness. That's all."

"Thank you," she said. "But I don't need it." They were at the door to the house, so she didn't have time to say more, and she didn't know what more she might have said. Gratitude and indignation fought for prominence, pounding in her chest to match the pounding of her temple.

Chapter 20

It took the teams and their steam-powered machines three weeks to have the county's grain ready for the mill. The air was littered with chaff. Clouds had threatened rain, but they only produced distant thunder and worry, then passed on. By the end of the harvest, Mother was able to do all the exercises Doc had left instructions for, and she could walk around the house with the help of her cane, but it was clear to everyone that her road to recovery was going to be a long one. Every night, Ella Bea rubbed ointment on Mother's hip, and every morning, Willie did the same.

Willie assumed that John Musick would be released from his work within days, but Father kept him on. The new crop had to be planted in only a few weeks, and they would need help once again. Mr. Musick had proven to be a good hand, and Father reasoned it would be easier to keep him on than to find a replacement to match him.

"Why do the rest of us have to work on Saturdays, but Mr. Musick gets the day off?" Ella Bea moaned as they ate their cornbread and sweet milk on the last Saturday of July.

"That was his condition for staying on after the harvest. I told him that was fine, as long as he didn't expect to get full wages."

"Why won't he work on Saturdays?" Edgalea asked.

"Didn't ask. Don't see as it's any of my business."

Willie expected Thurston to share what he knew about the baseball team, but he kept silent. Perhaps he suspected their father wouldn't approve. On Saturday mornings, Mr. Musick saddled up his horse and a large army-issued duffle bag and set out for town. He would still be gone when the last chores were finished, but his horse would be back in her pen on Sunday morning when it was time for the morning chores. Willie hadn't taken her brother to any more baseball games, but she had no doubt of John Musick's Saturday whereabouts.

"How was the meeting today?" Mother asked. Father's Saturday meetings of the committee to prevent the opening of the pool hall had taken a hiatus during the harvest, but they resumed the first Saturday afterward.

"Making progress. We've sent letters to every church leader, both local and across the state. They'll put pressure on their parishioners. The ladies want to hold a public rally, but I'm not interested in parading around the way they do, although I don't suppose I can stop them if that's what they decide. To be honest, I went to them for help, but they seem to be taking over the whole thing. I should have suspected as much. It's never enough for that sort of women. They started out wanting the vote, and now they won't be satisfied until they have their hands in everything."

"But won't the women's vote help the cause?" Gladys asked.

"My friends vote as their husbands do," Edgalea said.

"Of course," Willie said. "They can't be expected to act on their own."

"Exactly," Father said. He'd missed her sarcasm. "But there are enough around here determined to try, and they're starting to have influence. It's the only reason I'm putting up with this nonsense. Do you know, Ralph Armstrong's wife wears trousers?"

"I wish I could wear trousers. It would make work so much easier," Willie said. Father scoffed as Edgalea gasped, though Willie didn't understand what would be so wrong with it.

"Was Matthew Cash at the meeting?" Mother asked.

"He was."

"Any news?"

"Yes, in fact. Andrew bought the old Chester place. They've already moved out there."

"Already moved? But Violet just had the baby."

"Matthew didn't say anything about it."

"What kind of shape is the Chester place in? Mrs. Chester died when Thurston was still a baby. Has the house been sitting empty ever since?"

"Yes. I reckon it's a mess."

"Why would they be in a hurry to get out there, and with such a tiny baby?"

"Probably wanted to get out of town and have his own place. A man needs his independence and work to do."

"A woman needs her mother."

The room changed. The air was quiet, but it was not empty. Willie got the impression they weren't talking about the Cash family anymore.

"Was Mr. Parrish at the meeting?" Willie asked.

"He was." Surely her father knew she wanted news of Harold. He was still distracted by the direction of the previous conversation.

"Did he have any word about Harold?"

"A bit." Father grinned as he took another bite.

Willie knew now that he was teasing her, but she wasn't in the mood, so she refused to ask any more questions. She would wait for a letter and get news of her friend by his own hand. He was her friend after all; was it so strange that she was interested in his well-being? She should be allowed to ask after him without teasing. Perhaps this was Father's way of punishing her for not accepting his proposal. She wondered whether her father thought her refusal foolish, but nowhere was it written that if she wouldn't be his wife, she couldn't be his friend. While Willie made inaudible declarations to herself, the rest of the table moved on to other conversation.

After church the next morning, Mr. Belcher began telling stories about the size of the catfish in his lake.

"Jim, you ought to bring Thurston over. I've got catfish the size of dogs swimming out there."

"You don't say?"

"I do! Bet it'd take less than an hour to have a mess to fry for supper."

"We'll have to do that sometime when we can plan ahead for it."

"I could take him," Willie said. She loved fishing. It was one of the things she had always been invited to do until Thurston was old enough to take her place. She also loved eating fried fish.

"I guess that's right," Father said.

"Then I'll expect them this afternoon. Have Sarah save back some chicken livers for you. Catfish can't resist 'em." Willie and her father nodded, but Willie knew they'd have to dig up worms for bait. Neither of them mentioned that Edgalea was doing all the cooking or that the liver was Mother's favorite part of the chicken and there was no way she'd part with it, even in exchange for a mess of catfish.

At home with the family, Thurston hurried through his Sunday dinner even more quickly than usual.

"You're like an animal," Ella Bea said, wrinkling her nose. "At least wipe the gravy off your face." Thurston dragged the back of his arm across his mouth, creating a streak of gravy on his cheek and a matching one on his sleeve. "Disgusting." Ella Bea said, and she scooted her chair another inch away from him.

"Mind your manners, son," Father said.

"Yes, sir."

Thurston kept his face ducked toward his plate, and there were no more complaints, but Willie saw Aunt Chloe shake her head in disapproval. She was sitting at the table but did not have a plate of food. Instead, she sipped a cup of hot tea and pursed her lips at the children's every indiscretion. The girls didn't see why she still had to come over for Sunday dinner if she wasn't even going to eat, but she was Father's sister, and Mother enjoyed having her around.

Thurston used a biscuit to wipe his plate clean before he carried it to the basin.

"Are you ready to go?" Willie told Thurston.

"Go where?" Ella Bea whined. "I want to go!"

"I'm taking him fishing at the Belchers'," Willie answered.

"Oh. Never mind," Ella Bea said.

"I'll go find some worms," Thurston said. "Meet you outside!"

"Disgusting," Ella Bea said. "Everything he does is disgusting."

"You won't think it's disgusting when you're eating fish for supper," Edgalea said. Ella Bea crossed her arms over her chest in a pout.

"It's a nice day for fishing. I think I'll join you," Edgalea said. "Can you wait while I finish the washing?"

"Sure," Willie answered. "How 'bout you, Glad?"

"I'll stay with Mother," she said.

"Me too," said Ella Bea, though no one had invited her to do otherwise.

"I'll finish the washing," Gladys offered. "Y'all go on."

They found Thurston outside with John Musick. Both man and boy were kneeling on the ground, using an old ax handle to dig in the dirt at the base of the windmill. The chickens gathered around them, also looking for worms. When the girls approached, Mr. Musick stood.

"Mr. Musick says he could catch a catfish with his bare hands!" Thurston said.

"Sounds like a tall tale to me," Willie said.

"I'd like to see that trick," said Edgalea.

"I don't think I could do it in the muddy lakes around here. It's what we did in the creeks back home. The catfish like to hide in the rocks and tree roots. You can put your hand up under there and the fish will latch right on."

"Easy as that, huh?" Willie asked.

"I didn't say it was easy. But it's that simple."

"Can you come fishing with us?" Thurston asked the hired hand.

"Yes," said Edgalea, tapping the bridge of her glasses. "If you enjoy fishing, you should come along. Mr. Belcher won't mind."

"If you're sure. I always did like fishing," Mr. Musick said. He dusted his hands on his pants and straightened his straw hat on his head. "Let me run and grab my things."

The foursome set off out down the dirt road carrying homemade rods to the Belcher farm.

"Why are you taking a book?" Thurston asked, jerking his head toward the book in his hand. "Aren't you going to fish?"

"Yes, but while I'm waiting for a fish, I can read a bit."

"Seems like a waste of a good fishing trip."

"Don't you like to read?"

"Never had use for it."

"Have you always read so much?" asked Edgalea.

"No. It's something I picked up during the war. Silly as they were, the Western stories made me think of home."

"And the good guys always win," Willie added. She remembered him making this comment on the night they met. His half smile told her that he remembered it, too. The remark made more sense to her now, imagining him in a trench in France. "Were you ever afraid the good guys wouldn't win?"

"No, the writer knows everyone wants a happy ending."

"I mean during the war," Willie said. A shadow crossed Mr. Musick's face, and she realized he'd known what she meant and had tried to avoid the question. She wished she'd let it go.

"Yeah, there were times I wondered. Every day, in fact. By the end, I'm not sure any of us even knew who the good guys were."

"Our fellas, of course!" Edgalea insisted, but Mr. Musick didn't answer.

They walked in silence the rest of the way to the Belcher place. By the time they'd crossed the half mile of dirt road, the sunshine and freedom of a Sunday afternoon had cleared their minds of other worries and had them thinking about fishing again.

They chose a spot on the south side of the shallow playa lake, and Thurston pulled a handful of hooks from a pouch in his pocket. They each picked one up and tied their own lines.

"Those are good knots. I'm not sure my sisters could have done so well."

"We do fine for ourselves," Edgalea said. "How many sisters do you have?"

"Three sisters."

"Better than four," Thurston said. It was the first sign he'd been listening to their conversation at all.

"And six brothers," John Musick added.

Thurston pulled a handful of worms from his other pocket. Both of his sisters gave him disapproving looks, but John Musick smiled and thanked him for sharing. They fished in silence for several minutes.

"Where does Mr. Belcher get the catfish to put in this pond?" John asked.

"During wet years like this one, they stay here in the playa. When it starts getting dry, he seines out a good share and puts them in his stock tank until the next big rain. Then he casts the net in the tank and moves them back to the lake," Edgalea explained.

"During the last dry spell, he plowed a few trenches out in the middle so they'd hold enough water to keep the fish longer in dry times," Willie added.

"Sounds like a good system."

"Never thought of it that way," Willie said. "It's just how folks do things around here."

"Hey! I got one!" Thurston yelled. He alternated winding his line and raising his rod until he had the ten-inch whiskered fish on the bank. He slid his hand over its face and positioned his fingers to avoid the sting of the dorsal fin as he slid the stringer through the fish's gills.

"Looks like Thurston is winning the competition," Edgalea said.

"Maybe if y'all did less talking, you'd catch some too. One fish won't make much supper." For the next hour, they did just that. They each kept to their own thoughts and added fish to the bucket. John Musick was the one to break the silence.

"Your parents will be looking for you before long."

"I guess we'd better get home so we can clean the fish and start fryin'," Edgalea said. They each cut the hooks from their lines and gave them back to Thurston. Willie put the stringer of fish into a bucket. She strained to carry its weight.

"I'll get those," John Musick said. Willie protested at first, but the handle of the bucket was cutting into her hand, so she traded him for his fishing pole and book.

"Why do you talk funny?" Thurston asked Mr. Musick as they crossed the field toward home. Willie wondered the same thing.

"Thurston!" Edgalea said, "Don't be rude!"

"What do you mean, son?" Mr. Musick asked.

"Sorta fancy. You use them fancy words and different talk." Once again, Willie had wondered the same thing and was happy Thurston had voiced his curiosity.

"He's not the first to mention it," Mr. Musick told Edgalea. Turning toward Thurston he said, "Best I can guess, it's from reading so much. When I first started reading, I didn't know a lot of the words."

"Really?" Thurston asked, wide-eyed.

"I didn't get much schooling, and what I got was mostly figures. But the more I read, the fewer words I skipped over. After a while, I found myself using words I hadn't even known before. I'd go to say something, and a particular word seemed to be the one I needed, best said what I wanted to say. It happened over time, so I didn't notice. But my family did, and it frustrated them. I did my best to talk their way when I was with them. They liked that better, I think."

"Well, I'm gonna read enough books to talk fancy, too," Thurston said. "Especially around my dumb ol' family!" With that, he took off running toward the house. When the rest of them arrived, sweating and sun weary, Edgalea fetched the pliers and knife while Willie put away the rods.

"We'll get 'em all cleaned, Mr. Musick," Edgalea said when she returned. "You can go sit with your book, and we'll call you to supper when it's ready." Willie was irritated by her sister's offer. Why should he sit and read while they did the work?

"My mother would never approve of that," Mr. Musick said. "She always said if you catch 'em, you clean 'em. And that's a lot of fish for two girls."

"Edgalea and I are quite fast with the knife," Willie said. She wanted Mr. Musick's help, but not if he thought they needed it.

"If you're sure," he said. "Thank you for letting me join you this afternoon. I enjoyed it."

"You're welcome any time," Edgalea said.

With that, John Musick walked toward his dugout, and Willie and Edgalea took on the task of pulling the skin off nineteen catfish.

"Mr. Musick seemed to enjoy the fishing," Edgalea said.

"Maybe it reminded him of home," said Willie.

"He's good at a lot of things."

"Yes."

"And seems nice," Edgalea added.

"Yes."

"You'll probably think it's a wild idea—"

"I don't think it's wild at all," Willie said. Neither of the girls said out loud what was or was not wild. Sisters don't find it necessary to say everything out loud. Willie felt a sense of relief that of all the silly boys Edgalea did not win the favor of, she'd finally set her eye on someone like Mr. Musick.

The evening air was cooler outside than in the house, so while Willie and Edgalea cleaned the fish, their father built a fire under a metal frame in the front yard, and Gladys carried out the large cast iron skillet. Father carried Mother's chair outside and helped her down the stairs.

"Did you invite Mr. Musick to come over for supper? I know he doesn't usually join us on Sundays, but I hope he knows he's welcome."

"Yes, we invited him," Willie said. "But maybe Edgalea should go check on him to be sure." She risked a wink at her sister, who gave her glasses a nudge.

"I'll go!" Thurston offered, and he was off before anyone could answer.

No sooner than he'd left, Thurston came running back, excited to report that Mr. Musick had accepted the invitation. Sure enough, Willie saw his tall, lanky figure making his way over. He'd put on a fresh shirt. Edgalea looked down at her apron and announced she was going to clean up before dinner. Willie smiled as she watched her sister hurry inside.

Mother said, "Willie, aren't you going to clean up, too?" Willie looked down at her own apron spotted with blood and scale. It hadn't occurred to her to change, but maybe she would. "Go on, Willie," her mother said.

Willie walked in the house to find Edgalea pinning her red curls in front of the mirror.

"You've already impressed him by tying a fishing line. I think you can let the hair go," Willie said.

Edgalea dropped the hair pin. "What are you doing, sneaking in here?"

"I'm not sneaking. Mother sent me to clean up," Willie said. "But I'm only putting on a clean apron, not getting ready for the social."

"Don't tease me, Willie."

"Fine. It's no skin off my back if you want to get dolled up," Willie said. "but I don't think it's the sort of thing Mr. Musick cares about." She went to the kitchen and took a clean apron from the hook.

When Willie returned to the yard, she heard the crackling of cornbread batter and onions frying in the pan. As soon as the fish came out of the skillet, they were delivered onto the nearest plate. Thurston had clearly been standing closest to the fire for several helpings. Edgalea nudged him out of the way and held out two plates. She delivered them to Father and Mr. Musick. After all the fish were fried and plates were filled, the adults talked of farm business while Willie and Edgalea recounted their day of fishing to Gladys and Ella Bea.

"Mr. Musick is a famous baseball player!" Thurston said. Willie nearly choked on her cornbread. She couldn't imagine what led him to bring that up.

"If he's so famous, why is he living in our dugout?" Ella Bea asked. Once again, Willie coughed. She only hoped her father couldn't hear their conversation.

"Ella Bea!" Edgalea scolded. "He works here. He's not a baseball player." Her indignation on Mr. Musick's behalf made Willie laugh.

"He is, too!" Thurston said. Thurston was doing his best to defend the hired hand, too.

"Then why is he here?" Ella Bea demanded.

"Because he wants to be!" Thurston yelled. "Right, Mr. Musick?"

Willie groaned. She didn't want John Musick to be forced into joining their conversation.

"Yes, I like it here." Clearly, he'd been listening to the children's exchange, which meant their father had probably heard it all, too. She braced herself for one of his lectures.

Sure enough, Jim Tollett spoke. "Better for a man to earn an honest wage than to waste his life playing children's games," he said.

Willie recognized her father's tone. He was daring Mr. Musick to disagree with him.

"My father thought much the same," Mr. Musick said. "Told me farming was the most honest work there is."

And just like that, John Musick managed to appeal to Jim Tollett's pride and make him believe they agreed about the absurdity of men playing baseball. Willie wondered whether he knew how deftly he'd avoided a confrontation.

"Your father sounds like a good man," Jim Tollett said.

"He was. He's gone now."

"I'm sorry to hear that," Mother said. Willie was sure her mother was also aware of the challenge John Musick had avoided. She was an expert at this the sort of maneuver.

"Do you have any word from your people?" Mother asked, changing the subject.

"No ma'am," Mr. Musick said. Willie found it strange he called her ma'am since he was so near her age.

"That's too bad. It's hard when they're far away and you don't hear much."

"Yes, ma'am. Not many of my folks read or write, so I don't expect much."

"That's a shame," said Mother. "It's the same for my mother. She has neighbors who write for her, now and then. I worry one day we'll just lose touch."

Mother withdrew then, and her comment had a similar effect on Mr. Musick. In the days following her accident, Willie had begun to understand more of her mother's history and why she disappeared into her thoughts at times. She wondered what it was in the hired hand's past that would cause him to do the same.

They all had fish on their plates by now and were content to eat without talking. Willie broke a tail off and enjoyed its hot, salty crunchiness before using her fork to scrape the meat away from the bones. It was nice to eat something other than chicken and pork. When everyone had their fill, they continued sitting for a while longer, singing the hymns and folk songs they all knew.

Mr. Musick thanked Mother and Father for inviting him over for supper and sauntered to the dugout. Father helped Mother into the house, and Edgalea, Gladys, and Ella Bea followed them with the dishes.

Willie went with her father to make the rounds, checking on the Herefords, gathering eggs, and making sure everything was as it should be before turning in for the night. Thurston tagged along, taking the long way around to milking the cows.

One by one, as they finished their day's work, they gathered in the small sitting room. The girls had mending to do, Thurston whittled on a piece of century plant stalk, and Father marked pages in his Bible in preparation for the next meeting of concerned citizens.

"Father, why don't you read anything good?" Thurston asked.

"Son, there's nothing worth putting in your mind other than the Bible."

"John Musick—"

"Mr. Musick."

"Mr. Musick reads Westerns."

"What he does in his time off is none of my business. For myself, I see nothing good to come of it. It's nothing but laziness for a grown man to spend his time lying around reading when there are necessary things to do. Might as well take a nap." In Father's mind, napping was the sort of idleness the devil delighted in.

Chapter 21

The family used the final days between the wheat harvest and summer planting to get everything from the garden into a crate, barrel, crock, or jar. The work did not compare to the intensity of the wheat harvest, but the heat of August made it grueling work, nonetheless. Even while resting, no lap was without a bowl of beans or peas to shell.

In the early days of summer, the sisters argued over who spotted the first ripe tomato and whether she had to share it. By August, they had more than they could manage. They peeled them and boiled jars of them in the iron pot over the fire outside. The acidic smell of tomatoes filled the air, lingered on their clothes, and lodged into their memories.

Likewise, they chopped and salted cabbages and packed them in crocks to store in the cellar. They filled crates with knobby sweet potatoes, and they dug up, cured, and braided onions and garlic. They pickled cucumbers and peppers until their nostrils burned with the scent of vinegar. Thanks to the rain, it had been a good year. A visitor to their cellar might believe they'd never want for anything.

They took their meals outside to escape the kitchen's stifling air. At Sarah's prompting, John Musick joined them for dinner during the week. He was quiet, though he never appeared uncomfortable. They had all become accustomed to his presence even though he still behaved like a guest at the table. For her part, Edgalea treated him like one, always serving him first and offering second helpings.

Willie often saw Mr. Musick sitting outside the dugout when she went out for her nightly chores, and he almost always had a book in his hand. One night Willie waved at him just to see whether he'd notice. He nodded, then went back to his reading. She felt an impulse to interrupt him further, to make him leave the world of his book. Her family had always said she couldn't resist poking a bear. As she closed the distance between them, she imagined a bear holding a book.

"Another Western?" she asked when she reached the porch. He dropped the book to his lap and looked at her.

"Another one or the same one. It's hard to say. I have a small collection, and when I finish them all, I start again. But you know how Westerns are. They start to run together."

"I don't actually know. I've never read one." She felt self-conscious now that she had his full attention.

"Oh, I assumed you read."

"I do, but not Westerns." Willie hoped he wouldn't ask what she did read. The books she enjoyed seemed too juvenile to mention. Ola had gotten her to read part of a romance novel, but she didn't want to tell him that either. "I mostly read things assigned for school," she said, before he could ask for specifics. "I'm sure I'd enjoy a Western."

"You're welcome to borrow one of mine. I also have science fiction."

"Is that like school reading?"

"Oh no. It's about travel through space, life on other planets, ways of talking to folks far away as though they're standing right beside you."

"Sounds like nonsense."

"Might be. Or maybe it's what the future holds."

"You have an interesting idea of the future."

"I reckon I might," he said. "I get the notion you have interesting ideas of it, too."

Willie was not in the mood to explain or defend her picture of the future. She decided it was time to change the subject.

"Everybody talks about what a good baseball player you are," she said. "They all say you should have played in the big leagues."

"Is that right?"

"Didn't you want to?"

"Lots of boys dreamed of it."

"So why didn't you?"

"Promised my daddy I wouldn't."

"Why?"

"The way he saw it, he was protecting me."

"From what?"

"Wasted life."

Willie realized that books were the one topic that would keep Mr. Musick talking, and she always enjoyed a bit of chatter while she worked. It made the time pass more quickly. While they dug up potatoes one afternoon, she decided to try striking up a conversation by asking, "Have you always read Westerns?"

"No. I didn't read much till basic training. After a ball game we put together, a fella said I was a regular Zane Grey. I didn't know what he meant, so he loaned me a book, *The Young Pitcher*. My first Zane Grey book. It took me weeks to finish as I hadn't done much reading since I finished eighth grade. But it was a good story, and it kept my mind occupied."

Willie tried to conceal her smile. One question about reading had earned her a near soliloquy from Mr. Musick. Anxious to keep the conversation going, she said, "I thought Zane Grey wrote Westerns."

"Mostly, but other things too. He pitched for a school back east, so he's written a couple of baseball books," John said. "Anyhow, when I finally finished that one, I asked if he had another, and he did. Our training was up, but he let me take it. I must have read that book a dozen times over the next eleven months."

"Do you still have it?"

"I do. It's so tattered, it's not much good anymore, cover torn, pages falling out, been wet and dried out more times than I could count. I reckon it's trash by any account, but I can't part with it."

This was only the second time he'd mentioned the war. She understood his reluctance, but she was also curious. She knew of many men who had joined the Army during the Great War, but they'd all come back to their fields and families as though no time had passed. The women whose husbands had returned took food to the widows and mothers who would never see their husbands and sons again, and that was the only acknowledgment that anything had happened during their months on the other side of the world.

"What was it like in the trenches?" Willie asked. She felt bad for asking, but curiosity got the best of her.

"Worse than you can imagine," John Musick answered. "Like digging your own filthy grave then living in it."

"Were you surprised you survived?"

"Not really. We all knew death was only a step away, but it's easier to think it will come for the other guy."

"Still, it must have been a relief to get home."

"I was relieved to be alive. In some ways, coming home was the hardest part. You spend all that time imagining what coming home will be like. While you're over there, you start to forget anything bad. You remember the smell of fried chicken, the way your brothers clap you on the shoulder, the comforts of home. But when I came back, it was as though a rock had been taken out of the creek. The water kept flowing over and filled the space as though the rock had never been there at all. My brothers and sisters had found work or gotten married. My folks had become accustomed to farming without me, and there wasn't enough profit to split another way. I couldn't find a job or bank who would give a loan to a serviceman to buy a farm. Said I didn't have enough collateral or record of income.

I'd had daydreams of a big homecoming, but it didn't seem like there was a place for me at home."

"That's terrible," Willie said. "Is that why you came west? To your uncle?"

"Yep. I packed everything I owned into my army duffle and saddled up my pony. Daddy died within the year. I thought about going home then, but my brothers were taking care of our mother. By that time, I was working for Mr. Greathouse and didn't want to leave a good job. And I reckon I was afraid of being let down again."

Willie couldn't believe he was telling her so much. She hadn't intended to pry so far into his personal life. Maybe he needed to tell it to someone, and she happened to be the nearest who would listen.

"I'm glad you stayed," she said. She hoped she hadn't embarrassed him. Her boldness could make people uncomfortable. "It's been good for Father to have you here," she added.

"I'm glad too," he said. "I like your family, Willie."

Chapter 22

The next Saturday, as Edgalea and Willie shelled peas in the morning shade, Edgalea asked, "What do you think about Mr. Musick? I mean, now that he's been here a while, what do you think?"

"He's a good worker," Willie said. Seeing her sister wanted more, she added, "And kind. And funny in his own way. Not showy or clownish, but funny in quiet ways."

"I don't know how you can figure so much," Edgalea said. "I haven't heard him string more than a half dozen words together. I wonder about his life before he came here. What's his family like? Has he talked about them?"

Willie thought before speaking. It was true Mr. Musick didn't say much when they were all gathered for meals, but in the weeks since the harvest, he'd shared stories of his past, his brothers and sisters, and baseball games won and lost. He hadn't said it was confidential, but Willie had the impression that these weren't things he'd want her to share. She wasn't sure how to answer her sister, so she shrugged.

"Not much," Willie said. She felt like it was true enough not to be a lie.

"Could you find out?" Edgalea asked. "You have so much more time with him than I do."

"If it comes up," Willie said. Their mother called them then, and Willie felt relieved to be released from the conversation.

As was the habit every Saturday at supper, they heard an update on the latest meeting about the billiard hall. This was to be the last one until after everyone finished sowing their wheat. While not as big an undertaking as the harvest, it was still a significant season in the life of the community.

"Some folks wanted to have the decision wrapped up by the new year, but we need time to get everyone thinking right. If we rush, we'll get a result we don't want. I got everyone to understand. We'll put it off till early next year."

"Sounds like it was a good meeting."

"It was," he said. "And since I'm sure you'll ask, Andrew and Violet have moved back in with Matthew and Doris. I think Andrew is working out at the Chester place a good bit, trying to get the house fixed and a small plot of winter wheat started. I don't know that he'll get it done in time, but I admire his gumption."

"And the baby?"

"Doing fine. But the womenfolk agreed he'd be easier to tend if they stayed in town while Andrew gets the farm fixed up."

"I bet Doris is tickled to have them back."

Sarah smiled at her husband, and he lifted his chin. He was proud to have remembered to bring home a tidbit that pleased his wife.

Mother wasn't the only one anxious for the delivery of information. Every few nights, in the dark of bedtime, Edgalea asked Willie if she'd learned any more about Mr. Musick. It was several days before Willie had the chance to learn anything she felt comfortable passing along.

Rather than asking about a book, Willie decided it was time to take a more direct approach to get something she could report to Edgalea. "Do you miss your family?" she asked Mr. Musick while they were pulling up prickly okra stalks.

"I reckon I miss the familiarity. Even if someone gets under your skin, it's a comfort to know what you're gonna get."

"Were you close to your brothers and sisters?"

"I was always closest to my brother Rance. He was the only one who wrote to me while I was in France. Maybe it's because he was over there, too. Of course, that came at a cost."

Willie had to ask. "Did he die?"

"No, didn't die. But the gas. It messed him up." His voice trailed off then. Willie was afraid she'd pushed him to that distant place he went in his mind. After a beat he said, "You know, we used to get into some real trouble."

Willie looked up and smiled, glad to hear him continue.

"Once, after we'd been huntin' squirrels, we cut off all the paws and stuck 'em between the planks of the front porch so it looked like a bunch of varmints were reaching up to grab your feet. My youngest sister had fits over that one."

"Once, me and Harold caught a mess of fish and put them under May Bell Mason's porch."

"Why would you do that?"

"She'd made me mad, talking about my mother. Harold wasn't keen on the idea, but I needed a lookout, and he never could tell me no."

"Is this the same Harold that sends you letters?"

"Yes." Willie could tell there was another question coming, but he surprised her by not asking it. Then she surprised herself by answering anyway.

"He's a good friend. We've known each other all our lives. But there's nothing more. We have different ideas of the future." Mr. Musick still didn't speak. Willie was a bit unnerved by his silence. In her family, men said what they were thinking, even before the thought was fully formed. Somehow, his silence made her say more than she intended.

"He's going to be a lawyer and needs a wife. I'd rather have a farm." Mr. Musick still didn't speak. "He's a wonderful boy though. Man, I guess. But he's not for me. Although he'd like me to be. He asked. Back in the spring. I've wondered if I made the right choice, but not really. It was never meant to be. We were never like that. A couple, I mean.

"I think he'd rather go with someone he knows, is all. Beats starting from scratch with some girl waving a dainty fan. That's what I think he's thinking, anyway. I don't blame him. My sisters say I'll never find a husband if I don't act a little more like that, but Edgalea's tried it and she's not married either, so what does that say for their way of thinking?" Willie suddenly recalled her reason for beginning this conversation.

"Not that Edgalea's not the marryin' type. She'd be a great wife. She can cook everything you'd ever want. She's the tidiest person I've ever met. Won't allow a boot or hat set down out of place. And she's real smart. Got good marks all the way through school. I've thought more than once that she'd make a good match for you—"

Willie stopped. She'd never meant to say so much. She looked up at Mr. Musick. He looked amused.

"My sister's going to kill me," Willie said. She knew her cheeks were red, and not just from the heat, but she refused to lower her gaze. An unexpected fit of laughter came over her. She steadied herself with her hands on her knees. John Musick must think she's crazy. "Are you always so good at getting secrets out of people?" she asked, as she picked up her burlap sack and continued with cleaning the garden.

"I reckon if people have secrets, they're bound to come out," he said. "But don't worry about me. I won't say a word."

"In fairness, you should tell me something now. A secret of your own."

"I'd hate to be thought unfair," he said, "but I probably don't have anything worth telling."

She hoped he would say more, but he went silent.

Chapter 23

Schools in the county didn't resume until after the new wheat was in the ground, as not enough students would attend before then to make it worth the teacher's salary. Since the families only paid for the number of months their children attended school, they'd all agreed the year wouldn't begin until the end of September.

Planting the wheat was a mixed game of weather forecasting, superstition, and prayer. Willie had a hunch her father thought it all came down to hard work on their part. The Lord would reward their effort with good weather and good luck.

When the time came, Father and Mr. Musick did most of the planting. Willie's task to keep up with the work of the home place and herd gave her purpose, and she walked with her head held high. She was not a helper but the primary workforce, and she hoped she'd proven her value. Willie had waited weeks to bring up her idea of staying home again. The night before their father took them to Portales for the first week of school, Willie saw her chance. She joined him at the windmill before going inside for supper.

"Father, I can't go back to school."

"Of course, you can. I'll take you to Portales tomorrow."

"I mean I'm not going back. I'm going to stay here to work. To help you. The killing frost is right around the corner. I could be here to get the sorghum cut."

Jim Tollett turned to his daughter and studied her face. She couldn't remember having his undivided attention before. She knew her boldness could set him off. She changed her tone, but not her position. "You know there's no school learnin' as useful as what I'll get here. Plenty of boys quit school to work their farms."

"That's different. Those boys are going to be farming by the next fall. They've got all the schooling they need."

She tried a different approach. "If I'm only meant to be a wife, don't I have all the schooling I need? Wouldn't you rather have my help?"

Willie watched as his face contorted almost indecipherably. He furrowed his brow. His eyes drew together, and his mouth twisted. He rubbed his chin, then wiped his hand over his face and dropped his head.

Willie could see she'd won. She'd found the crack in his argument, and they both knew it. But when he looked up again, his face was smooth, and he looked right at her.

"You'll finish school," he said.

Willie returned his placid look. She searched his eyes for any sign he might change his mind and found nothing but twin seas of ice-blue. She felt anger welling up in her own brown eyes and walked away before it overflowed. Her chores needed to be done, even if her father didn't think her contribution was essential. On her way to the barn, she nearly collided with Mr. Musick on his way to the dugout.

"Your dad died," she said without kindness or preamble. "Why won't you play in the big leagues?" Willie watched as the question landed and Mr. Musick struggled to make sense of more than her words. He was reading her face, no doubt noticing the tears running down her cheeks. She wiped them away and raised her chin. To his credit, he didn't mention the tears or ask her what was wrong. He answered her question.

"A couple of scouts have asked me the same thing, but those dreams are finished for me. My dad died, but my promise didn't."

"I don't think I could promise away my dreams," Willie said.

"Even for your father?" Mr. Musick asked.

Willie didn't answer. Until today, she'd always thought of her father as the patron of her dreams, not a detractor.

She finished her chores and returned to the house for supper. Her anger still brewed under the surface, but she had control of it now. No one else would see her cry. Fortunately, her father was still out completing his nightly rounds so she didn't have to face him right away.

Gladys handed her a bowl of black-eyed peas and cornbread. "What's wrong?" she asked.

"Father is making me go back to school! Even when he knows I'd be more use to him here!" She kept her voice low, knowing she'd be in trouble if he happened to hear her.

"Willie, I don't think Father's the one you should be angry with," Gladys said.

"Of course he is! I'm sixteen years old. The school isn't forcing me to return. Only Father is."

"It's Mother."

"What's Mother?"

"I heard them talking about it weeks ago. Mother told Father that you need to go back to school. She told him not to let you quit."

Willie was stunned. If what Gladys said was true, there was no hope left. It wasn't often that Sarah Tollett expressed her opinion, but when she did, in matters of weather and children, he didn't argue. Willie felt the tears coming again.

Chapter 24

Willie did not speak to her mother beyond necessity that night or Sunday morning. They'd all been busy enough that it didn't draw attention. Willie did her chores, went to church, helped cook and clean, and packed her bag for the school week. She was disappointed that her mother hadn't noticed her withdrawal. She wouldn't dare provoke her mother, but she wished she could speak her mind.

Before they loaded the truck Sunday evening, Willie got what she wanted. Sarah took her hand. "Sit down, Willie," she said.

Willie considered ignoring her mother and going outside, but she welcomed the opportunity to confront her. And, despite her anger, she'd never been disrespectful to her mother.

"You have a chance for education right now that you'll never get again. One I wish I'd had. I can't let you squander it."

"It's not squandering if it's worthless anyway."

"It will only be worthless if you don't have it." Sarah released Willie's hand then. Willie wanted to fire back with a remark that her mother's life would be no different with more schooling, but there was a disarming look in Sarah's eyes, neither fighting nor giving in, only full of knowing. Willie couldn't think of a retort.

"Yes, ma'am," was all she managed to say.

Before Father left them at Aunt Xenia's, he told Willie to follow him out to the truck. For an instant she thought he might invite her to return to the farm with him. When she saw his pinched face, she knew that wouldn't be the case.

"I know you don't want to go back to school," he said, "but it's what your mother thinks is best, and maybe it is. And when you finish, you'll get your quarter section."

"And two of the Herefords?" she asked.

Father laughed. "My daughter," he said, and his smile told Willie he was proud of the fact. Jim Tollett put out his hand and Willie shook it.

On their first night in town, Willie hoped for news of the Howler, but there was nothing to report. The nighttime noises ceased for long stretches, then came back again without a discernable pattern. The town was perplexed. The girls in the house on Railroad Street were bored with the speculation. The mystery *they* wanted to solve was John Musick.

Willie squirmed in her chair as they talked. She told herself it was out of concern for him, but a quiet voice admitted she was also concerned for herself. Over the summer, by everyday increments, John Musick had become part of her life. His stories had opened her eyes to a world outside Roosevelt

County. She had no interest in leaving, but knowing how big the world was had made her feel more secure with her place in it. It felt odd to hear them speak of him with such detachment. When the conversation turned to romantic notions of a hero-soldier in need of a good woman and speculation about why he hadn't found her yet, Willie bristled.

"The war was horrible," she said, trying to crush their notions of heroic fighting. "Mostly waiting in rancid mud for enemy fire."

"What a brave man," said Lois. "He deserves to come home to a family and a good dinner now."

"He came home to a world that had moved on without him," Willie said. "That's why he's here. He deserves to live how he pleases."

"You've gotten to know him pretty well?" asked Jimmie. It sounded more like an accusation than a question.

"They've spent a lot of time working together," Gladys said.

"Too bad Edgalea isn't getting more time with him," Ola said.

Willie felt a question or maybe a hunch forming around the edges of her mind, but she didn't allow it air to breathe. She excused herself to bed, leaving her sister and cousins to sort out the fate of the hired hand. Now that she wouldn't spend her days in the fields or be in her seat at the dinner table, Willie wondered when she might see John Musick again.

The next morning, Willie was the first of the girls up. Her aunt was in the kitchen, putting away dishes from the night before.

"You went to bed so early, we didn't have time to visit," said Aunt Xenia. "How is your mother doing?"

"She's good. It's been a long row, but she's determined." Willie thought about her mother's look from the morning before. "We had more time together this summer. She told me about her early days with the Tolletts."

"Uh oh," said Aunt Xenia.

"So it's true? You all gave her a rough time?"

"Worse than that, I'm sorry to say. Your father stood by her, though. He knew she'd make a fitting partner for him. And she has."

"Here, I'll help with that," Willie said, placing a jar on a high shelf.

"Thank you."

"Mr. Musick is his partner now," Willie said. She had hoped to be her father's new partner. Without John Musick, she might still be at home. She knew her resentment had crept into her voice, so she added, "He's been a lifesaver, really." As she said the words, she realized how much he'd been her partner as much as her father's.

"Your mother will always be his partner, but it sounds like Mr. Musick has impressed you," Aunt Xenia said.

"Yes, I guess he has." Willie felt the niggling thoughts from last night beginning to take shape again, so she shifted the conversation. "I'm keen to find ways for him to spend more time with Edgalea. I think they would make a pair."

Xenia turned her head, and Willie could feel her aunt's eyes studying her.

"Are you sure that's what you want?"

"Well, I know he's quite a bit older than she is, but men marry younger women all the time."

"Yes, that's true," Aunt Xenia said, but Willie still thought she looked skeptical.

"He doesn't go to church, but he really is a good man. He'd make a fine husband."

"Oh, I don't doubt that." Aunt Xenia grinned as though a joke had been told, but Willie couldn't discern what it was. Perhaps her aunt needed to spend more time with John Musick to be convinced of his merit. She was about to say so when Lois came in and tied on an apron. The morning routine unfolded in the same sequence as it had four months ago.

In fact, everything seemed the same except Willie. Something had changed over the summer, though she couldn't name what it was. The transition from farm work to schoolwork, which was always hard, felt tortuous. Since her mother's accident, she had taken on more responsibility for the farm. She'd also taken the lead in caring for the herd, *her herd*, as she liked to think of it. She'd received more independence and the renewal of her father's promise for a quarter section of land. Willie went through the motions of her school days, but her mind never left the farm.

As they filed into the high school on the third Monday of the term, her friends' chatter seemed a million miles away. She took her seat on the back row between Glenn and Clyde. Mr. Thompson was already in the front of the room reading a newspaper while the students filed in. He either noticed that the seats were filled or that the noise level reached a peak, because he shook the paper straight with a deliberate pop and folded it neatly. He cleared his throat and stood with his arms folded across his chest until the noise subsided.

"Good morning, students," he said.

"Good morning, Mr. Thompson," they replied in chorus.

"I trust you remember everything we covered last term and are ready to pick up where we left off." The students did not reply but looked down at their desks. He directed them all to a new page in their textbooks and assigned a set of problems to complete on their slates.

"When you've completed your figures, raise your hand and I will come to check your work. Only then may you erase and go to the next. Please begin."

Willie was surprised at how much she recalled from the previous year. The figures were easy for her to complete. Mr. Thompson checked each one, and in no time she had completed the assignment. Clyde had also finished and was reading a book. Willie could see from the spine that it was a Zane Grey novel. She smiled at this reminder of John Musick.

"Do you like Zane Grey?" she asked him. She'd never seen him reading a Western, but maybe she hadn't noticed because it meant nothing to her.

"Yeah," he said. "I only read them at school though. Pop says a man worth his salt shouldn't have time to read."

"My father thinks the same."

"I have another one. You want to borrow it?"

Willie really didn't want to borrow a book, but before she could say so, Clyde lifted his desktop and took out a book that looked similar to the one he was reading. She thought about what John Musick had said about them all being pretty much the same.

"I guess the good guy will win, right?" Willie asked.

"Well, sure. He always does," Clyde answered.

Willie read as her classmates worked on math problems. When class was over, she asked Clyde if she could keep the book for a couple of days so that she could finish it. John Musick probably owned this same one, and she could have borrowed it from him over the summer. He always enjoyed talking to her about books. Willie regretted that she'd never asked him. She imagined how that conversation might have sounded.

"What are you reading?" Ola asked when they were settled in Aunt Xenia's sitting room.

"Whatever it is, it has her under a spell," said Lois. Her curls were tucked under a nightcap that matched her pink nightgown.

"You know, some people can only *read* about romance," Minnie said as she brushed her straight black hair.

Ola threw a pin cushion at Willie. "What *are* you reading?" she asked again.

"Oh," Willie looked up and was surprised to see all the girls looking at her. "*Betty Zane.* It's by Zane Grey."

"A Western?" Minnie said. "Only boys read Westerns. You really are the most peculiar thing, Willie Tollett. It's hard to believe we're kin."

"Don't be silly, Minnie. Of course girls read Westerns," Lois said. "Probably before the men. I've read Zane Grey serials in the *Ladies' Home Journal* for years. One I read last year was especially good. A city girl from the East was engaged to a man who went West after the Great War to get himself right again. Of course, it all ended well."

"It's fine to read from *Ladies' Home Journal*, but it's unattractive to carry a book that you only see boys reading," Minnie said.

Willie didn't respond. She put her eyes back onto the page and tried to continue reading, but it didn't hold her interest.

By the end of the week, she returned the book to Clyde unfinished. She couldn't get through the long, descriptive passages, and it didn't fit her idea of a Western, though she didn't know what the rules were for being such. She supposed she'd expected cowboys to play a prominent role. She couldn't understand why John Musick found it so appealing.

She was determined to talk to him about the book, but for weeks, he was in the field when she got home from school on Friday evenings. On Saturday mornings, she'd tend to her chores, but she never crossed paths with him despite the adjustments she made to the timing and order of her work. By afternoon, his pony was gone, and he would not return until sometime in the night. He kept to himself on Sundays now. As the weeks became a month, she wondered if she'd only imagined their friendship.

She dared to ask Edgalea about him one Saturday evening while they churned butter in the front yard. Gladys and Ella Bea were doing laundry with Mother, and they had a rare moment alone.

"Do you see Mr. Musick much during the week?"

"Now and again," she said. "He eats dinner with us, but he hardly speaks except to Father. I've tried to start up a conversation, but I don't want to be too obvious."

"Too obvious about what?" Willie asked.

"You know," Edgalea said. "Too forward."

"Of course," Willie muttered. She had taken for granted that Edgalea could engage in conversation naturally and without worry. When a woman had romantic intentions, she had to veil them while simultaneously making them recognizable to a man who might have the same ones. Romance was complicated.

"Of course," Willie said out loud. "Is he getting along well?"

"He eats well, and Father doesn't complain about his work," said Edgalea. "I think next week, I'll make an effort to get around him more. I know his routine well enough. Maybe I can meet him coming in from the barn."

Willie was struck with resentment toward her sister. She couldn't name the source, but it was similar to the way she often felt around Thurston. She wished she knew Mr. Musick's routines well enough to encounter him on Saturday mornings.

"You'll send him running scared with that sort of boldness," Willie said. She'd intended a playful tone, but it landed with a bite. She could see that she'd hurt Edgalea and knew she should apologize, but she was so puzzled by her own feelings that she couldn't do it. Both girls churned their butter with vigor. They did not speak of Mr. Musick again.

Chapter 25

After dinner on the third Saturday of October, Willie stood in the cow lot with a shovel and bucket. She had been sent out to collect cow patties for the stove, but she was taking a moment to examine the herd. Carl, almost full grown now, stood by his mother looking out across the plains.

"If you stand there long enough, maybe they'll come fill your bucket for you."

Willie smiled as she turned in the direction of the familiar voice.

"You know, it's a special place where the cows cut the grass and fuel the fire," he said. It took her moment to understand his meaning, then she smiled again. It was easy to smile with Mr. Musick.

"What are you doing here?"

John Musick laughed. "Would you like me to leave?"

"No," Willie said. The word jumped out with unintended force. "Of course not. It's just that you're usually not around on Saturdays."

"I will be for a while. Baseball ended, and I told your father I'd work six days if he needs it. Speaking of which—" He tossed a burlap sack over his shoulder. Willie noticed he was wearing a new shirt under his denim overalls. "Time to harvest corn."

"I have the same orders. I'll join you after I get this bucket filled."

"I'll be glad for the company," he said. Willie smiled as she watched him walk away. She filled her bucket with cow patties faster than usual.

It was the first time she'd worked with John Musick since school started. At first, she felt awkward being alone with him. They'd shared so many conversations about family and dreams for the future, but more than a month had passed since they'd spoken at all.

"I tried to read a Western," she said. He looked up, catching her watching for his reaction. "I couldn't get into it, though. It's so unrealistic. The West isn't really like that."

John Musick laughed. She had forgotten its sound. She remembered how it once confused her, never knowing if he was mocking her. His laughter erased the weeks of separation, and she admitted to herself how much she had missed him.

"No one reads Westerns for their accuracy," he said. "People back east want to believe in the cowboy tales, and people in the West want to believe they'll be heroic when their time comes."

"What do you mean, 'cowboy tales'?"

"You know, that men are strong, women are virtuous, and the good guys always win."

"Is there a tale about men being virtuous and women being strong? That's the one I want to read."

John Musick laughed again. "Which one did you try, anyway?"

"*Betty Zane.*"

"No wonder you didn't like it! It's more of a historical than a Western. You should have started with *Riders of the Purple Sage*. I'll loan it to you."

"It's probably better than what I've been reading for school."

"Tell you what, when I get back to the dugout, I'll set one out on my porch and you can pick it up in the morning."

The next morning, as the family hustled to get ready for church, Willie forgot about the book. Thurston realized that his trouser button was missing, and since she was the first one dressed and ready to go, Willie had to sew one on while he stood by the stove in his underpants. When they got home, they had dinner and gathered their bags to head to town for the week. On the way to the truck, Willie saw John Musick leaning against the fence, smoking. He raised his hand to her, and Willie's heart skipped a beat. She hurried toward the dugout.

"I'll be right back!" she called over her shoulder.

She returned a minute later and breathlessly climbed over the tailgate. "Sorry, I had to check on something." They didn't notice that she was carrying a book she hadn't had before.

Once she was seated in the truck bed, she opened it and found a note written on the bottom half of an invoice from Aunt Chloe's store.

> *Miss Tollett–*
> *This is the one you should have started with. Hope you like it.*
> *–JHM*

Willie turned to the first page. The story began with Jane Withersteen, a wealthy, landowning woman. John Musick was right; this was the book for her. She'd only meant to read the first page or two, but she'd been so taken in by the intensity of the conflict between Mormons and Gentiles that she didn't notice when the roads became smooth or when the sounds of cows on farms were replaced by the noise of people on the roads in town. It came as a surprise when the truck stopped and her sisters stood to go into Aunt Xenia's house. She used John Musick's note to mark her page and slid the book into her satchel.

Willie had another chance to read when they all gathered in the sitting room after supper, Lois with her *Ladies' Home Journal*, Jimmie and Ola crocheting, and Minnie brushing her hair. The household had become accustomed to her habit of reading in the evenings, so they didn't notice when she opened the book and studied John Musick's note. She wondered what the H stood for.

Willie went to bed with the others, but sleep eluded her. She slid off the shared mattress and removed *Riders of the*

Purple Sage from under her pillow. She lit the kerosene lamp in the kitchen, poured a small glass of milk, and took a seat at the kitchen table. Again, she read the note marking her page before she resumed the novel. Once she started reading, she found it difficult to stop. She continued to be intrigued by the trouble with the Mormons and Gentiles. In her Sunday school classes she'd learned of the distinctions between Jews and Gentiles, but this brutal clash was new to her.

Even more gripping was the mysterious rider, Lassiter. From the moment she read the description of his intense gaze with its "piercing wistfulness of keen, gray sight, as if the man was forever looking for that which he never found," she pictured John Musick. *John H. Musick.* Willie was surprised at first when she realized the description had brought Mr. Musick to mind. Could it be that like Jane Withersteen, Willie's "subtle woman's intuition, even in that brief instant, felt a sadness, a hungering, a secret"? She laughed away the thought. It was the stuff of romance novels and perhaps Westerns, but not for practical young women. Regardless, as she hailed Lassiter's fiery speeches, cheered when he agreed to be Jane's rider, and sighed every time he gave Jane a gentle smile, Willie imagined John H. Musick.

Willie had no idea how much time had passed before she decided she better get to bed, but she was sure she'd only closed her eyes when she heard Aunt Xenia start the morning coffee.

Chapter 26

The next sound Willie heard was the front door opening and closing—Jimmie leaving for work. She closed her eyes one more time and woke to Gladys shaking her shoulder.

"Willie?" she said. "Are you sick?"

"What?" Willie sat up. It was fully daylight.

"It's time to leave for school," Gladys said.

"Time to—Great day in the morning!" Willie leapt out of bed and pulled her dress on. She grabbed her shoes and fumbled with the laces. "Glad, what are you still doing here? You're going to be late!"

"I thought you were sick!"

"No! We'll run together!" Willie grabbed her bag and ran for the door. When they were almost out, Willie stopped and turned back into the house.

"What are you doing? I hear the school bell ringing!"

"I forgot something!" Willie grabbed *Riders of the Purple Sage* from under her pillow and stuffed it into her satchel as she ran out the door.

Before they crossed the street, Willie saw a small crowd gathered outside the school building. The front doors were open, but no one was going inside.

"What's going on?" Willie wondered out loud.

She pushed her way to the front of the crowd. She realized right away why no one was entering the building. The noxious smell wafting from the open door was enough to keep everyone several yards away. Clearly, someone had set off a stink bomb.

The students lingered outside for most of the morning while the building aired out. Mr. Cooper instructed freshman boys to brave the smell and open every window and door in the building. If he couldn't find a particular culprit to punish, he would be satisfied to make all of them suffer.

Some of the students who lived close by went home. The senior high girls gathered in groups at the far edge of the yard. Willie considered joining Joyce and May Bell, but she decided against it. Instead, she found a sunny spot near the road and took out *Riders of the Purple Sage*, escaping with the fictional riders to a hidden valley, until the clanging of the school bell signaled that the air was clear enough to begin classes.

The sulfurous odor still lingered but was bearable now, unlikely to make anyone's eyes burn. Willie settled into her desk in Mr. Thompson's room. She half-listened to his demonstration on graphing. She didn't see much sense in learning the algebraic expressions he was teaching, but they came easily to her, so she went through the steps and earned herself ten more minutes to read. She became bogged down in descriptions of canyons, sage, and pinyon and grew frustrated, knowing she had limited time. She skimmed the pages until the action resumed.

The students were dismissed to their lunch recess only an hour after they'd begun classes. Most of the girls reclaimed their posts on the far edge of the school yard, so Willie carried her lunch and *Riders of the Purple Sage* out to her sunny spot and read alone while she ate her biscuit and potato. She had just opened the book, anxious for Venters's exploration of Surprise Valley, when Ola sat down next to her. "What's going on with you?" she asked.

"What do you mean?" Willie said.

"You've been acting very strange."

"How's that?"

"Well, you were late to school for one thing. And I've never known you to oversleep. You've had your nose in your book all day, and you never miss a chance to tell news and stories. And you hardly commented on the prank from this morning. I thought you'd have figured out who did it."

"If I'm guessing, it was a freshman boy. Boys will settle for obvious and gross every time. And this one is so crude. Had to be a freshman."

"Yes! Didn't you hear? Dale Mason confessed before lunchtime!"

"Makes sense."

"May Bell is fit to be tied. At first, she denied that it could have been her brother, then she denied that he was her brother at all!"

"I guess she likes to do the talking. Not be the family everyone is talking about."

Ola nodded in agreement. "We should remember her in our prayers." Both girls laughed. "What are you reading, anyway?" Ola asked.

"It's a Western."

"From Clyde? Is this how you flirt?"

"No. From our hired hand."

"Your hired hand reads?"

"Any time he's not working."

"Hmm."

Willie got the impression that Ola was waiting for her to speak, but she didn't have any more to say. Her cousin looked toward the other students in the yard then looked back at Willie and sighed.

"Go on," Willie said. "I'm good."

Ola tilted her head and narrowed her eyes at Willie as though looking for confirmation that she wanted to be alone. Willie opened the book, and Ola got up to join the crowd in their lively recounting of the stink bomb incident. Willie read the note on the invoice again. Flirting? she thought. Ola had the strangest ideas. She slid the invoice between pages in the back and read until it was time to go inside.

Willie felt obligated to return John Musick's book before spending another week in town, and she knew that once she got home on Friday, she wouldn't be able to read again. More than that, she didn't want to wait until Sunday night to learn the fate of Jane, Lassiter, and little Fay or Venters and Bess.

Willie was surprised by how caught up she'd become in the story, as she silently encouraged the horses to ride harder and pleaded with Lassiter to "*Roll the stone!*" Undeterred by Monday morning's mishap, Willie ignored the heaviness of her eyelids and did not close the book on Thursday night until she'd finished the last page.

As Friday dragged on, the only thing that kept Willie awake was replaying the final scenes of the book in her imagination. She was relieved to finally make it to the ease of her English class. They were assigned a set of grammar exercises that Willie completed easily. Then she slid the invoice from the pages of the book and wrote a reply to John Musick.

> *JHM—Thank you for the book. It was better than* Betty Zane. *Thrilling, though I skipped some of the sage and pinyon parts. I don't know a thing about Mormons, but I've known mean men in our church, so I guess they're like anybody else. Mr. Grey sure paints them as villains. I suppose good guys sometimes dress like bad guys, and folks who should be good can be of the worst sort. Don't you wonder what happened after they rolled the stone? Can they really live in Surprise Valley forever? And what about Venters and Bess?*
>
> *—Willie*
>
> *P.S.—What does the H stand for?*

In the truck on the way home and later when she did her chores, Willie imagined what the fictional citizens of Cottonwoods might be doing now. She wondered how Jane, Lassiter, and Fay fared in Surprise Valley and whether she would have the courage to seal herself off from the rest of the world. She decided it would depend on who was in the valley with her, and then wondered who the best companion might be. Gladys? Ola? Harold? She had to force herself out of her reverie before going inside for supper.

Willie followed her father and brother into the house as the sun went down. Their entrance set activity into motion, like the cogs of a machine turning the gears. Edgalea took the skillet of cornbread out of the oven and placed a generous wedge in each bowl, Gladys ladled beans on top, and Ella Bea carried the bowls to the table, all while Mother poured milk into glasses. Father said grace, and the girls shared the details of their week in town as they ate.

"Sounds like a great deal of folderol," Father said in response to the story of the stink bomb. "I'll have to speak to Mr. Cooper at our meeting tomorrow."

"Didn't you also meet today?" Mother asked. "Willie, that reminds me, you received a letter from Harold on Wednesday. I put it on the dresser."

"Yes, but we have work to do before we're ready to call a vote. We're ready to put pressure on those who would support the moral decay of our town."

Willie wondered how her father could see the world in such black-and-white ways. In his view, a man was either hardworking, honest, and good or lazy, corrupt, and wicked. In his calculation, no amount of good on one side of the equation could balance a single word or deed toward the bad. As a child, she had appreciated the simplicity and clear expectations. As she drew closer to adulthood, however, she questioned his logic. John Musick, for example, was a capable and hard worker. Despite this, his habit of reading, playing baseball, or going to the pool hall on his time off would land him squarely on the lazy side according to her father. The older Willie got, the less the math worked.

After supper, Willie slipped into the bedroom while her sisters cleaned the kitchen. The sun already touched the western horizon, but Willie had enough light at the window to read Harold's letter. She was surprised to find a small print, not more than two by three inches, between the folded page of the letter. It was a picture of a man standing on a tree-covered hill. On the back, in Harold's script, it said, "Has anyone seen my cow?" She laughed at his ludicrous caption. In the letter, Harold described the changing colors of the leaves and shared stories of his university friends and boring days of work at the law office. There was nothing to engender envy or longing to join him. In fact, every letter he sent confirmed that she'd made the right decision. She could not deny that she missed her friend, but she'd also had the companionship of John Musick since he left.

Early Saturday morning, Willie tucked *Riders of the Purple Sage* under the waistband of her calico skirt and went to the dugout. Rocks were stacked around the porch, and she used one to keep the cover and pages from flapping in the wind.

With a sense of satisfaction for having completed the book and returning it so promptly, she walked to the barn to start milking. When she passed the dugout on her way to strain the milk, the book was gone.

The winds howled on Sunday afternoon, bringing in a cold front from the north. Willie pulled on her wool stockings, a wool scarf, and her only coat. She wanted to check on the frost-coated calves and make sure they were faring well before heading to Portales for the week. Carl, like the others, was huddled against his mother, his head bowed toward the south. Willie couldn't help but worry. The calves were big, but severe weather could be deadly.

Gladys walked to the truck carrying a pile of quilts. No doubt mother was warming potatoes and sadirons to keep their hands and feet warm on the ride.

As Willie hurried to the truck, she glanced at the dugout. Smoke danced in the wind above the small chimney. A book sat under the rock on the porch, though she was certain it hadn't been there last night. Father hadn't come out of the house yet, so Willie ran to the dugout for a closer look. She picked up the book and opened it, anxious to confirm that it had been left for her.

Miss Tollett—

I didn't think you were going to have much time to read. You must have enjoyed Riders of the Purple

> Sage. *I don't have to wonder what happened to our heroes, as Zane Grey did us the kindness of writing another book about them.*
>
> *—John Horry (sounds like sorry) Musick*

Anxious to check for a note, she hadn't paid attention to the cover. She tucked the scrap of paper inside the book and read the spine. *The Rainbow Trail.*

Willie startled at the sound of Gladys calling her name.

"Come on! It's time to go!"

Willie tucked the book under her arm, hoping it wouldn't draw attention. She was about to climb into the truck when Edgalea pulled her aside.

"Willie, I learned something about Mr. Musick."

Willie's heart pounded. It felt as though the book might burn a hole through her arm.

"Do you know where he goes on Saturdays? When he's not working?"

"The ball fields," Willie said.

"No. Worse." Edgalea looked over her shoulder, as though afraid someone might hear her. "The pool hall," she whispered. "The one in Portales."

"Oh, Saturday nights," Willie said. "Sure, go on." She was impatient for Edgalea to tell her story so she could get out of the wind.

"What do you mean, 'go on'?" Edgalea asked. "He goes to the pool hall. What sort of man does that?"

"I don't know, Edge. The sort who fought in a war? Who works hard all week? Who doesn't have a family? And according to Aunt Xenia, the same kind who goes to church every Sunday." Willie was cold and growing impatient.

"Surely not!"

"Did you ask Mr. Musick about it?"

"No. He's so quiet. Never says a word about himself."

"Oh, right," Willie said. She thought it better not to argue this point with her sister. "How did you find out then?" she asked.

"Mr. Belcher's hired hand was over here helping get the last of the corn in. I took coffee out to them and overheard their plans to meet there."

"I see."

"Yes, now you see. But I guess he's still a reasonable consideration, given my age."

"Edge, you're not old."

"You know what I mean."

"Don't sell yourself short. Mr. Musick is a good man, but he's not the only man."

"I hope you're right. He's awfully old, isn't he?"

"Not really," Willie said. Plenty of girls married older men, often with a passel of children they needed help with, but this was not the point. "Edge, it's freezing out here. We'll talk next week, all right?"

Willie squeezed into the truck and closed the door before her sister had the chance to respond.

Chapter 27

"You're still reading that Western?" Jimmie asked when the girls gathered in Aunt Xenia's sitting room. Despite the warmth from the kitchen's stove, they were wearing their flannel gowns and wool stockings and sitting in pairs under quilts. Willie started to tell her cousin that it was a new one but remembered Ola's question about flirting with Clyde.

Willie felt Ola's elbow poke her rib under the quilt as she answered, "Yep, still reading it."

She decided she'd have to be more inconspicuous about her reading if she wanted to continue. Borrowing one book from a boy was fine, but borrowing a second one would raise eyebrows. And how much more if they knew it was not from a boy but from the hired hand! She was lucky no one had paid enough attention last week to notice the title. Willie slowed the pace of her reading and didn't finish *Rainbow Trail* until her second week with it. She wrote a reply to Mr. Musick during her civics class on Friday. When she got home that evening, she ran to the dugout and placed the book under the rock.

Mr. John Horry Musick—

Zane Grey likes surprise identities! This time I was expecting it and still didn't get it all figured out before the end. At first, I didn't care about Shefford or his plight, as I only wanted more of the Cottonwoods folks I'd come to know, but I was rooting for him after he stuck out his trials in the West. I'm afraid I turned on him again after he left Fay to the Mormon women. TWICE! Now what about Zane Grey and the Mormons? I can't tell whether he likes them or not. At times he paints them villains, then he comes to their defense at the turn of a page. I couldn't tell whether I should be on their side or against. I don't pretend to understand all of what they were accused of, but enough to want Fay Larkin far away! And the Indians. Either all bad or more capable than anyone could really be. Does he confound a person on purpose? What's he up to? Do you know? I never guessed Westerns gave a person so much to think about. Sure more than Regency romances, but I guess you wouldn't know about that. Thank you for sharing the book. I'd like another if you don't mind.

—Willie

Willie thrilled with nervous excitement as she went about her chores. She hoped for John Musick's approval in a way she never had with anyone other than her father. In contrast to her father, however, she wasn't desperate for his agreement, only that he found her thoughtful. She didn't care that he might judge her clothes, hair, or even her personality, but she couldn't bear the thought that he might think her naive or foolish. She thought of the note she'd left as the supper conversation went on around her.

"It looks like we're making good progress with the vote," Father said.

"Oh?" asked Mother.

"Yes. We'll put the issue on the ballot in February."

"Speaking of progress," Mother said, and she turned her face from Father. "Girls, I think it's time for Edgalea to start looking for work, and I have a job in mind." Willie began paying attention.

"The first Tuesday of February," Father said, clearly not ready for a shift in conversation.

"That's a relief," Mother said. Then she continued. "My hip's nearly right, and you have Mr. Musick helping you. I believe we can spare her."

Father opened his mouth then closed it again. He blinked and tilted his head like a dog does at an unfamiliar sound, catching up to Mother's side of the conversation. "Maybe we can, but why would we?" he said at last.

"Edgalea needs to get out. She's still young and full of potential." Willie wondered which potential her mother hand in mind. Potential to find a husband or to earn money?

"I reckon you're right," he said. "It would be easier for her to find a husband if she were in town now and then." His idea of potential only followed one path.

"I was thinking it might be important for her to start saving money so that she could live well on her own, as your sisters have."

"My sisters have the help of their brothers."

Mother and Father both looked at Thurston, slurping as he raked beans from the bowl into his mouth, oblivious to the expectations for his future. Father pressed his lips together and tilted his head. Edgalea would not have a brother able to support her for many more years. She either needed to marry or find a way to provide for herself.

"I'll talk to Chloe on Sunday," Father said. "I'm sure she could use an extra hand."

"I mentioned it to Chloe last week, and she said she couldn't take on help right now. She did tell me George McCormick might could use someone in his general store in Portales."

The girls all kept their opinions to themselves. They were accustomed to their parents making decisions for them as though they weren't in the room. Willie tried to make eye contact with Edgalea to get her opinion on the matter, but her sister was studying her cornbread with the intensity of a fly on manure. That was enough to tell Willie that Edgalea and Mother were in on this plan together. Edgalea's assignment was to keep her head down and let Mother handle Father.

When Willie finished her first round of chores on Saturday morning, she found *The Man of the Forest* waiting for her under the rock.

Miss Tollett—

I imagine Zane Grey is trying to figure it all out himself. There's good and evil in every group and person. Maybe he leans more on what he saw first. Or what he was told about first. Then life shows him something new, but it's hard to change that first idea. Savvy?

I forget that you are still young. I wonder that I gave you such material to read. But if the Bible is approved reading, I can't see much harm. Scarier stories in there than in any Zane Grey.

Can't say I've read any Regency romance, but I can loan you another Western. You'll have to tell me whether you're a Nell or a Bo.

—JHM

Willie tucked the book into her waistband. She didn't understand his query, but it heightened her anticipation. Unfortunately, her curiosity would have to wait. She worked until the sun went down, her hands growing numb with cold, then joined her family singing the songs carried from Father's Tennessee hills and Mother's people in North Carolina. Next to hearing Father's news from town, singing with her family on Saturday night was her favorite part of the week. They hadn't done it often since mother's accident, which made it even sweeter now.

Sunday followed the rhythm of Sabbath, and Willie did not start the new book until she was back at Aunt Xenia's house.

The other girls stayed in the kitchen, preferring the warmth of the stove. Willie settled into one end of the sofa, pulled a crocheted afghan up to her shoulders, and put her hands out just enough to hold the book. She saw immediately that Milt Dale would be the leading man, and she had no doubt he would save the day by the last page. The plot surprised her in that an old man was dying and leaving his ranch and livestock to his niece. Willie thought through the list of her extended family, searching her mind for an uncle or cousin who had no children and might leave her an inheritance. It was no use. The Tollett men all had many children, and even if they didn't, there would be plenty of nephews in the line. It was a pointless daydream.

It took a week of reading in town for Willie to be introduced to the characters of Helen, called Nell, and Bo Rayner. By Friday, Willie had her answer to John Musick's query. Anxious to continue their correspondence, she wrote it on the back of a General Electric bulletin and tucked it between the pages of *The Man of the Forest*. She considered how to deliver her reply without returning the book.

On Sunday morning, she found her solution. When the family returned from church, Willie lingered in the back of the truck while her father and sisters went inside. Then she ran to the dugout and placed her Bible, with the GE bulletin tucked between the pages, under the rock.

Mr. JHM—

I am not a Nell or a Bo. I am not dutiful and proper, and my mind is not set on chasing boys. I don't imagine either of these two would be suited to manage the ranch. I would be, if only I had a wealthy uncle ready to die.

—Willie

Chapter 28

Willie's evenings were filled with homework now, and by the time she picked up *Man of the Forest* after supper, her eyes were heavy with sleep. Despite her weariness, the thrill of an outlaw gang plotting to kidnap two women, and the surprise when they get swept into the forest by a lone mountain man, compelled Willie to open the book every night. Once she began reading and considering what her next note to John Musick might say, she turned page after page until she dozed off, still sitting up on the sofa.

"Willie, put that light out and come to bed," Gladys said.

"I will after I read a few more pages."

"You're not reading; you're sleeping."

"I'm not sleeping," Willie protested. "I'm checking my eyelids for holes."

Gladys rolled over and left her to it.

When they arrived at the farm on Friday, the sun was already setting, taking the last touch of warmth with it. Willie went directly from the truck to check on the Herefords. Passing the dugout, she noticed a book under the rock, their rock as she thought of it now. She scanned the horizon until she found her father and Mr. Musick walking through the spent corn field. She approached the dugout.

Willie retrieved her Bible from under the rock. She'd forgotten all about leaving a note in it last Sunday, and her heart pounded in her head. Had it been left out all week? What if her father noticed or it had been damaged by the wind? As quickly as the thought entered her mind, she dismissed it. John Musick would never be so careless. He must have returned it to its spot knowing that she'd be home today.

Willie picked up the Bible and smiled at John's handwriting below hers on the GE bulletin.

Miss Tollett–

I hope I didn't offend you with my question. You are quite unlike any young woman I've known, including Nell and Bo. I have no doubt you could run a ranch on your own. I guess you didn't take a shine to either leading lady. Maybe you'll change your mind.

I wonder if you meant for me to read the Bible this week. I'm afraid I'd need more time than you could be without it. Maybe it will be some comfort that I've read it before and find most of it very good.

–JHM

Willie laughed. She'd stopped worrying about whether John Musick was making fun of her. She understood that his wit was good-natured, never unkind. She also understood that his apology and concern of offense was genuine. She would have to assure him that she was not so easily offended.

At the end of the night, Willie went to the barn to milk and found Father telling Mr. Musick his plans to sell the male calves and buy one new bull. She was irritated that her father hadn't told her this plan, but of course there hadn't been time. Willie noticed how intently John Musick listened, how he nodded to show his agreement and narrowed his eyes but kept silent when he differed. Without an excuse to linger in the barn, Willie carried the milk to the house and washed for supper.

"What has you so cheerful?" Edgalea asked Willie as they sat down to eat.

"Change in the air, I guess," said Willie.

"Cold front won't hold much longer," Father said. "Warmer days next week."

"Speaking of change," Mother said, "Edgalea has news." She looked at Edgalea, who sat a bit taller. Mother nodded, indicating that Edgalea should be the one to share.

"I'll start work in Portales on Monday," she said. "Chloe was right about George McCormick wanting help. Gussie's been nervous about working alone ever since the Howler business started."

"Edgalea's experience at Chloe's store made her an easy hire," Mother added.

The conversation continued, but Willie did not follow it. Her mind was occupied with how she could get a reply to Mr. Musick without waiting another week. When the idea finally came to her, she reveled in both the obviousness—it had worked before—and the risk it entailed.

Before supper on Saturday, Willie tucked her Bible into the waistband of her skirt and carried it to the dugout on her way to the barn. She knew that John Musick might not see the book when he returned late that night. And even if he did, there was no guarantee that he'd return it before church in the morning. She relished the fluttering in her stomach. Farming on the plains involved danger but provided few opportunities for daring.

JHM—

I am not so easily offended. Thank you for your confidence.

You say you've read the Bible, but you don't go to church. Why?

Another question for you. Would you like to live at Paradise Park, as Milt Dale does, among wild animals instead of people? I believe I'd be lonesome.

—Willie

P.S. I'm surprised there's so much romance in these Westerns. I didn't know men were interested in that sort of thing.

The next morning Willie got out of bed even earlier than usual, anxious to retrieve her Bible. She'd felt bold after dinner, but in the stillness of the night and the nearness of Sunday services, she'd recognized her foolishness. She shivered as she slipped out of the warmth of the quilts and the nearness of her sisters' bodies.

Mother was already awake and starting the coffee. "You're up early," she said.

"Yes," Willie said. "I wanted to get a start on the day."

"Well, bundle up. It's cold enough to freeze the hair off a hog."

Willie did as she was told, thinking how easy it would be to hide the Bible under her layers of clothing. She stepped out and gasped at the biting wind. She walked toward the dugout but didn't see her Bible. The sky was still gray with only a hint of light on the eastern horizon. Perhaps, she thought, it's too dark to see from a distance. She dared to walk right up to the stoop and bend down, but there was nothing under the rock. Her stomach tightened. On one hand, Mr. Musick had noticed the Bible and picked it up. On the other hand, he hadn't returned it, and there was no way to know when he would.

Willie hurried through her work, using a shovel to break the thin layer of ice over the stock tank, throwing out hay, and milking the cows. Despite her gloves, her hands were so cold by the time she got to the barn, she had to rub them together before she began the milking. Penny and Polly did not appreciate cold hands on their udders, and they would make milking difficult if they were put out.

While she milked, Willie formulated a plan. She would not have her Bible for church. Whether she said that she misplaced it or that she forgot to bring it, Father would be angry. Her only option was to make it through the morning unnoticed.

By the time she'd milked and cleaned around the stanchion, Willie's hands were warm, and she had taken off her coat. Despite having worked up a sweat, she bundled up again before stepping outside. She took a full bucket of milk in each hand and ducked her head in anticipation of the cold wind.

As she stepped out of the barn, she bumped headfirst into John Musick. She let out a quiet yelp as milk sloshed over the sides of the buckets.

"I'm sorry," he said. "I didn't mean to scare you."

"You didn't scare me," Willie said. "Only startled."

"I meant to catch you before you milked, but you're done early."

"Got an early start."

"Thought you'd probably need this today," he said as he held out her Bible. Relief flooded Willie's body, washing away the thoughts that had troubled her sleep. She set down her buckets and took the Bible from him. She unbuttoned her coat and tucked the book into her waistband.

"Yes, thank you." She looked up at him for the first time and noticed how tired he looked. His wool hat was pulled down, but she could see dark circles under his eyes. His coat and trousers were covered in dirt as though he'd already been out in the fields.

"You look like you haven't slept."

"Got in late. I was afraid of missing you this morning, so I stayed up to wait for sunrise."

"You didn't have to do that."

"I know how your father feels about Sundays and Bibles. I wouldn't want you to get into trouble on my account."

"I'm the one who left it out for you. If I got in trouble, it would be my own doing."

"But I picked it up and carried it in."

"I suppose it would be on both our consciences then." Willie looked up and smiled. She wanted to keep him in this conversation. Unlike passing along information or even stories as he did with all her family, this banter was unique to the two of them. Forgetting the cold, she wished she could spend the day working with John Musick.

"Speaking of trouble," he said, interrupting her thoughts, "You'd better get inside with that milk."

"Oh! Yes, I better."

John Musick stepped aside, and Willie took up her buckets and stepped out of the barn. The cold wind took her breath away. She had been so warm standing in the barn with John, she hadn't thought to button her coat after taking the book. By the time she got in the house, she was chilled to the bone.

"Sit a spell by the stove and warm yourself," Mother said. "Get 'hold of some coffee. I always think the first freeze is the hardest."

Willie pulled off her gloves and did as she was told though she was anxious to get the Bible out of her skirt. As soon as her mother stepped toward the bedroom, she pulled it out.

Her numb fingers struggled to open the cover, but her effort was rewarded.

Miss Tollett—
I reckon I see mankind the way Milt Dale does. Living with wild animals seems a safer choice. At least they're bound by laws of nature. Greedy men are bound by nothing. I also think of God and religion much like Dale.

—JHM

P.S. Men I know like to imagine they could be a woman's hero. If that's romance, then yes, we like it.

Despite her still-cold hands, Willie felt her cheeks burn at the mention of romance. She read the note again, beginning with her own words. She'd brought up romance first, she remembered, and was pleased with her nerve, though she'd meant nothing by it.

"Getting an early start, I see." Father's voice cut through Willie's pride, and she startled, dropping the note. On impulse, she stretched her right leg, covered the bulletin with her shoe, then slid it back toward her chair.

"Yes, sir," she said.

"I like to see that," Father said. "An early start gives you more time in the scriptures. I'd like to see your sisters take your lead."

"Yes, sir," Willie said again. She forgot that she had the Bible in her lap. She held it tight to steady her hands.

"Might need to move away from the stove now. Your cheeks are starting to burn."

"Yes, sir," Willie said, once more aware of the heat in her cheeks even as she shivered with cold. Her father was distracted by his own cup of coffee, so she reached down to pick up the note. Her fingers fumbled, still cold, but after three attempts, she got the paper tucked between the pages of her Bible and hurried to the bedroom.

Edgalea and Gladys were dressed, but Ella Bea was still in the bed with a pillow over her head.

"Out of bed," said Edgalea. "You'll miss breakfast."

"But it's so cold!"

"Where have you been?" Gladys asked Willie.

"I couldn't sleep, so I went out early and got the milking done."

"The wind sounds awful," Gladys said. "Is it as cold out there as it sounds?"

"Why don't you ask Ella Bea?" Willie said. In a swift movement, she placed her cold hands under Ella Bea's pillow and onto each of her cheeks. Her youngest sister squealed and jumped out of the bed swinging her fists at Willie.

"Well, Ella Bea," Edgalea teased. "Is it cold out there?"

Ella Bea fumed as her three older sisters laughed. She started to crawl back under the quilts, but Edgalea yanked them away from her.

"Oh no, you don't!" she said. "Time to get up and dressed."

"You are all horrible!" Ella Bea yelled. By this time, her sisters were all dressed and filing out of the bedroom. They left her to sulk and recover on her own.

"What have y'all been doing to your sister?" Mother asked.

"Nothing she didn't deserve," Willie said. Gladys put biscuits from the night before on a plate for each of them.

"Whatever it was, I hope it gets her out here. Your father will be ready to go soon, and he won't wait."

"Can I have her biscuit?" asked Thurston.

"No. I'm sure she's up now," Willie said.

Ella Bea came into the kitchen with a scowl on her face. Edgalea and Willie laughed again, but Gladys pushed the butter toward her.

"Oh, El. Don't hold it against us," she said. It was no wonder she was everyone's favorite.

Chapter 29

Ella Bea and Thurston sat in the cab with Father on the way to church. The three oldest girls huddled together under quilts in the truck bed. Unlike the first cold snap, the girls were accustomed to the cooler temperatures and didn't need so many layers or the heat of the irons. With the sun shining bright overhead, the morning was turning pleasant.

"You tossed and turned all night," Edgalea said. "What's on your mind?"

"Nothing in particular," Willie answered. "I suppose it was the change in the weather."

"Change does seem to be in the air," Gladys said. "Around you at any rate."

"What's that supposed to mean?"

"Don't rightly know. Only there's something different about you this fall."

Willie shrugged in response. She had noticed feeling more out of place than usual, both at school and at home. Is this what her sisters noticed, too? Or could they see the effect

John Musick and his books had on her? She decided the best course was to change the subject.

"Are you glad to be working in Portales?"

"Mother is set on the idea of my earning wages, and Father believes I can catch a husband."

"But are you glad?"

"They're right, I suppose. But I might lose an obvious candidate."

"Oh? Who is that?"

"Mr. Musick, of course!"

Willie's eyes widened, then she blinked away her surprise. Caught up in her own world, she had assumed her sister's interest in the hired hand—an interest she had been the one to spark—had waned. They hadn't spoken of him since the summer day shelling beans. The idea of John and Edgalea together seemed absurd now, and Willie felt her breakfast sour in pit of her stomach.

"Have the two of you been talking more?" She couldn't resist asking.

"Not alone, of course. He's usually outside while I'm in the house. And when he comes in for dinner, he and Father are full of farm talk. He always says hello to me though, and I hear a particular kindness in his voice. A little extra just for me, I think."

Willie knew there was no need to be jealous of Edgalea. Still, when Edgalea greeted her Sunday school pupils, Willie felt the hair on her neck stand at attention. When she heard Edgalea singing during the worship service, she clenched her jaw. Willie imagined the sound of John Musick saying hello to her sister with *particular* kindness. By the time they returned to the bed of the truck, Willie needed nothing more than her envy to keep her warm.

"You know you have the support of Charlie Baker," Aunt Chloe said when they were seated around the dinner table. She'd continued fasting on Sundays, allowing herself a glass of milk and nothing more while the rest of the family filled their plates with fried chicken, fried potatoes, and gravy. Father brought up the idea of joining her in the weekly fast, but Mother gave him an extra scoop of potatoes in response, and that was the final word on the matter.

"I wasn't sure where he would land, but I'm glad to hear it. He holds sway over his three brothers, so that could tip the numbers."

"Not to mention he's the wealthiest man in the county. He and Polly were in the store last week placing a large order for silk. Preparing Eula's trousseau, probably. I required payment up front as I'd never sell that much to the entire town in a year.

"Anyhow, I asked her outright what Charlie was likely to do. Turns out their oldest boy was seen coming out of the billiard hall in Portales. When word of it got to Polly, she told Charlie if he didn't state his intention to vote against the one in Inez, she'd be holding a sign at the next Ladies' League gathering."

"I reckon she might, too," Father said.

The afternoon passed in similar fashion, with Father and Aunt Chloe going back and forth with talk of votes and righteousness while Mother and the girls sipped their coffee and listened. Willie envied Thurston's freedom to bundle up and go outside to play. She preferred work to this version of rest, and what she really wanted was to read her book. Finally, Father announced that it was time to load the truck for Portales.

If Edgalea expected a fuss to be made over her return to Railroad Street, she was surely disappointed. All the talk was about the Howler.

"It's back! We heard it again last night!" Ola squealed as soon as Jim Tollett left the house. Everyone doubled up under quilts and settled in as Ola continued. "The whole town probably did!"

"Did anyone see it?" Willie asked. She wished the excitement could have waited one more night.

"Some say it looked like a man!" Lois said.

"Others swear it's an animal walking upright!" Ola added.

"I've been saying all along it's a werewolf," Minnie said. "Mark says he could rid the town of the beast in no time if everyone were willing to face the fact that it will have to be dealt with in supernatural ways."

Everyone's chatter stopped as they turned to look at Minnie.

"Surely you can't believe that," Aunt Xenia said.

"Mark says there are documented cases further west. Only we're too limited in our beliefs to accept the obvious truth."

"Mark is full of hogwash," Jimmie said.

"He isn't. He's been places and met people."

"Will someone tell us what happened?" Edgalea asked.

"Did someone really see the Howler?" Willie asked again.

"It started yesterday after sundown," Lois said. "We were making our way to bed when we heard it the first time. It was only one howl or cry or whatever. So short that even though we all heard it, we wondered if we'd imagined it."

"Yes, but we hadn't imagined it," Ola said. "We were in our beds when we heard it again, right outside the house. Or so we thought. We gathered at the windows—"

"Mother wouldn't let us go outside," Minnie interrupted.

"It didn't matter though, because as soon as we were all up, it was quiet," Jimmie said.

"I checked around the house," Aunt Xenia said. "All I found was a pair of marks across the dirt in the yard. Looked like someone dragged a couple of potato sacks across it."

"You went out alone?" Gladys asked. "Weren't you scared?"

"Alone, not unarmed. Anyhow, a great number of people have tried to spot the creature with no luck. Figured I wouldn't fare any better. But if I did, I was prepared."

"We came in and got settled. After we'd been asleep a while we heard it again, but this time from a distance," Lois said.

"That time it went on and on, but it sounded like it was moving," Ola said.

"We probably wouldn't have woken up except for the excitement earlier," Lois said.

"And in all that time, did anyone see it?" Willie said.

"Not that I've heard," said Aunt Xenia.

"Was anyone hurt?" Gladys asked.

"Not a soul," Xenia said.

"How strange," said Willie.

"I hope it's not out tonight," said Gladys with a shiver. The other women agreed, but not Willie. She wanted to hear the sound again and see the monster for herself.

"After the excitement of last night, I believe we could all use an early bedtime," Aunt Xenia said. At the mention of bed, Willie realized how tired she was. She'd had her own restless night and early morning and felt it catching up with her. Despite the excitement in the house and the thoughts swirling in her mind, she fell asleep as soon as her head was on the pillow.

The Howler was quiet for the rest of the week, but the town's speculation had reached new volume after Saturday night's episode. It was the only topic of conversation at school, and Willie's friends gathered around the long oak table in the library during lunch to compare what they'd heard.

May Bell, of course, had the most to say. "My daddy says if the deputy doesn't form a posse, the townsfolk will."

"The deputy better do something," Glenn said. "There's talk of an election to have him replaced."

"I've heard that the mayor's been talking to a man from Santa Fe who specializes in this sort of thing," said Joyce, almost in a whisper.

"A supernaturalist?" Willie asked. She'd assumed Minnie and her boyfriend were only making that up.

"Yes! So, you've heard the same thing?" Joyce asked.

"Not from a reliable source," Willie answered. She wondered whether the same unreliable information could be repeated often enough for everyone to assume it was true.

"I think before we call on a supernaturalist, we should call on the Lord. I'm organizing a prayer meeting for this weekend," May Bell announced.

"Something's got to be done about it," repeated Glenn.

"But why?" Joyce asked. "Other than satisfying our curiosity, why is it so urgent that something be done about a creature that's done no more than wake people up and make a mess of a few yards? There are dogs in town that have done worse, and no one gets worked up."

"Because we know the dogs," Glenn said. "We don't know anything about the Howler."

"And that's reason enough?" Willie asked. She was as anxious as anyone to have her curiosity satisfied, but Joyce made a good point.

"Yes!" the others responded, and Joyce flinched.

Speculation about the Howler brought *Man of the Forest* to Willie's mind, although she couldn't say exactly why. She had a notion that it was related to Nell and Bo's discussions of nature, religion, and mankind with Dale in his forest refuge. She'd never heard the men and women in her life exchange ideas in this way. While her father and Aunt Chloe sometimes discussed matters of religion over Sunday dinner, their conversations lacked the complexity or opportunity for dissent that she found in these fictional discussions. Likewise, her gut told her that the problem of the Howler would be more complicated than anyone guessed. Could the townsfolk tolerate something they didn't understand, or was removal the only option?

By the end of the week, word of the Howler had made its way to the Tollett farm. Over their potato soup on Friday night, Father told the girls that when they were in town, they were to return to Aunt Xenia's house immediately after school or work.

"No doubt it's the ruffians leaving the pool hall," he speculated. "Mark my words, the town is going to reap what they've sown. They made a deal with the devil, and now he's parading in their streets. Hopefully, the people of Inez will learn from their folly."

"I can't wait till I live in Portales," said Thurston between loud slurps of soup. He'd abandoned his spoon and held the bowl in front of his face. "All the good stuff happens there."

"Nothing good will come of this," Father said. Willie noticed the edge in his voice.

"Yeah, but at least it's exciting," Thurston said. He had apparently not noticed Father's tone. "I'm going to work in town when I get grown."

"That's enough," Father said. He didn't raise his voice, but his tone was serious. He put down his spoon and lifted his milk glass. "You can't run a farm from town, son. Your home will be here."

"But I don't want—"

"Enough!" Father said, slamming his glass on the table.

"I'll run the farm," Willie said. Surely her father could finally see that she'd be a better owner than her brother.

"Yes, no doubt," Father said with pride and approval, "but as owner, Thurston will need to stay close."

Could her father honestly think she would do all the work on land her brother owned? It was an intolerable suggestion, perhaps as bad as marriage. She needed to get her quarter section and start showing her father what she could do with it. Graduation could not come soon enough.

Willie noticed her sisters' eyes on her. The heat rising up from her bowl met the heat gathering in her chest.

"He'd better stay close enough to run his own operation, as I'll be busy running mine," Willie said.

"Ha!" Father laughed without humor.

Willie did not laugh. Was her father saying he would not give her the land he'd promised? She stayed at the table but didn't eat another bite.

Although she rarely read her Westerns at home, after supper Willie picked up *Man of the Forest*. She needed to escape to a world of happy endings. Unfortunately, the book took a sour turn. Helen and Bo would suffer men's betrayal as well. The world was a cruel place, and now even Zane Grey offered no better place in which to escape.

When she went out to do her final chores, she returned the book to the rock, but she kept John Musick's last note. She gave her reply on a fresh page of writing paper she'd taken from school.

JHM—

I've decided to quit on this book. Why does Zane Grey go to the trouble of introducing these women and convincing us to like and trust them if, in the end, their uncle is looking for a man to run the business? Why doesn't Uncle Auchincloss leave his ranch to a man if he wants a man to run it?

Anyhow, I don't want to read further. The story of men not taking women seriously is the story of real life. Like you, I want the happy ending.

—Willie

The book was gone in the morning.

Willie kept watch on Saturday for a new book to appear. It was a sunny day, mild after days of severe cold, so she found reasons to be outside most of the day. She checked for a book again on Sunday before church, but there was nothing on the stoop except the rock. She regretted returning *The Man of the Forest* so soon. What if John Musick thought she was quitting Westerns altogether? She would miss the escape Zane Grey novels provided.

"What's wrong?" asked Gladys as they loaded the truck to return to Portales.

"Nothing," Willie said. "Why do you ask?"

"You've been moping all weekend."

"Have I?"

"Yes. At first, I thought you were still upset by what Father said, but that's not it. You look like you've lost something."

"No, you were right. I'm still thinking of Father."

"You've never let his comments stick. Don't start now," Gladys said. "He'll come back around. He always does."

Willie shrugged and climbed into the truck. As they rode into town, she sank deeper into her thoughts. Her mood was related to her father's words, but it was more about the loss of her books and letters. In truth, she missed John Musick. She'd come to understand that her connection to him had filled a loneliness she'd felt for as long as she could remember. She had always been different, among her family members and at school. Harold accepted her difference, but with John, she'd felt normal, as though her dreams were perfectly reasonable, even if unusual. Without their books and the notes that accompanied each exchange, their contact would be limited to chance encounters.

By the time they arrived at Aunt Xenia's, Willie was in a true malaise. The thought of ending each day without a few pages of escape and having nothing to occupy her mind other than schoolwork and town gossip cast a shadow over her. She lamented the impetuous nature that compelled her to act without thinking. John probably thought of her as a child, prone to tantrums.

Willie went to bed early and began the new week with nothing to look forward to. In class, her mind drifted, as it normally did, but there was no satisfaction in the old reverie. She tried setting her mind on cattle breeds, farm implements, and crop rotations, but to no avail. Until a few weeks ago, farming had been the sole source of her daydreams. They offered little comfort now that her father might withhold his promise in an effort to restore his sense of control. Now, her mind only returned to thoughts of John Musick.

By Thursday afternoon, she'd turned from sullen to unkind, and when she walked in on a conversation between Minnie and Edgalea, she found an easy target for her meanness.

"You can't possibly believe your prospects are better now!" Minnie was saying. Edgalea chopped an onion, but Willie didn't think it was the source of her red, watery eyes. Minnie wore an apron, but didn't appear to have a task at hand. "No man wants to marry the woman working behind a shop counter. How has that worked for Aunt Chloe?"

Willie stepped between her sister and her cousin. "Why wouldn't a man want a smart, hardworking wife? You have to believe men prefer an empty-headed girl because that's all you have to offer!"

With that, Willie walked out the front door and continued down the street with no destination in mind. She knew she had overreacted. Minnie picked on Edgalea, but she had no more certainty for her future than any of them did. Surely she was smart enough to see that her railroad man offered no guarantees. Minnie understood how the world worked.

Willie stopped in her tracks. For the first time, she regarded Minnie in a new light. Her cousin's arrogance was fear in disguise. She bullied Edgalea to cover the fact that she was scared to death of her own future. A block later, Willie admitted to herself that maybe her anger was also a symptom of fear. Between her father's outburst and John Musick's silence, she felt untethered. It was a new feeling, and one she didn't enjoy.

By the time Willie finished her walk, she was no longer angry at her cousin, but she wasn't happy to see her sitting on the porch either. She considered passing by the house without stopping, but the sun was already going down, and she had homework and chores to get to. She took a deep breath and reminded herself to use restraint. She did not, however, plan to apologize.

Minnie stood as Willie approached the porch. Her clothes and hair were as tidy as ever, but she had a crumpled appearance. "I'm sorry," she said.

"For what?" Willie asked. She knew she should accept the apology and offer her own, but she couldn't bring herself to do it.

"For what I said to Edgalea."

"Then you should be apologizing to her."

"I did," Minnie said. Willie noticed the shadows under her cousin's eyes. They were the source of her disheveled look. She seemed to be waiting for Willie to answer, but Willie had nothing kind to say. "How do you do it, Willie?"

"Do what?"

"Walk around without a care for what people think of you."

"I do care. I just don't assume people are thinking of me all that much."

Minnie didn't respond. She stood facing Willie, blinking her big brown eyes like a sow who knows she's bound to be pork. Willie wanted out of this conversation. Vulnerability from Minnie was more difficult to bear than conceit. Willie knew there was only one way to end the tortuous moment.

"I accept your apology," she said.

Minnie's countenance changed immediately. Her shoulders dropped and light returned to her eyes. She stepped toward

Willie and gave her a hug, and as she did so, Willie felt her defenses melting. Her own hostility was the result of loneliness. She began to understand her cousin's years of striving and manipulation. They were more similar than Willie wanted to admit, both motivated by fear of isolation.

"I'm sorry, too," Willie said.

Minnie released her and smiled. With a sigh, Willie reached for the front door.

"Don't forget your book," Minnie said. Willie paused with her hand on the door and turned to look. Her cousin was holding *Man of the Forest*. Now it was Willie's turn to stand in silence.

"Isn't it yours?" Minnie asked. "You're the only one who reads this sort of thing."

"Where did you get it?"

"It was under the chair. You must have left it out last night."

"Oh," Willie said. She examined her cousin's face, searching for signs of a trap. Did she know more about the book than she was letting on?

"Well? Are you going to take it?"

Willie grabbed the book from her cousin's hand. "Thanks," she said, and she walked through the door as though the events of the last hour had never happened.

Inside the house, everyone was intent on their own tasks. Evenings were never quiet enough to hear the clock in the kitchen, but its steady ticking told Willie that the other women had either been talking about them or listening to their conversation. She pretended not to notice. Minnie went to the bedroom. Willie carried her satchel to the kitchen table. Before trading the Western for her grammar textbook, she opened the cover.

> *Miss Tollett—*
> *Didn't you also doubt Nell's ability to run the ranch? Perhaps it is not her womanhood, but her lack of experience that gives her uncle pause. Land ownership is no small gift, particularly for a woman, if you'll allow me to say so. Having an owner separate from the foreman is not uncommon among the wealthy. Try to see it through.*
>
> *—JHM*
>
> *P.S. I was afraid you wouldn't see the book in time to pick it up on Sunday. I gather you do most of your reading in town, so I hope you don't mind that I left it at your aunt's house when I came on business for your father. He's had me in town during the week since there's less for me to do in winter.*

Willie allowed a smile spread across her face as she put away the book and began her homework. The other ladies soon joined her in the kitchen, serving up the stew they'd left to simmer while they eavesdropped.

"You must have had a good talk," Gladys said as she sat next to Willie.

"Not really," Willie said. "Same as always. Minnie behaves poorly, feels bad that the world doesn't adore her, then apologizes so she can feel better."

"Looks like it made you feel better, too. Sometimes I wonder if you just need a fight once in a while."

"Maybe." Willie met Gladys's eyes and smiled like a possum. In thinking she'd lost her connection to John Musick, she'd come to realize how valuable it was to her. The insight was intoxicating. She might smile forever. And if they thought her relief was the result of her talk with Minnie, she would let them.

Willie waited until after supper to retrieve *Man of the Forest* from her satchel. The kitchen was clean, and everyone had settled in with their handwork, homework, and letter writing. Willie was so relieved to have a book, and especially a note, from John that she would have read anything he asked her to. She would not allow her connection to him to be broken again. She turned to the page where she'd stopped—it felt silly now that she'd ever done so—and resumed her reading. By the end of the week, she was ready to give him the answer to his query.

JHM—

I finished Man of the Forest *and I'm glad for it as I can give your question a full answer now. I am not a "thinker" as Helen describes herself. It doesn't take any effort for me to act rather than brood. In that way, I suppose I'm more like Bo, but without the silly, romantic notions. Like Bo, I find it "glorious" to get out from the domestic life and feel my blood burning. I do possess Nell's directness and admired it in her. I bring Bo's energy to Nell's sensibility. Since you posed the question, I had it in mind as I read the book. I admit that I was surprised to find qualities in both women that I wish to see in myself. That voice that keeps Nell from forgetting herself. The courage to love so openly like Bo.*

You are the Milt Dale of Roosevelt County. Do you see that? A solitary man who reads. I tried to understand religion through his eyes. How church folk can lie, cheat, steal, and kill, but nature has no cruelty. Nothing dies in vain, and God is in that somehow. Maybe that's how my mother sees religion, too. Of course, she loves the Bible as much as any church-going ladies. Maybe more. Reads it different, I guess.

Kindly, Willie

P.S. Since you'll be in town more, I'll leave a Sears Roebuck catalog on Aunt Xenia's porch. If I finish a book, I'll leave it underneath. Is it ok if I write even when I haven't finished a book?

Miss Tollett,
You don't strike me as lacking courage for anything. I see myself in Dale a bit. Reckon we see the world similar. Maybe it was always in me or maybe reading Zane Grey books put the ideas in my head. For sure there aren't many people around here who want to talk about such things. Maybe that's the reason for my loneliness.

Try The Light of Western Stars. *Another one about a courageous woman. I'll leave an International Harvester under our rock. Write any time.*

–JHM

Chapter 30

November 15

JHM,

Madeline Hammond's arrival in El Cajon recalled to me my cousin Zenia. She left by train to meet her brother in Idaho. I wondered how she might have handled such a cowboy on her arrival. Good thing she's not from New York City! Is the city as Zane Grey describes it? Are there truly women with so little to do?

You'll think it's odd that I see myself in Madeline Hammond. I get the same feelings of "future revolt." The lives people think women want are not for me. It's why I'm so stubborn about marriage. I want something of my own from life. Do you remember the line, "It was the woman in her that obeyed—not the personality of proud Madeline Hammond"? Maybe I don't have that obedient woman in me. I buck against the bridle. All personality!

I also find myself drawn to Stillwell. "When my time comes to die I'd like it to be on my porch smokin' my pipe an' facin' the west." Can you imagine a woman smoking on her porch?

Truly, Willie

November 19

Miss Tollett,

You do possess that woman. It's the daughter in you that obeys. But ambition is admirable. Both are. Knowing when to call on each might be the trick of it. Is avoiding marriage the answer? That seems less like going after something and more like running from something else.

We sailed out of NYC in 1918 and stayed a spell again on our way home. Have I told you that? I didn't meet any women such as Madeline Hammond, but I saw cars driven by men in suits with proper ladies stepping out in fine clothes onto streets lined with buildings twice the size of city hall. I was told they were homes, so I suppose Zane Grey's take is factual. I'll take the West over what I saw there. I'd rather see the sky.

And, as a matter of fact, my mother enjoys chewing tobacco while sitting on her porch. Given the chance, I suppose she'd smoke it in a pipe.

Kindly, JHM

November 23

JHM,
Your mother sounds like someone I'd like to meet. You never told me you were in NYC. I gather you didn't enjoy it.

Jane, Helen, Madeline, even my Aunt Xenia own land and don't have a husband. I don't know any women with a husband and land. From what I can see, a woman must avoid one to gain the other.

Still, you're right. I am an obedient daughter. You might say Father keeps my personality in check. I should warn you then that he's going to Amarillo to sell half the calves—not Carl, I'm glad to say–and bring back a new bull. Could be gone a few weeks—what will the obedient daughter do with her father gone? Ha! I'll tell you. We're staying in town till school lets out for winter. Don't know how you'll manage all the work at the homeplace. Sure, I'll miss it. The herd especially.

I used to enjoy being with the girls and hearing all the town talk, but lately I feel a bit lonesome even surrounded by them. I start reading a little sooner after supper and stay up a little later each night. No one's noticed. Their minds are all on the Howler. They share what they've heard from the store, Grandpa Sam's, and school. I half listen for a while but get drawn into The Light of Western Stars. *I would like to see the Howler though. A little danger to make me feel alive. Like Madeline Hammond on the mustang.*

Please call me Willie. I like to think we're friends now.

Truly, Willie

November 26

Miss Willie,
You're better off getting caught in Light of Western Stars *than any talk of the Howler.*

To tell the truth, I was excited the first time I saw the big city. I'd never been far from Bosque County, Texas, so it was exciting to see everything lit up. The hustle and bustle looked like important people with important things to do. But by the time we got back from fighting, the shine had sure enough worn off. I'd had enough of noise and people piled on top of each other. Most stars disappear when you're looking at the sky in NYC.

Your father agreed to hire Andrew Cash to help while he's gone. He's a good kid, good worker. We'll get it all done. Your father sure wanted to get the castrating done before he left, but the weather's been too warm. Plenty of neighbors willing to help when the time is right. Don't worry, your herd is in good hands.

Kindly, JHM

November 28

JHM,
A night sky without stars? No wonder Madeline Hammond loved the West. The stars call to me, haunt me like they do her. Give me that hunch I'm missing something. Maybe it's the "woman of me" again, calling in the mustang's ear or unable to resist "forbidden fruit." Funny that in the same book, the "woman" in Madeline Hammond makes her obedient, but also makes her daring. Did you see that?

You could work for a woman like Madeline Hammond. Her cowboys read books and stopped cussin' and drinkin'. Sounds like you. I'm not sure whether they still gamble though. Might have to give that up.

My friend Joyce announced she'll marry Bill on the day of graduation. Said she had to promise as much, or he'd take her to Elida and get 'em hitched over the weekend. He can't savvy her commitment to finishing school. To tell the truth, I can't either. There's nothing she'll learn between now and graduation that she doesn't already know. Certainly nothing more she'll need to know to be Bill Carter's wife. Anyhow, if you have opportunity, could you let Mother know? Just say you heard it in town. I bet she's lonesome for news.

Truly, Willie

November 30

Miss Willie,
You read Zane Grey different than me. See things I'd never noticed. Maybe God gave women different eyes than men.

Got the branding done last week. Your mom made a mess of calf fries. Sure was good eatin'. Next week Red Sam, the Belchers, and the Clarks are coming over to slaughter hogs. It will be a long, messy ordeal. Might be easier done on our own.

This morning I bought an old Model T with winnings off a man from Roswell. He didn't know when to call it quits. I tried to tell him he'd lost enough, but he wouldn't admit it. When he lost the final hand, he looked surprised. I felt bad enough to give him a break, but all the fellas who'd seen his foolishness wouldn't hear of it. Best I could do was give him money for a ticket home and see him to the depot. I don't guess I'll quit on gambling.

I suppose I wouldn't make the cut for Madeline Hammond. Maybe a woman around here could hire me to work her land, one who wouldn't be bothered by a game of pool and dominoes.

Kindly, JHM

December 1

JHM,
A truck! Great day in the morning! That will make your trips to town a whole lot faster. Wish I could have been there for the branding. I know it's hard, dirty work, but there's something to it that makes me feel like I'm part of it all. Like the herd is yours, the community is yours, you get to belong because you put in the work. But maybe that's all wishful thinking.

I'm still reading The Light of Western Stars, *and it's veered toward absurdity. And you know what? I loved it! I laughed and laughed at the cowboys putting on airs at playing golf. I've never seen a golf game. Have you?*

One upside to staying in town—I'll finally have my chance to hear the Howler. Maybe even see it. Minnie's been saying I'll have to wait for a full moon, but Xenia said it's more frequent on the weekends. Sure enough, I saw her pull her chair closer to the front door and sit up later last Saturday night. I suspect it's also why Xenia has entertained more conversations with the widower Mullins next door. Glenn says the townsfolk are making plans. May Bell is planning another prayer meeting. I suspect she's counting on the chance to collect town gossip more than she expects divine intervention for a nighttime disturbance.

Oh! And speaking of nighttime disturbance, last night, Aunt Xenia told Minnie that she'd arranged a job for her at the high school. Minnie was fit to be tied! Hysteria! Minnie accused Xenia of giving up on her being married (we were all thinking it) and that she was ruining her chances of a proposal. Aunt Xenia wouldn't budge.

Truly, Willie

December 2

Miss Willie,
I know what you mean about belonging. Work is what brings a man purpose. I figure that's about the same.

I'd forgotten that bit in The Light of Western Stars. *No, I've never seen a golf game either. Unless cowboys were playing, I can't say as I'd care to. I'm glad it gave you something to laugh about. Zane Grey must have written those scenes particular for the womenfolk to enjoy. He has a knack for bringing prideful men to humility. The action scenes for the menfolk are coming back soon.*

Kindly, JHM

December 3

JHM,
You were sure right about the action! I do believe Zane Grey set us up with the golf and campfire storytelling so he could stir us up good. The action scenes aren't just for the menfolk, you know. That's what I'm always getting at. We want to see life! It's men who confine women to the kitchen or in Madeline's case to meaningless days of leisure with no purpose. Maybe all women don't want to work a ranch or be kidnapped by bandits, but they don't want a lifetime of nothingness either.

I think Edgalea is noticing this urge in herself for the first time. She's working at the McCormick's store, and even though she gives her pay to Father, I think it's going to her head that she can earn money. She's been asking Aunt Xenia how she paid for her house.

Truly, Willie

December 4

Miss Willie,
I never gave a thought to women wanting something different than what they have. Maybe you're right, but I've never heard a woman say so. Women know how to care for babies so much better than menfolk.

It appears the natural way of things. You make me wonder.

The first time we met you were ready to marry Edgalea off to me. Do you recall?

Kindly, JHM

December 5

JHM,

Of course, women know how to care for babies! Same as you know how to rope and ride or plow and hoe. But not all men are farmers. And what woman is given the chance to say what she wants? I first thought of the idea when Harold—remember my friend?—decided to go to school to be a lawyer. He said that just because he was the son of a farmer didn't mean he had to farm. It got me to thinking about what I might want to do if I had a choice about it.

I laugh to think of our first meeting. I did try to make a match of you and Edge. I told her the same, and I'm afraid she took me at my word! She even had ideas that you showed her special favor at the house. Did you?

I'm nearing the end of The Light of Western Stars. *I'm tempted to stay up reading so I can see how it all works out, but I won't let myself. I've enjoyed this book most of all, and don't want to come to the last page. Silly, isn't it?*

One curiosity of The Light of Western Stars. *The cowboys are all so protective of Madeline Hammond. In the other books, the women from the East are thrown into action and danger as though they must prove themselves or be proved by the West. I wonder why Zane Grey treats Madeline Hammond differently.*

Truly, Willie

December 6

Miss Willie,
If it's silly, then I'm a silly man because I've done the same thing. When I only had a couple of books of my own, I would read slowly because I never knew when I'd have a new one to read. Maybe you'll feel okay to finish The Light of Western Stars *if I deliver the next book early.*

I never noticed the difference in Madeline Hammond's treatment. I think all men have an instinct to protect a woman. And perhaps the rough treatment of the other women has been for their protection, too? Sometimes a man has to get a woman on the horse first and explain later.

I don't believe I gave Edgalea any particular attention. It was never my intention, anyhow.

Kindly, JHM

December 7

JHM,
I got Wildfire. *It's a little wet, but I think it will dry out okay. It's been quite the afternoon! At lunch, the sky was bright blue overhead, but a thunderhead darkened the horizon.*

In home ec, Mrs. Thompson was going on about suit jacket collars, and the wind ripped the pattern right out of her hands! Sewing notions rolled all over the room before we got the windows closed. She thought she'd just keep going, but a flash of lightning startled us all. Mrs. Thompson tried to get control, but it was all giggling and crowding around the windows. When another thunderclap rattled the walls, she gave up. Told us to hurry on home. All the other classes let out too.

Well, we left, but we didn't hurry. Guess we were struck silly by the storm. I met Ola and Gladys in the school yard. We all stood talking until the bottom sure enough fell out of that cloud. At first, we stood there like idiots, stunned and laughing, getting completely drenched. Then, rain turned to hail.

We gathered our skirts, held our books overhead and skedaddled! Got to Aunt Xenia's porch drenched and with knots from the hail on our heads and knuckles. Curly-haired, drowned rats—that's what we looked like! Couldn't get out of our wet coats and boots what with the swollen laces, numb fingers. Just fell in a pile by the door.

Anyhow, that's when I noticed Wildfire. *Being under the chair, it didn't get too wet, but it'll take a day or two to dry out. It'll give me time to finish* The Light of Western Stars. *(There was no note inside. Did you leave one? I hope I didn't drop it, or it's surely floated down to Mexico by now.)*

You might think the excitement stops there, but you'd be wrong. Minnie came in two hours later, dry as a bone and talking about her students cutting up during the storm. Aunt Xenia asked questions and kept her talking. Gave her enough rope to hang herself. Minnie finally noticed the way we were all watching and excused herself to the bedroom. We're all waiting to see what comes of it.

Better close now.

Truly, Willie

December 9

Miss Willie,

Your aunt has her hands full.

I didn't leave anything in Wildfire *that could blow away. Have you started it yet?*

Kindly, JHM

December 10

JHM,

I haven't started Wildfire *because I only finished* The Light of Western Stars! *Married and didn't know it! Can such a thing be possible? And can it be possible that I both love it and hate it? I must admit, I only made half the journey in the car to Mexico before my patience ran out. I let my eyes trace the words until our heroine and her cowboy heroes finally made it to Aquas Prietas. What an ending!*

Truly, Willie

December 11

Miss Willie,

I forget you've only had Wildfire *a few days. Seems like longer. I've wanted to give it to you from the start. I think you may find yourself in Lucy Bostil, even more than Zane Grey's other leading ladies. Like you, she wants something of life that is not often handed to women. Maybe because she doesn't have a mother, she's never learned those ways. So maybe there is something to your idea that we're prone to do what we see our mothers or fathers do.*

Kindly, JHM

December 12

JHM—
I finally started Wildfire! *I saw a line on the first page was underlined: "longing for something to happen. It might be terrible so long as it was wonderful." First time I've seen a marking in one of your books. Did you intend to bring it to my attention or was that done before you were loaning books to me? I like to think it was meant for me either way. I feel all those things, though I suspect you're the only one who knows it. I wonder if I didn't know it myself till I met you. Not to say you caused it. Just that I didn't think on things the way I do now. Could I have been so simple a girl less than a year ago?*

Lucy Bostil is quite a character. I may have her spirit, but I envy her britches! How much I could accomplish unhampered by skirts! I don't care for this Slone fellow. And the riders! What an impractical lot! The riders in Purple Sage *seemed noble, like protectors and workers. In* Wildfire, *they seem more like men who need to find jobs. But boy, wouldn't I like to be one of them, just for one ride! We've never had horses that run fast. Only ones that could work hard. Have you ever seen wild horses?*

Someday, I'd like to see the West that Zane Grey writes about. The Four Corners or any place in Arizona. I want to see sage and pinyon and great canyons. I've never been out of Roosevelt County, unless you count the day I was born in Hereford and the days it took to get from there to here.

I admit that I miss Madeline Hammond, Stewart, and their cowboys. Sure, I'll grow to love these characters as I have the others. Have you ever felt a longing for the friends you made in books?

Truly, Willie

December 13

Miss Willie,
I underlined that line the day I delivered the book. Had a hunch it would mean something to you. Once again, you've put words to a thought I've had but never spoken out loud. Sometimes, I've wondered if the friends Zane Grey created are more real in my mind than the folks that live around me. Especially after rereading the books so many times.

I've never seen wild horses. Imagine they're quite a sight. I'm satisfied to read about far-off places, even the ones out west. I've found a home here and don't have a mind to leave it. I'm sure someone young and energetic like you has all sorts of plans for leaving. I know I did. But when I was over there, I decided if I ever got to settle in a spot, I'd be happy to stay put.

Kindly, JHM

December 14

JHM,
Reckon a lot of dreams died during the war. Playing in the majors would have taken you to all sorts of places. Did that ever sound fun? Before France?

I was sure glad to see Lucy show up on the scene with Wildfire. *I couldn't believe Zane Grey pointed out the difference in how a girl would handle the mustang. He must have had a good mother or sister; he gives girls credit for a lot of things I didn't think men noticed.*

I gave you the wrong idea if you think I'd want to live anywhere but here. My father has promised me a quarter section, and I figure I can build on that, buy up other sections as I can. My dream is not to go anywhere big but do big things right here.

Speaking of—how's the herd? How's Mother? I wish I could send a message to her through you, but that might raise questions.

Truly, Willie

December 15

Willie,
Sure, I had dreams. As Zane Grey says, "men who live lonely lives are dreamers" or something to that

effect. My dreams were something to think of at night, that's all. I knew I'd never go against my pop. You talk of your dreams as though they're plans. That's altogether different.

With all your big plans and no desire to go someplace else, why does The Light of Western Stars *wake up a sense that you're missing out? What's missing?*

Everything at your homeplace is fine. Not much to report. The Herefords have eaten the last bits of dry grass they could find. Giving them hay now. Lucky your father planted last spring with plans for the growing herd. They'll be fine over winter. Your mother's hip is aggravated by the cold weather. Not that she ever complains. I only notice her limp more.

Kindly, JHM

December 16

John,
I come off more confident than I am. It's how I hold on to my dream. In truth, I worry that Father won't give me the quarter section he's promised. It may all be Thurston's someday. And if I get married, it will give him more reason to skip over me. He'll think I'm settled up.

I get the sense of bad news coming in Wildfire. *Lucy is wild, and there are bad guys for sure, but her father seems the most dangerous. To be so single-minded. Sure, he loves his daughter and horses, but his true love is winning. I remember what you said about Zane Grey humbling proud men. Reckon that's what I'm getting sight of.*

Remember my friend, Harold? I received a letter from him yesterday. He's getting married. I cried when I read the news. I'd never confess that to anyone but you. I'm happy for him, of course, but I feel like I lost something. My best friend. Something else? I'm afraid it's put me in a glum state. Poor Gladys is fussing over me, but I won't even tell her the cause.

One thing to look forward to—this will be our last week in town and last week of the school term. Father will return on Saturday, and we'll go home with him Sunday after church. I know you say all's well, but I want to put eyes on the herd myself. I'm also in a mood to see my mother.

Only downside—I never did see the Howler. In all the time we've been in town, no one has even heard it.

Truly, Willie

Chapter 31

Despite the fact that they'd started writing every day, Willie doubted that she would receive another letter from John for the same reason that she hadn't written to him in three days. She worried that if she left a letter, but he didn't pick it up in time, someone else would find it during the weeks that she stayed home for the Christmas break. It didn't stop her from checking several times a day and every night before she went to bed.

They were spending the weekend in town so their father could tend to the business of the billiard hall vote, and Friday night she was disappointed, but not surprised, when there was nothing under the Sears Roebuck catalog on the porch. The night was clear, and a full moon cast long shadows across the yard. She looked up and thought of Madeline Hammond and her cowboy hero, handsome and loyal Gene Stewart. She sighed.

Her next breath caught in her throat. Willie had the undeniable feeling that she was being watched. She shivered.

From her peripheral vision, she saw someone standing among the junipers between Mr. Mullins's yard and theirs. Excited by the possibility of seeing the Howler and not wanting to spook him, Willie avoided a direct look. Then from the corner of her eye, she saw the bright flash of a match. Within seconds, she recognized the scent of a spring social, a hot summer, and every book and letter she'd received that fall. She knew without having to look that it was John Musick.

She waved, and he nodded and smiled in return. She looked away, and it struck her that she was now more comfortable expressing herself to him in letters than standing in his proximity. The intimacy they'd shared was buffered by the exchange of the books. Here, with him so near, she felt exposed. And excited. Without thinking, she stepped off the porch and walked to him.

"Hi there," she said. She tried to make her voice sound casual and steady, not at all the way she felt.

"Good evening."

"Were you coming to leave something?"

"I was passing by when I heard someone come out. I stopped, hoping it was you."

Willie glanced over her shoulder. Everyone in the house was already sleeping. No one would notice her absence right away. Perhaps all night.

"Would you like to go for a walk?" she asked.

"Should you ask if anyone would like to join us?"

"They're all asleep. I was up reading."

"Then lead the way, Majesty."

Willie smiled at his reference to Madeline Hunter's nickname. She walked away from Mr. Mullins's house and the heart of town. She had never had occasion to stroll, so she walked with the same speed and determination as always. John Musick had no trouble keeping pace. He walked close beside her. *Close enough to brush hands,* Willie thought. She crossed her arms over her chest, which slowed her pace. John removed his coat and handed it to her. She tried to refuse, but he insisted. The warmth of his coat melted her insides. Or was it his smell, wrapped around her?

Willie knew it was risky for them to be out together. If they were noticed, the darkness would shift from her ally to her accuser. The thrill of adventure emboldened her, and she took John Musick's hand. His fingers were colder than her own. Maybe that's why he didn't let go.

She was about to speak when John stopped and put a finger to his lips to signal silence. Another shiver, unrelated to the weather, came over Willie. She heard the Howler.

Competing fears struck her at once—the possible threat of the Howler and the certain peril of Aunt Xenia getting up with her shotgun. Like the darkness that hid them, John Musick would be her defender or her indictment, depending on which danger presented itself.

"Come with me." John said in a low voice. She expected him to take her back to her aunt's house, back to safety. He led her by the hand toward the Howler's sounds.

Willie couldn't believe what she saw when they turned the corner. At first, she thought it was an odd-shaped shrub in the middle of Gussie McCormick's garden. When it moved, she decided it was an animal. As they stepped closer, she realized that it was Andrew Cash on his knees with his back arched. His muddy hands covered his head as he extended his face toward the sky and let out another mournful wail.

Willie remembered then that the only time she'd heard the sound for herself she wasn't sure whether it was a song or a cry. Townsfolk always talked as though it was an animal, so it was all she'd been able to hear. Now she saw the truth. There was no animal intent on destruction; here was a tortured soul.

John let go of her hand and stepped toward Andrew. As he walked, Willie watched his posture change. He stood taller, straighter, and he put out his chest.

"Private!" John said. His voice was not a yell, but it was full of authority. Andrew stopped his wailing. His arms remained up. "Private!" he said again.

Andrew looked at him. His left arm dropped to his side and his right hand went into a salute as he stumbled to his feet. Willie couldn't make sense of anything she was watching.

"Second line's here. Time to clear out."

John turned and walked toward Willie, and Andrew followed him, marching right past as though he couldn't see her. She stood frozen for a beat, then fell in line behind Andrew, having no idea where John was leading them. She knew that Andrew and his wife, Violet, lived with Andrew's parents, next to the filling station, but John was taking them in the opposite direction.

The two men looked like little boys playing a game of army.

They walked and crawled in formation. Willie did too, though she couldn't say why. It was clear that John was keeping Andrew in the shadows.

Willie realized they'd circled back to Mr. Mullins's yard. John turned around. He placed his hands on Andrew's shoulders and looked him in the eyes, searching for something, though Willie couldn't imagine what. He put a hand on either side of Andrew's face and leaned in closer.

"Andrew?" he said. Andrew did not respond. John gave the young man's cheek a slap, and Willie flinched. "Andrew?" John said again. Still no response. From the window, Willie saw the light of a lamp coming toward Mr. Mullins's door.

"John, Mr. Mullins," she said. John pulled Andrew to the ground with him. Andrew emitted a guttural sound, and John's clapped his hand over his mouth.

"We need to get him into your aunt's house."

"What? She'll be at the door with the gun. There's no way we'd get in without getting caught."

"I know. But we have to get Andrew inside."

Aware that she didn't have any better ideas, Willie followed the two men as they crouched in a low run through the neighbor's yard and up the steps to her aunt's front door.

As odd as it felt to do so, Willie knocked softly. Aunt Xenia opened the door immediately. Her expression followed her attempts to understand what was happening. She narrowed her eyes in confusion, widened them in castigation when she saw Willie, then narrowed them once more as she recognized Andrew, crouched on her porch.

"I'm sorry to intrude, Mrs. Webb. But my friend needs a place to clean up before he goes home."

"Have you all been to the billiards?" Aunt Xenia asked. Her eyes took in the men's dusty shirts and khakis. "Willie, were you out with them?" Willie hadn't considered her own appearance until that moment, and resisted the urge to dust off her blouse and skirt.

"Yes, ma'am," John said before Willie could answer or offer explanation. "And no, ma'am," he added. "Andrew and I have been playing dominoes. We encountered Miss Tollett outside your house." Willie could see by her aunt's expression that she was skeptical of his half truth.

"I thought I might have left a book outside and came out to fetch it." Willie thought adding a bit more truth might add credibility to the story.

"Clean up and go on to bed," Aunt Xenia said.

"But—" Willie couldn't think of a reasonable argument she could put forward. She didn't understand the situation enough to protest. She looked at John, but he was bent in front of Andrew, holding his friend's face in his hands as she'd seen him do in the garden. As she turned to go inside, she heard Andrew speak for the first time.

"John? Oh, no. It's happened again, hasn't it?" Willie heard him break into a sob as she closed the door.

As Willie undressed for bed, she recalled for the first time that she was still wearing John Musick's coat. Had Aunt Xenia noticed? She laid on the mattress in the sitting room, straining her ears to tune out the crickets and her sisters' breathing so she could listen to the conversation between the men and Aunt Xenia. She couldn't make out what any of them were saying, but she fell asleep trying.

Chapter 32

Willie woke Saturday morning prepared for a reprimand from her aunt and news that she would report Mr. Musick and Andrew Cash's behavior to her father. Instead, Aunt Xenia whistled as she fried up eggs and bacon and went about cleaning the kitchen as though nothing was out of the ordinary. Willie began to wonder whether she'd dreamed the events of the night before.

Edgalea went to the McCormicks, Lois and Jimmie went to Red Sam's, and Gladys and Willie stayed behind to pack their belongings and prepare to return home until mid-January. In the afternoon, they'd take dinner to Edgalea and pick up a few things for their mother at the store. Willie had started to relax when her aunt called her into her bedroom.

"Aunt Xenia—" Willie began before she'd even passed the threshold, but her aunt cut her off and waved her into the room. Then she closed the door.

"Willie, it's important that you don't say a word to anyone about what happened last night. Understand?"

"Yes, ma'am." The truth was, Willie did not understand at all. Her aunt must have seen as much on her face because she went on.

"That young man has enough trouble without the town knowing his business." Willie wondered how much of Andrew's business Aunt Xenia knew. She was also relieved that her aunt wasn't suspicious about her being outside.

"Yes, ma'am," she said again. She started to leave the room, relieved by her aunt's unexpected response to the situation. She was at the doorway when Xenia spoke again.

"And I think it's best you let me return Mr. Musick's coat."

"Yes, ma'am."

As Willie and Gladys walked to the store, the chill in the air felt refreshing compared to the heat of the kitchen conversation. Her heart rate returned to normal until she saw the same lean silhouette in the store window that had startled her the night before.

"Good afternoon, ladies," John Musick said when Willie and Gladys walked in.

"Good afternoon," they said together.

"I'm in the middle of counting flour sacks," Edgalea called from behind the counter. "Get Mother's order put in and I'll be finished."

"Why don't you go look at the thread, and I'll put in the rest of our order," Willie told Gladys. Gladys was all too glad to gaze at the thread selection in its range of thickness and color. Willie met John Musick's gaze and walked to the back of the store. He understood her meaning.

They stood shoulder to shoulder, looking at a wall of hardware. "Are you going to tell me?" Willie whispered. "About Andrew?"

"What do you want to know?"

"What made you tell my aunt that you two had been at the pool hall rather than tell her that he's the Howler."

"Willie, dear, don't call him that." John's voice was gentle, but she detected the sorrow and sincerity in his request. The reprimand stung, but she was moved by his tenderness.

"Sorry," she said. "But why didn't you tell her?"

John turned his body so that he faced the opposite direction, looking now at the shelf of udder salve and antiseptics.

"He doesn't want his family to know. Doesn't want anyone to know. Can't say I blame him. Willie, it's important that you don't tell anyone what you saw last night. Not even your sisters."

"I know. That's what Aunt Xenia told me. But why does he do it?"

John knelt down, as though reaching for something on the bottom shelf. Willie joined him, still facing the opposite wall.

"I saw it happen to men in the trenches. They'd see one too many fellas get their head blown off or spend one too many nights sleeping in their own muck. The mind can't handle it, even if the body survives. They just sort of break on the inside."

Willie turned to look at him, not knowing how to respond. He glanced at her, then turned back to the shelf of chain links.

"I'm sorry. That was too crude."

"It's okay," Willie said. "Sounds like war is a gruesome thing."

"It's hell. And, in Andrew's case, sometimes his mind thinks he's back in France. He lost a close friend when a nearby recruit lit a cigarette. Sniper took his head off. Andrew's mind takes him back there, nothing but darkness and the remains of his buddy on his face.

"Most times I can get him back by calling his name. Other times, I speak to him like a commanding officer. All soldiers know how to obey orders, and the training to obey overrides everything else. Once I can get him to look at me, really see me, the spell breaks. I help him get cleaned up and sneak him home. Of course, I can only keep an eye out for him when I'm in town." John returned to standing and moved to Willie's opposite side, examining a collection of nuts and bolts.

"But why would he rather folks think he's a drunkard? Surely Violet would want to know the truth. Maybe she could help him."

"It's hard to understand if you weren't there. There's no scar, no limp, nothing to show for the suffering you endured. Only the shame of being broken."

"You could explain it to her, like you are now. She would understand."

"I'm sure she'd try. But eventually she'd want him to get better, and when he didn't, she'd grow impatient and bitter. I've heard it happening to plenty of the boys. And no parents want to know their daughter is married to a crazy man. The Howler, was it?"

Willie was flooded with shame. John leaned toward her, bumping her arm with his elbow. He wasn't mad. He was only making his point.

"So, what's he going to do? Can he get better?" she asked.

"I don't know," John said. He walked a few steps past her and took a hammer off the wall as though giving it a closer look.

Willie didn't want to press this conversation any further. Not in person anyway. She closed the gap between them and picked up a tin of wound ointment.

"Aunt Xenia said she'd return your coat."

"I wondered about that," John said. "What else did she say about it?"

"Nothing," Willie said. "Yet."

"Would you like me to talk to her?"

"No!"

"I'll have to say something when I get the coat."

"How about 'thank you'?" From the corner of her own eye, Willie saw crow's feet gather in the corner of his. She imagined the way his eyes danced when he found something amusing.

"I'll start there and see how it goes," John said. "I think Gladys is ready for you. Better get your shopping done."

Willie wanted to say more, but John was right. Gladys was finished with the thread, and Edgalea was ready for dinner. John took her hand and squeezed it.

"It'll all work out," he said. She wasn't sure whether he was referring to Andrew or their nighttime walk. And she didn't know which one should concern her most. All she knew was that she couldn't wait until the next time he might take her hand.

Willie watched him leave as Edgalea called out, "Goodbye, Mr. Musick! You should have worn a coat!" As Willie ate her cold chicken and biscuits with her sisters, she savored the taste of something finally happening.

That night, as the women of Railroad Street made their way to bed, Willie approached Lois. "Didn't you say you'd read Zane Grey's serials in your *Ladies' Home Journal*?"

"Yes, several."

"There was one in particular. About a woman engaged to a man who'd come back from the Great War?"

"Oh sure. They can start to run together, but I remember that one."

"Would you mind if I read it?"

"Can't get enough, huh?"

"Guess so. Do you remember which issue it was in?"

"Oh, I haven't the slightest," Lois said, "but you're welcome to go through them."

"Thank you."

Willie knew that it was too late to begin rummaging through stacks of magazines, but she was anxious to see what Zane Grey had to say on the matter of men's lives after the war, and she preferred not to answer any of her cousins' or sisters' questions about her motives.

She laid on the mattress and waited for her sisters to fall asleep. Then she slipped out of the blankets, wrapped her robe around her shoulders, and carried the heavy basket of magazines to the kitchen table. Her cousin had first mentioned the stories in October, and she spoke as though it had already been a while since she'd read the story. So Willie started with June 1923 and went issue by issue, checking the table of contents for anything written by Zane Grey. She found *The Vanishing American*, but a quick scan told her it was not the story she was looking for.

As her fingers grew numb with cold, she struggled to turn the pages. She was about to give up her search for the night when finally, in the February 1922 issue, she found the last segment of a serial called *The Call of the Canyon.* Even from the final paragraphs, she knew this was the one she needed. She pulled out the four issues the story spanned and straightened them into a neat stack. These would become her at-home reading, she decided.

Chapter 33

By the end of December, work on the farm was limited to feeding the livestock and making sure their water didn't freeze over. The shoots of winter wheat would lie fallow through February. The cellar shelves were stocked with the fall harvest of meat and vegetables. Shorter daylight hours forced the family inside together more often, mostly in the kitchen, even when they weren't cooking or cleaning. The stove was the only source of heat in the house, and Mother kept a lamp at each end of the kitchen table. Willie worried it would be a long winter.

Father sat at one end of the table with his Bible opened while Thurston whittled the stalk of a yucca plant at the table's other end. The girls filled the seats in between and worked on Christmas gifts for each other. They'd given up trying to be secretive about their gifts. Looking around the kitchen, everyone could see that they would receive a scarf from Ella Bea, socks from Gladys, a hat from Willie, and gloves from Edgalea. Mother was the only one who kept her gifts a secret.

The children only ever saw her work on mending their clothes, but they knew that on Christmas morning she would produce handwork that must have taken months to complete in secret.

Willie appreciated her issues of the *Ladies' Home Journal*, which she read any time she wasn't crocheting hats. Though excited to read *Wildfire*, she believed *Call of the Canyon* held answers, not only to Andrew's troubles, but to John Musick's heart as well. Besides that, *Wildfire* would be harder to explain to everyone.

Willie resumed the jobs that Thurston did when she was in town for school, determined not to let him prove himself more valuable than she was. She needn't have worried. He was happy to stay inside while one sister did his chores and another cooked his breakfast.

Working in the milk barn a week after school dismissed, Willie heard someone approaching. Then she smelled the Camel cigarette.

"I hoped it would be you," Willie said.

"I was about to say the same. Though I do enjoy morning talks with your brother. He's not as lazy as you all make him out to be. I think he has different ambitions is all."

"Well, that suits me fine. As long as I get my piece of land come spring, he can have whatever ambitions he wants."

John examined the tack hanging on the walls.

"You haven't left any notes since you came back," he said without looking at her.

Willie chewed on her bottom lip. She hadn't started *Wildfire* or decided whether to tell him about reading *Call of the Canyon.*

John spoke again. "I'm sorry about what happened in town. I shouldn't have taken that walk with you."

"Is that why you think I haven't written?" she asked. "No one's said a word about it. I've been busy, that's all."

"Still, I should have thought about—I forget that you're so young."

Willie redirected the conversation. "I see you got your coat," she said.

"Yes, your aunt found me at the post office. She was gracious, as always."

"No trouble?"

"No."

"Did she say anything about—anything?"

"She asked after Andrew. But nothing about you."

"That's good," Willie said.

"Better get back to work," John said.

"I'll write this week," Willie said.

"If you want to," John said, "I'd like that."

JHM,

I'm sorry I didn't write sooner. Truth is, I haven't been reading Wildfire*, so I didn't know how to start a letter. Other truth is, I've been reading a Zane Grey from* Ladies' Home Journal. Call of the Canyon. *It's about a New York City woman whose intended goes*

West because he's not right after coming home from the war. I hope you're not sore. I didn't intend to keep it a secret, exactly. Only, I didn't want you to think I was snooping into AC's business.

More truth? I feel like I'm snooping into your business, too. I know you don't like to talk about it, but I know the war hurt you, too. I want to know what brings the shadows under your eyes and why you sometimes retreat even when you're standing right next to me. Suppose I want to know how to pull you back from wherever it is you go. Like you do for Andrew.

I'm not sorry exactly. I think I understand better, and going back, I'd do it again. Can I still ask forgiveness?

Truly, Willie

Miss Willie,
There's no need for forgiveness, but if it's what you'd like, I'll happily give it. I'm not sore. I'm glad you told me. You're a sharp girl—I should have known I couldn't fool you into believing I didn't have my own troubles. Not like Andrew's, but none of us ever really escape the trenches. It's a lonesome feeling. Less lonesome when I'm with you.

Wonder how long it will be before Call of the Canyon*'s printed as a book. Might be hard for me to carry* Ladies' Home Journal*!*

Kindly, JHM

By Christmas Eve, everyone had completed their gifts and tucked them into drawers, under mattresses, and behind crates for the night. Father read from Isaiah and the Gospel of Luke and lead them in hymns and carols. At the children's urging, he also told stories of his Tennessee childhood.

"Tell us one of your stories, Mother," Ella Bea said.

"No, sing us one of your songs," Thurston said. The two youngest had been arguing all day.

"Why don't I tell you a story and then sing you a song?" Mother suggested. The children nodded in agreement. They were all intrigued by Mother's stories of her family in North Carolina. The trees and rivers of her childhood captured their imaginations as much as her family's chants and songs.

"Back home, there was an order that all the Cherokee people had to give up their homes and go West."

The word "West" hit Willie like a punch in the gut. In all Zane Grey's writing, the West was what saved people. It restored their spirits, brought them to life. This was the first time she'd understood the West as a death sentence.

"My great-grandmother was allowed to stay in North Carolina because she had married my great-grandfather, who looked White enough, but that winter many others were forced to go. They weren't given time to pack and left with nothing but the clothes they were wearing. She never heard from many of her friends and family members and learned later that many of them died of cold and starvation. She never recovered from the heartbreak of it all. Her life had been spared, but she died of heartsickness only a few years later, when my grandmother was only four years old."

"That's terrible," said Gladys.

"Do you have another story?" asked Thurston.

"That's not the end of the story," Mother said. She continued, "When she knew her time was coming to an end, she gave her bead necklace to her mother with instructions that it be split between her young daughters so that they would always remember where they came from and what had been lost.

"My grandmother gave each of her daughters a portion of the strand when they married, and my mother did the same. When your time comes to get married, you'll have the strand for your wedding."

Everyone looked at the floor to avoid looking at their eldest sister. Mother did not look away. "Edgalea, your time will come. The beads are not a prize for getting married. They're a reminder of how mothers, daughters, and sisters care for each other, wherever life takes us."

"Yes, and if the boys around here are too dumb to realize what a catch you are, I'd say you're all the better for it," Willie added.

"Yes, I agree," said Gladys.

"But Mother," Ella Bea said, "if the necklace has already been divided so many times, what will be left for us to give our own daughters?"

"If you have daughters, I reckon you can decide for yourself. You can split the beads again or they can take turns wearing your strand."

"What about me?" Thurston asked. "What do I get?"

“Everything else,” Willie said. No one argued.

“It’s getting late,” Mother said.

“What about the song?” Ella Bea asked.

“One song,” Father said. Mother began her song in a language they’d never spoken and had mostly forgotten. Father joined in, humming a baritone harmony. The words meant nothing to Willie, but the sound stirred her emotions, nonetheless. The minor key matched the bittersweet tone of Mother’s story.

As Willie listened, she thought of Andrew Cash. She wondered if his howling was a song for his friend. Maybe this was his way of remembering where he’d been and what he’d lost.

Chapter 34

On Christmas morning, the family gathered in the kitchen at sunrise for hot cider. Willie had hardly slept. She'd received a folded letter from John Musick two days before with a note on the outside, *"Do not open until Christmas."* It was silly, she knew, and he'd never know if she cheated, but she liked the thrill of suspense and the fun of the surprise. She reached under her pillowcase at the same time that Ella Bea sat up with a jolt. "Merry Christmas!" she squealed.

Unlike every other morning of the year, the girls came to the kitchen in their nightgowns and robes. Thurston came out in nothing but his long underwear; however, Mother told him he'd catch his death of cold and made him get dressed. Father passed out stockings filled with oranges, nuts, and hard candy. Thurston popped the candy into his mouth and bit down, earning a glare from Ella Bea. Edgalea and Gladys shared an orange and passed the peels to Willie, who liked to scrape the pith and zest with her front teeth.

Aunt Chloe arrived just as Mother took biscuits out of the oven. "Looks like I got here right on time," she said. She pulled a jar out of her bag. "I've been saving this honey since the fall. Made a potato trade with a man from Texas."

Next, she pulled out five wrapped packages. Willie knew not to expect much. Despite the fact that Aunt Chloe owned a successful store and had no one to care for but herself, she was not one for frivolous gift-giving. Still, Willie was aware that her aunt did not share gifts with any of her cousins, so she tried to be grateful. The packages were stacked in the sitting room next to the ones her parents had put out during the night.

"Can we open our gifts before we eat?" Ella Bea asked.

"No! I'm too hungry to wait!" Thurston said. He loved gifts, but he loved nothing more than mealtime.

"We'll eat first," Mother said.

After they ate and washed the stickiness from their fingers, the girls cleared the table, and Father brought the gifts from the sitting room into the warm kitchen. Each of the children ducked into corners of their rooms to retrieve their gifts from the drawers, mattresses, nooks, and cabinets where they'd kept them hidden. The fact that they knew what they were getting did not diminish the joy of expectation.

They began with Edgalea's gloves, Willie's hats, Gladys's socks, and Ella Bea's scarves. Next, they all opened the small wooden figures Thurston had whittled for each of them. He was frustrated that he had to identify the shapes for them, but their effusive thanks lifted his spirit.

When the children finished their exchanges, Father invited Aunt Chloe to share her packages. There was no mystery to the size and shape of the newsprint wrapping. Clearly, she'd brought them all books. Ella Bea groaned audibly, earning a disapproving look from the adults. Thurston surprised everyone by tearing into his gift with enthusiasm.

"Now I can carry a book under my arm like John Musick does!" Willie felt heat rising in her cheeks for reasons she didn't want to explain. She kept her eyes on the gift in her hands and wondered what expression her father's face wore.

"Don't get carried away," he said. "It is not my intention to instill laziness in my son." Thurston took the wrapping off his package.

"Oh. The New Testament." Thurston said, not masking his disappointment.

"Now that you're beginning to read, it's time for you to have your own copy of the Good Book," Aunt Chloe said.

Edgalea received a book of recipes for dishes they would never eat, and for Ella Bea, a book of etiquette. Willie wondered whether her aunt meant anything by her book selections. Willie opened her package and saw a new copy of *Emily of New Moon*. She recognized the author's name from the *Anne of Green Gables* serial she'd read when she was younger.

"Thank you, Aunt Chloe," Willie said. "I'm sure I'll enjoy it."

"Well, good. Honestly, I'm trying to get rid of the books in the store. People don't buy them, and they're taking up space that could be used for better things."

"Funny, George and Gussie decided to start selling books in their store. Mostly novels though. Wonder how they'll do."

"Hmph," Aunt Chloe responded. Her disapproval, whether at their business acumen or taste in books, was evident.

Sarah gave each of her children a bundle wrapped in calico remnants and tied with twine. Willie opened hers to find a cream-colored collar crocheted with thread so thin she thought she could mend a shirt with it. It was too fine to wear with the dresses she owned. The impracticality of its beauty stirred Willie's emotions. Although she was dumbfounded by the impracticality, receiving such a fine gift made her feel beloved despite herself.

Jim handed Willie a second package. She lifted the bundle and unwrapped it slowly, feeling the family's eyes on her. Inside she found a folded piece of silk the color of coal, a shade that her sisters refused to wear, saying it made their skin look too pale. However, it was the perfect complement for Willie's darker skin and black hair.

It was the finest fabric she'd ever had to work with, the first that wasn't salvaged from flour sacks or someone else's castoffs. It was beautiful.

Willie met her parents' eyes. Her mind had been on Zane Grey, John Musick, and Andrew Cash. She hadn't given any thought to graduation, much less a graduation dress. In their faces, she saw enough pride and love to make her feel both humbled and invincible. Having two daughters graduate high school was an accomplishment her parents would take pride in.

As soon as they'd all unwrapped their gifts, Willie slipped away to the bedroom, saying she better get dressed and get her chores done. She sat on the bed and hugged her pillow to her chest, relishing another moment of anticipation. Then, in a sudden rush, she slid John's note out and unfolded it.

Dear Willie,
Merry Christmas! I'm not good with words, so I'll borrow from our friend Zane Grey. I know you felt a kinship to Madeline Hammond, so I hope you'll forgive me for taking liberties with her sentiments.

When I met you, Willie, "I became conscious of faint, unmistakable awakening of long-dead feelings—enthusiasm and delight. When I realized that I experienced an inward joy. And I divined then, though I did not know why, that henceforth there was to be something new in my life, something I had never felt before, something good for my soul in the commonplace, the natural, and the wild."

Your friendship has been the surprise of my life.

Kindly yours, John

Chapter 35

The family put on their Sunday best to attend the Christmas service and dinner at the Inez Church. Of course, they also had new hats, gloves, and scarves to display. Even Willie decided against her everyday dress.

"Willie, you look so nice!" Gladys said.

"I wanted to wear Mother's lace."

"I think you look fine," Father said. "So much like you mother at this age."

"Careful or the boys might take notice," Mother said with a wink.

Everyone endured the Christmas service, enjoying some readings and hymns more than others, but the potluck that followed was the highlight of the holiday. The meal was an unspoken competition between the ladies of the congregation, and it was the one day each year that Mother attended the service with her head held high. No one could match the flavor of her smoked pork, the flakiness of her pie crust, or the balance of sweet and sour in her plum pie filling. The men, Jim Tollett included, claimed bragging rights any time their wife's dish was superior to the other wives'. Willie found it interesting that even in this, the men managed to take credit for the women's work.

Brother Greathouse led them in a blessing to close out the service and bless the meal. Then he solicited help from the men to arrange the room for the Christmas Tree Social while the ladies arranged their dishes.

Willie brought out the cast iron pot with the lid down tight to keep the pork from drying out, but Mother didn't allow anyone else to handle her plum pies. She had picked the tart sandhill fruits in June and combined them with the sweeter crop from the orchard three weeks later. The result was a tangy combination that couldn't be beat. As soon as she finished the canning, Mother would select the best-looking jars and set them apart in the cellar to only be taken out for the Christmas dinner at church. She gave other jars as gifts throughout the year or bartered them for other goods and services. After her summer accident, she'd sent Willie with two jars for Doc and Mrs. Burton.

Willie turned to see John Musick, wearing a blue shirt she'd never seen and brown britches cinched tight with a belt, sitting in one of the pews against the wall, and she was glad she'd worn a nice dress. She felt dizzy at the collision of her worlds. Strangely, she believed that the one that existed with John in the pages of their letters and Zane Grey's novels was the truest. John knew and understood Willie's dreams and fears better than anyone. In fact, although most of the people in this room had known her all her life, they would be shocked to know what thoughts occupied her mind. Her heart fluttered as she recalled the words of his Christmas letter.

When all the people in higher pecking order had filled their plates, Willie started toward the food line. She noticed that John hadn't served himself when the other men his age did. She was surprised when he joined her in the line. She warmed at his nearness.

Willie could match every dish on the table to its cook. John put his hand on the serving spoon stuck in Mrs. Burton's pie pan.

"I wouldn't," she said quietly.

Willie had known Mrs. Burton would save the jars of Sarah Tollett's plum pie filling for the Christmas potluck. That's why Willie had tampered with the jars before she delivered them.

"Why?" he asked. Willie didn't say more, but she shook her head, so he shrugged and put down the spoon. Her gaze lingered on his hand.

When Willie reached the end of the line, Joyce waved and pointed to an empty seat she'd saved at their table. Willie smiled at John as she carried her plate toward her friends. She hated leaving him. She was certain he had friends, but she doubted any of them were in this crowd. She thought of his note about being lonely.

"Did you hear about the plum pie Mrs. Burton brought?" asked May Bell as soon as Willie sat down.

"Her plums must have turned," said Joyce. "Or her jars didn't seal?"

"I don't know, but anyone who missed out on your mother's pie and took hers instead got the sore end of that!" May Bell said.

"It's too bad," said Willie. "I guess she'll have to be more careful next time."

Willie and her friends shared news of their respective Christmas gifts and caught up on the gossip they'd heard from their parents since school let out. They admired the heart-shaped charm necklace Bill had given Joyce. May Bell showed off her dropped waist dress that was very fashionable but Willie thought impractical for winter.

"Who are you looking for?" May Bell asked.

"What?" said Willie. "I'm not looking for anyone."

"Yes, you are. You keep looking over your shoulder like you're checking to see if someone is there."

Willie looked back again and saw John Musick walk out the door.

"I'll be back in a bit," she said. She grabbed her coat and went outside.

Willie found John leaning against the north wall of the building, smoking a cigarette, just like the first night they'd met. Could it have only been a few months ago? She was glad she'd made a show of putting her new gloves and hat in her coat pockets. She pulled them out now and put them on.

"Let me try that again," Willie said, holding out her hand.

"Are you sure?" he asked. She reached for the cigarette and put it to her lips.

"Breathe in, but not too deeply. Hold it a beat then breathe out." She tried to follow his instructions but ended up coughing as soon as she started to inhale. Unlike their spring encounter, John's laughter set her at ease, and she laughed too.

"I'm glad you came," she said.

"It's Christmas," he said. "Not the sort of day you want to spend alone. Your father invited me to come out, so here I am."

"Is that the only reason?"

John looked at his feet then met Willie's eyes. "You know it's not."

"You could have ridden over with us."

"I don't think that would have been a good idea."

"It wouldn't have been a problem." He looked at her, and Willie felt electricity in the space between them, the way the air crackles during a thunderstorm.

"Well, maybe a little," she said.

"Did you all have a good morning?"

In answer, Willie held out her gloved hands then pointed to her hat. Finally, she opened the top of her coat to show the lace on her collarbone. "My mother made us these. She must have started last Christmas to get them all finished. Plus, socks and a little wooden calf—or so I was told—from Thurston. And my parents gave me silk for a graduation dress."

"Quite a haul," John said.

"It was." Willie wasn't sure how to respond. No one in their county was wealthy, but she was aware that her family was better off than most. They stood without talking until John finally broke the silence.

"Thanks for the tip on the plum pie. I heard some rumbling about it from the other men."

"You're welcome." Willie smiled.

"The pie hadn't been cut yet. How did you know it wouldn't be good?" John couldn't see the lift of her chin or her sly grin.

"Let's just say a pie is only as good as what you put in it. I had a hunch there was a little something extra in her jar of plums."

"Six months ago?"

"The most satisfying victories take time."

John threw his head back and laughed out loud. She wished she could make him laugh like that all the time.

"You are something else!"

Willie laughed too, all coyness gone.

"Does anyone else know this side of you?"

Willie stopped short. She'd been thinking earlier how much better John knew her compared to her family and friends. Now he'd spoken the thought out loud.

"Mostly they don't," she said, "but some day they will."

Willie could feel their time running out. She decided to say her words in a rush rather than fret over how to put them in writing.

"Thank you for your Christmas letter," she said. "It's the nicest thing anyone's ever said to me. And I feel the same thing about you being my friend. The truth is, I'm not lonely when I'm with you."

John cleared his throat as he dropped his cigarette butt and twisted his toe on it.

"There was more I wanted to say . . ." John's voice trailed off.

Willie held her breath. She wondered if she'd said too much. She wondered if he would take her hand.

He started again. "I know you don't want to be married, and I understand. You have other dreams. But after you finish school and establish your farm and herd, maybe you'll reconsider. I won't ask you to give up anything. I'll do a share of cooking and washing so that so you never feel trapped in the kitchen. I know what it's like to be the hired hand. I don't want that for you. Maybe we could be partners."

For the first time in her life, Willie was speechless. Laughter and tears swelled, but she wouldn't allow either to come out. She felt competing impulses to run away and to fall into his arms. She'd always known exactly what she wanted, and she'd had to fight for it. In this moment, everything she wanted was too much for one lifetime. If only they lived in a Zane Grey Western.

"Please don't answer," John said. He took her hand, and she thought her knees would fail her. "You've told me your dreams. Don't hold it against me that I spoke mine."

"Life is but an empty dream," Willie said with the tone she'd used to recite the Longfellow verse in seventh-grade elocution. She shrugged and forced a half smile as she shook her head.

Then she walked away before the tears rolled down her cheeks. She rejoined her friends, sang the hymns, and washed the dishes. She was silent in the truck, mumbling about Mrs. Burton's pie. When they got home, she stayed outside, saying she needed fresh air. She stood on the front stoop, watching for the hired hand's return, ready to rush inside if she saw him.

In the light of Roosevelt County stars, she allowed herself to admit that she was in love with John Musick. As soon as she acknowledged that truth, she questioned everything else she thought she'd known. She leaned against the closed door, and like Madeline Hammond, wondered who she was now that she was in love. *Was she still Willie Tollett?*

Chapter 36

A bleak January winter settled over Roosevelt County. Fields of native grass ranged from brown to gray, making the soaptree yucca the stand-out feature of the landscape. Cattle huddled together in the pastures, just as their owners nestled under quilts and around cook stoves. A few dustings of snow provided flashes of novelty, but after the holidays, every day felt much like the other. The sisters all looked forward to returning to school.

Willie had her own reasons to be glad. She'd done her best to avoid Mr. Musick since the Christmas social. When she was with him, everything seemed possible. She imagined she could be in love, married even, and still get the other things she wanted from life: purpose and identity beyond a husband. Away from him, she knew it was impossible.

Distance kept her safe. Now that she was going back to school, she was comfortable leaving a note for him under the International Harvester catalog on the dugout porch. She picked up their correspondence as though no time had passed and his Christmas confession never happened. She desired the warmth of his familiarity without the risk of being burned. She'd stepped too close to the fire and recognized her need to be cautious. John seemed to understand her unstated request because he also picked up as before.

January 5

Dear John,
I don't care a lick about school, but I'll be glad to read again. Once I finished Canyon *I was without escape. What a shame it is to be stuck inside and unable to go away into the pages of a book! Mother joked that one of us girls might not survive the winter. She was right. If we'd had to endure another day of Ella Bea's complaining, we would have had a new round of fighting over who got to bury her out back. I don't remember a winter so long! When I get to the house in town, I'll wrap myself in a quilt and enjoy my time in Bostil's Ford!*

What do you hear of Andrew?

Yours truly, Willie

January 5

Dear Willie,
Yes, I can hear the cat fights from the dugout. Ha!

I'm glad to be out of the fray, but the sounds of family give me comfort. The noise of a family is the sort of detail I can imagine. If there's to be a dream for us, the details will sort themselves out.

I'm rereading The Light of Western Stars *after seeing it through your eyes. At times I wondered if you were reading a different book altogether. I'm anxious to hear how you read* Wildfire.

Andrew is doing well, I think in part because of your aunt. She's paid visits to their house and enlisted her widower neighbor to take special interest in him.

Yours kindly, John

January 8

Dear John,

My plans of spending long evenings with Wildfire *have been dashed. Aunt Xenia, no doubt with my mother's urging, has been on me to work on my graduation dress. Working with such fine cloth is both exciting and intimidating. Mistakes are high stakes. I bring it out every night and study the pattern, but I haven't brought myself to cut the pieces yet. Besides, it seems a shame to put so much effort into a dress I'll only wear once. Though I suppose I could wear it again to all the weddings stacking up. Joyce, of course, will be married the same day we graduate.*

May Bell won't be far behind. And then Minnie. She says her fella has proposed, but she's real cagey about details. Ola thinks they'll run off to Fort Worth in the night. Sad to say, but I wonder if he'll run off and forget to take her with him.

I regret to report that we heard Andrew last night. Perhaps the loneliness of winter after the warmth of holidays is to blame. The long nights and shorter daylight hours have everyone feeling blue. And I suppose Aunt Xenia has returned to her everyday life, which doesn't leave as much time for social calls. Funny, when we heard the sound this week, she immediately went out to the porch with her shotgun. I don't know if it's worry over the Howler or on account of me wearing your coat.

Yours truly, Willie

January 8

Dear Willie,

I believe both of your hunches are right. Your aunt keeps watch for Andrew. Whether to keep him on the narrow road or because she knows more than she lets on. Good thing, too. I get the hunch that Andrew's problems will only get worse. The improvement we saw around Christmas has reversed. I'd like to bring him out to work here again, but if he had a spell, your father might not take as kindly to helping a struggling man as his sister does. And it will be weeks still before there's much work to do.

You wrote of your friends' weddings. Is there nothing in marriage that calls to you? I thought women had natural interest in being a wife and mother, things only women can do.

Yours kindly, John

January 10

Dear John,

I hate to admit, but you're right about Father. He sees things in black and white. No gray.

I chose a pattern for my dress and that seems enough to satisfy Aunt Xenia, so I've picked up Wildfire *again. I thought the horse race would happen in the final chapter, but there it was, only halfway through. I don't know what Zane Grey has planned for the second half. Is it normal to see yourself in every book you read? How is it that I felt such kinship to Madeline Hammond and now feel the same toward Lucy Bostil? And those two so different?*

Your thoughts on women and marriage echo those in Call of the Canyon*. They sound right. Why, then, do I find myself resisting the notion? Something in it won't settle.*

Sure there's something in marriage that appeals to me. Something in you that appeals to me. To have endless time together, a friend and partner in work and life. But the more I try to imagine the details, the fuzzier it gets. Like trying to stare at a single star. The only thing I can imagine is the two of us on a sofa, each reading a book. But then how would we get any work done? My farm would go to rot!

Yours truly, Willie

January 12

Dear Willie,

Could it be that Lucy is closest to the girl you are and Madeline closest to the woman you plan to be? I hope it's not too bold for me to say so. Zane Grey has plenty of excitement left for the folks of Bostil's Ford, and not all good. Not for them anyhow. For a story to be good, Zane Grey has to bring folks near to breaking. I'm anxious to read Call of the Canyon. *Maybe my thoughts on marriage are selfish. Could be all men's thoughts on women and marriage are.*

I like to imagine us reading together. More than that, I like to think of you imagining it. I suppose your farm might do well enough that we could hire men to help with the work so we would have time to read.

You didn't mention Andrew. I hope that's good news. I haven't been to town much lately. Roads are too muddy.

Yours kindly, John

January 12

Dear John,
Yes, good news for Andrew. Talk in town is dying down again. We can be glad for the townfolk's short memories.

Slone working for Bostil seems too good to last. A good man winning the trust of the girl's father and becoming his top hand? It appeals to me, but I also liked their secret meetings in the desert. Is it a girl's lot to be squeezed between her father and the next man she loves?

Yours kindly, Willie

January 12

Dear Willie,
I can see how Slone's arrangement might appeal to a girl, but a man will always want to chart his own course and not be beholden to another man. Particularly the father of his sweetheart. At some

point, a girl has to decide whether she's going to stay in her father's house or her husband's.

Yours kindly, John

January 14

Dear John,

There it is again. The choice between her father and a husband. When does a girl get to choose herself? Can't you see why marriage looks like a trap?

You're right, of course. I should have seen the trouble sooner. Such an arrangement could only last so long. Too many secrets and strong feelings living in the same household. It was bound to end in fisticuffs. It's all falling apart in Bostil's Ford!

Yours truly, Willie

January 14

Dear Willie,

I hope you don't think I mean to trap you. I've taken notions of marriage for granted. I've never heard of a woman wanting to choose herself. I can't even imagine what that looks like, though I'm sure you have. Forgive my old habits.

Yours kindly, John

January 15

Dear John,
To bet a woman! The nerve of these men—both of them! And yet, my heart leaps at the revelations tumbling out all in a row. Everything in the open. Time to choose sides and prove where their devotions lay. Such romance! More exciting even than the horse race!

Only trouble now is that I've read too quickly, and the end of another book comes right as I've become good friends with the folks. Again, I worry that I may not become so well acquainted with the next bunch. I'm determined to slow down and make the last pages last! The winter is long. I can't imagine it without the friends Zane Grey brings me.

Yours truly, Willie

January 15

Dear Willie,
Like a good card game. The game is fun, but the height of fun is the moment when all the cards are on the table.

I'm afraid you've read every Zane Grey Western I have. I could loan you a couple of books he wrote about baseball, but I'm afraid you wouldn't find them as interesting. You could do like me and start over at the beginning, reading them all again.

Yours kindly, John

January 17

Dear John,
I'm no good at slowing down. Instead of starting over, I believe I'll retrace my steps. I'd like to read The Light of Western Stars *again if you're finished with it.*

At home last weekend Mother mentioned your birthday is coming soon. I expect she's planning a special dinner for you Saturday. Funny to think of you at our table. It's been so long.

How often I've described this winter as long.

Yours truly, Willie

January 18

Dear Willie,
Your mother was kind to think of it. Can't recall the last time anyone marked my birthday. Being with your family will be a real treat.

Yours kindly, John

Chapter 37

On the morning of the birthday dinner, Mother gave the girls instructions to clean the house with extra vigor. Whether she cared about the hired hand's birthday or only wanted to keep them too busy to bicker, Willie didn't know. They shook out the curtains, swept the floors, and beat the rugs without complaint. Thurston even swept the front stoop without being asked. He may only be the hired hand, but they all had a soft spot for John Musick, and the flurry in the house proved it.

John arrived for dinner wearing the same blue shirt he'd worn to the Christmas social. He greeted each of the Tollett girls, with equal kindness, Willie noted. He bent down to Thurston's eye level and shook his hand. Then he stood straight and shook each of her parents' hands.

"Thank you for going to all this trouble," he said to Jim and Sarah.

"No trouble at all," Jim answered. Willie suspected John had noticed them outside in their coats, shaking curtains and beating rugs on the fence. He'd probably even noticed Thurston holding a broom. Had her father noticed?

They took their seats around the table, Jim and Sarah at each end, Mr. Musick next to Jim, Thurston and Ella Bea on the same side, and Gladys, Edgalea, and Willie on the opposite side. Willie always sat closest to their father. She'd never worried before that this put her directly across from John.

She listened to Father dictate his plans for the spring and to her sisters chatter over town news. Thurston peppered John with questions about spring baseball, which he managed to answer without drawing attention to his chosen pastime. Mother tended to all of the conversations, introducing a subject change if the girls' talk became gossip or the topic might raise her husband's hackles. At the same time, she refilled plates and coffee cups until everyone had their fill.

Through it all, Willie worked to avoid giving John Musick too much attention. Or too little. She tried to hear her voice as those at the table might. *Was she too familiar in her tone with John? Too quick in her responses to Father? Too silly in her talk with her sisters? Did everyone at the table know what was really on her mind?* She hardly tasted her food.

Everyone lingered at the table, picking bits of meat from chicken bones and using biscuits to clean gravy from their plates. With her hands under the table, Willie removed the slip of paper she'd kept tucked in her sleeve.

She'd wanted to give John his birthday gift as soon as she arrived home from Portales on Friday, but she'd resisted running after him. It had been a week since she'd purchased a book for him from the McCormicks' store. In the inside cover, she'd written, *For your birthday, 1924, Yours truly, Willie*, then stuffed it into her pillowcase. She could have left it on the dugout porch this morning, but she wanted to give it to him in person. She recognized the heat spreading from her chest. She was taking risks on several fronts.

Father leaned away from the table with a satisfied sigh. "Better get movin' before we're caught sleepin'." This was the sign Willie had been waiting for. She stood, knocking her chair off balance in her rush. She righted the chair and began gathering plates.

When she reached for John's plate, she nudged his hand where it rested on the table and slid her note underneath it. She stood only for a second to see his hand close around the note and slide to his hip pocket.

"Thank you all," John said as he stood up. Everyone exchanged a round of well wishes, despite the fact that they would spend the rest of the day working in close proximity. Willie didn't dare make eye contact. She wondered how long it would take him to read her words.

> *Meet me in the barn in the first minutes of your birthday. I have something for you.*

Willie had no way to be certain whether or not John would meet her in the barn. At bedtime she kept her stockings on and pulled her nightgown on over her blouse. She shoved her coat and hat under the bed. She crawled under the weight of the quilts, feeling the book inside her pillowcase. She heard her sisters come in minutes later. She tried feigning sleep, but Gladys wasn't fooled.

"Willie, are you feeling all right? Have you taken ill?"

"No, I'm fine. Only tired." She didn't want her sisters to worry as that would only lead to more attention. "I'm already feeling better now that I'm in bed. I'm sure I'll fall asleep as soon as you do." She rolled toward the window and pushed her hand under the pillow so that it rested under the book.

When the other girls were in the bed, she heard Edgalea speak in a hushed voice. "You know, I used to think John Musick was a possibility, but I don't anymore."

"Oh?" Gladys said. Willie didn't answer, but she wondered whether her sisters could hear her heart pounding.

"Yeah. I'm afraid he's been alone too long."

"I know what you mean," said Gladys. "Although he seemed cheerful today."

"I noticed that, too," said Edgalea.

Willie tried to think of a way to respond that would not raise suspicion. Then as too much time passed, their conversation gave way to slow breathing. Her sisters were asleep.

Willie drifted off several times, waking up worried that she'd slept too long. Each time, she held Harold's pocket watch to the moonlight coming through the window. When it read eleven fifty-three, she slipped her legs off the side of the bed, took out the book, and moved her pillow to the place her body had been. She pulled her coat over her nightgown, tucked the book inside, and took a tentative step. She felt her way along the bed to the door. As long as she could get past her sisters, she'd be fine. Her father couldn't hear, even when wide awake, and thanks to the bedtime tea Mother had been drinking since her accident, she wouldn't be disturbed by creaking floorboards.

Willie pulled on her hat and boots and stepped into the cold night. The moon provided just enough light for her to walk the familiar path from the house to the barn.

When she stepped inside, John Musick laughed, and she immediately forgot about the risks she was taking. She knew she would walk right into the fire if it meant hearing his laughter.

"You really came!" he said. "I wondered if I'd been set up!"

"I wouldn't do that!" Willie said. "Well, I might. But not to you. At least, not this time."

"You know your father will fire me if he finds us meeting in the middle of the night." He took a long drag on his cigarette.

"He won't," Willie said. "He'll shoot you."

"Yes, and some birthday that would be."

"Oh, that's right!" In her excitement at seeing him, she'd almost forgotten the reason for the occasion. "Happy birthday!"

"Thank you. I can't imagine a better way to begin the year."

"I have something for you," Willie said.

"Yes, so you said."

She reached into her coat. "I didn't have time to wrap it. You'll have to close your eyes so it can be a surprise."

"No live animals?"

"Promise."

John closed his eyes. Willie took his hands, wishing he wasn't wearing gloves so she could feel his skin on hers. She wrapped his fingers around the book. She let her fingers linger a moment then forced herself to let go and take a step back.

"Now you can open them." He held *Wanderer of the Wasteland* toward the moonlight coming through the barn door and ran his fingers over the glossy dust jacket.

"A new Zane Grey," he said.

"The newest," Willie said. "One we've never read before, so I can't guarantee that the good guys will win," she said. His laughter came again.

"I don't remember the last time I got a birthday gift," he said. His eyes were both sad and bright. "I don't know how to thank you."

Willie took a step, closing the space between them. Closer to the risk. Close enough to get burned. John did not move way.

Willie looked up and held his gaze. She feared that he might kiss her. The silliness of her classmates' conversations about boys always referred to the feelings in their hearts. No one ever mentioned the churning she felt in her stomach now. It was like jumping off the hay barn into the hay. Something you knew was foolish but would do again in a heartbeat.

The moment expanded to eternity, and Willie couldn't stand it any longer. She placed a hand on John's shoulder, raised up on tiptoes, and pressed her lips to his. She felt his hands go to her waist as his mouth answered hers.

Then, quite before she was ready, he pushed her away and took a step back. His eyes were wide with fright.

"I'm sorry," he said.

"I'm not," she answered. Her usual bluster was gone, but not her assuredness in what she wanted.

"I shouldn't have done that. You need to go." Stunned by the turn of events, Willie almost did as she was told. Almost. Instead, she closed the gap as before, put a hand behind his neck, and pulled him into another kiss.

Before he could apologize again, she released him and hurried to the house. Before she opened the front door, she stopped and looked back toward the darkness of the barn. She would not be satisfied with only one dream in her life. She thought of Madeline Hammond and one of the lines that had first stirred her spirit. "*I hope I have found myself—my work, my happiness—here under the light of that western star.*"

Chapter 38

When Willie went out to milk the next morning, she couldn't resist looking in the direction of the dugout. She knew John would already be working, but her eyes were drawn to the place he occupied. She watched the thin line of smoke rising from the chimney and imagined him drinking his first cup of coffee. Had she been his first waking thought the way he had been hers? In the barn, as she sat on her stool and milked, she stared at the place where they'd been only hours before. She felt the sensation of falling again. Was this what love was supposed to feel like?

She remained in her reverie as she carried her buckets of milk into the kitchen.

"Willie, did you see Mr. Musick this morning?" Mother asked. Willie almost dropped the buckets.

"No, ma'am," she said after she recovered herself.

"Your father needs to speak to him this morning."

"What about?" Willie asked. Surely there was no way her father could know about last night. She considered her comment last night about him shooting John Musick. Surely, he wouldn't. But she knew that he would.

"Something about the Belchers' mules."

Willie sighed in relief.

"Are you feeling well?" Mother asked. "Gladys thought you might be coming down with something. Your cheeks do look flushed."

"I'm fine. Going from cold to warm is all. It's awfully warm in here, isn't it? I better get changed for church."

The Tollett family had followed the same routine as every Sunday Willie could remember. For Willie though, there was nothing routine about it. Her entire life had changed overnight. Sunday school, the sermon, her sisters' talk on the way to and from church faded into the background. Everything before last night was like a monochromatic brown cloth cover. She imagined her future like a full-color jacket.

She hardly noticed her father's animated talk of Tuesday's vote over the billiard hall. It had mattered in the *before*. Now, she was only glad the issue was coming to an end. By next week, the matter would be settled, and she wouldn't have to hear any more about it.

When the time finally came for them to make the drive to Portales, Willie got out of the house before her sisters so that she could run to the dugout. She smiled at the sight of a book under the weathered International Harvester. John had returned *Wildfire*. And he'd included a note. She placed a slip of paper between the catalog and rock and hoped he would notice it. She imagined his expressions as he read it.

Dear John,
I hope you didn't mean it when you said you were sorry. I meant it when I said I wasn't. Lucy never regretted meeting Slone at the bench in the Cottonwoods.
Yours truly, Willie

She was eager to know what he'd written, but she tucked the book in her satchel. Her delay was due in equal parts to fear and hopeful anticipation. Supper dragged on until she worried that she would never know what he'd said. She hurried through her cleaning and at last took her seat on the sofa and opened the book. Edgalea was the next to come in the room, and she interrupted her before she could read John's note.

"What are you up to?" Edgalea asked.

"I'm reading."

"You've had a dodgy look about you all day. Tell me what you're up to."

"I'm not up to anything."

"Where did you go last night?"

Startled, Willie dropped her book with a thud that echoed on the wooden floor. Edgalea knew more than she'd let on and would play it to her advantage. Willie knew she needed to keep her cool, despite the heat radiating from her chest. "I had a dream that something happened to the steers, and I needed to check on them or I wouldn't be able to sleep again."

Willie reached for the book, but Edgalea snatched it first and thumbed through it. More heat. "Didn't you already read this one?"

"Yes, but I really liked it, so I'm reading it again." Willie assumed no one was paying attention to what she read. What else had her sisters noticed?

Edgalea turned the book over in her hands as though it might have a latch that would unlock all her sister's secrets.

"Fine. Enjoy your book," Edgalea said, handing it to Willie. "I'm going to work on my table runner."

Willie opened the book, but there was no way she could read. She waited until the room was full and Edgalea was distracted by conversation and her handwork. Then she leaned over the side of the chair and felt around the floor. Without even knowing what John's note said, she knew she was lucky it had fallen out when she dropped the book. Her fingers finally brushed against the slip of paper. She picked it up and unfolded it over the open pages of the book.

Dearest Willie,

I've written many letters of regret and apology and

thrown them into the fire. I should regret what I did, but I don't. I would do it again a hundred times over. I didn't die in the war, but I haven't felt this alive since I got home. And still, I'm sorry. I don't mean to disrespect your family. I promise it won't happen again. That is, unless you'll reconsider the offer I made on Christmas. It stands as long as you need.

Kindly yours, John

Chapter 39

Willie would have liked to spend more time thinking about John and the kiss they shared, but on their next night in Portales, Lois held up her hand, signaling everyone to be quiet. They ceased their reading, stitching, and stories for a few seconds before they heard the unmistakable sound of wailing. Her sisters and cousins scrambled to the windows, but Aunt Xenia told them to sit back down. She took the shotgun from its place above the door and went outside.

Willie couldn't help picturing Andrew somewhere out there reliving the worst minutes of his life. They waited for an hour for something more to happen, but the sound eventually died down and faded completely. Then Aunt Xenia came inside and put the shotgun away without offering any report. She only asked what they were all still doing up. By Friday morning, Willie was desperate for a word from John. She left a note for him under the Sears Roebuck catalog, hoping he would notice.

January 25

Dear John,
We've heard Andrew three nights this week. Aunt Xenia has taken to sitting on the front porch every night. You've probably seen her. I'm afraid he'll be found out soon.

Willie

January 30

Dearest Willie,
I'm coming to town as often as I can. I've seen your aunt sitting outside, even when Andrew is not out. I believe she's keeping watch for him. Not for your protection but his. This cold, gray February brings France to mind. I've no doubt that's the reason for Andrew's recent troubles.

I don't know whether you've got news of the vote in Inez. It didn't pass. The billiard hall will be allowed. Your father's taking it hard.

John

January 31

Dear John,
Things are getting more tense. There's talk now of a citizen patrol to walk the streets at night. You have to figure a way to keep Andrew at home long enough for things to cool down.

I imagine Father is outraged. Righteous living is his highest aim. For everyone.

Willie

February 2

Dearest,
Beyond moving in with Andrew, there's nothing more I can do. He's heard the talk in town, and he's terrified he'll be found out. Fear is probably making him worse. I only hope he doesn't lose hope.

John

February 4

Dearest,
Relay a message to your aunt. There's a group of men planning to flush out "the Howler" Friday night. They'll start at one end of town and spread

out, walking in a line like the wolf hunts up north. They'll beat every bush until they find him. If he is out Saturday night, he'll need friends. I'll be in town.

John

February 5

Dear John,

No need to deliver that message. Word is all over town. The boys at school are amped up like it's the big ball game. What can Aunt Xenia do? I believe you are his only friend and a loyal one, but what do you have planned? Sounds like it could be dangerous. Be careful.

We're all to stay here Friday night and ride home with Father on Saturday. He says "the Howler" is the townspeople's problem, brought on by their own wickedness, but he doesn't want Aunt Xenia and the other girls here by themselves in case the hunt gets out of hand.

Willie

Chapter 40

The ladies of Railroad Street gathered in the sitting room Friday night, but they were not settled. The male intrusion to their routine had them all on edge. Each of the girls tried to attend to her usual evening activities, but Jim Tollett's presence filled every space. He'd ranted through supper over the result of the vote. Willie couldn't remember when she'd seen him so angry. Aunt Xenia, usually impervious to her brother's rants and gloom, convinced him to take a cup of tea in the sitting room, but she couldn't sit still. She paced the straight path from the front door to the back door, looking out the windows at each turn. Willie wondered whether she was more nervous about the Howler, the men hunting him, or the man who insisted on protecting her household. As for herself, Willie was consumed with worry for the man protecting the Howler.

"I'll need to be at Grandpa Sam's early tomorrow, so I'm going on to bed," Jimmie said.

"Yes, I think I'll go on, too," said Lois. Willie knew they were looking for an escape from her father's presence. She wished she could do the same, but she had to see how the night would end.

"Already?" Minnie asked. "Why, it's still early. You'll miss the excitement!" For Minnie, it seemed, excitement trumped discomfort.

Time ticked on without incident until one by one, Ola, Gladys, and Edgalea excused themselves to bed. Jim's head tilted back, and Willie heard him snoring. Minnie looked at him, then stood with a huff and went to the kitchen for a cup of tea. When her cup was empty and Jim was still snoring, she gave up on excitement and walked to the bedroom.

Another hour later, Willie heard scraping sounds outside. She looked at her father to see if he'd heard it, but of course he hadn't. He was still asleep. Aunt Xenia leaned forward in her chair. She looked at Willie and put a finger to her lips. They both sat frozen and straining. Then they heard it again. Willie couldn't be sure, but she thought she also heard men's voices. She looked at Aunt Xenia, who looked at her brother, still sleeping in the chair.

Xenia crept to the front door and slipped out. Willie heard the beginnings of the distinctive wail. She held her breath, willing her father to keep snoring, but he was off the couch and out the door before her next heartbeat. Willie heard a scuffle as she stepped toward the open doorway.

Aunt Xenia went out, but Willie didn't follow for fear she'd be sent to the bedroom. From inside the door, she heard hysterical laughter followed by her father's yelling.

"You! What are you doing here?" Jim Tollett demanded.

"Jim, they're likely out for a walk," Aunt Xenia said. Again, the absurd laughter.

"Hello, Mr. Tollett!" There was an odd quality to John Musick's voice. It reminded Willie of the voices the students used when they were acting out the spring performance. "Me and Andrew were out for a walk. Got to telling stories and got carried away."

"I'm no fool! You're trying to sober up. It was one thing to hear about you playing pool on Saturday nights. I've let it slide because you do good work during the week. Figured your day off was none of my business. But this crosses the line. Here at my sister's doorstep, lurking around this house full of girls. And corrupting one of our best young men. This is what comes of giving the devil a foothold!" Her father's pent-up anger over the vote spilled out in a string of prophetic curses aimed at anyone who was still awake at this hour.

Willie couldn't stay hidden anymore. She stepped outside and saw Andrew's arm draped over John's shoulders, with John supporting his weight. Andrew looked half asleep, as though he was unaware of his surroundings. In contrast, John was making lively gestures and speaking more loudly than necessary. It would be easy to believe the two men were drunk.

"Father—"

Jim didn't take his eyes off of the men as he answered her. "Go inside, Willie. These men won't bother you anymore.

"John, you'll gather your belongings and be off my property by dawn."

"But Father—" Willie said, a bit louder this time.

"Yes, sir," John yelled, looking at Willie as he cut her off. His gray eyes widened with meaning.

He looked back to Jim, but Willie was certain his next words were meant for her. "Say no more. I won't leave anything behind."

Willie saw a group of men coming toward John and Andrew, drawn by the noise. Two of them, Mr. Lancaster and Mr. Carter, waved. As they got closer, Willie saw Bill Carter, Joyce's fiancé, in the group.

"Any trouble, Brother Tollett?" Mr. Lancaster asked.

"None I haven't taken care of myself."

"Not the Howler then?" asked Mr. Carter.

"No, just a couple drunks," Jim answered.

Willie watched as John half-dragged Andrew past the men hunting for the Howler. Her father put his arm around her shoulders. She couldn't hear the words exchanged by the men as their paths crossed, but they sent John away with a quick clap on the back.

Aunt Xenia turned to her brother. "James Ebby Tollett, has it ever crossed your mind that maybe you don't know everything?" Not for the first time, Willie wondered how much her aunt knew.

"Not once," he replied. "I've suspected for weeks that something was out of sorts. I should have acted sooner."

Willie wanted to run after John and make him tell the truth. She wanted to turn to her father and tell him everything she knew. Surely he would have compassion once he knew the full story. But she had seen in John's eyes his commitment to keep

Andrew's secret, no matter the cost. And with her silence in that moment, she agreed that she would too.

She let herself be led into the house, trapped by her father's protective arm. The election had wounded his pride and threatened his sense of order in the world. He was taking control where he could find it.

True to John's word, the dugout was empty before they got home Saturday morning. Willie made an excuse to go near it when she went out, half hoping she'd find a note, but the International Harvester was gone. There was no sign that John Musick had ever been there.

Chapter 41

Willie found it unimaginable that a day could be so ordinary after the events of the night before. Father set about his chores as though nothing of significance had happened in the past week. He asked for her help mending a section of fence while the sun was out, and she had no choice but to follow him into the cold, gray day. It was tedious work, made more challenging by the fact that with her gloves on, she had trouble manipulating the pliers and wire, but without them, her numb fingers fared no better. Father hardly spoke as they worked, though this was not unusual. What was strange was the way he kept looking toward the dugout. Willie wondered whether she'd started it or he had. Either way, John Musick was evidently on both of their minds.

As they ate their ordinary supper, completed their ordinary chores, and endured an ordinary Lord's Day, Willie waited for someone to mention that extraordinary things had happened. Even when Father left them at Aunt Xenia's house, they exchanged simple hellos and no more. Jim did not give his sister advice or instructions, and she did not give him any of her mind. No one said a word about the failed vote, the empty dugout, or the rage steeping in the silence.

Willie didn't know what became of John after he left the Tollett farm, but she was certain he was still in the county. As soon as her father drove away on Sunday evening, she placed a note for him in the pages of the Sears Roebuck.

Dear John,
What's happened to you isn't right. I don't know what there is to be done about it. What will you do? Where will you go?

Truly, Willie

Willie felt a surge of relief when she returned from school to find a new note tucked in pages of the catalog. Everyone's silence was starting to make her feel crazy. She needed reassurance that she hadn't imagined the world coming apart at the seams. She dropped her satchel and picked up the note, not caring anymore who might see her.

Darling,
All will be well. We're lucky Andrew didn't have time to get going fully before your father came out. Andrew and Violet have taken me in but I don't plan to stay long. I can tell Violet's nervous about it all. I'm doing what I can to keep an eye on Andrew without being seen myself. He doesn't need me to tarnish his reputation. When I hear him leave

the house at night, I get him home quick as I can. Working on a better plan.

Yours truly, John

Willie was surprised to notice her tears dripping onto the paper as she shivered on Aunt Xenia's front porch. She's read John's words over and over, but repetition didn't make them any more believable. If he didn't plan to stay with the Cashes long, where would he go? When would she see him again?

The men of Portales planned to sweep the town looking for the Howler again the next Friday, and once again, Jim Tollett came to keep watch over the ladies of Railroad Street. Willie was prepared for another tortuous night, but she didn't have to wait long this time. Right after supper, they heard yelling from down the street. Jim took off toward the high school shouting instructions for the girls to stay inside. Xenia went out to the porch, and after a brief pause, the other girls followed her. Willie imagined she smelled John Musick's cigarette. Then the evening fell quiet again.

"What do you think that was all about?" Ola asked.

"It's too early for the Howler," Jimmie said.

"The posse probably came across Widow Jenkins looking for her cat," Aunt Xenia answered. "Bet they all scared the daylights out of each other."

"Do you think they'll find the Howler tonight?" Gladys asked.

"Men tend to find what they're looking for," Aunt Xenia said. "Or something close enough to satisfy."

"Come on Ola, let's get the dishes done," said Lois.

"Yes. Nothing but foolishness out here," Aunt Xenia said. Everyone followed her inside, but Willie lingered on the porch. She heard a rustle in the junipers before she saw John's silhouette separate from the trees. She wondered if Andrew was nearby. She only hesitated on the porch for a moment before, without care for the consequences, she went to him. She couldn't help it. She wanted to be near him more than she wanted anything else.

As soon as she reached him, he wrapped his arms around her, and she buried her head in his chest.

"You shouldn't be out here," he whispered.

"You shouldn't either. Of all the yards to hide in, you're least welcome in this one."

"I needed to see you."

Willie pulled away then and looked at John's face. The circles under his eyes were even darker than usual. He looked like he hadn't slept in the past week. There was so much she wanted to say that she couldn't say any of it.

Instead, she took his hands and asked, "Is Andrew out?"

"Not yet. Still having supper. Said he might join the posse later." John laughed without humor.

"Where are they?"

"All around. The way I understand it, they're gathering at the four corners of town plus the high school. If they hear something, they'll fan out and move toward it, then close in like a net."

"Quite a plan."

"A good plan, I'm afraid." The words hung in the cold air between them.

"You need to get back in the house, and I need to get back to Andrew," John said, giving her hands a squeeze and then releasing them.

"I know," she said. "But John—"

"I know, darling." He kissed the top of her head. "But you have to go."

She was halfway to the porch steps when the familiar wailing stopped Willie in her tracks. Without thinking, Willie raced back to the juniper. She wrapped her arms around John and held him close. They heard Andrew again, and she released John from the safety of their hiding place.

"Be careful!" she whispered to him. He turned back and locked eyes with her but did not consent to her request. Willie watched him run toward Andrew, then she saw her father coming from the other direction joined by the same group of men they'd seen the week before.

John called out to Andrew, who was howling loudly now. John called his name with the authority of an army officer as Willie had heard him do before. Andrew walked toward John but continued to wail.

Ignoring Andrew, Jim Tollett walked directly to John Musick. "What are you doing here?" he demanded. "Some nerve you have! Lurking around my sister's house again! What's on your mind, fella?"

Instead of responding to the Jim Tollett's questions, John looked at Aunt Xenia, who had come to the porch with her shotgun, and yelled, "Mrs. Webb, I think you better send for Violet!"

Aunt Xenia called inside, repeating the instructions to Ola. She ran down the steps, gave wide berth to the men, and headed down the street. The other ladies of Railroad Street came out onto the porch. As Ola left, more townsmen arrived. Willie recognized many of her classmates. Neighbors came out of their homes, anxious for their chance to see the Howler up close. The widower Mullins stepped from his porch into his yard.

The growing posse surrounded Andrew but were unsure how to approach him. The ones who had seen him as he first appeared as the erect, menacing Howler stepped forward as though to grab him, but he looked anything but dangerous now. He was still wailing, but his shoulders slumped and his head was in his hands. The men who were coming on the scene called to the ones in front to grab him but seemed reluctant to make any move themselves.

Aunt Xenia stepped into her yard, pointed her shotgun to the sky, and pulled the trigger. John used the distraction as an opportunity to place himself between Andrew and the mob. Andrew dropped to his knees, head back, arms in the air, and filled the street with his lonesome sound.

"He's not a threat to anyone!" Aunt Xenia said now that she had their attention. "The young Mrs. Cash will be here soon and shouldn't have to see him like this, surrounded by a pack of wolves."

"Maybe she should!" Joe Carter yelled. "If she doesn't already know she's married to a monster, she should know it now!"

"He's not a monster," John said. "Look at him. He's not hurting anyone. He's the one hurting."

"How do we know you're not in cahoots with him?" Bill Carter asked.

"Yeah, I heard you got him so drunk last week you had to carry him home!" yelled another voice from the crowd.

"Where'd you come from anyway?" demanded William Terry. "Aren't you usually at the pool hall? You sure weren't out with us. Only showed up quick-like with the trouble."

"He came out of the shadows by the house," Jim Tollett said.

"Come on, now! In cahoots for what?" John asked. "This young man is suffering. He was a soldier, remember? One of the boys who went across the world to buy your security. You'll parade in honor of his courage, but can't find it in you to care in his sorrow?"

"We should take him in," Deputy Barker said. He made a move toward Andrew and the other men joined him. Andrew curled up in a ball on the ground with his hands over the back of his head.

"Grab 'em both!" Jim Tollett yelled. "Whatever Musick's got to do with this Howler business, he's certainly a drunkard and a nuisance. I suspect he's got Andrew into this somehow."

Following Brother Tollett's lead, the men who were not occupied with Andrew descended upon John. He didn't resist as men grabbed his arms and forced him to his knees next to Andrew.

Willie knew her silence could no longer protect Andrew. His secret was out. But perhaps speaking up now could save John Musick. She stepped out from the shadow of the juniper tree.

"Willie Josephine!" her father yelled. "What are you doing out here?"

"John is not a drunkard! He only acted that way to try to protect Andrew. He's been trying to help him."

"What do you mean? How do you—" A shadow of understanding came over Jim Tollett's face.

Willie watched her father furrow his brow. Then, his eyebrows raised, and she knew he had guessed why she was outside. He punched John square on his jaw, sending his head back. The men who were holding John let go. They weren't about to let a man take a beating without the chance to defend himself.

John put up his arms to block further blows from Jim Tollett, but he did not fight back. After a whirlwind of unanswered blows, the men who had held John moved in to restrain Jim. Willie ran to John and turned to face her father. Jim dropped his fists, and Willie saw the fury in his eyes.

"How long?" Jim asked through clenched teeth. His words were barely audible. It took Willie a second to realize he'd spoken to her. Then he yelled. "How long?"

"John is a gentleman!" she said. She hated the way her voice cracked.

"A gentleman doesn't lurk in the dark with a child!" he yelled. "The shame you'll bring on us!" The look in her father's eyes made Willie cower. She'd always been his favorite, his righthand man, his pride and joy. The disgust she saw now was unbearable.

Before Willie could answer her father, Violet Cash came through the crowd, holding her skirt and running. Her face was stricken with the knowledge that something terrible had happened without yet knowing what it might be. When she reached the men surrounding Andrew, she looked from one face to another, pleading for an explanation. Getting no answers from them, she pressed into the circle, and they made way for her to pass. She knelt next to her husband running her hands over his chest and back, examining him for injury or explanation as she continued asking questions of the crowd, of Andrew, of anyone who could make sense of what she saw.

Willie observed a moment right out of *The Light of Western Stars*.

"*Quite suddenly the rapid-fire questioning ceased; Andrew choked, was silent a moment, and then burst into tears.*" Violet held him close, as though she could shelter him from the war inside his mind.

While all eyes were on the scene between Andrew and Violet, Willie watched John Musick back away and disappear into the darkness.

She turned back to the couple on the ground. Andrew's pain was reflected in Violet's eyes, but she did not turn away.

Her small frame, wrapped around his body, followed his progression from heaving sobs to quiet whimper. She didn't speak out loud, but Willie recognized that Andrew understood his wife's commitment. She would stand by him.

The bystanders seemed stunned into silence and stillness. He was their hometown soldier, home but not whole.

Aunt Xenia came down from the porch and spoke into the silence. "Which of you is going to tell her? Who wants to tell the story of how you saved the town from this great danger?"

The men who had been so eager to expose a monster backed away from the broken man being held by his young wife. They seemed unsure of what to say or do next. Aunt Xenia walked through the crowd, straight to the couple. She put her arm around Andrew's waist on the opposite side of Violet, and together the women supported the fallen soldier up the steps and into the widow's house.

The men looked at the ground, at each other, and up the street. Folks from the neighborhood began to turn back to their homes.

"We've done what we set out to do, gentlemen," Deputy Barker said. "We found the Howler. Let's all go home now." The group seemed relieved to have their next step provided. They turned and walked away without a word. No one wanted to speak of the scene they'd witnessed. Willie was reminded of watching men walk away from a burial. Sympathy, finality, and above all gratitude that tragedy hadn't struck their own family.

Chapter 42

Jim Tollett had not spoken to or even looked at Willie since he'd yelled at her in Aunt Xenia's yard. He'd brought her home with her sisters, but Willie would not go back to Aunt Xenia's or to Portales High School again. Jim was arranging for her to move in with one of his sisters in Tennessee, where Willie would help care for the family's children to earn her keep in their household. He would take her to meet the train in Amarillo on the first of March.

Sarah had delivered this news to Willie on Saturday night, along with instructions for her to stay home from church. Willie cried herself to sleep while Gladys gently stroked her back. She entered the kitchen Sunday morning after she heard the truck drive away. Mother urged her to eat, but she had no appetite. Her stomach roiled with aching for John, anger at her father, and grief for Andrew and Violet Cash. Above all, she grieved the possibility for a life of her own.

Willie understood, as her mother and sisters must, that moving to Tennessee could remove her from the family's life forever. Their relationships would be limited to letters exchanged a few times a year, assuming her father would allow correspondence. By going to church without Willie, Brother Tollett communicated to the whole community now that no daughter of his would be involved in scandal or corruption. If it also meant that Willie was no longer his daughter, so be it.

She completed her chores then went to the cow lot. In two weeks, her father would send her away from everything she'd known, including the Hereford cattle she'd worked so hard for, thinking they would be hers. A year ago, she'd had it all figured out. Now, she realized, nothing was ever certain. She thought of John and wondered where he was and what he might be doing. If she could only see him again, he could help her see a way through.

Mother came out with a biscuit, encouraging her to eat, but Willie refused.

"He'll come around," Mother told her. "Give him time."

"Two weeks?" Willie asked. Willie was not in the mood for her mother's attempts at reconciliation. She needed time to think.

"He's doing what he thinks best. He only wants to protect you."

Willie didn't answer.

Mother tried again. "You know, this is hard on him, too." Willie knew that it was. Sending her away changed the plans for the future they both had.

"He could stop it," Willie said.

"That's just it. He does everything he can to protect the ones he loves, but sometimes it's out of his control. That's the hardest part."

“Like losing the vote.” Willie said. Mother didn’t answer but Willie knew she was right. “I don’t need his protection,” she went on. “Or his control.”

“He’ll come around,” Mother said again.

How could Willie explain to her mother that “coming around” could not change the last ten months of her life? She no longer believed in her father’s world where everything existed in black or white. She’d seen the vivid colors of Zane Grey’s West. It might be fiction, but it rang truer to her than anything else.

At her mother’s suggestion, Willie stayed in the bedroom during dinner. She pulled *Wildfire* from her satchel and reread her favorite passages. Suddenly, an idea struck her. Her father might have given up on her, but she wasn’t giving up on herself.

That afternoon, Willie stood on the front stoop and watched Edgalea and Gladys load the truck.

After Gladys put her bag in the truck, she returned to Willie and held out her arms. As they embraced, Willie spoke into her sister’s shoulder.

“Glad, I need you do something for me.”

Gladys pulled away and looked at Willie. “What is it?”

Willie pulled her close again. “I still have this book of John’s—Mr. Musick’s,” she said. She took the book from her waistband and tucked it into the back of Gladys’s as she hugged her. “I’d feel terrible not returning it. Could you deliver it for me?”

“I don’t know, Willie. When would I even see him?”

“Leave it on Aunt Xenia’s front porch, under the Sears Roebuck catalog. He’ll find it.”

"I see," Gladys said. Then she let go.

"Thank you," Willie said. She could only hope her sister didn't get curious enough to notice the dogeared corner of a page in the book.

Come next Thursday before dawn to the bench in the cottonwoods. I'll meet you there. My heart is breaking. It's a lie—a lie what they say. Oh, come! I will stick with you. I will run off with you. I love you!

"I can only assume he means it to be a gift," Gladys said when she returned *Wildfire* to Willie on Friday night. "The book was gone when I got home from school on Monday afternoon, but it was there again this afternoon."

Willie was grateful for her sister's lack of curiosity and acceptance of the most innocent explanation, but she was confident the book was more than a gift. She tucked it under her coat and turned as though rushing to finish her chores.

As soon as she got to the other side of the barn, she ducked out of sight. Her fingers trembled, though not from cold. As she'd expected, there was a folded sheet of paper tucked in the pages of *Wildfire*. When Willie unfolded it, she was surprised to find it blank. In her initial haste, she'd missed a charcoal circle around a portion of the page and the line John had underlined.

Have you ever been so madly in love with a man that you could not live without him?

And Slone could not but know, too, looking at her; and the sweetness, the eloquence, the noble abandon of her avowal sounded to the depths of him. His dread, his resignation, his shame, all sped forever in the deep, full breath of relief with which he cast off that burden. He tasted the nectar of happiness, the first time in his life. He lifted his head—never, he knew, to lower it again. He would be true to what she had made him.

In the margin, so small she almost missed it, he'd written, *We'll need a witness.*

Willie's legs could no longer hold her upright. She crumpled against the side of the barn and slid to the ground, holding the book to her heart. She laughed and cried in turn. Anyone walking by would have thought she'd lost her mind. She read the passage again and again, letting its meaning sink it. They'd never need to write in secret again. On Friday, she would be Mrs. John Musick.

Two days later, on the last Sunday of February, Willie watched Edgalea and Gladys loading the truck again. They didn't know that when they finished their week in town, she would be a married woman.

Her mother came outside and stood beside her. "My girls," she said, and Willie could see the unspoken grief in the lines around her eyes. She took her mother's hand, and they both cried in silence as they kept their eyes on the older girls as they loaded their bags. When the door opened behind them, Sarah dropped her hand and went inside as Jim Tollett stepped out.

He passed Willie and walked to the truck without a word, then Edgalea and Gladys ran back to her. They took in her tear-streaked face, and Gladys wrapped her arms around her. In that moment, she was tempted to share her secret, but the stakes were too high. They'd know soon enough.

"Willie?" Gladys said into her ear.

"Yes?"

"I'll always be there when you need me."

"I know, Glad."

Edgalea stepped forward then wrapped them both in her arms. "We'll see you soon, Willie," she said. "We'll have one last night together."

A blast of the truck's horn cut through the air, jarring them out of the intimacy and intensity of the moment. Knowing better than to test their father's patience any further, Edgalea and Gladys turned and hurried to the truck. There would have been room for both of them in the cab, but they huddled close under a quilt in the back instead.

Only after the truck was lost in a cloud of dust did she consider the meaning of Gladys's whispered promise. *I'll always be there when you need me*. Had her sister been curious after all?

The days ahead loomed like a storm between Willie's old life and a new one. The air was still but heavy and charged with electricity. After Friday everything would change, including her name. Willie found herself lost in daydreams, not noticing when anyone spoke to her. Of course, Ella Bea was the only one who said much. She looked for chances to be alone with Willie, still trying, without success, to learn the details of what had happened at Aunt Xenia's house. Thurston made himself scarce as soon as he returned from school each afternoon. Willie knew it couldn't last. Eventually, he'd have to learn to be Jim's right hand, but not now. Brother Tollett didn't want anyone's company and took his supper alone in the bedroom.

Mother instructed Willie to clean and mend her clothes in preparation for the move to Tennessee. Willie approached the domestic tasks with energy, knowing she was actually preparing her trousseau. She was an attentive student in the kitchen, as she imagined herself sharing cooking duties with her new husband. She heeded Mother's warnings not to overwork the biscuit dough or burn her clothes when using the iron.

"I always knew you could take to household chores if you needed to," Mother said, attributing her domestic diligence to preparation for the new life she imagined for her in Tennessee.

"I'll do my best," Willie assured her. It was the only comfort she could think to offer.

On Tuesday morning as she took inventory of tasks that still needed to be done, she pulled out the silk she'd been given for her graduation dress. She hadn't done anything with it, but now she held it up and imagined how it might look as a wedding dress.

"It's a shame we won't see you wear it," Mother said, standing at the door. For an instant, Willie imagined her mother had read her mind.

"Yes, it is," Willie said. She thought of her mother learning of her marriage only after the wedding. "Oh Mother!" Willie said dropping the fabric to her lap. Tears filled her eyes and she sank onto the bed. Mother sat beside her. Willie put her head on her mother's shoulder and sniffled like a child. She wanted to tell her mother everything, to beg her to be part of it, but she resisted. Sarah and Jim Tollett did not keep secrets from each other.

Sarah stroked Willie's unkempt hair and Willie let her. For the second time that week, mother and daughter cried together without exchanging a word. If they'd spoken, or even looked at each other, they might have discovered they were grieving different losses.

Willie noticed that her mother's body was softer than when she had last leaned into her this way. She also smelled different. Less like fresh earth and more like coffee and stale dust. Willie tried to remember the time before. Before the accident, before John Musick, before Zane Grey. Life was simple and her future seemed certain. It was a nice memory, but she was ready for something new.

Willie remembered the silk in her lap. She sat up straight and wiped her eyes with the back of her arm. "Mother," she said. "Could you help me make a new blouse before I leave? I know that's not what the silk was for, but I might need something nice. It won't take the whole length. Edgalea or Gladys could use the rest."

"I think that would be fine," Mother said. "Real fine."

Willie immediately measured and cut the pieces she would need and set her mind on finishing the blouse in the next three days. Luckily, this was one part of her wedding her mother could join her in. Every night, after Willie had completed her regular chores and learned what she could about running a house, Mother poured them each a cup of tea and sat in the lamplight with her as Willie prepared for her wedding.

On Thursday evening, as Willie washed the supper dishes, she saw Aunt Xenia's car coming up their road. Willie's stomach dropped. Mother went outside to meet them. Willie stood beside her and watched Edgalea and Gladys get out of the car.

"Willie!" Gladys said, and she wrapped her sister in a hug.

"What are y'all doing here? What's wrong?" Mother asked.

"Nothing's wrong," Edgalea said. "We just asked Aunt Xenia if she'd bring us home a day early, so that we could help Willie get ready."

"Sarah, they needed more time together before—" Aunt Xenia's voice trailed off and she hugged Mother. It was unusual for the two women to show such affection.

Willie hugged each of her sisters again before they went inside. Edgalea saw the blouse on the table.

"Willie, you've done a fine job," she said. "These are the best stitches you've ever made.

"I like the points on the sleeves," Gladys said.

"And look at the drape of the neck!" said Edgalea.

"Thanks. Mother helped with those," Willie looked at Mother standing behind her sisters and noticed she was crying. Before Willie could go to her, she opened the door at her back and slipped into her bedroom.

"I'm down to the piping," Willie said.

"What will you wear with the blouse?" Edgalea asked. Willie thought it was curious that neither of her sisters had asked her where she would ever wear such a blouse.

"Mother gave me her black wool skirt." Willie said, pointing at the skirt on the table. "It needs to be let out, but it'll do."

Gladys held up the full gathered skirt. "You know, you could use the same trim on the skirt you're using for the blouse to make it a matching set."

Willie knew she wouldn't have time to add embellishments to the skirt. This was her last night, and she'd be up late finishing as it was.

"We'll help," Edgalea said. She took the roll of grosgrain piping and began measuring it against the skirt. Willie searched her sisters' faces for any clue that they knew her secret and were giving her their blessing in their own way. She couldn't be sure, and there was too much at stake to ask.

Before she went to bed, Willie packed the garments she'd been working on, four dresses, clean stockings and underthings, and two aprons into a suitcase. As she took inventory of the practical garments in her suitcase, Willie took pride in knowing she'd paid attention to the right things all along. She would not be the type of wife who existed only to adorn the household with lovely, useless things, including herself. She would be of worth in her own right. John had seen her covered in cobwebs and cow patties, and even wearing trousers.

Satisfied, she tucked the suitcase under the foot of their bed. By all appearances, she was ready for the trip to Tennessee. For the first time, she wondered where she would sleep tomorrow night and all the nights after. She decided she didn't care, so long as John was by her side.

Chapter 43

Willie didn't dare sleep. She didn't dare close her eyes. She listened to her sisters' breathing, to the owls and bullfrogs, and finally to the crickets' song. The wind picked up and whistled through the crack around the window. Must be a cold front coming in. She clutched Harold's timepiece and watched the long hand tick away the minutes. Sunrise was still hours away. She held the watch under the quilts to keep her hands warm and pulled it out every half hour until the short hand finally made its way down to the five.

Willie knew Gladys would agree to be her witness, but to eliminate the risk of revealing her secret too soon, she waited until the last possible moment to ask her. She crept over to Gladys's side of the bed and shook her.

"Gladys, wake up," Willie whispered. "Glad, I need to tell you something."

Gladys squinted at her sister. "Is it time?"

"Glad, I'm getting married today, and I need you to be a witness."

"I know! I've hardly slept a wink!" Gladys whispered back. Willie realized Gladys must have looked inside *Wildfire*. She tucked the suitcase under her arm, then they crept silently through the house, grabbing coats and boots on their way out. The cold of the morning burned in Willie's lungs as she pulled on her boots. While she was pulling on her coat, she heard movement inside the house.

"Run!" she whispered to Gladys.

Willie hugged the suitcase to her chest and ran to the barn with Gladys by her side. She could see the puffs of their breath against the dark sky. By the time they reached John, Willie's tears had frozen against her cheeks, but she didn't notice. She felt like Lucy reunited with Slone.

For the first time, Willie looked at John's face. She'd watched her father hit him, but she hadn't seen him since that night. His left eye was still puffy, and his cheeks bore yellow and green bruises. Lucy's words from *Wildfire* came to her: "*I know everything—what they accuse you of—how my dad struck you.*" As much as she'd found a kindred spirit in Lucy, she'd never imagined that these words would fit her own life.

John interrupted her thoughts with his low voice. "Horses are ready. Let's go."

"Horses?"

"Yes, we need to leave quietly. Truck's parked at the Belchers'. We'll tie the horses there for the morning."

They hurried around the corner, where two horses Willie didn't recognize were saddled and ready. Edgalea sat on one of them.

Willie stifled the scream in her throat. Without a sound, John mounted the other horse and reached for Willie's hand. She threw up her leg behind him and hissed, "You can't stop us, Edge!" John clicked his tongue and the mare took off. Gladys mounted behind Edgalea, and the sisters made chase.

They rode hard over the two miles to the Belchers' place, where John's truck waited by the side of the road. Edgalea and Gladys reached them before John could get their horse tied up and the Ford's engine running.

"How am I supposed to be your witness if you won't let us catch up?" Gladys said, panting.

"But you told Edgalea!"

"She'd already guessed you were up to something. She asked if I knew what you were planning."

"But how did you know?"

"Ladies, we've got to go," John said.

"I'm coming as a witness!" Edgalea said.

"Me, too," said Gladys.

"Let's go!" John repeated.

They crowded into the truck's cab. Willie relished the closeness to John, but her joy was diminished by the fear that came with realizing her sisters had known her plan.

"How—" Willie started to ask.

"You haven't been as sneaky as you thought," Edgalea said.

"You didn't fight the move to Tennessee, and we knew the fight wouldn't go out of you so easily," Edgalea explained.

"Which meant you must have another plan," Gladys said.

"Then, when Mr. Musick sent the book back—" Edgalea added.

"We knew you needed witnesses—" Gladys said.

"So, we asked Aunt Xenia to bring us home early," Edgalea finished, giving her glasses a satisfied nudge.

They drove until pink light splashed across the flat landscape. John slowed to a stop on the side of the road.

"What are you doing?" Willie asked. She had expected to race all the way to Elida.

"Sun is coming up. There won't be another place for you to change, and I'd rather not ride into Elida with the three of you in your nightgowns. It doesn't look like anyone is coming after you, but if they do, it's going to look like I stole you out of your beds."

"You mean robbed the cradle?" Willie couldn't resist the joke. And John couldn't resist laughing.

He stepped out of the cab and walked away from the truck. Edgalea and Gladys pulled off their nightgowns, revealing their Sunday dresses underneath.

"A bit wrinkled, but they should do," Edgalea said. "Willie?" she asked, looking at her sister.

Willie pulled the carefully folded charcoal blouse and skirt out of her suitcase. She slipped out of her nightgown and changed into the wool skirt and the loose cowled, drop-waisted silk blouse she'd worked so hard on.

Edgalea stepped toward Willie and placed a familiar leather pouch in her hand. "You'll need these," she said.

"The wedding beads," Willie whispered. "How did you get them?"

"Yesterday while everyone was busy with their own doings. Don't worry. No one saw me."

"But they're supposed to be for you," Willie argued.

"They're for the daughter who's getting married. Mother would want you to have them. If I ever need them, you can split the strand."

"Thank you," Willie said. "For everything."

"You girls ready?" John called out. He was standing with his back to them. Willie saw by his raised shoulders and folded arms that he was cold.

"Yes, ready!" she called back. The party did not exchange any words as they rode the last five miles into Elida. John parked in front of a café across from the courthouse.

"Coffee?"

"You want coffee? I'm ready to go to the courthouse," Willie said.

"I'm ready, too, darling. But the courthouse won't open until eight o'clock. We'll be there as soon as they open the doors. In the meantime, I could use coffee."

The foursome walked into the café, drawing the attention of a table of men drinking coffee and catching up on weather. All of them nodded at John. Willie had never been inside a café. It smelled like their kitchen at home, like coffee and bacon but with the addition of cigarette smoke. Tiny trails of smoke danced above every occupied seat.

The girls followed John to the counter, where he ordered four cups of coffee. Willie began to regret wearing her graduation clothes. It was drawing more attention than her work clothes might have. All of their clothes left little doubt that something out of the ordinary was happening.

"Morning, John," one of the men said as he leaned forward across the counter.

"Morning, Bill," John answered.

"Special occasion?"

"Could be."

"I don't like the way they're staring, Willie," Edgalea whispered. "Let's go wait in the truck."

"What about our coffee?" Willie asked.

"Leave it," Gladys said. "I need to fix your hair."

Willie didn't want to walk out. She didn't want to leave John's side or let these nosy men push her from a hot cup of coffee to the cold truck. Then she heard one man speak a little louder than the others. "Looks like Jim's getting his oldest married off after all," he said. The other men laughed.

Willie's cheeks grew hot. She took offense for her sister, who didn't need pity from old men in a café, for their father, who seemed to be looked down upon for not having rid himself of any daughters, and most of all for herself. Why did none of them assume she was the one getting married? Of course, she knew the answer, but such logic escaped her in the moment.

She led the way outside, and they sat in the truck cab. Willie found the brush and hairpins she'd tucked into her suitcase. Willie knew that little could be done with her dark, wiry hair, but she knew from the set of Gladys's jaw that she was determined to try. She sat between her sisters and let them press and pin to their satisfaction. Gladys gave her a final look.

"Thanks to the cold, you definitely look the part of a blushing bride."

Willie took the string of tiny seed beads out of their leather pouch. "Turn around," Edgalea said, taking the necklace. Willie turned and scooted down in the seat as her older sister put the necklace around her neck and fastened it in the back. She sat up and took her sisters' cold hands.

"I wish Mother could see you on your wedding day," Edgalea said.

"I do, too. But you know it wouldn't have worked," Willie said.

"I know."

"Oh, but she will see you!" Gladys said. She reached down to the floorboard and held up their mother's Kodak.

"Oh, Gladys!" Willie said.

"It was Edgalea's idea," Gladys said. "She grabbed it when she went for the beads"

Willie lifted her arms as much as her coat would allow and put them around both of her sisters. They wrapped her in their arms and she knew their mother had been right. The women would take care of each other, wherever life took them.

Suddenly, Willie broke loose from the embrace. She saw the county clerk unlocking the courthouse door. "It must be eight o'clock!" she said. "I'll get John." She walked into the café, and John stood when he saw her. She walked directly to him, raised up on her toes, and kissed him on the cheek.

"Let's get married, darling," she said loud enough for the table of men to hear.

Outside, she took John's elbow with her left hand and locked arms with Edgalea and Gladys on her right. They walked across Main Street and up to the small, red-brick courthouse. From the tiny atrium, a person could follow one oak door to the deputy's office or another to the judge. The clerk was a short, slender man with receding hair. Willie suspected he was younger than his disgruntled appearance suggested. He sat at a broad table in the open area laying out folders and marking each one with a pencil.

"We'd like to be married today," John said. Willie gave his elbow a squeeze.

The clerk didn't look up. He only sighed and shook his head. "Let me make sure the judge has his robes on." He stood and put the pencil behind his ear then stepped into the judge's chambers. When he returned, he still didn't make eye contact, but said, "He's ready for you." Then he went back to organizing his folders.

"Good morning, folks," the judge said. Unlike the clerk, his eyes lit up as Willie and John entered the room as though he'd been expecting them. He had gray hair and a mustache and wrinkles around his eyes and mouth similar to John's.

"Good morning, Judge," John said. "I hear you'll perform rites of matrimony."

"I can and often do. I have to ask though, how old is the bride-to-be?"

"Almost seventeen," John said. "I heard that won't be a problem here."

"No, sir. Not usually. I am going to ask you to step out for a minute while I have a chat with the young lady." He looked from Edgalea to Willie to Gladys. "Which one of you might that be?" The man's voice was kind, but Willie grew nervous at the thought of standing before him by herself. She stepped forward with shaky legs.

"Okay, then, you're the only one I need." He nodded toward the door, and John, Edgalea, and Gladys stepped back out into the atrium.

"It's no secret I'll do weddings for girls under eighteen without a parent present," the judge said, "but I like to make sure everything's aboveboard. Are you sure you want to marry this man? He appears to be a bit older than you."

"Yes, I'm sure."

"Are you really? I can see to it you get back home if you don't want to do this."

"No, I want to. I'm sure." Willie had never been so sure of anything, and it felt good to say so.

"In that case, tell your fella to come back in."

"And my sisters?" Willie asked.

"Yes, them, too," the judge answered.

Willie opened the door and waved the others in. The wedding party entered and stood shoulder to shoulder in front of the judge. She noticed that John was wearing a suit, complete with a vest and tie. She guessed he'd had it on all morning, but she hadn't seen him without his coat. That's when she realized she was still wearing hers, quickly shook it off, and draped it over a chair. They faced each other and John took her hand in his. Willie took a deep breath, creating space for every emotion that filled her body. The judge began.

"Name of the groom?"

"John Musick."

"The ball player?"

"Yes, sir."

"Well, I'll be!" The judge wrote on a certificate. "Bride's name?"

"Willie Tollett."

"Uh-oh. What's your daddy's name?"

"Jim Tollett, sir."

"I was afraid of that," the judge said. "Guess that explains the shiner." He leaned forward and spoke to John. "Any chance I can talk you out of this?"

"No, sir," John said. Willie smiled, despite herself.

"Lordy, I'm gonna have hell to pay."

"And I am sorry."

"I see you don't deny it."

"No, sir. I reckon we'll all have hell to pay," John said.

"Let's get it done then."

Willie never had expectations for a wedding, but she thought there'd be more to it. It was remarkably easy to sneak away and get married. The exchange of vows took less than five minutes. The judge declared them husband and wife, and John turned to face Willie. He closed the space between them and she looked up at his bruised face.

"'I'll kiss you,'" she whispered, quoting *Wildfire*. "'If kisses will make it well—it'll be well!'" Then he kissed her as though daring the world to change what they'd done.

The clerk stopped them on their way out of the courthouse.

"You're not official without a marriage certificate. I'm not saying you have to, but you might ask a pastor to fill it out. That sort of thing might matter to her folks."

Willie wondered if Brother Thurston might be willing to do such a thing. She wondered if it would make any difference to her parents.

"We'll do that," John said.

"Alright then. Take this with you. If he will or if he won't, either way, bring it back next week and I'll sign it."

"Much obliged," John said.

"You'll have to wait four years for your first anniversary," the clerk said.

"How's that?" John asked.

"Leap year. February twenty-ninth. Won't see that date again for another four years."

"If you live that long," Gladys said, and they all laughed; all except the clerk. He only shook his head.

They walked out of the courthouse less than ten minutes after the time they'd arrived, yet the world looked completely different to Willie Musick as she strolled hand in hand with her husband. It was fully daylight now, and with spring only a few weeks away, everything looked especially vibrant. There was nothing romantic about the barren courthouse lawn, but Willie felt like the heroine in any one of the Westerns she'd read. The girl got her fella, and the good guy won.

"How about breakfast, Mrs. Musick?" John asked. "Edgalea? Gladys? What do you say?"

"I'd love that, Mr. Musick," Willie answered. Her sisters nodded in agreement. Willie slipped her hand into the crook of John's elbow. He leaned over and kissed the top of her head.

"Well, Wildfire," John said. "'There will be consequences to face when we get back.'"

She felt disappointed that he was casting a shadow over their moment of joy. Then he gave her a wink. "'It might be terrible—'" he started.

Then Willie recognized the line he'd marked for her in the first page of *Wildfire*. She met her husband's dancing gray eyes and answered, "'So long as it's wonderful'!"

Epilogue

Monday, March 2, 1964 The Portales News-Tribune Page 5

AFTER 40 YEARS of marriage, Mr. and Mrs. John Musick prepare to celebrate their 10th anniversary on Feb. 29th at their home near Rogers. (News-Tribune Photo)

John Musicks Observe 40 Years of Marriage

The 40th is known as the ruby anniversary, so Mr. and Mrs. John Musick chose ruby-red as the color to use in decorating for their open-house when they observed their wedding anniversary Sunday.

February 29th was the actual date, so, strictly speaking, they have had only ten anniversaries. They were married at Elida on that date in 1924.

They have two sons, Claude of Idaho Falls, Idaho, and Gordon, of Granite, Okla. neither of whom were here for the anniversary. Their daughter, Mrs. Lowell Wilhoit, and eight grandchildren helped them plan their celebration and greet the friends who called.

The Musicks have their home on the homestead filed by her father, J. E. Tollett, in the Rogers community. Her brother, Thurston Tollett, and her father, were also present for the open house. She had two sisters, Mrs. Estin Scearce of El Paso and Mrs. Lester Pitt of Sweetwater, Texas.

Asked if she had lived all her life in the county, Mrs. Musick replied, "Not quite—I was three weeks old when we came here."

Mr. Musick came to the county in 1920 from Hamilton, Texas.

Author's Note

John and Willie (Tollett) Musick were my maternal great-grandparents. I grew up hearing the story of their elopement. Though John Musick died before I was born, Willie lived until I was thirteen years old. By the time I knew Great-Grandma, she was an "old lady" who often repeated the same "old" stories. I can't count the number of times I've wished I'd paid more attention.

Careful readers will notice that I changed some historical and geographical details to create this work of fiction. Most notably, I chose to consolidate the communities of Rogers and Inez, New Mexico. I also took liberties with John Musick's birthday, January 22. At times, I chose to use surnames common to Roosevelt County in the 1920s. The real Tollett Family Tree is extensive, but I only included the branches relevant to my telling of John and Willie's story. Beyond the names, all renderings are a work of fiction.

John was almost twice Willie's age when they married. While this would not be acceptable or legal in today's society, there was no indication in decades of stories, letters, and memories that their marriage was based on anything except love and mutual respect.

Willie's Reading List

Betty Zane

Riders of the Purple Sage

The Rainbow Trail

The Man of the Forest

The Light of Western Stars

Wildfire

The Call of the Canyon

Endnotes

p. 306 Grey, Zane. *The Light of Western Stars*. New York: Grosset & Dunlap, 1914.

p. 321 Grey, Zane. *The Light of Western Stars*. New York: Grosset & Dunlap, 1914.

p. 353 Grey, Zane. *The Light of Western Stars*. New York: Grosset & Dunlap, 1914.

p. 361 Longfellow, Henry Wadsworth. "A Psalm of Life." In *Voices of the Night*. New York, Burst & Co.: 1839.

p. 379 Grey, Zane. *The Light of Western Stars*. New York: Grosset & Dunlap, 1914.

p. 405 Grey, Zane. *The Light of Western Stars*. New York: Grosset & Dunlap, 1914.

p. 411 Grey, Zane. *Wildfire*. New York: Grosset & Dunlap, 1917.

p. 420 Grey, Zane. *Wildfire*. New York: Grosset & Dunlap, 1917.

p. 428 Grey, Zane. *Wildfire*. New York: Grosset & Dunlap, 1917.

Acknowledgments

I owe the completion of this book to many people. First, to the Ad Hoc Group of Lubbock, Texas, for teaching me how to write fiction. To the Friday Group of Nashville (Michelle Hasty, Ally Hauptman, and Rachael Milligan) for reading, rereading, and staying tuned through the fits and starts of this project. To Danielle Peters for keeping me sane and productive during COVID. Also, to the Women Writing the West for providing a warm welcome and support.

To Nathan Dahlstrom, Jennifer Cortez, Dennis Wilhoit, Clyde Wilhoit, and Walter Wilhoit for reading early drafts. It was a team effort to fill my gaps in farming and ranching know-how. Any mistakes or inaccuracies are mine.

To Johnnie Berhhard, Mikee Delony, and Ellen Morgan for your editing services. Also, to Dawn Woods, Bruce DeRoos, and Eric Peters for making the book beautiful.

Thank you to my dad, for thinking to ask how my writing is going. Special thanks to my mom, who taught me to love, appreciate, and be curious about the people and places that made me.

To my children, Hank and Josephine, for sharing the writing life. *I love you today and I'll love you tomorrow . . . You can always come home to me.* Finally, to John. Thank you for living the adventure with me. Our kids and grandkids will have a good story to tell.

About the Author

Sheila Quinn grew up in West Texas and spent significant time in Eastern New Mexico listening to the stories of her grandma, upon whose life and family her fiction is based. Now she lives and writes in Franklin, Tennessee. She is the author of *This Year, Lord: Teachers' Prayers of Blessing, Liturgy, and Lament*. Her short stories have been featured in *Cricket Magazine*, *The Concho River Review*, and *El Portal*. Sheila has twenty years of experience working with public schools and teacher preparation programs. She enjoys gardening, hiking, and reading good books with her husband and children.

You can learn more at
sheilaquinn.com
or subscribe at
sheilaquinn.substack.com

Made in the USA
Coppell, TX
29 February 2024